# PATH OF
# THE OUTCAST

'RUN,' LECHTHENNIAN SAID, pointing to the windows ahead of the group, his voice cold and calm. 'We are discovered.'

Aradryan looked down the corridor and his blood froze and his skin prickled with a chill of utter dread. At the arched windows stood dozens – hundreds – of pale-skinned figures. They had androgynous faces and single-breasted bodies, with eyes like polished coal that stared at the eldar with rapt hunger. Forked tongues slithered in anticipation over needle-thin teeth. Instead of hands they had elongated claws, like some monstrous lobster, and these they tapped against the window panes while narrow faces snarled and grinned and leered.

Aradryan's waystone was like a nail being driven into his heart, piercing hot as it burned through his chest. A chorus of voices sang in his head, beautiful and terrible, alluring and yet filling him with disgust. Though he had never laid eyes on the creatures before, he had heard tales from his earliest memories and knew in his gut, in the deepest pit of his spirit, the nature of the apparitions that confronted him: servants of the Great Enemy, daemonettes of dread Slaanesh.

A WARHAMMER 40,000 NOVEL

PATH OF THE ELDAR SERIES
BOOK THREE

# PATH OF
# THE OUTCAST

## GAV THORPE

BLACK LIBRARY

*This book is dedicated to Kez, without whom I might still be wandering as an Outcast.*

**A BLACK LIBRARY PUBLICATION**

First published in Great Britain in 2012 by
Black Library,
Games Workshop Ltd.,
Willow Road, Nottingham,
NG7 2WS, UK.

10 9 8 7 6 5 4 3 2 1

Cover illustration by Neil Roberts.

A CIP record for this book is available from the British Library.

UK ISBN: 978 1 84970 197 6
US ISBN: 978 1 84970 198 3

See Black Library on the internet at
**www.blacklibrary.com**

Find out more about Games Workshop
and the world of Warhammer 40,000 at
**www.games-workshop.com**

Printed and bound by CPI Group (UK) Ltd, Croydon, CR0 4YY

IT IS THE 41st millennium. For more than a hundred centuries the Emperor has sat immobile on the Golden Throne of Earth. He is the master of mankind by the will of the gods, and master of a million worlds by the might of his inexhaustible armies. He is a rotting carcass writhing invisibly with power from the Dark Age of Technology. He is the Carrion Lord of the Imperium for whom a thousand souls are sacrificed every day, so that he may never truly die.

YET EVEN IN his deathless state, the Emperor continues his eternal vigilance. Mighty battlefleets cross the daemon-infested miasma of the warp, the only route between distant stars, their way lit by the Astronomican, the psychic manifestation of the Emperor's will. Vast armies give battle in His name on uncounted worlds. Greatest amongst his soldiers are the Adeptus Astartes, the Space Marines, bio-engineered super-warriors. Their comrades in arms are legion: the Imperial Guard and countless planetary defence forces, the ever-vigilant Inquisition and the tech-priests of the Adeptus Mechanicus to name only a few. But for all their multitudes, they are barely enough to hold off the ever-present threat from aliens, heretics, mutants - and worse.

TO BE A man in such times is to be one amongst untold billions. It is to live in the cruellest and most bloody regime imaginable. These are the tales of those times. Forget the power of technology and science, for so much has been forgotten, never to be re-learned. Forget the promise of progress and understanding, for in the grim dark future there is only war. There is no peace amongst the stars, only an eternity of carnage and slaughter, and the laughter of thirsting gods.

Life is to us as the Maze of Linnian was to Ulthanesh, its mysterious corridors leading to wondrous vistas and nightmarish encounters in equal measure. Each of us must walk the maze alone, treading in the footsteps of those who came before but also forging new routes through the labyrinth of existence.

In times past we were drawn to the darkest secrets and ran wild about the maze, seeking to experience all that it had to offer. As individuals and as a civilisation, we lost our way, and in doing so created the means for our doom, our unfettered exploration leading to the darkness of the Fall.

In the emptiness that followed, a new way was revealed to us: the Path. Through the wisdom of the Path we spend our lives exploring the meaning of existence, moving from one part of the maze to another with discipline and guidance so that we never become lost again. On the Path we experience the full potential of love and hate, joy and woe, lust and purity, filling our lives with experience and fulfilment but never succumbing to the shadows that lurk within our thoughts.

But like all journeys, the Path is different for each of us. Some wander for a long while in one place; some spread their travels wide and visit many places for a short time while others remain for a long time to explore every nook and turn; some of us lose our way and leave the Path for a time or forever; and some of us find dead ends and become trapped.

– Kysaduras the Anchorite, foreword to
*Introspections upon Perfection*

# PROLOGUE

DEATH AND REBIRTH played out across the heavens, every star a furnace of creation and an inferno of destruction. They stretched out in every direction, spiralling around the galactic core, seemingly timeless yet ultimately as mortal as any creature. Birth and demise, all of it cycling again and again, giving rise to life and civilisations, and destroying them as quickly as they appeared. Stability was an illusion. There was no stasis, just an everlasting dance of elements that would outlast any mind capable of comprehending it.

Opening his eyes, Aradryan surfaced slowly from the dream, feeling the weight of air upon him, the press of darkness on flesh as he lay still on the thin mattress of his bed, the silence suffusing every fibre of his being. It was utterly black in his chambers; not the least glimmer of light existed to intrude upon his thoughts.

The cosmic nature of the dream continued to spiral slowly in his thoughts as unconsciousness gave way to waking. Responding to his state, Aradryan's chambers suffused him with the barest glow of light, slowly brightening to bring him out of his mental submersion. Limbs tingling, the dreamer twitched his fingers and wriggled his toes, the first of several exercises that would enable him to lock his thoughts back to his physical body.

Aradryan sat up, his breathing becoming faster and shallower, his body reacting to the sudden influx of soft stimuli. Half sleeping, latched on to the core essence of the dream, Aradryan stood up slowly. He clothed himself without conscious effort, drawing on a long robe of dark blues and purples. Slipping his slender feet into a pair of knee-high boots, he left the dreaming room and went into the main chamber. Here the light was brighter still, though a fraction of its normal intensity, causing Aradryan to squint for a few moments while his eyes adjusted.

The after-images of the dream lingered still and he felt small and unimportant. The dream had shown him the vastness of the universe, and against that he was nothing, a tiny conglomeration of cells and thoughts that would be extinguished.

The chambers felt too constricting, so Aradryan left quickly, his heart yearning for something that would recapture the soaring majesty of the galaxy. Without conscious regard, he made his way to a skyrunner. Placing his hand upon the activation jewel, he let his desire pass into the machine's matrix, which in turn drew power from the infinity circuit: the psychic network of Alaitoc Craftworld.

The skyrunner interpreted his will as best it could, rising swiftly from the balcony-like docking bay to skim across the white grass fields that covered the floor of the Dome of Swift Longings. Realising that the skyrunner was taking him towards the dock towers on the craftworld rim, Aradryan chuckled to himself. The semi-sentient craft had felt his yearning for the wide galaxy and was taking him to the berths of the starships.

Aradryan's quiet laughter stilled. Perhaps the skyrunner was more intelligent than he was. He had experienced many dreams, but none had left an impression as strong as the one he had just woken from. Part of him was glad for that fact. The Path of Dreaming existed to tap into the power of the unconscious and subconscious, bringing forth fears and desires that it was impossible to recognise while awake. For nearly two passes he had trodden the Path of the Dreamer, alongside his friend Korlandril, and they had shared many special moments of pleasure and regret, their dream-bonds tighter than any ordinary friendship. Was this dream the Moment of Realisation? Had the dizzying vistas of the galaxy been the culmination of his searching for purpose?

Such thoughts, only partially constructed in his semi-fugue state, occupied Aradryan until the skyrunner arrived at its destination, furling its guiding sail to slip into a mooring at the Tower of Winding Destiny. Aradryan stepped from the craft and followed the passageway that led up to the heights of the docking spire. The few eldar that he encountered immediately recognised the half-alert state of a Dreamer and stepped nimbly out of his path, allowing him to follow his whims unimpeded, until they brought Aradryan to a broad expanse alongside one of the main quays.

It was hard to disassociate from the dream-images, but Aradryan was conscious of there being many other eldar around him. There was a ship docked at the quayside. It was massive, its hull towering above them, its stellar sail even higher still, stretching towards the glimmering force dome that held the ravening vacuum of space at bay.

Looking up, Aradryan saw the stars, scattered across the outer sky like diamonds on black velvet, enticing and bewitching.

Someone bumped into him, shaking him from the last vestiges of the dream's grip. A little disconcerted, Aradryan looked around and found himself in a large crowd thronging the dockside. More eldar were coming down the ramps that led from the open gateways of the starship.

Aradryan was aware of a solemn mood; he sensed it even before he heard the first sobs and saw the glistening tears in the eyes of those around him. He felt an emptiness, and when he looked again at the eldar disembarking from the ship he realised why.

The first to alight were Aspect Warriors. A wave of grim anger and deep hatred washed over Aradryan as Khaine's anointed killers strode down from the gangways, still armed and armoured. Striking Scorpions in heavily plated armour of greens and yellows bore three of their number amongst them, the corpses carried on floating biers, guided by the hands of the living. Dark Reapers in black and red followed, also accompanying their dead. And then came the Dire

Avengers, so bright in their armour of blue, white and gold, yet so sinister with their faceless masks.

Aradryan wanted to back away, but there was someone behind him. The Aspect Warriors were apparitions of death to his half-dreaming mind, each an incarnation of the part of Khaine they represented. Howling Banshees filled his thoughts with screaming images of flashing death; Fire Dragons set his mind ablaze with an inferno of destruction.

It was almost too much to bear in his fragile state, but Aradryan stayed, morbid curiosity getting the better of him. From images glanced in the infinity circuit and snatches of conversation, he saw a blue sun and a yellow sun, gleaming down on a still lake. A white building, human-made, was wreathed in death and fire. The brightly-armoured Aspect Warriors stormed through doors and windows, cutting down the humans within without mercy.

After the Aspect Warriors, others came from the ship: Guardians and seers. These were not the grim-faced fighters that had come before, and it was their grief that suffused the crowd around him. The feeling of lament grew stronger and stronger as more of the dead and wounded were carried down to the dock-side, each a life lost or damaged.

Aradryan stared at the blood-flecked blue and yellow armour of a Guardian. He could not say whether the blood was eldar or from their foes, but each glistening droplet, every ruddy stain, held within it some hidden secret of mortality.

The dream and the current surroundings melded in Aradryan's thoughts, forming a whole. Even the stars die, he thought.

Yet the eldar who had fallen were not yet wholly dead. Upon the chest of each glowed a spirit stone, containing the essence of each slain warrior. From here the stones would be taken into the depths of Alaitoc and placed upon the nodes of the infinity circuit. The spirits would flow free from the stones and mingle with the psychic energy of generations who had come before, becoming both the lifeblood and the nervous system of the craftworld.

The thought suddenly terrified Aradryan. To be trapped on Alaitoc for eternity, bodiless and voiceless, seemed to his dreaming mind a fate worse than death.

He stopped short, for there truly was a fate worse than death that awaited all eldar: She Who Thirsts. The creation of the eldar's depraved past hungered after their spirits, and would devour them all if given the chance. The spirit stones, the sanctuary of the infinity circuit, were the only defence against such a nightmare; the only bastion secure against an everlasting torment of spirit that terrified every eldar.

Yet even that fear could not fully cut through the sense of entrapment that had seized Aradryan. With glassy eyes he stared at the corpses as they floated past, body after body after body. Questions crammed into his thoughts, of who the slain had been and how they had died. Had there been pain? Had their lives been happy and complete, or had death taken them before their ambitions had been fulfilled, their desires sated? Would they linger ever after in the infinity circuit regretting the missed opportunities, now denied to them as much as the utter silence of true death?

'Save me...' Aradryan whispered, falling to his knees. Alaitoc was a prison, keeping him from a life amongst the stars. Worse than that, he realised. The craftworld was a place of the dead, fuelled by the spirits of the deceased, consuming their life force with a hunger every bit as ravenous as the Great Enemy's.

Aradryan surged to his feet and grabbed the nearest person, a maiden a little younger then himself with auburn hair that fell to her knees, and eyes of violet. She wore the robes of a healer, the white of death marked by handprints of dried blood.

'They cannot stay here!' snapped Aradryan. 'There is no more room. The dead, they are so many, we cannot have any more.'

'You are dream-touched,' said the healer, gently removing Aradryan's grasp. 'Leave me be.'

Aradryan staggered away, but wherever he looked there were more dead eldar. Each was a meaningless mote snuffed out of existence, and the thought threatened to tip him from his teetering state into the darkest abyss of madness.

A hand fell upon his shoulder, turning him. Aradryan looked into a pair of wise grey eyes and heard a soft voice.

'What is wrong?' said the other eldar, his face full of concern.

'I do not want to die here,' Aradryan replied simply. 'The stars call to me, and I do not want to die before I have seen them.'

'Then do not stay.' The eldar smiled and stroked his hand down Aradryan's arm, bringing a sense of stability and calm. 'This ship, she is called *Lacontiran*. She will leave again in four cycles' time, why not come aboard with me?'

'Come aboard?' Aradryan turned to look at the starship. Amongst all the blood and ugliness she was beautiful; sleek and purposeful.

'I am Nairnith, a steersman,' said the other eldar. 'It seems that you have dreamed enough. If you wish to see the stars, I will take you to them.'

'Yes, to see the stars,' said Aradryan, his panic fading into memory.

# Part One

---

## Steersman

# FRIENDSHIP

*The Endless Valley – There is a place, on the distant rim of the galaxy, where the darkness between stars stretches further than anywhere else. Beyond lies the gulf that separates galaxies, where the cold blackness seems to spread for eternity. It is here, in the Endless Valley, that the webway fades and the light of stars is nought but a glimmer. The Endless Valley is home to many secrets, of eldar and other, more sinister creatures, and empty save for the relics and ghosts of the distant past.*

AN AURA OF shimmering gold enveloped the *Lacontiran* as the starship passed out of the webway portal. The curving, spired mass of Alaitoc appeared in the spectral display that hovered in front of Aradryan, filling the steersman with mixed emotions. It was

almost impossible to believe that twenty passes had
turned since he had last seen the craftworld, but he
had felt no homesickness on the long journey and
seeing Alaitoc filled him with trepidation as much as
familiarity.

Sitting in the rainbow glow of the pod-like steering
chamber Aradryan moved his fingers lightly across
the jewelled panel in front of him, trimming the aft
sail to better catch the dying light of Mirianathir:
the ruddy star about which Alaitoc slowly orbited,
drinking in the rays of the huge orb. The star and the
craftworld could be seen via a holo-projection that
surrounded the steersmen, so that it seemed they
floated in space, the unending firmament stretching
out beneath and behind them even as Alaitoc grew
larger beyond the undulating console of the controls.
In a small sub-display at the heart of each eldar's
controls the *Lacontiran's* position was shown by a
gleaming rune amidst an ever-changing web of four-
dimensional telemetry. Beside Aradryan, Nairnith
and Faethrunin adjusted the course of the *Lacontiran*, the three steersmen working in concert without
spoken word, their minds subtly connected by the
psychic skeleton of the starship.

The three of them guided the *Lacontiran* along the
rim of Alaitoc, passing gracefully between arcing
bridges and over glistening force domes through
which could be seen vast plains and ranges of hills,
artificial seas and twilit forest glades. Swarms of
smaller craft moved aside for the starship as it glided
down towards the docking spear of the Tower of
Eternal Welcomes. Aradryan smiled at the name,
and his unease dissipated a little; news of the vessel's

arrival had been heralded for some time and he had received contact from Thirianna that she would be there to greet him. To see her again, and his dream-companion Korlandril, would ease the hurt that nestled deep in his heart. Part of him still felt as though he was returning to a prison, but the terror that had accompanied his departure had been assuaged by the voyage, with the aid of Faethrunin and Nairnith.

Passing through the rainbow field surrounding the dock, the *Lacontiran* slid alongside a curving quay, effortlessly coming to a halt under the urging of Aradryan and his companions. The stellar sails were furling themselves and already there was much activity aboard the ship: passengers moving to the gateways to disembark, the handful of crew ushering their charges through the passageways.

'We are back,' said Nairnith, the chief steersman, veteran of more than a score of voyages.

Aradryan met the old eldar's gaze and they shared a moment, their thoughts connecting across the membrane of the *Lacontiran*. Memories flashed past, of sights seen and encounters shared. There was something else present too: the vast psychic power of Alaitoc's infinity circuit merging with the spirit of the starship, drawing in its experiences, updating its semi-conscious essence of all that had transpired in its absence.

Aradryan ignored the influx of information and turned to Faethrunin. The other steersman extended a hand and the two of them lightly touched fingers in a gesture of parting. Almost immediately Aradryan felt a sense of loss as he drew his fingers away, knowing that he would miss Faethrunin's dry wit and easy words of encouragement.

Not willing to draw out the parting any longer, Aradryan stood and left the steering chamber. His bag was already packed, a few clothes and souvenirs picked up on his travels, but the real treasures he had gained were locked in his mind: sights of swirling nebulae and the spectacle of stars being born. It had been everything he had dreamed of and more, and as Aradryan joined the crowds filing out of the ship's dozen gateways, he knew that nothing would ever replace the majesty and wonder of the galaxy.

Bathed in the iridescent light spilling from *Lacontiran*, he walked down the gangway and was confronted by a wave of life; the quayside was filled with hundreds of eldar who had come to meet the ship, either because friends or loved ones were on board or simply to welcome the returning voyagers. Amongst the throng he caught a glimpse of Korlandril, though his friend's gaze passed over him initially. Beside Korlandril, Thirianna was stood on the tips of her toes to peer over the shoulders of those around her.

Seeing the two together as they were gave Aradryan a moment's pause and conflicted emotions raged inside him for a moment: happiness at seeing them, jealousy of what appeared to be a close relationship. When he had left, Thirianna had been a Dire Avenger, dedicated to the Path of the Warrior. Though always willing to share a joke or come on an excursion, there had been a coldness about her; yet that coldness had made the moments of warmth shared with her that much more special and intimate. Turning his attention to Korlandril, Aradryan saw nothing of the

Dreamer he had left behind. There was no sign of the distant gaze of the dream-swept; instead Korlandril's eyes were in constant motion, taking in every movement and detail.

Aradryan realised that he must seem a strange sight, perhaps unrecognisable. His hair was cut short on the left side, almost to the scalp, and hung in unkempt waves to the right, neither bound nor styled. He had dark make-up upon his eyelids, giving him a sunken gaze, and he was dressed in deep blues and black, wrapped in long ribbons of twilight. His bright yellow waystone was worn as a brooch, mostly hidden by the folds of his robe.

He met Thirianna's gaze and smiled, and her expression of delight at seeing her friend returned momentarily expelled Aradryan's doubts about his homecoming. Aradryan waved a hand in greeting and made his way effortlessly through the crowd to stand in front of the pair.

'A felicitous return!' declared Korlandril, opening his arms in welcome, palms angled towards Aradryan's face. 'And a happy reunion.'

Thirianna dispensed with words altogether, brushing the back of her hand across Aradryan's cheek for a moment, lighting up his skin with her soft touch. She laid her slender fingers upon his shoulder, an exceptionally familiar gesture of welcome usually reserved for close family. Though taken aback by this display of familiarity, so at odds with the cool repose she had shown before, Aradryan returned the gesture, laying his fingers upon her shoulder.

The moment passed and Aradryan stepped away from Thirianna, laying his hands onto those of

Korlandril, a wry smile on his lips.

'Well met, and many thanks for the welcome,' said Aradryan.

He looked at Korlandril as the other eldar kept his grip longer than was normal, perhaps seeking to reinforce the gesture with its duration. Looking into Korlandril's eyes, Aradryan saw that he was being scrutinised, not unkindly but openly, bordering on the impolite. With a slight smile to hide a quiver of discomfort, Aradryan withdrew his grasp and clasped his hands behind his back, raising his eyebrows inquisitively.

'Tell me, dearest and most happily-met of my friends, what have I missed?'

A FEELING OF unreality pervaded Aradryan's thoughts as he accompanied Thirianna and Korlandril, walking away from the docks. So different had the steersman's life been aboard the starship, it felt as if he was stepping back into a memory. He had spent the last cycles on Alaitoc in an almost constant dream state, and it was no wonder that he now felt that the craftworld was somehow half imagined. Korlandril offered to pilot a skiff to convey the trio back to the habitat domes, but Aradryan declined. He had sailed interstellar gulfs for a long time and until he felt Alaitoc beneath his feet, until he walked its boulevards and plazas, he would not truly believe that he was back.

So it was that they sauntered along the Avenue of Dreams, through a silver passageway that wound beneath a thousand crystal archways into the heart of Alaitoc. The dim light of Mirianathir was caught in the vaulted roof, captured and radiated by the intricately faceted crystal to shine down upon the pedestrians below, glowing with delicate oranges and pinks.

Korlandril was being garrulous, speaking at length about his works and his accomplishments. He could not help it; the mind of the Artist had no place for circumspection or self-awareness, only sensation and expression. Aradryan felt Thirianna looking at him occasionally and met her glance, sharing her patient amusement at their friend's talkativeness, while Korlandril continued to extol the virtues of his sculptures.

Aradryan was more curious about Thirianna's transformation than Korlandril's parroted profundities on artistic merit.

'I sense that you no longer walk in the shadow of Khaine,' said Aradryan, nodding in approval as he looked at Thirianna.

'It is true that the Path of the Warrior has ended for me,' she replied, For a moment she seemed distracted, and Aradryan saw a flicker of emotion, a hesitant moment of pain, mar her fair features. It was gone in an instant, but it was a sign of weakness, of vulnerability, which he had never seen in her face before; it speared into him with its delicacy, making Thirianna appear even more beautiful. 'The aspect of the Dire Avenger has sated my anger, enough for a hundred lifetimes. I write poetry, influenced by the Uriathillin school of verse. I find it has complexities that stimulate both the intellectual and the emotional in equal measure.'

'I would like to know Thirianna the Poet, and perhaps your verse will introduce me,' said Aradryan.

Korlandril's change from Dreamer to Artist was not unexpected, but Thirianna was as different from the friend he had known as a warm star-rise was to a cold twilight. 'I would very much like to see a performance, as you see fit.'

'As would I,' laughed Korlandril. 'Thirianna refuses to share her work with me, though many times I have suggested that we collaborate on a piece that combines her words with my sculpture.'

'My verse is for myself, and no other. It is not for performance, nor for eyes that are not mine,' Thirianna said quietly. Aradryan noticed her cast a glance of irritation at the sculptor, suggesting that this was not the first time the subject had been broached, and rejected. 'While some create their art to express themselves to the world, my poems are inner secrets, for me to understand their meaning, to divine my own fears and wishes.'

Admonished, Korlandril fell silent for a moment and Aradryan felt a stab of pity for the Artist, who could not help but express every passing thought, such was the state of the Path he walked. He existed in the present, an ever-moving observer and creator, neither looking forwards nor glancing back.

'Have you come back to Alaitoc to stay?' asked Korlandril, his enthusiasm quickly returning. 'Is your time as a steersman complete, or will you be returning to *Lacontiran*?'

The question was hard for Aradryan, and it was not one that he wanted to – or could – answer so soon after arriving. Rather than show his discomfort, Aradryan decided on a shot of good-humoured retaliation for the indelicate question.

'I have only just arrived, are you so eager that I should leave once more?'

The look of shock and horror on Korlandril's face was worth the risk of offence. Realising that his friend was gently mocking him, and acknowledging that he had been deserving of such treatment, Korlandril bowed his head, accepting the joke. It was almost possible to forget the nightmarish moments that had nearly sent Aradryan spiralling into madness, taking him back to a time when he and Korlandril had cared not for a thing in all the craftworld, save to dream and joke and enjoy life.

'I do not yet know,' Aradryan continued, seeing that Thirianna was keen to hear a proper reply. How could he express the uncertainty that crowded his thoughts; would they be able to understand the dilemma he faced? 'I have learnt all that I can learn as a steersman and I feel complete. Gone is the turbulence that once plagued my thoughts. There is nothing like guiding a ship along the buffeting waves of a nebula, or along the swirling channels of the webway to foster control and focus. I have seen many great and wondrous things out in the stars, but I feel there is so much more out there to find, to touch and hear and experience. I may return to the starships, I may not. And, of course, I would like to spend a little time with my friends and family, to know again the life of Alaitoc, to see whether I wish to wander again or can be content here.'

Thirianna nodded with understanding, and Korlandril regarded Aradryan's reply with uncharacteristic silence and poise. Before the quiet became awkward, the Artist spoke again.

'Your return is most timely, Aradryan,' Korlandril said. 'My latest piece is nearing completion. In a few cycles' time I am hosting an unveiling. It would be a pleasure and an honour if both of you could attend.'

'I would have come even if you had not invited me!' laughed Thirianna. 'I hear your name mentioned quite often, and with much praise attached, and there are high expectations for this new work. It would not be seemly at all to miss such an event if one is to be considered as a person possessing any degree of taste.'

Korlandril's invitation sent a shiver of apprehension through Aradryan, but he masked it instantly. Amongst his fellow steersmen there had been few secrets, but each of them had mastered the means to withdraw their emotions, lest a rogue thought unsettle their companions during a delicate manoeuvre. It was this technique that Aradryan employed now, shielding his friends from his moment of fear. The thought of attending such a gathering unsettled Aradryan, as he was convinced there would be some there who remembered his near-collapse so many passes ago.

Korlandril looked earnest, and Thirianna seemed eager that Aradryan accompanied her, her body turned towards him, eyes wide with expectation and hope.

'Yes, I too would be delighted to attend,' Aradryan said eventually, trying to make the words sound natural. 'I am afraid that my tastes may have been left behind compared to yours, but I look forward to seeing what Korlandril the Sculptor has created in my absence.'

* * *

AFTER THEY HAD become reacquainted, Aradryan parted from his friends and returned to the quarters where his family had lived before his departure. It had seemed odd to him that none of his family had come to meet him at the Tower of Eternal Welcomes – adding irony to the name – but the reason became clear as he arrived at the Spire of Wishes. All of Aradryan's extended family had gathered from across Alaitoc to welcome him back, including several half-sisters and cousins he had never met before, but his father had died while he had been away and his mother had left Alaitoc, travelling to Yme-Loc Craftworld to visit an old lover who was an autarch there.

The celebration was genuine and his family happy to see their wandering relation returned, but for Aradryan it was too much, too soon. The news of his father's death was a shock, though they had not been especially close. That his mother had left Alaitoc, perhaps for good, worried him more than he thought it would have done. He had thought more about returning to friends rather than family, but that was because, he realised, he had taken their presence for granted. Without his parents it seemed as if a foundation of his life, one that had sat comfortably unnoticed until now, had suddenly been pulled away.

He had grown accustomed to the peace and contemplation of shipboard life, and the sudden attention and activity taxed his endurance as well as his patience. He stayed at the festivities for as long as he could bear it and then made his excuses, fleeing the Spire of Wishes to seek solace in one of the garden domes.

His thoughts awhirl, Aradryan wandered the woods and riverbanks of the Dome of Subtle Rewards, which was kept in a permanent dawn-like state, the pre-day glow casting fire and gold upon the leaves and water. Even this beauty was a mockery of the genuine grandeur of nature, he thought. He had watched stars rise above worlds so pristine, no life had yet sprung up from their azure oceans. He had seen supernova consuming planets and listened to the strobing call of pulsars that had died before even the eldar had known sentience. It was impossible to reconcile such experiences with a simple miniature sun held in stasis like a cheap conjuror's trick.

Eventually, Aradryan's whimsical feet brought him to a platform at the foot of the Bridge of Yearning Sorrows. The massive field-clad arch rose high above Alaitoc, and as he stood looking up at the silver towers at its pinnacle, Aradryan's thoughts were flooded with memories. This was one of the most popular haunts of Dreamers, who could go to the transparent hab-spaces at the apex and fool themselves into thinking that they slept floating amongst the stars. Aradryan had spent many cycles there, and there was something about that illusion of freedom, no matter how false it was in reality, that lured him there again.

He summoned an open-topped carriage, which glided along the monorail from its hangar with barely a whisper to announce its presence. Stepping inside, Aradryan smirked to himself as he looked at the simple controls: three touch-sensitive gems of which one was the self-guidance activator. On the *Lacontiran* Aradryan had mastered a board of nearly seven hundred different controls. He laid a fingertip on the automatic drive and sat back, trying to relax.

The carriage accelerated quickly, encasing Aradryan in a dampening field so that the strengthening wind of its passage was dulled, allowing the steersman to feel the air through his hair and on his face as a pleasant breeze while beyond the bubble it sped past as a gale. From several other stations, more rails ascended towards the peak of the arc, coming together like the outer threads of a web to form an intricate, overlapping conjunction inside the lowest level of the apex tower.

A few eldar drifted about the terminal with the glazed look of the half-dreaming. Just coming here stirred memories and desires in Aradryan. He had spent many cycles here, lost in the wonder of his own subconscious, exploring the possibilities of imagination. Out of instinct he crossed the concourse and took a moving rampway to the next level.

Here there were open-fronted chambers where dreamers could procure all manner of stimulants and tranquilisers to change their mood and alter their dreams. Little had changed since Aradryan had first come here, though as he walked along the parade of archways he saw no faces he recognised. It was the way of the Path, that an eldar delved into part of themselves for a time, but then moved on, broadening their experience and developing control of their fierce emotions.

Entering one of the dens, which Aradryan's memory told him served intoxicating beverages to bring about a lighter sleep to enable the blending of dreaming and reality, the steersman felt a sudden craving. It was not a physical need, for there were traps aplenty for a careless eldar without the snare of physiological addiction; it was an old yearning in his heart to step aside from the woes and cares of the world.

Aradryan fought the urge. Dreaming had brought him to an understanding of reality that could not be hidden from. His revelation amongst the dead and dying of Alaitoc had lain heavily on him ever since, and no amount of carefree fumes and liquors would expunge them.

There was nothing here for him, but as Aradryan turned back towards the central boulevard he spied a face he recognised. In the glow of a deep blue lamp, he saw one of the Dreamers, slouched upon a low seat, eyes half open, mouth pursed as if blowing a delicate kiss.

'Rhydathrin?' said Aradryan, crossing over to the somnolent figure. The other eldar's eyelids flickered and then opened. Unfocused eyes regarded Aradryan for a while before a slow smile crept across the lips of the Dreamer.

'It's Aradryan, is it not?' said Rhydathrin. He blinked slowly, surfacing from his half-sleep. 'Yes, it is. I thought you would never come back.'

'I took aboard a ship,' said Aradryan, sitting in the chair opposite his companion. He laid a hand on the other's arm as Rhydathrin tried to sit up. Aradryan knew well what his friend was experiencing: a fugue-like trance that was hard to break. 'It has been a long time, but I have returned.'

'The stars,' said Rhydathrin. 'The stars call to us all, do they not? I went to the stars too. I danced in the corona and swam in their hearts.'

'Yes, I remember,' said Aradryan. 'But that was just

a dream. We dreamt that together, many times.'

'I was incinerated. So were you. I recall it precisely. Ash we became, blown away by the stellar winds.'

Aradryan shuddered, remembering the experience with a mixture of elation and horror. It had felt so peaceful yet terrifying, stripped away by one's own subconscious, the blaze of the imagined stars becoming a metaphor for self-revelation.

'I have been gone a long time, friend, but you are still here,' said Aradryan, suddenly concerned. 'Have you been Dreaming all of this time?'

'Of course not,' said Rhydathrin. He giggled and slumped to one side. 'Well, perhaps. It is hard to remember. Hard to remember what happened. Hard to... Didn't you go to the stars?'

'Yes, I have just told you that,' said Aradryan. He stood up, shaking his head gently. He had seen such a thing before, when an eldar became so enamoured of his dreams that his grip on reality was weakened almost to breaking. Time becomes meaningless, a cycle lasting an age or a moment, the present and the past no longer divided by the conscious mind.

There was little help that could be offered, and as he watched, Aradryan saw Rhydathrin slipping again into the half-sleep, his hand held up briefly in parting.

With swift steps, Aradryan left. There were no answers here, and coming to this place had served only as a reminder of the temptations he had overcome. Like the exarchs on the Warrior Path, or the bonesingers or farseers, the Everdreaming were trapped. Why could nobody else see how dangerous the Path was? For Aradryan it was clear. The Path was nothing more than an unending series of tempt-resses, each with her own lures, paraded through the life of an eldar until one snatched him up and held him captivated until death. It was a prison, no less so than the infinity circuit to which they were all destined to be sent. The tenets of discipline, obedience and focus were a sham, shackles invented to keep the eldar from being themselves.

Agitated, Aradryan left the Bridge of Yearning Sorrows and fled for the sanctuary of the docks at the Tower of Eternal Welcomes.

He could not stay on Alaitoc.

# DISLOCATION

*The Well of Harmonies – All things have a beginning, and for the webway that beginning took place at the Well of Harmonies. Some legends claim that this world was where Eldanesh first sired the eldar people, and where Khaine cast down his bloody spear to create the War in Heaven. There are some philosophers who say that the Well of Harmonies never existed, except as a metaphor, for everything is a cycle and begins nowhere, never ending. The truth may never be known, whether once there was a single place from which sprang the existence of the eldar empire, or if ever it was so, born into tragedy and reborn again and again in every subsequent generation.*

THE LOWER LEVELS of the Tower of Eternal Welcomes gave a second meaning to the name. It was amongst these twilight corridors that the eldar of Alaitoc made fresh liaisons, most of a temporary nature. Starship crews from other craftworlds mingled with pleasure-seeking Alaitocii, while the young and the naive moved from drinking establishment to eateries to apartments seeking congress with like-minded spirits.

Aradryan had never been drawn to this place before, occupied as he had been by the more existential delights of the Dreamrooms, but he hoped to find someone from the *Lacontiran* that he would know. It was not entirely unpleasant to walk along the curving passageways and flame-lit balconies, just one stranger amongst many, as lost as the Ulthwé-nese, Saim-Hannian and Biel-Tani traders and crews who shared the space with him.

As he walked past the open doors of the tower's various concerns, Aradryan was greeted by a melange of different moods. Songs and poetry, laughter both delicate and uproarious, music and silence played out, accompanied by the smells of cooking and fine spirits, perfumes and incenses. If there was anywhere on Alaitoc where it was possible to feel free from the Path, this was it, but still its presence could be felt. Attendants who trod the Path of Service moved from patron to patron with trays of sweetmeats and wines, while those on the Path of the Merchant came to terms with their greed and materialism through hard haggling and double-dealing.

In just a short time, Aradryan saw dozens of different costumes and fashions, some old, some so new they had freshly arrived from other craftworlds. Colours in dazzling rainbows fought against bleak monochromes. Pale visages stared at him amongst crowds of highly painted faces, while all manner of exotic pets – feline gyrinx, sinuous silversnakes, bipedal sconons and many others beside – purred and yowled and yapped as a backdrop to the constant conversation.

In contrast to the cloying crowd of his family, the throng of the Tower of Eternal Welcomes did not intimidate the steersman. Aradryan felt comfort in his anonymity, and with his courage bolstered by this, he ventured into a drinking hall. The interior was lit with a glow of bright neon blues and pinks, low couches forming broken circles around fountains encircled by constantly refreshing glasses.

Aradryan spied a gap at one of the drinking benches and crossed through the room to sit down. After inquiring with the eldar already seated whether the space was intended for an absent occupant, Aradryan was assured that it was truly available. He gingerly sat down, slightly embarrassed by his lack of experience at such things.

He looked at the glasses close at hand. They were like upended bells in shape, upon a belt that slowly but constantly travelled from one couch to the next. The silver liquid of the central fountain splashed into each glass, diluting the elixir already in the bottom, filling the glasses with blues and reds and oranges. Hesitantly, Aradryan snared a glass filled with an amber fluid and raised it to his nostrils. It smelt like burned honey, not altogether pleasant.

'I would avoid that one, if I were you,' said a voice to his right. He looked up and saw a female eldar sitting on the bench next to him. Her hair was black as night, save for a stripe of gold tucked behind her right ear. Golden too was the paint above her eyes, which were a piercing violet, and sable was the colour of her lips. Unlike many that Aradryan had seen since arriving, she eschewed colour on her cheeks, leaving her almost white skin unmarked. She was dressed in a high-necked robe, which clung tightly to the curves of her body as she leaned forwards and plucked the glass from Aradryan's trembling grasp. She replaced it with another, filled with a vermillion drink. Aradryan caught the scent of kaiberries and slightroot.

'This is my favourite,' the female eldar said, her dark lips forming a warm smile. 'Try it.'

Aradryan did as he was told, sipping the drink. It was sweet but not sickly, the liquid evaporating in his mouth as it was warmed by his breath, creating a swirl of flavour across his tongue. His eyes widened in appreciation and his companion laughed quietly.

'My name is Athelennil,' she said, touching her fingers to the back of Aradryan's hand. 'That is a good one, but do not drink it all, there are some other delights worth savouring.'

'I am not sure I should get intoxicated,' Aradryan said, feeling self-conscious. Athelennil smiled again.

'There is no fear of that here,' she said. 'Only taste and sensation from these drinks, nothing more. You can drink until you weep or your heart is contented, whichever you prefer.'

'Why would I weep?' Aradryan said sharply.

'I do not know, stranger,' Athelennil said pointedly. 'If we were to get to know each other, perhaps you would tell me.'

'My apologies, I have been very coarse. I am Aradryan, recently of *Lacontiran*.'

'A steersman, yes?' said Athelennil.

'Yes, how can you tell?'

The eldar waved a hand at Aradryan's hair and dark ensemble.

'The morose always feel drawn to steersmanship. It gives one a sense of control, yet brings untold wonders.'

'You speak as if out of experience.'

'Not of being a steersman. I was a navigator, though, for many passes.'

'And now?'

'Now? Now I am outcast,' said Athelennil. She grinned at Aradryan's shocked reaction. 'Of Biel-Tan, originally, though it has been some time since I trod upon the decks of my home. Do not look so shocked, Aradryan of *Lacontiran*. I would say a third of those around you are outcast, one way or another. There has been a bit of an impromptu gathering on Alaitoc in recent cycles.'

'Outcast tells me that you do not tread the Path,' said Aradryan, recovering his composure, 'but it does not tell me what you actually do with yourself, when not recommending drinks to strangers.'

'See? You can be charming when you try. I am mostly a ranger, my friend. I have spent the last three passes out amongst the Exodite worlds of the Falling Stair, learning about their ways.'

'An odd people, for sure,' said Aradryan. 'I myself have been along the Endless Valley, and so did not encounter Exodites, but all that I have heard marks them as a strange people.'

'The Alaitocii are a strange people,' said Athelennil, seeming to take no offence. 'When viewed from far enough away, that is.'

'Once I would have disagreed, but I have travelled enough to know that what you say is true,' said Aradryan. He took up a pale blue drink and offered it to Athelennil, before seizing a ruby mixture for himself. He held the rim of the glass to his lips in toast and then lifted it to eye level so that he looked at his companion through the translucent contents, turning her pale flesh scarlet and her eyes to deep purple. 'By our differences are we judged, by our shared heritage are we known.'

'A fine sentiment,' said Athelennil, one eyebrow raised in amusement. 'Though not one I feel you composed yourself.'

'I must confess the words belong to an old philosopher, called Kysaduras the Anchorite. You may have heard of him.'

'He is somewhat discredited on Biel-Tan, I must tell you,' said Athelennil. 'His *Introspections Upon Perfection* are sometimes dismissive of the role played by Asurmen in the forming of the Path. Biel-Tan has many Aspect Warriors, and they did not take kindly to such treatment.'

'You have been a Warrior?' asked Aradryan. He took a gulp of his drink when Athelennil nodded. It was delicately spiced, leaving a warm aftertaste that slowly seeped into his gums and down his throat. 'I have a friend who has also suffered the wrath of Khaine. She has moved on now, but perhaps it would be good for me to discuss it with her, do you think?'

'I would not,' Athelennil said, her mood becoming sombre. 'We don our war-mask for a reason. It is not wise to pry beyond that mask.'

The pair sat with that uncomfortable truth for a

little while, until Athelennil raised a more humorous topic. Soon they were laughing as they shared old exploits and scrapes. Athelennil was a fount of tales from across the known galaxy, and there was a richness to her stories that intrigued Aradryan. He longed to know more about the life of the outcast, but Athelennil grew tired. To his surprise, she invited him back to her quarters.

To his further surprise, Aradryan accepted.

IT WAS LATE in the cycle before Korlandril's grand unveiling of his latest masterpiece when Aradryan realised he had not been in contact with his friends since he had first arrived; nor his family, though that was of less concern. The previous few cycles had been a welcome distraction, spent in the company of Athelennil. They had shared a bed frequently, but also made a more telling acquaintance with each other in the establishments of the Tower of Eternal Welcomes and a few other well-chosen spots that Aradryan had used for romantic encounters prior to his departure.

He had remembered the unveiling as he had left Athelennil's apartment and a sudden guilt filled him at the thought. Firstly, he knew he should mention the event to Athelennil. It was, he had come to realise, something of a society occasion amongst the artistic circles of Alaitoc, and to be on good terms with a sculptor of Korlandril's renown was a matter of high regard. For all that she had shown him over the previous cycles concerning the underbelly of the Tower of Eternal Welcomes, Athelennil deserved an invite to this noteworthy celebration.

Secondly, he felt guilty because he knew he would

never offer that invite; he would accompany Thiri-anna. Athelennil was vivacious and engaging, but on more than one occasion in her company Aradryan had caught himself wondering what it would be like to share a similar experience with Thirianna. As a Warrior she had intrigued him; as a Poet she enticed him. The time he had shared recently with Athelennil had reawakened in Aradryan a desire for closeness; not the harmonious friendship he shared with his fellow steersmen, but something of a less temporary nature, a bonding with a kindred spirit. Athelennil was good company, but Thirianna stirred his heart in a way he had not felt for a long time.

So it was that he left Athelennil's apartment as Alaitoc settled a false twilight over its inhabitants. Not far away was a node for the infinity circuit, as could be found all over Alaitoc. Aradryan had not yet interfaced with the psychic network of the craftworld, and remembering the brief contact he had felt when *Lacontiran* had docked, Aradryan approached the ter-minal with a little trepidation.

He placed his palm upon the gently pulsing gem, and at the instant of his touch the node came to life, glowing energy filling the crystal threads that ran up into the slender pedestal. Immediately Aradryan was connected to all of Alaitoc, and felt its immensity sur-rounding him. He blocked out the surge of signals, the chatter of countless eldar exchanging informa-tion, and settled himself, fearing to be overwhelmed by the rush of flowing data.

He concentrated, focusing on Thirianna. The infin-ity circuit responded, his thought rippling across the crystalline matrix. No more than two heartbeats later he felt a connection with the poet, though it was only a faint echo of her spirit, imprinted upon the psychic circuitry of her chambers. Still cautious of the wider network, Aradryan feared to search further for her and instead left an impression upon the matrix expressing his desire that they meet.

Taking his hand away, Aradryan broke the connection. He stepped back, wondering what to do next. It was still almost a full cycle until Korlandril's unveiling and he felt no desire to do anything in particular. It was tempting to return to the embrace of Athelennil, but he resisted the urge. Instead, he made his way up to the pinnacle of the Tower of Eternal Welcomes and from a viewing gallery there watched the procession of ships coming and going through the swirling webway gate that lay astern of Alaitoc, wondering where those vessels came from and where they were going.

NOT LONG AFTER mid-cycle, Aradryan entered the Dome of Silence Lost. He had never come here before, it being one of the smaller domes on Alaitoc, situated away from the main habitation domes and thoroughfares. He was to meet Thirianna, who had responded to his message with the location of their rendezvous: the Bridge of Glimmering Sighs.

Most of the dome was made up of golden-grassed hillsides, the artificial sky coloured as if lit by pale dawnlight. Slow-moving aerethirs glided on thermals rising from concealed vents, their four wings utterly still, craning long necks to the left and right as they snapped at high-flying insects with their slender beaks.

Bisecting the dome was a wide river, its banks steep and filled with fern fronds. As he made his way towards the gurgling water, Aradryan spied solitary figures elsewhere in the semi-wilderness: poets sitting or meandering in contemplation, seeking inspiration from the sigh of the wind and the flitting shadows that passed across the undulating hillsides.

At the heart of the parkland, a silver arc crossed over the ribbon of white-foamed water that cascaded through the Dome of Silence Lost, its span curving as it rose to the crest high above the river. Green and blue snapwings and red-crested meregulls trilled and squawked as they dived beneath the bridge and swept along the banks, skimming just above the water.

There were no other eldar nearby and no sign of Thirianna, so Aradryan walked up the Bridge of Glimmering Sighs, its surface reflecting the cloudy twilight above. There was no wall or rail on either side, but such protection was not needed by the sure-footed eldar. Aradryan reached the crest and took in a deep breath, catching the subtle fragrance of the winter grass far below.

He stepped to the edge of the bridge, leaving only his heels on the span. Looking down between his feet, Aradryan saw the swirling waters far below. Turquoise and azure, flecked with foam, the river sped past jagged rocks, the silver and gold of fish glinting beneath the surface.

All Aradryan had to do was step forwards.

He sneered at himself for the thought. There was no resolution here. In purely physical terms, Alaitoc would not allow him to be dashed upon the foam-sprayed boulders. The craftworld would act to save his life, dulling the artificial gravity or perhaps generating a buffer field to smooth his fall.

Even if that were not the case, to throw himself from the bridge would be a pointless act. His fate was the same, whichever way he died. His spirit would be absorbed by the waystone hanging on his chest and in turn would be interred into the infinity circuit, to be trapped in the limbo of undeath forever.

'Aradryan!'

He looked over his shoulder at the sound of Thirianna's voice. She was not far away, striding purposefully up the bridge. Her smile was enchanting and instantly dispelled his morbid thoughts. Though there was no sign that Thirianna had guessed his self-destructive intent, Aradryan felt like a child who had been caught doing something forbidden. He smiled and waved at Thirianna, disguising the knot of guilt that tightened around his stomach.

The gesture reminded him of the time when he had left. Korlandril had been unable to bear the thought of him leaving, so it had been Thirianna who had accompanied Aradryan to *Lacontiran*, waving him goodbye as he had boarded the starship, happy for him yet her eyes betraying concern. Now those eyes looked at him with a questioning gaze.

'A very pleasant location,' he said, stepping back from the edge of the bridge to face Thirianna. 'I do not recall coming here before.'

'We never came here,' Thirianna replied. 'It is a well-kept secret amongst the poets of Alaitoc, and I trust that you will keep it so.'

'Of course,' said Aradryan. He looked out over the edge again and the thought that he might simply step from the bridge returned. 'It reminds me a little of the gulfs of space, an endless depth to fall into.'

'I would prefer that you did not fall,' Thirianna said, reaching out a hand to Aradryan's arm to gently tug him back. 'You have only just come back, and we have much to talk about.'

'We do?' he said, delighted by the thought. 'Perhaps you have a verse or two you would like to share with me, now that Korlandril does not intrude upon us.'

'As Korlandril told you, I do not perform my poems.' Thirianna took her hand away from Aradryan's arm and cast her gaze into the distance. Aradryan did not know what she looked at, but her lips parted gently. Her face in profile was remarkable, as if drawn by an artist's hand.

'I thought perhaps they were written for a very select audience,' said Aradryan. 'It must be such a gift, to compose one's disparate thoughts – to embrace them and order them in such a way.'

'They have an audience of one,' said Thirianna, still not meeting Aradryan's gaze. 'That one is me, no other.'

'You know that we used to share everything,' said Aradryan. 'You can still trust me.'

'It is myself that I do not trust. I cannot allow any fear that my compositions might be seen by another to restrict my feelings and words. I would be mortified if my innermost thoughts were put on display to all-comers.'

'Is that what I am?' said Aradryan, hurt by her words. How could she not trust him? He reminded himself that she remembered him as a Dreamer, and knew nothing of the bond and mutual faith he had formed with his fellow steersmen. He took Thirianna by the arm and turned her towards him. 'One of many?'

'It is no slight against you, nor against Korlandril or any other,' explained Thirianna. 'I choose to share what I share. The rest is mine alone, for no other to know. Please appreciate that.'

'Such an attitude does not sit well aboard a star-ship,' said Aradryan. 'One is part of the many, and in confinement with others most of the time. It takes several to pilot such a vessel, and we must each trust the others implicitly. I have learnt that friendship is not the only thing that must be shared. Cooperation, the overlapping of lives in ways beneficial to all, is the key to understanding our place in the universe.'

'A grandiose conclusion,' laughed Thirianna. 'Per-haps there is something of the poet in you!'

Aradryan realised his words had been a bit pomp-ous. He let go of her arm and glanced away, ashamed. She had not responded as he had hoped, and he could tell that there was nothing deeper than friend-ship between them. It seemed obvious that Korlandril had seen earlier what Aradryan had missed. Trying not to think about that, he looked at her again, hid-ing his feelings.

'Korlandril will not be entertaining us until the dusk of the cycle begins,' he said. 'If you will not grace me with your poems, perhaps you could sug-gest other entertainments that will divert us until the unveiling.'

Thirianna did not reply, but looked keenly at Aradryan, trying to penetrate the calm veneer he had assumed. Small twitches at the corner of her mouth and a slight narrowing of her eyes betrayed some internal dissent, but it passed in a moment and she forced a smile. Thirianna laid a palm upon the back of Aradryan's hand.

'The Weathering of the Nine takes place later today,' she said. She spoke of the carnival that took place aboard drifting sky barges, touring the nine great domes of inner Alaitoc. It was a haunt of adolescents and tourists. 'I have not been for many passes.'

'Nostalgia?' said Aradryan, smiling at the memories of the parade, an eyebrow rising in amusement.

'A return,' Thirianna replied. 'A return to a place we both know well.'

Aradryan considered the invitation for a moment, unsure whether it was wise to revisit old memories. If he declined, Athelennil would surely give him welcome instead. Yet that would be unfair on Thirianna. It was not her fault that she only sought friendship. It was the least Aradryan could do to attempt to enjoy some time with her.

'Yes, let us go back a while and revisit our youth,' Aradryan said. 'A return to happier times.'

'It is a truth that as we progress, our grief increases and our joys diminish,' said Thirianna.

The two of them started down the slope of the bridge towards the coreward bank. Thirianna's words seemed to be a general declaration rather than directed at him, but Aradryan felt them like a barb all the same. He could not allow his own depression to infect the happiness of a friend.

'It does not have to be so,' said Aradryan. 'The universe may have grief in plenty to heap upon us, but it is in our power to make our own joy.'

Thirianna looked to reply for a moment, but stayed silent, brow gently furrowed as she considered his words. They walked on a little further, close to each other but not intimately so.

'Yes, you are right,' said Thirianna, with a smile of genuine pleasure. 'Let us recapture the past and create some new happiness.'

THE STATUE WAS bathed in a golden glow and tinged with sunset reds and purples from the dying star above. It depicted an impressionistic Isha in abstract, her body and limbs flowing from the trunk of a lianderin tree, her wave-like tresses entwined within yellow leaves in its upreaching branches. Her face was bowed, hidden in the shadow cast by tree and hair. From the darkness a slow trickle of silver liquid spilled from her eyes into a golden cup held aloft by an ancient eldar warrior kneeling at her feet: Eldanesh. Light glittered from the chalice on his alabaster face, his armour a stylised arrangement of organic geometry, his face blank except for a slender nose and the merest depression of eye sockets. From beneath him, a black-petalled rose coiled up Isha's legs and connected the two together in its thorny embrace.

'She is so serene,' Thirianna said. 'Such calm and beauty.'

Aradryan's fingers flicked in agitation at his companion's words, for he saw nothing of the sort. Korlandril's creation had the same ostentation as its creator. Its name was no more humble either: *The Gifts of Loving Isha*, it was called. Aradryan looked at the sculpture, which was perfectly executed, and felt nothing. The weaving of organic and inorganic was intriguing, and the lines were pleasing to the eye, but there was nothing new to stir the steersman's heart.

'It is self-referential,' Aradryan explained, his gaze moving from the statue to Thirianna. 'It is a work of remarkable skill and delicacy, certainly. Yet I find it somewhat... staid. It adds nothing to my experience of the myth, merely represents physically something that is felt. It is a metaphor in its most direct form. Beautiful, but merely reflecting back upon its maker rather than a wider truth.'

Aradryan found it hard to express himself. The words he sought did not come easily and by the look that passed briefly across Thirianna's face he realised she thought his opinion scornful. She took a deep breath before replying, obviously choosing her words with care.

'But is not that the point of art, to create representations for those thoughts, memories and emotions that cannot be conveyed directly?'

'Perhaps I am being unfair,' said Aradryan, speaking sincerely. He saw movement in the crowd behind Thirianna and out of the corner of his eye spied Korlandril advancing on them. His face was a mask of anger, and Aradryan realised his criticism had been overheard. And not taken well at all. He sought to temper his comments as Korlandril stormed closer. 'Out in the stars, I have seen such wondrous creations of nature that the artifices of mortals seem petty, even those that explore such momentous themes such as this.'

'Staid?' snapped Korlandril, stepping next to Thirianna, who turned with a look of shock which swiftly became one of guilt, as though she shared the blame for Aradryan's critique. 'Self-referential?'

Korlandril's childish outburst was embarrassing, but there was nothing Aradryan could do to take back the words; just as there was nothing to stop the Artist feeling the hurt he did. Aradryan tried to offer some advice.

'My words were not intended to cause offence, Korlandril,' he said, offering a placating palm towards his friend. 'They are but my opinion, and an ill-educated one at that. Perhaps you find my sentimentality gauche.'

Korlandril hesitated, blinking and glancing away in a moment of awkwardness. The pause lasted only the briefest heartbeat before his scowl returned.

'You are right to think your opinion ill-informed,' Korlandril said. 'While you gazed naively at glittering stars and swirling nebulae, I studied the works of Aethyril and Ildrintharir, learnt the disciplines of ghost stone weaving and inorganic symbiosis. If you have not the wit to extract the meaning from that which I have presented to you, perhaps you should consider your words more carefully.'

Korlandril's accusation was misplaced, and it irked Aradryan that he should be blamed for not being stirred by the Artist's pedestrian creation. The steersman noticed Thirianna stepping back as he crossed his arms and met Korlandril's glare with a stare of his own.

'And if you have not the skill to convey your meaning from your work, perhaps you need to continue studying,' Aradryan snarled. 'It is not from the past masters that you should learn your art but from the heavens and your heart. Your technique is flawless, but your message is parochial. How many statues of Isha might I see if I travelled across the craftworld? A dozen? More? How many more statues of Isha exist on other craftworlds? You have taken nothing from the Path save the ability to indulge yourself in this spectacle. You have learnt nothing of yourself, of the darkness and the light that battles within you. There is intellect alone in your work, and nothing of yourself. It might be that you should expand your terms of reference.'

The two of them had shared a bond of Dreamers, and had left imprints upon each other in ways that simple friends could not. Yet Korlandril had changed beyond recognition. His arrogance was towering, his self-importance colossal. The Artist's venomous words felt all the more like a deep betrayal because of the past they had shared.

'What do you mean by that?' said Korlandril, every syllable spat with anger.

'Get away from this place, from Alaitoc,' Aradryan said, trying to be patient, remembering that it was not Korlandril's fault; he had discarded all self-awareness when he had become the Artist. Aware of Thirianna's scrutiny, Aradryan made a show of seeking accord with Korlandril, for it did Aradryan no favours to appear the aggressor in the eyes of his would-be lover. 'Why stifle your art by seeking inspiration only from the halls and domes you have seen since childhood? Rather than trying to look upon old sights with fresh eyes, why not turn your old eyes upon fresh sights?'

Korlandril parted his lips for a moment, but then shut his mouth firmly. He directed a fierce glare at

Aradryan, before stalking away through the blue grass, scattering guests in his flight.

Aradryan turned towards Thirianna, hands raised in apology, hoping that she did not attach any blame to him for Korlandril's tantrum.

'I am sorry, I d– ' he started, but Thirianna's scowl cut him off.

'It is not I that deserves your apology,' she said curtly, the words like barbs of guilt in Aradryan's gut. 'Perhaps such behaviour is tolerated on a starship, but you are back on Alaitoc. You are right, you have become gauche.'

With that parting remark, she left Aradryan, ignoring his call after her. As he watched her walking away, the steersman knew that he had made a grave error. His two closest friends had turned from him, and Alaitoc seemed even less like home than it did a few moments before.

# FATE

*The Deserts of Sain-Shelai* – The black sands of Sain-Shelai spread to the horizon, lifeless and bleak. At their centre stands a solitary hill, and in that hill is the opening of a small cave. Inside that cave burns a small fire. The pall of its smoke spreads out across all of the desert, joining it as one with the flames. From the smoke comes the tale of what goes by, and so into the flames stares the one-eyed hag, Morai-heg. Seeing what passes, the Crone weaves the skein of fate, choosing the length of the thread of life for each mortal, binding it to the destinies of others in the great pattern of existence. On occasion, a great storm will sweep the black sands and Morai-heg will be blinded. She throws her weavings upon the flames, casting fate adrift for those poor spirits, until the storms have passed and she can see once more.

ARADRYAN FOUND ATHELENNIL in one of the vapour lounges of the Tower of Eternal Welcomes. After his confrontation with Korlandril he was in no mood to relax, inhaling narcotic and hypnotic incenses and fumes. Taking note of his agitated disposition, Athelennil bid farewell to her companions and took Aradryan back to her quarters. Seeking some sense of release, the steersman took her arm and stepped towards the bed chamber but she twisted from his grip with a frown and pointed to the low couch that ran along one curved wall of the chamber.

'You misunderstand our relationship,' she said. 'I do not exist solely to salve your troubled thoughts. What we share must be mutual.'

'I am sorry,' said Aradryan, taking one of Athelennil's hands in his, bowing in apology. 'I meant no offence, my love.'

'My love?' her laugh was edged with bitterness. 'Love has nothing to do with what we have. Do not seek to woo me with false words.'

Aradryan was taken aback by her forthright denial and realised that he had said the words idly, without even considering them. She was right to rebuke him.

'I am disconcerted and dismayed,' Aradryan confessed. 'I have had a sorrowful parting with friends.'

'Not sorrowful,' said Athelennil. She took Aradryan by the arm and led him to the couch, pushing him to be seated. From an alcove in the wall she took up a crystal bottle and two glasses, pouring two measures of the lavender-coloured drink. 'Your agitation is not sorrow, it is something more than that.'

Knowing that the burden of the evening's events would stay upon him until he confided in another,

Aradryan told the sorry tale of the unveiling, and confessed his regret for not taking Athelennil as his partner.

'Korlandril and I parted with angry words, and I fear I have also lost Thirianna,' he finished.

'Ah, sweet Thirianna,' said Athelennil. She held up a hand to Aradryan to silence his protest about her tone of voice, which was gently mocking. 'Do not think to deny that you have feelings for her. I say this not out of jealousy, but out of friendship. If you wish to be with her, you will have no complaint from me. I am due to leave Alaitoc in two cycles' time anyway, so it is irrelevant.'

'Two cycles?' Aradryan had known that Athelennil would leave at some point but he had not thought it would be so soon.

'I travel aboard *Irdiris*,' she said, sitting beside Aradryan.

'Bound for where?' he asked. 'Will you return?'

'I have no answer for either question, and I care for no answer.' Athelennil stretched an arm along the back of the couch and arched her back, her eyes never leaving Aradryan's 'That is the point of being outcast – to have no bonds to fetter one's travels.'

'I will come with you,' declared Aradryan.

'Will you?' replied Athelennil, assuming a pose of mock subservience. She flicked her hair from her face in annoyance. 'What if I do not want you to come with me?'

Aradryan had not thought of such a thing and slumped in the chair, shoulders sagging. He felt fingers on his knee and looked up to see Athelennil smiling at him.

'You are in such a sorry state, Aradryan.' She stroked a hand up his leg and then put her fingers to his cheek. 'Do not make a drama out of circumstance. I would be pleased if you chose to come with me, but be warned that we need no steersman. We are outcasts, not mentors, and if you leave on *Irdiris* you are choosing the Path of the Outcast too.'

'I am not so sure...'

Aradryan was changing his mind with every heartbeat. He wanted to see the galaxy, and to spend time with Athelennil; he also wanted to stay with Thirianna. Evidently the conflict was clear to Athelennil.

'I will take no umbrage if you wish to explore where the water flows,' she said, withdrawing her hand. 'Speak with Thirianna. Make inquiries of the other starships if you wish to continue to be a steersman.'

'There is no reason to contact Thirianna, save to give her fresh opportunity to share her scorn for me,' said Aradryan, standing up. 'You did not see the disdain in her face, disdain I deserved.'

'It is deserved if you think so little of your friends that they would judge you so harshly on a single episode.'

'You think she would speak with me?'

Athelennil waved a hand dismissively and looked away.

'It matters not what I think. If you fear further rebuke, then do not speak to her. If you have any courage at all, you will put aside your fear and seek her out.'

'Then I shall, if that is your feeling on the matter,' said Aradryan, heading for the door.

He hesitated a step but there was no further reply

from Athelennil. Stung by the sentiment of her words, Aradryan headed to the infinity circuit node, seeking to link with Thirianna. As before, she was not to be easily found and so he left his imprint, conjoined with the desire for reconciliation.

Knowing that to return so swiftly to Athelennil would be an invitation for further mockery, Aradryan instead headed into Alaitoc, away from the dock towers and quay spires. The outcast's words accompanied him, though, distance no object to their pursuit. The offer to leave Alaitoc – properly leave as an outcast – preyed on his mind as he rode a spear-car from the Dome of Tranquil Reservations to the Boulevard of Split Moons.

The proposition filled him with fear for the most part, but in a way the fear added to the thrill of being outcast. It was safety that cloyed and coddled his thoughts, and so perhaps he needed to make the ultimate break from their safety, giving himself no refuge. If the Path was the trap he thought it to be, the only escape was to become outcast: to eschew the teachings of the Path altogether. It mattered nothing if he voyaged far from Alaitoc for the rest of his life if he did so on the ships of the craftworld, which though distant were still merely extensions; detached limbs of the same body.

Aradryan wandered the stalls that lined the Boulevard of Split Moons, named so for in shape the thoroughfare resembled two crescents backed onto each other. There were all manner of small trinkets on sale; gewgaws of pretty gems and polished jewels that caught the light in dazzling rainbows. The traders here were not mercantile in the true sense, but mostly artisans giving away their wares to make room for future projects. When one lived as long as an eldar, there was a great deal of clutter to be periodically cleared.

Some stalls had ancient artefacts that passed from generation to generation, some of them dating back hundreds of passes. Antiquity in itself held little value for the eldar, but some aesthetics, some designs had a timeless quality, and there were those who preferred to possess the purity of their original incarnations rather than objects created in the style of the old schools.

Also on display were clothes, of styles both fashionable and old. Aradryan had given little thought to his wardrobe of late and lingered awhile at these stands, studying the cut and cloth of loose robes and tight jackets, studded leggings and belted shirts. His own attire had earned him a few strange glances and a couple of admiring looks. He wore a wide-shouldered jacket of dark blue, flared at the hips, fastened by a line of tiny buckles from waist to neck and wrist to elbow. A heavy kilt of subtly blended greens and blacks covered his upper legs, above narrow boots studded with golden buttons. It was a style that had not been widely popular even before his departure, and now looked very out of place.

Thinking of how long he had been away aboard *Lacontiran*, it occurred to him that if he were to accept Athelennil's offer, he might never come back to Alaitoc.

Never.

He tried to summon up a little grief at the thought. He tried to imagine what it would be like never to come here again, but as Aradryan looked at the petty merchants and their meaningless wares he could find no enthusiasm for the place of his birth.

Into these thoughts came the apparition of Thirianna. At first, Aradryan thought that it was not strange that she should appear in his thoughts when he considered leaving the craftworld, but after a moment he realised that her appearance was not a creation of his imagination; she was touching upon his mind via the infinity circuit.

He was guarded at first, offering cordial greetings to his friend. In reply he received a wave of warmth, and sensed a desire to make amends and seek comfort. This was much to his liking, and Thirianna detected as such. She would come to him, he knew, and he would wait for her.

The connection dissipated, leaving Aradryan slightly out of touch with reality for a moment. He regained his senses, the lingering effect of the psychic connection ebbing away.

Aradryan did not have long to wait. Thirianna found him as he looked at a pair of plain golden earrings. Turning at the sound of her voice, Aradryan was stunned by the vision that appeared before him. Thirianna wore a tight bodysuit of glittering purple and silver. On her arms she wore several bejewelled torcs, with long white gloves up to the elbow. Her boots were of the same material, and about her slender throat was wound a light scarf, which hung down to a wide belt studded with blazing blue gemstones. Her hair and eyes had been coloured a subtle jade green, matched by the colour of the small waistbag that hung at her hip.

Aradryan smiled broadly as she approached and held up the earrings, which were shaped vaguely like two leaping fish.

'Not really to my taste,' said Thirianna as they touched hands in greeting.

'Not for you, for me,' said Aradryan, nonplussed.

'I know,' said Thirianna, laughing softly. She took one of the earrings and held it up to the side of Aradryan's face. The curve of the jewellery matched well with his features and she nodded. 'Yes, they would look very good.'

'Then it is decided,' said Aradryan, recovering his composure. The steersman signalled his desire to take the jewellery to the stallholder, who nodded his head in appreciation of a choice well made and waved for the pair to continue on their way.

The two of them spoke little as they moved between the stalls and stores, examining gems and scarves, robes and headdresses. Thirianna's silence unnerved Aradryan and he found himself making inconsequential utterances to fill the quiet, yet the more he talked about the wares on display, the more distant she seemed to become. He tried to engage her with a commentary on the latest fashions, which were a trifle plain, boring by his standards, but she did not want to participate.

She was similarly quiet when he tried to hint at his dissatisfactions with craftworld life. He heard her sigh more than once, and the harder he tried to explain how distant he felt from life on Alaitoc, the more annoyed she became. Eventually it became too much for her.

'What is it about life here that chafes so badly

that you must constantly gripe and find fault?' she snapped, taking Aradryan by the arm and guiding him to a small alleyway between two stores where they would not be overheard.

'I am sorry if I have broadened my view beyond the petty baubles on display here,' Aradryan replied, though he bit back a comment about the pettiness of spirit that pervaded the Alaitocii if they praised the baubles filling the market, realising that such a sentiment would include Thirianna. He paused and calmed himself. 'No, I am genuinely sorry. You say that life here chafes, and I can think of no better word to describe it. It rubs against my spirit, binding my thoughts like a cord around my limbs. Alaitoc is safe, and controlled, and suffocating. It offers comfort and dependability. I no longer desire these things.'

'So why did you return at all?' Thirianna asked, showing genuine concern. 'There must have been a reason to come back.'

Friendship had been the reason for his return, but his friends had gone by the time he got back, replaced by a Poet and an Artist. Love, of a deeper kind than he had felt for his friends, had grown in his heart when he had met Thirianna the Poet, but how could he tell her that? She had made it clear she did not feel the same, and so such a declaration was both selfish and pointless, serving to hurt both of them for no obvious gain. Aradryan clamped down on the emotions that raged through his breast, forcing himself to appear unperturbed though inside his thoughts were in tumult.

'My memories of Alaitoc were fonder than the reality,' said Aradryan. 'Or perhaps the reality has changed to one of which I am less fond.'

'You speak of Korlandril,' said Thirianna. The mention of the Artist's name caused a brief flicker of annoyance in Aradryan, which quickly turned to shame when he admitted to himself his part in angering the Artist.

'And you,' said Aradryan. He sighed and leaned back against the wall of the alley, crossing his arms over his chest. Though he could not confess all, there was something of his state of mind that he could share with Thirianna. Something she had to know if he was going to leave. 'I do not know my place here any longer.'

'It will take time, but you will adjust again and learn anew to find the delight in each moment that passes, and meaning in the things you now find trivial,' Thirianna assured him. 'Alaitoc is your home, Aradryan.'

'Is it?' he replied. 'I have no family left here, and my friends are not those I left behind. Why should I choose to stay here when all of the galaxy is open to me?'

'Though it would sadden me to see you leave again, I cannot argue against your desires,' said Thirianna, and her agreement served to dishearten Aradryan further.

'Is there some reason I should stay?' he asked. He made no attempt to hide his thoughts this time, directing a look of longing, of desire, at Thirianna. She was shocked and took a moment to reply.

'I have only my friendship to offer,' Thirianna said. Aradryan's disappointment was instant, showing as a furrowed brow and parted lips for a moment before the emotionless mask descended again.

'Friendship was once enough, but not now,' said Aradryan, his tone even and quiet. He directed a quick bow of the head to Thirianna, in deference to her feelings, eyes closed out of respect. The rejection hurt, but it was not unexpected. He had met her on a fool's errand. Perhaps Athelennil had known this all along, and so had forced him into confirming his fears rather than harbour baseless hope. 'It seems that even friendship is not possible with Korlandril. He has grown arrogant, I think, and he has no time for others. Thank you for your candour, Thirianna. I hope I have not caused you undue embarrassment or woe.'

His embarrassment growing, Aradryan fled, leaving Thirianna with quick strides. He stalked along the Boulevard of Split Moons, heading back to the transport that would take him to the Tower of Eternal Welcomes. As he thought of joining Athelennil on her travels, his heart lightened a little and so too did his step.

Approaching the platform of the carriageway, Aradryan smiled, suddenly feeling free of the burden he had been carrying since he had seen Thirianna and Korlandril waiting for him beside *Lacontiran*. He owed them nothing. They had not waited for him, but had moved on with their lives, as they were right to do. Now he would move on with his life too. Thirianna was not unique, he told himself. If he spent more time with Athelennil the two of them would grow more alike. Freed from the constraints of the Path, Aradryan was sure he would become a more compatible companion.

It was better to leave Alaitoc. There really was nothing for him here.

THE IRDIRIS WAS a small skiff, with a single stellar sail, her hull displaying a mottled green and black as Aradryan approached along the dockside. Cargo was being loaded into her hull, and a stepway arced up to an opening in her side not far from her slender nose. For all that she was considered small by starship standards, the *Irdiris* was still large enough to take some time to walk from tail to nose. Her golden sail stretched high between the beams of the docking wharf, on the outer edge of the Bay of Departing Sorrows.

The name meant nothing to Aradryan as he walked with Athelennil by his side. She was dressed in a tight bodysuit of yellow and blue, her hair coloured black and white in alternating stripes, tied into an elaborate braid that hung to the small of her back. Aradryan's eyes danced over the curve of her waist and hips, enjoying the spectacle.

'You have company,' murmured Athelennil, a moment before Aradryan heard a familiar voice calling his name. 'I will see you inside.'

Athelennil parted from him as he looked ahead, seeing Thirianna walking quickly along the dockside. His heart leapt at the sight, not with hope but with fear. He was so close to leaving now, he could not turn back. It did not bother him to disappoint Athelennil and her companions, if disappointed they would actually be, but he was on the brink of finally quitting Alaitoc and if Thirianna showed a change of heart he might never escape.

He stopped, hands on hips. Thirianna broke into a run. He heard a derisive snort from Athelennil moments before Thirianna reached him, before she turned up the boarding ramp.

'This is madness,' Thirianna said as she reached her friend. She reached out a hand to his arm but he stepped away, avoiding the contact.

'It is freedom,' he replied, glancing over his shoulder towards the open, iris-like door of the starship. He looked back at Thirianna and he realised that there was no need for his last words to her to be so harsh. 'I did not wish to be parted like this. It is too painful to say goodbye.'

'It does not have to be this way,' said Thirianna. 'Do not leave.'

'You wish me to stay?' said Aradryan, one eyebrow raised. He could tell from the way she held herself and the tone in her voice that she had not suddenly developed feelings for him. He was intrigued to hear what argument Thirianna would present. 'Would there be a purpose in remaining on Alaitoc?'

'There must be more to this than your desire to be with me,' she said. 'How can you hate Alaitoc, who has raised and nurtured you and given you so much?'

'I do not hate her. I am merely bored of her. Perhaps in time my thirst for new vistas and experiences will be sated and I will return.' A thought, half-formed, came to mind and Aradryan spoke it without hesitation; a solution to both of his problems. 'Would you come with me?'

'Be safe,' she said. 'See the stars and come back to us.'

'I will, Thirianna,' Aradryan replied. He strode close

to her and laid his hands on her shoulders. 'Take care of Korlandril for me. I sense that he needs a good friend at the moment, if only to save him from himself.'

'And who is going to save you from yourself?' Thirianna asked, tears moistening her cheeks. She could not look at Aradryan and kept her gaze on the marble-like floor of the docking pier.

'Nobody,' Aradryan said. I do not need anybody, he told himself. He let go of her and stepped away, knowing that he had this one chance to do so. If he held her, if he comforted her, it would be too much and he would have to stay, to still the guilt that was even now stirring in his heart.

Luckily she did not look at him with her beautiful eyes, and he turned away, taking quick steps to the boarding gantry. He did not look back as the door hissed shut behind him, leaving him alone in a short passageway.

Like all eldar ships, the interior of the *Irdiris* was more organic than constructed. The vessel had been grown into being by the bonesingers and their choirs: first the wraithbone skeletal core and then the smooth weave of psycho-plastic that formed the hull, bulkheads and walls. The floor merged seamlessly with the walls, which merged seamlessly with the ceiling, forming a continuous enclosure of softly gleaming yellow and green. At regular intervals the walls bulged slightly around the internal rib-like bracing of the wraithbone skeleton.

The light from the walls was ample for the eldar to see by, suffusing the ship with a gentle, constant glow of dappled colour. Underfoot the floor was slightly soft and yielding to Aradryan's tread, and spaced between petal-like doorways were bulges and blisters of storage lockers, some small, others larger than Aradryan. Here and there were crystalline clusters set into the walls: interfaces with the ship's psychic matrix. The pulse of the energy network was a sensation in the spirit rather than heard or felt. Aradryan detected the telltale quickening of the wave passing from the ship's core along the hull, as the engines generated power to slip aside from Alaitoc's artificial gravity field.

OUTSIDE, LIGHTS SPRANG into life along the length of the *Irdiris*, bathing the dock in a warm aura of oranges and reds. With barely a sound, the breeze of its passing ruffling Thirianna's hair, the voidrunner lifted from the platform and tilted starwards. The forcefield enclosing the dock shimmered into silvery life as the *Irdiris* passed through it. *Irdiris* swiftly accelerated, diving towards the golden-edged circle of the webway gate swirling aft of Alaitoc. It became a shimmer against the stars as its holofield activated, and then it was gone.

# Part Two
---
## Ranger

# FREEDOM

*The Exodite Worlds – First to escape the Fall were the Exodites. They saw the shadow that had fallen upon the hearts of the eldar and they took to their ships and fled the empire. To the newest worlds they travelled, seeded in recent generations, primordial and harsh. They tamed the reptilian beasts they found there, and named them dragons after the grand serpents of old. With them they took the secret of crystal networks and into the rock of their new homes they bound their world spirits, so that when the Fall came and She Who Thirsts came into being, their souls were captured by the crystal webs of their worlds and not devoured. Yet the world spirits that sustain the settlements of the Exodites are not without their own hunger, and into them must be passed the spirits of every generation sustained by their energy.*

THOUGH THE IRDIRIS was not as large as *Lacontiran*, Aradryan was immediately familiar with the layout of the starship. Like all eldar vessels, she had been grown by the bonesingers from a central wraithbone core, resembling the spine and ribs of some large beast, though inverted. A dorsal passageway ran the length of the ship, with sizeable compartments to either side, the pastel blue psycho-plastic of the walls gently mottled with green. Curving bulkheads separated the chambers, extruded from thicker rib-like spars that bulged gently from the walls.

The structural core was also the power plant of the ship, suffused with psychic energy from Alaitoc's infinity circuit for transit in the webway, during which the stellar sail was furled and the mast retracted and lowered into the fuselage of the vessel. This energy matrix could be felt by Aradryan as *Irdiris* powered away from the craftworld, a gentle thrum throughout the ship that came to his mind rather than his other senses.

Athelennil waited from him in a small arched hallway at the end of the entry passage, near to the slender nose of the ship. She said nothing, but her expression showed a little surprise that he had joined them.

'There is nothing to keep me on Alaitoc,' Aradryan said as he joined her.

'It will always be your home, whatever happens,' said Athelennil. 'I have travelled to many worlds, but part of me still belongs to Biel-Tan. You cannot deny that.'

Aradryan shrugged dismissively and Athelennil took that, rightly, as a sign that he did not wish to continue with the topic of conversation.

'There is plenty of space, *Irdiris* is berthed for at least twenty, and there are only five aboard,' Athelennil told him. 'You are free to choose whichever space you prefer from those that are unoccupied. Come, I will show you the rest of the ship.'

Turning sternwards, she led Aradryan down the central corridor, which was broken by archways every dozen paces or so. Some were open and led into storage areas, curving ramps dropping down into the depths of the starship. Others were closed off by slit doorways. Athelennil stopped in front of one of these and it opened, responding to her mental command, revealing a communal eating area. An oval table dominated the room, supported on a wide leg that grew up from the floor, like green-veined marble in colour. On the far wall were crystal-fronted cabinets filled with dishes and utensils, many of which were unfamiliar to Aradryan.

'We all have to fend for ourselves here,' said Athelennil, noting his bemused expression. 'There is no Path of Service to tend to your needs.'

Aradryan nodded in understanding. It was not a consideration that had occurred to him, and this minor revelation made him realise just how different his life would be. Even aboard *Lacontiran* his lifestyle had not been much different from that experienced by the Alaitocii throughout their lives. As an outcast he would have to be all things: steersman, cook, warrior, navigator, messenger.

'Through there is the crop vale,' Athelennil said, interrupting his thoughts. She pointed at a doorway to their right. 'We have four bays set aside for growing food, and another with a freshwater pool. Everybody contributes their time.'

'Of course,' said Aradryan. He smiled faintly. 'You will have to teach me what to do.'

'And you best be a quick study, my friend. With only five of us, there is a lot of work to go around, even with the supplies we have in biostasis in the hold.'

She continued the tour, showing him several communal areas, all but one of which were bare save for low couches and tables. The fourth was furnished more fully, with an abstract tapestry hanging on one wall, its iridescent threads changing subtly in the breeze of the artificial air, creating a permanently shifting, wave-like pattern of greens and greys. Alcoves in the walls contained a few keepsakes and trophies: vases and small statuettes; crystal decanters containing a variety of glistening drinks; a child's animadoll which turned its doughy features towards Aradryan as he entered, its crude face scrutinising him without eyes.

On one of the couches was another eldar, dressed in a short robe of heavy black cloth. He eyed Aradryan with curiosity and stood up, his scarlet pantaloons billowing, tucked into short lizard-hide boots. Aradryan guessed him to be older by a generation.

'Jair Essinadith,' said the other eldar, raising a palm in greeting. His grey eyes never left Aradryan's and the former steersman met his stare without hesitation.

'Aradryan.'

'Of course you are,' said Jair. 'Athelennil has told us about you.'

'I hope she was flattering,' said Aradryan, glancing at his companion.

'Not really, my would-be vagabond,' said Jair. His tone was not overtly hostile, but Aradryan was in no doubt that he was entering a close-knit group and his arrival would cause disruption.

'And where do you hail from, originally?' Aradryan tried his best to be cordial. This was a new start for him, and if he was to make the most of the opportunity it would go well to be on friendly terms with his shipmates.

'Alaitoc, like you,' said Jair. 'Though I left many passes ago. I was once mentored by Naerithin Alaimana. The waterfalls in the Dome of Unintended Pleasures – I created them. Perhaps you know them?'

'A modern wonder, for sure,' said Aradryan. 'I spent three cycles dreaming on the viewing gallery there.'

'There will be plenty of time to exchange old tales, I am sure,' said Athelennil, taking Aradryan by the arm. 'You should meet the others first.'

Aradryan nodded his goodbye to Jair as he was gently guided from the room, receiving the same in return. When they were back in the main passageway, Athelennil slipped her arm under Aradryan's and leant closer.

'I do not think Jair will remain with us for much longer,' she said quietly as they headed aft. 'He speaks ever more about his past accomplishments, and the longing for Alaitoc's peace is growing stronger with every journey we take. His reminiscences are becoming repetitive, so it will be good for him to have another ear into which he can pour them.'

'I do not wish to hear of Alaitoc,' said Aradryan. 'It is to leave the craftworld behind that I have joined you. I fear constant reminder will only irritate me.'

'And so you must learn some patience. On the craftworld we can lose ourselves, for our entire lives if we wish, allowing petty grievances and grating encounters to pass us by. If you wish to remain on *Irdiris* you must accept the rest of us as we are.'

'I am not insensitive,' argued Aradryan. 'On *Lacontiran* I was in close proximity to many others and managed to make friends and remain civil.'

There was no reply from Athelennil, but in the absence of her voice Aradryan could hear the sound of music. The distinctive lilting notes of a summer-flute drifted along the passageway from an open arch ahead.

'That is Lechthennian,' explained Athelennil, smiling as she tapped her fingers on Aradryan's arm in beat to the lively tune. 'He plays all manner of instruments, and composes his songs himself. He spends most of his time back here on his own, playing to himself or writing his music.'

Aradryan listened to the melody and could appreciate the complex harmonies that filled the corridor. The tune stirred his heart in a way that little else had done in the last few cycles, lifting his spirit, promising excitement and contentment in equal measure.

'Perhaps we should not disturb him,' Aradryan said. 'I would not like to intrude.'

'He will not mind,' Athelennil assured him. 'If we did not interrupt his playing, we would never get to speak to him. He is the oldest of us, by far. *Irdiris* has had many crews, changing over the passes, but as far as we can tell, Lechthennian has been here for at least two arcs.'

'He must be as old as the ship, almost,' exclaimed

Aradryan. Even as he said the words, not far from the archway, he realised that the music had stopped.

'Not even close,' said a voice from the chamber beyond, soft and assured.

Aradryan and Athelennil stepped through the doorway to find Lechthennian standing by the wall, placing the arm-long summerflute into a purpose-shaped niche. There were other instruments on shelves, in alcoves and on stands upon the floor. Aradryan recognised some: a fourteen-stringed half-lyre, next to an arching holoharp; the red, white and black keys of a chime organ; a set of half a dozen lapdrums. Others were unknown to him, a variety of stringed, blown and percussion devices.

The eldar was barefoot, clad in loose trousers and a tight-fighting jacket of white that glimmered with a cross-thread of silver, which struck Aradryan as odd, for white was the colour of mourning and normally shunned by right-thinking folk. Lechthennian was old, to those who knew what to look for; the slight thinness of his hair and skin; the lines at the corners of his eyes; the flare of his nostrils and tapering of his ear tips. Yet none of these purely physical attributes betrayed his age as much as the weight of his gaze, which measured Aradryan in an instant.

'*Irdiris* is nearly as old as Alaitoc,' said Lechthennian, seating himself again on a stool to one side of the room. There were other plain chairs arranged facing him, set in a semicircle to the left of the archway. 'Her first voyage came just half an arc after the Fall.'

'I did not mean offence,' said Aradryan hastily.

'Why should I take offence, I am old, as you say,' replied Lechthennian. He waved a hand for the pair to seat themselves and produced a thin, whistle-like instrument from a pocket inside a robe. He tootled and tweeted for a few moments, the notes reminding Aradryan of a nursery tune from his childhood. Lechthennian then looked hard at Aradryan, the whistle spinning slowly between his fingers. 'Escape is not what you think it is.'

'I... I am not sure what you mean.'

'There is no need to be coy,' said Lechthennian. 'You are outcast now, and it is no cause of shame, just as my age is no cause of shame. You want to be away from Alaitoc, and that is no bad thing. Be careful, though, that in running from one trouble you do not pitch yourself headlong into another.'

'I am in no trouble,' said Aradryan. 'I do not know what Athelennil told you about me, but I came on board free of any dark cloud.'

'We both know that is not true, Aradryan,' said the aging eldar, his expression stern. 'I know only what I read in your eyes and I see that darkness comes with you, but it is not all doom and gloom.' He made another couple of toots on his whistle, like the call of the grasswitch frog, and grinned. 'You have good company, a fast ship and a desire to see the galaxy. There are worse fates.'

'You are an accomplished musician,' said Aradryan, glad for the opportunity to change the subject to his companion.

'No, I am not a musician,' said Lechthennian. 'As you would know it, a musician dedicates himself to the perfection of his composition and performance. I have simply had a long time to dabble and pick up a thing or two.'

'If you are not a musician, what are you?' said Aradryan. He felt Athelennil's fingers tighten on his arm, as though he had said something wrong, but Lechthennian continued to smile.

'I am a traveller, that is all,' he said. 'Welcome aboard *Irdiris*.'

THE LAST MEMBER of the crew, Caolein, was also the pilot, and Aradryan did not see him for some time as he guided the ship through the webway, navigating the traffic of ships coming and going this close to Alaitoc. Younger even than Aradryan, Caolein sported blond and black hair to his waist, tied in three long locks that were bound with silver thread. He wore a pale grey steersman's suit studded with small gems of blue and purple, and flopped down with a sigh on the couch opposite Aradryan and Athelennil, who had been in the common area drinking sour whitenut tea and discussing the cooking arrangements.

'I'm glad that is done,' declared the pilot. He reached out and poured himself a cup of the whitenut tea from the steaming ewer. 'Out into the open webway, heading for the stars!'

'Towards Kha-alienni, like we discussed?' said Athelennil, eyes narrowing with suspicion.

'More or less,' Caolein replied defensively.

'Jair warned you about this before,' Athelennil snapped, standing up. She turned towards the door, and Aradryan was not sure whether he was meant to follow or not.

'Relax!' Caolein held out a hand. 'We are heading to Kha-alienni, for sure. I thought it might be nice to go by way of the Archer Cascades, that's all.'

Athelennil stopped and turned back in the archway.

'For truth? We do not need another of your wild detours, Caolein.'

'For truth. We have someone new on board, and I bet he has never seen the Archer Cascades.'

Aradryan shook his head.

'No, I do not think *Lacontiran* passed that way,' he said.

Caolein invited Aradryan to accompany him to the pilot's chamber, in a small blister just in front of the mast. Though smaller, with space only for two eldar, the control panel seemed similar to the one Aradryan had used on board the *Lacontiran*. In some ways it was simpler, there being only one stellar sail and the ship being smaller. In other ways, there was a lot more to think about, with various trim and attitude controls all being interconnected, rather than handled by separate pilots. For the moment, the spirit circuitry was piloting the vessel, guiding it along a straight, broad stretch of the webway. A display glowing from an oval crystal screen above the console showed a white tube stretching ahead and behind, rendered from the feedback the ship was receiving across the psychic connection with the webway.

'When we next have to manoeuvre, I'll let you practise,' promised Caolein.

Running his hand along the edge of the black console, feeling the slight thrum of the ship around him, Aradryan very much looked forward to that. A ship, guided by a single hand, capable of going anywhere in the galaxy... He looked at Caolein, who was grinning, and Aradryan found that he was smiling himself.

'Welcome to freedom, Aradryan.'

FOR SEVERAL CYCLES, Aradryan immersed himself in the new routine of the ship. He picked fruit and cut down cereals in the bio-cabins, and learnt how to operate the cooking equipment in the galley. He spent a cycle tending to the freshwater system, marvelling at the miniscule fish that lived within the filtering pond and streams, feeding on contaminants.

At the end of each cycle, he would return to his bed chamber – or share Athelennil's – and would find sleep coming swiftly, brought about by a deep contentment. There was something therapeutic about fending for himself, of being himself and not a Dreamer or a Poet or an Artist; just Aradryan.

As time passed, Aradryan felt the harmony of ship-borne life soothing his concerns about mortality. There was no pressure here to prove himself, and he was no longer subjected to the overbearing presence of the infinity circuit. Alaitoc had a strong tradition of the Path, and since Aradryan had been born he had been lectured on its importance and his continual development. As an adolescent he had been drawn to the Path of Harmony, facilitating the callings of others. He had quickly bored of that, falling into the Path of the Dreamer, and when that had come to its abrupt end, it had been without thought or effort that he had changed to the Path of the Steersman. Now he was on no Path. He could do what he wanted, experience any emotions he wanted to feel, explore wherever his whim took him.

During a mid-cycle meal, Aradryan was in the company of Athelennil and Caolein, and he felt ready to confess his enthusiasm for the life of the outcast. He did not know his companions all that well, but in a way it did not matter; they had each experienced their own release and would understand how he felt.

Finishing his meal, Aradryan opened his mouth to say something but stopped. He had felt a shiver pass through his body: a faint tremble that set his teeth on edge. He had felt nothing like it before, and as he turned to Athelennil to ask the question he saw that she was already crossing the room, heading for the wraithbone interface terminal.

'You'll get used to it,' said Caolein, who saw Aradryan's confusion and continued to explain. 'You wouldn't have sensed it in something as big as *Lacontiran*, but here we're so close to the core, you can feel the pulse of the webway itself. It makes a joy out of flying, being there in the moment as we surge across from one web tunnel to the next, feeling the flow around you. Anyway, something's disturbing the webway, something quite significant.'

'It's bad,' said Athelennil, drawing her hand back from the terminal. 'Come feel for yourself.'

Caolein waved for Aradryan to precede him. Placing his fingertips onto the opalescent psychic node, Aradryan allowed his consciousness to touch upon the psychic core of *Irdiris*. As Caolein had warned, the ship was so much smaller, more compact then anything he had experienced before. The network upon *Lacontiran* had been interfacing with hundreds of spirits at any given moment, blocking out the background connection to the webway. Here the psychic network of the ship was flimsy, almost skittish in its spirit; agile and inquisitive.

Aradryan could feel where the boundaries of the warp and reality blurred, just beyond the rune gates and warding walls of the webway, bleeding into each other, forming the tunnels through which the eldar travelled. The network of the ship extended out into the void, psychically reaching for the webway material to find purchase; as a bird uses its wings to catch the breeze so *Irdiris* fastened on to the immaterial pulsing of the webway through its matrix.

The webway was rippling, recoiling strongly from sensations that emanated not far away. Sensations that filled Aradryan with a deep-seated dread.

All of this he took into himself in a moment, and before he could pull back he felt himself drawn along the webway, delving into the effect that had caused the ripple, iterated for him via the ship's psychic network.

He felt pain and loss, and his body spasmed at the magnitude of it. Thousands, hundreds of thousands, of spirits were in torment, their hurt and their misery sending shockwaves across the webway. The agony engulfed Aradryan, just for an instant, and he was witness to its cause.

Green-skinned beasts ravaged his body and slew his family. They crawled upon him like parasites, biting at his flesh, leaving welts and wounds in their wake. The towers of his cities toppled, falling into ruin, the bodies of the dead crushed beneath the white stone or hacked apart or burned on massive pyres that choked his air.

He was dying.

With a gasp, Aradryan pulled himself away from the node, his fingers tingling, mind reeling.

'Was that... Were they orks?' he said, his throat dry. Licking his lips, he looked at Athelennil. 'What was that?'

'That is the cry of an Exodite world spirit,' she said, a tear glistening in her eye. 'I know it well. Eileniliesh. The world is under attack.'

'Eileniliesh is only a few cycles from here,' said Caolein. 'Seven cycles at most.'

'We must speak to the others,' said Athelennil.

'We felt it,' said Lechthennian, standing at the doorway. He stepped through, Jair just behind.

'We have to help, don't we?' said Aradryan. 'I mean, we should, shouldn't we? If we're just seven cycles away?'

'It is not as simple as that,' said Jair. 'We are only five, we cannot turn an army of orks. That message was intended for Alaitoc, a cry for help. They will respond.'

'So what does that mean for us?' said Aradryan, turning his gaze from one companion to the next. 'We just ignore it?'

'No,' said Caolein. 'But we will have to meet with the others first, join forces with the crew of other ships.'

'What other ships?'

'There will be other outcasts adrift in the webway who will hear the distress of Eileniliesh and respond,' explained Jair. 'We will gather our strength and consult on the best course of action. But for you, I am afraid that means an early return.'

'A return to where?' said Aradryan, and then

meaning dawned. 'The mustering, it will be on Alaitoc?'

'Yes,' said Athelennil, laying a hand on Aradryan's.

'I cannot go back, not so soon,' said Aradryan. 'I would look like a fool. No, I do not mean that.' A memory of the Exodite world spirit's message surged into his thoughts. 'Looking like a fool is nothing compared to the pain I felt in that call for aid. You have to go back to help, even if I cannot. I suppose I could just stay on the ship.'

'If that is what you wish,' said Lechthennian.

'We will be joining the ranger cadre,' said Athelennil, stepping away from Aradryan so that she was next to Jair. 'If you want to help the people of Eileniliesh, you might come with us.'

'Be a ranger?' Aradryan laughed. 'I know nothing of war or scoutcraft.'

'It was just an idea,' said Athelennil.

Aradryan could sense disapproval in the stance of the others, and knew that he was acting out of turn, but he could not see how he could help. Then he remembered Athelennil's earlier statement: everybody does what they have to for the needs of all. Aradryan sighed and smiled.

'Back to Alaitoc it is, I suppose,' he said. He looked at Jair and then Athelennil. 'Being a ranger, what does it entail?'

BEHIND THE PILOT'S chamber a stairwell led down into the lower levels of *Irdiris*. With Athelennil leading the way into the hold area, Aradryan walked alongside Jair as the older eldar explained the principles of the ranger.

'It is the rangers that keep an eye out for threats to the craftworlds and Exodites,' said Jair. 'There is no duty, no oaths or vows, but we take it upon ourselves not to wholly abandon the rest of our kind. This attack, the ork invasion of Eileniliesh, is a call to arms.'

Aradryan was horrified by the idea of war and it must have shown in his face.

'I forget that you have never trodden the Path of the Warrior. I would say not to be afraid, but that is a lie. Fear is a great motivation that will help you to stay alive. Not all rangers confront the enemy directly, you do not have to fight if you do not wish. We will be consulting with the seers and autarchs of Alaitoc, to coordinate our efforts with those of the Aspect Warriors and fleet. What that might require, I cannot say, but if you stay by my side I will ensure you come to no harm.'

Aradryan was not sure Jair could guarantee his safety, not wholly, but he was reassured a little by the ranger's words.

'If I was to choose to fight,' Aradryan said quietly, 'how would that work? Where do we get weapons from?'

As if in answer, Athelennil stopped by one of the storage bay doors, which whispered open at her touch. Lights flickered into life, revealing the contents within.

The storage space was semicircular. Around the walls were hung coats and cloaks of curious design, each uniquely patterned with grey and white, matching the colour of the room. Beside each was a rifle, almost as long as Aradryan was tall, with a slender stock and complex sighting arrangement. There were shuriken pistols, long knives and slender swords also, holstered and scabbarded between the cloaks and coats. Knee-high boots, folded grey and black bodysuits and drab brown packbags were stowed on top of locker bins at the juncture of wall and floor, and hanging from the ceiling was more equipment: breathing masks and magnifying monocles; slender ropes and grapples; aquatic gear like artificial fins; furled airwings made of near-transparent thread.

Inscribed into the ceiling was an image of Kurnous, the Hunter God, once enemy of Khaine, consumed by She Who Thirsts like the rest of the ancient pantheon. Aradryan thought it a little superstitious to find such a picture here, celebrating a dead god, but said nothing.

'This is the gear of a ranger,' said Jair, waving a hand to encompass everything. 'Here is all that you need to survive, wherever we go, whatever we have to do.'

'I have never fired a gun nor swung a sword in my life,' said Aradryan. He stepped into the chamber and reached out, fingers stroking one of the cloaks. It shimmered, the cloth he touched taking on a pinkish hue to match his skin. 'So, this is cameleoline?'

'Yes,' said Athelennil. 'Do not be concerned about your military experience, or lack of it. It is irrelevant. The task of the ranger is to fight from a distance. We locate the enemy and guide the true warriors to their target. The longrifle is the preferred weapon. Remember that the foes we fight, be they orks, humans or whatever, are far less physically adept than we. With a little training you will be a match for their best marksmen, and your coat and cloak will hide you from retaliation.'

'I said I will keep you safe, and I will,' said Jair.

'It is not my life I fear for, only my sanity,' said Aradryan. 'I have never killed before, what if I cannot do it?'

'Whether you join us as a ranger or not, you will learn to kill,' said Jair. 'We will hunt for food, and you must slay what you wish to eat if you desire meat. The farm chambers can sustain us indefinitely, but you will grow bored eventually. That is when the fresh meat of a kill tastes the best! Life is but part of the cycle, and death its only end. You know this already.'

Aradryan accepted this with a silent nod. His hand moved from the coat to the rifle beside it. He picked it up, lifting the weapon from its hook. It was surprisingly light, easily hefted in one hand. Orange and red jewels set into the blister-like housing above the trigger glowed into life at his touch, and a faint purring signalled the energising of a powercell. Aradryan turned to Athelennil.

'Show me how it works,' he said.

THE IRDIRIS WAS one of the first ranger ships to reach Alaitoc, having received the distress call from Eileniliesh not far from the craftworld. Jair and Athelennil were to meet with the ruling council of farseers and autarchs, who were no doubt already aware of the tumult coursing across the webway. Aradryan did not feel comfortable attending the meeting, and remained with Lechthennian and Caolein aboard the ship.

It was Caolein who convinced him to step out onto the craftworld again. The two of them sat on the couches of the common area, sipping iced juice.

'You left in pain, twice,' said the pilot.

'And why would I return to the source of that pain?'

'To rid the place of its power over you. You have a rare opportunity, Aradryan. The last time you departed Alaitoc, it was twenty passes before you returned and your friends had changed much. Now you have the chance, knowing that you have a chance for happiness, to see them and assure them you are well.'

'What if they do not care to see me?' said Aradryan, placing his goblet on the low table by his feet. 'The wound will reopen.'

'The wound may fester if not addressed,' replied Caolein. 'The worst that happens is that you come back to *Irdiris* without success. You do not have to see any of them ever again, and none aboard will think the less of you for the attempt.'

Thus reluctantly persuaded, Aradryan headed into Alaitoc once more, far sooner than he had expected. He did not trust himself to use the infinity circuit – and in a way did not wish to warn his former friends of his presence – and so he travelled directly to Thirianna's chambers. Here he was informed by the young family that now lived there that she had relocated, to quarters close to the Dome of Crystal Seers at the heart of the craftworld.

After making discreet inquiries, Aradryan located Thirianna's new abode and took a sky shuttle there. He stood outside the door for some time, summoning up the courage. When he was finally ready, though he did not know what he would say, the door detected his intent and signalled his presence with a long chime.

The door slid soundlessly open, revealing the main chamber of the apartment. Thirianna was standing in the middle of the room, putting something into a pouch at her belt.

'Aradryan!' she said, turning towards her visitor. 'This is unexpected.'

Not for the first time, Aradryan was aware that his appearance was somewhat irregular. Though he had not worn the cloak or coat, his ranger undersuit was a shifting pattern of holo-generated greens and blues, adopted from the sky and park beyond the balcony outside Thirianna's door.

'Hello, Thirianna,' said Aradryan, stepping into the apartment. He smiled and offered a palm in greeting. Thirianna laid her hand on his for a heartbeat, obviously nonplussed at his arrival. 'Sorry I could not warn you of my return.'

'I did not expect to see you again for much longer,' said Thirianna. She sat down and waved to a cushion for Aradryan to sit but he declined with a quick, single shake of the head.

'I cannot stay long,' he told her. In truth, just seeing her stirred up confusing emotions, and he was coming to the conclusion that Caolein had been wrong; this was a mistake. 'It seems my attempt to get far away from Alaitoc was destined to be thwarted. The *Irdiris* intercepted a transmission from Eileniliesh. It's an Exodite world that has been attacked by orks. We thought it wise to return to Alaitoc with the news.'

'Preparations are already under way for an expedition,' said Thirianna. 'Farseer Latheirin witnessed the impending attack several cycles ago.'

'Such is the way of farseers,' Aradryan said with a

shrug. He laughed. 'Of course, you are becoming a seer now. Perhaps I should choose my words more carefully?'

'I do not take any offence,' replied Thirianna. 'They are an enigmatic group, that is sure. I have been around them for some time and I do not yet understand their ways.'

Aradryan did not know what else to say. He shifted his weight from one foot to the other and back again, unwilling to make small talk but uncertain of broaching any deeper subject.

'How have you fared?' Thirianna asked.

Aradryan shrugged again.

'There is not much yet to say,' he said. He gestured at his outfit. 'As you see, I have decided to join the rangers, but in truth I had not set foot off *Irdiris* before we had to return. On Eileniliesh we will fight the orks.'

'That would be unwise,' said Thirianna. 'You have never trodden the Path of the Warrior. You have no war-mask.'

'It is of no concern,' said Aradryan with a dismissive wave of the hand. 'My longrifle will keep me safe. It seems I have a natural talent for marksmanship.'

'It is not the physical danger that concerns me,' said Thirianna. She stood up and approached Aradryan. 'War corrupts us. The lure of Khaine can become irresistible.'

'There are many delights in the galaxy. Bloodshed is not one that appeals to me,' said Aradryan. He had expected his friend to be more supportive; it had been partly Thirianna's choices that had sent him from Alaitoc again. 'I never realised how blinkered you could be. You see the Path as the start and the end of existence. It is not.'

'It is,' said Thirianna. 'What you are doing, allowing your mind to run free, endangers not just you but those around you. You must show restraint. Korlandril, he has been touched by Khaine. His anger became too much.'

'He is an Aspect Warrior now?' said Aradryan, amused by the news. He could not suppress a laugh at the irony of the sculptor's last work being a testament to peaceful Isha whilst gripped by inner anger that had burst free. 'I did not realise my critique of his work was so harsh.'

Thirianna flicked her hair in annoyance, her fingertips pushing a stray lock behind one ear. Aradryan calmed himself, realising that he was the cause of her irritation.

'Why have you come here?' said Thirianna. 'What do you want from me?'

'Nothing,' said Aradryan. It seemed a self-centred question to ask. He had come to assure Thirianna that he was doing well, but she was clearly too involved with her new rune-casting to care about him. 'You made it very clear I should expect nothing from you. I came as a courtesy, nothing more. If I am not welcome, I shall leave.'

Weighing up her answer, Thirianna said nothing for a few moments, regarding Aradryan with a cool gaze. Her expression hardened.

'Yes, I think you should leave,' said Thirianna. Aradryan felt a stab of disappointment, anger even, but he nodded his acquiescence. Thirianna's harsh stare relented slightly. 'Please take care of yourself,

Aradryan. I am pleased that you came to see me.'

Aradryan took a step towards the door, summarily dismissed, but Thirianna's last words fixed in his thoughts; she did care about him. Caolein had said that this was a second chance to part on better terms, but Aradryan had managed to squander the opportunity. Should he make amends, he thought? Did he need to tell her that he missed her?

'Goodbye,' he said, one hand on the edge of the open door. 'I do not expect us to meet again. Ever.'

Aradryan meant what he said. He wanted Thirianna to know that this was likely the last time she would see him. As a ranger he would travel far away, and he had no desire to come back. If he died, lost and forgotten on some distant world, he would be happy with such a fate.

'Goodbye,' Thirianna replied. 'Travel well and find contentment.'

With a sigh, Aradryan turned away and moved out of view. The door swished across the opening, and Aradryan headed along the balcony with a swift stride, annoyed with himself; for listening to Caolein and for letting Thirianna have the final say

As he was about to take the turn towards the stairwell, he heard Thirianna calling his name. His heart raced in his chest for a moment, but he kept his expression impassive as he turned to look over his shoulder at her.

'Please see Korlandril,' Thirianna called out to him. Aradryan nodded and raised a hand in acknowledgement. She was more concerned about Korlandril than him. So be it, thought Aradryan.

\* \* \*

PERHAPS IT WAS egotism that prevented Aradryan returning directly to *Irdiris*; the thought of reporting his failure to Caolein nagged at him. The encounter with Thirianna, while not an absolute disaster, had left Aradryan feeling a little raw and unable to face the questions Caolein would have for him if he came back without achieving at least some kind of understanding with his former friends. Also, he had promised, tacitly, to see Korlandril, and so to the ex-Sculptor's home Aradryan travelled next.

The door opened before Aradryan just in time to show Korlandril stepping into a side chamber. He waited for a moment, but there was no word of welcome, nor any call to leave.

'Things change again,' said Aradryan, calling out the first thing that came into his head in lieu of anything more profound. Korlandril stepped back into the main room, eyes widening with shock.

'Things change again,' agreed Korlandril. He stared at Aradryan for some time before gesturing for his guest to seat himself. The ranger declined with a slight shake of the head.

'I have come out of courtesy to the friendship we once shared,' said Aradryan. 'I thought it wrong to come back to Alaitoc and not see you.'

'I am glad that you have come,' said Korlandril. 'I owe you an apology for my behaviour the last time we met.'

Aradryan was taken aback by this outright confession. Of Thirianna and Korlandril, it was the latter Aradryan considered he had wronged the deepest, but his dreaming partner seemed sincere in his sorrow.

'It was never the case that we wronged each other intentionally,' replied Aradryan, feeling that he needed to meet honesty with honesty, 'and neither of us owes the other anything but respect.'

'I trust your travels have been fruitful?'

Aradryan smiled and nodded. And lied.

'I cannot describe the sights I have seen, the thrill of adventure that has coursed through my veins. The galaxy has been set out before me and I have experienced such a tiny fraction of the delights and darkness it has to offer.'

'I too have been on a journey,' said Korlandril, cleaning his hands with a cloth.

'I have heard this,' said Aradryan. Korlandril looked at him and raised his eyebrows in question. Aradryan was not quite sure how to bring up Korlandril's change of Path, and chose his words carefully. 'Thirianna. I met with her first. She told me that you are now an Aspect Warrior.'

'A Striking Scorpion of the Deadly Shadow shrine,' said Korlandril. He delicately rinsed his hands and dried them under a warm vent above the sink. 'It does not anger me that you saw Thirianna first. My parting from her is an event of the past, one with which I have wholly come to terms.'

Aradryan's eyes swept the living quarters, taking in the Isha statues arranged around the room. Each of them wore the face of Thirianna, or close representations of the same. Aradryan smiled and darted a doubtful look at Korlandril.

'Well, perhaps not *wholly*,' the warrior admitted with a short laugh. 'But I truly bear you no ill-will concerning your part, unwitting as it was, in the circumstances that engulfed me.'

'Have you seen her recently?'

Korlandril shook his head.

'It would serve no purpose. If I happen to cross her path, it will be well, but it is not my place to seek her company at this time. She and I travel to different places, and we make our own journeys.'

'Someone else?' suggested Aradryan.

Korlandril seemed confused for a moment, and then his lips parted silently in an expression of realisation.

'Aha!' laughed Aradryan.

'It is not like that,' Korlandril said hurriedly. 'She is a fellow warrior at the shrine, it would be entirely inappropriate for us to engage in any deeper relationship.'

Aradryan was aware of no such convention amongst Aspect Warriors and allowed Korlandril to see his doubt rather than say anything out loud. The two of them stood in silence, comfortable if not pleasant, before Aradryan realised that as a Striking Scorpion, Korlandril would be bound for Eileniliesh too. 'I have also come to give you advance warning that you will be shortly called to your shrine.'

'How might you know this?' asked Korlandril, frowning fiercely. 'Have you spoken to Kenainath?'

'I would not tread foot in an Aspect shrine! And your exarch does not venture forth. No, it is from first-hand knowledge that I am aware of this. I have just returned from Eileniliesh. It is an Exodite world not so far away. Orks have come to Eileniliesh and her people call on Alaitoc for help. I have come back as their messenger. Even now the autarchs and farseers debate the best course of action. There is no doubt in my mind that they will issue the call to war.'

'And I will be ready to answer it,' said Korlandril. At the mention of war, his whole posture had changed. His eyes had become hard as flint, his jaw set. It unsettled Aradryan, who had last seen that look just before Korlandril's outburst at the unveiling. The ranger thought it better to depart before the good grounds he had established with his friend were destroyed by some chance remark or perceived difference.

'I have my own preparations to make,' said Aradryan, taking a step towards the door. 'Other rangers are gathering here to share what they know of the enemy. I must join them.'

Korlandril nodded his understanding. Aradryan was at the door before Korlandril spoke again.

'I am glad that you are alive and well, my friend,' said the warrior, sincerity in every word.

'As am I of you, Korlandril.' Aradryan replied out of instinct but realised he meant it. The bonds of dreaming-partner went deep, deeper than ordinary friendship, and Korlandril had once meant a great deal to him. 'I do not know if I will see you on Eileniliesh or before we leave. If not, then I wish you good fortune and prosperity until our next meeting.'

'Good fortune and prosperity,' echoed Korlandril.

Aradryan stepped out of the apartment with a lighter step than he had entered. As the iris-door closed behind him, the ranger took a deep breath. Alaitoc would be in his past now. He would discover what the future held at Eileniliesh.

# DISCOVERY

*The Maze of Linnian – In the ancient days before Ulthanesh and Eldanesh were sundered from each other and Khaine wreaked his bloody vengeance during the War in Heaven, Eldanesh looked to the protection of his people while Ulthanesh turned his gaze out to the wider world. Intrigued, Ulthanesh left the house of his family and searched far and wide in the wilderness. It was slow work, though, for the winds were strong and the terrain harsh. Seeking shelter one night on the slopes of Mount Linnian, Ulthanesh came upon a golden gateway in a cave. At first he was afraid, and he left the cave, daring the cold twilight. The next night he came upon another golden gateway, behind a magnificent waterfall. Still Ulthanesh was too afraid to pass the portal. On the third night, when he*

*saw a glimmering gateway atop a distant hill,
Ulthanesh resolved to himself that he would not
be frightened any more. He passed through the
gateway, and found himself in another place:
the Maze of Linnian. The labyrinth stretched
across the world, above and beneath it, with
many turning passages and dead-ends to frus-
trate Ulthanesh. There were hidden chambers
where monsters and other perils awaited, and
mighty were Ulthanesh's deeds to overcome
these foes and obstacles. All was worthwhile, for
the Maze of Linnian brought Ulthanesh unto
glorious highlands and fertile hills, spanned the
stars with rainbow bridges and delved into the
sparkling depths beneath the world of the eldar.
In time, Ulthanesh returned to the house of his
family and gathered his followers. Now that he
knew they were there, Ulthanesh saw the gleam
of the golden gates everywhere, and with his
sons and grandsons he explored their secrets.*

OVERHEAD, THE SUN was hot, sending steam rising
from the primordial forest. It was a real sun, and
its real heat also touched the skin of Aradryan as he
stepped from the docking ramp onto the soil of a
real world. The first planet he had set foot on in his
long life. He had been raised on Alaitoc and during
his travels aboard *Lacontiran* he had never left the
starship. As his boot sunk a little into the mud, he
wondered why he had never done this before.

The wind tugged at his coat, his garments shifting
to brown and green to blend with the surroundings,
and it occurred to Aradryan that this wind was not

generated by some hidden vent or artificially stirred by climatic engines, but the result of impossibly complex pressure and temperature interactions in the atmosphere of Eileniliesh. Far to his left, a dark smudge on the horizon could have been smoke, or perhaps storm clouds.

Covering his eyes against the glare of the sun, which on second consideration he decided would benefit greatly from being dimmed a little, Aradryan thought about the sky. There was no dome to hold it in place. The mass of the world and the physics of gravity bound the atmosphere to the planet, with no force shields required. It was a magnificent thing, and listening to the squeal and screech of birds – really, truly *wild* birds – sent a thrill through him.

'Ex-dreamers,' muttered Jair as he walked past. 'Always with their heads in the clouds.'

Aradryan turned to respond, but his harsh answer died in his throat as he saw the smile on the other ranger's face.

'I once actually had my head in a cloud,' Aradryan said, shifting the rifle slung over his shoulder into a more comfortable position. 'It was on the skybridge above the Gorge of Deep Regrets.'

'Fascinating,' said Jair. He pointed to a slender tower not far ahead, rising above the canopy of the trees surrounding the clearing where Caolein had set down *Irdiris*. The Exodite building was a light grey spear thrust into the indigo sky, widening to a disc-like platform pierced by arched windows not far below its narrow summit. The deep blue leaves of the forest fluttered in the wind around its base, showing their silvery undersides, their whisper drifting to Aradryan's ears.

'This is where we were told to meet the others?' said Aradryan.

'The Exodite elders will be speaking to all of the rangers in the first wave,' replied Jair.

'And when will Athelennil and the others arrive?'

The two of them started walking, passing into the shade of the immense trees. Having visited Eile-niliesh before, Athelennil was amongst the outcasts who had remained with the craftworld army, to act as guides to the Aspect Warriors and seers. Aradryan missed her already, though Jair was proving to be a witty and informative companion.

'Tonight, I expect,' said Jair. 'The Alaitocii battle-ships are not so swift as our ranger craft, and the autarchs deemed a night attack to be the best course of action.'

'I am still not sure what I will be able to do,' said Aradryan. The soft mulch of leaves gave way slightly under his light tread and the not-unpleasant fra-grance of gently rotting leaves surrounded him. It was autumn here, due to the planet's position in its orbit around the star and its particular axial tilt. Within the controlled climate of Alaitoc, seasons were a mat-ter of whim or design, winter snows a marvel to be conjured up and then disposed of once the entertain-ment they provided grew wearisome.

'We have to find out where the orks are, and if they are on the move,' said Jair.

'How do they cope?' Aradryan asked. 'The Exodites, I mean.'

'Cope with what?'

'The randomness of their world,' explained Aradryan. 'A storm could sweep away their crops, or an earthquake could topple their towers and swallow their cities. How do they endure such unpredictability?'

'Some would say it is stubbornness,' said Jair. 'I think it is more deep-rooted than that. Once, before the Fall, our people commanded the stars and worlds were shaped to our whim. Like Alaitoc, there was nothing that we did not control. It was that laziness that allowed our bane to whisper in our ears, spreading the moral decline that brought about the Fall. The Exodites will never again trust themselves to be masters of their surrounds. Its capricious ways, the untamed weather and the vacillations of tectonic and volcanic activity, humble them and stave off the risk of idleness and ultimately a return to depravity.'

'A slightly masochistic temperament, by the sounds of it,' said Aradryan. They had come to another clearing, the solitary tower soaring into the sky above them, tall doorways open at its base. 'Why did they not simply adopt the Path as the craftworlds did?'

'You, who walk here as an outcast, ask that question?' Jair's laugh was of incredulity. 'The Exodites see the Path as a trap – an illusory control that masks an inner darkness. They think that there is purity in their hard lives, and that only constant denial of their emotions will eventually set them free from the taint of... Well, you know.'

'The Great Enemy? She Who Thirsts? The Prince of Pleasure? We both know to what you refer, why so suddenly coy?'

'Even those names are best left unsaid, Aradryan,' said Jair, stopping to take hold of his arm. 'You are not behind the wards of Alaitoc, protected by the warp spiders and barriers of the infinity circuit. It is not wise to tempt the gaze of that power, especially in jest.'

Aradryan was suddenly scared by Jair's earnest warning and stepped back, pulling his arm free. For a brief heartbeat he thought his waystone glowed a little brighter in its golden setting, a moment of warmth touching his chest. It was probably imagined, but Aradryan glanced around nonetheless, disturbed by the sensation.

'The trees are glowing!' he exclaimed, thoughts of the Great Enemy dispersed by this sudden revelation.

It was perhaps an overstatement, but there was a light from the trees around the tower, an aura strongest at the roots, gleaming between the folds of the bark, glimmering along the serrated edges of leaves. Now that his attention was drawn to it, Aradryan noticed the faint light elsewhere, similar to the silver glow that came from the uppermost storeys of the tower. Crossing to one of the trees, Aradryan knelt down and examined its roots. There was a miniscule vein of crystal running along the wood.

'Careful, that is the world spirit,' Jair said when he noticed what Aradryan was doing. 'This tower must be some kind of node point, where the crystal matrix is close to the surface.'

'And it delves into the ground, going deeper?'

'A world spirit makes the infinity circuit of Alaitoc look small,' said Jair, crouching to run his hand through the dirt. 'It stretches across the whole planet, seeping into the cracks between rocks, like the rootlets of a plant.'

Concentrating, Aradryan tried to feel the presence

of the world spirit, as he would a ship network on the infinity circuit. He felt nothing, expect perhaps the slightest background awareness. Closing his eyes, he tried to home in on the spirit, opening his thoughts to it, but there was nothing to hear but the sighing of the wind. Aradryan remembered the moment of contact he had felt aboard *Irdiris*, but that shared experience created no connection here.

'A matrix that size, that could send that message across the webway, must be powerful indeed, but I cannot sense it at all,' he said, opening his eyes.

'The world spirit is vast in size, but its potency is exceptionally diffuse,' said Jair. He motioned that they should continue across the glade to the tower. 'Originally, perhaps less than a thousand Exodites fled to this world. Even after generations, the energy that has been stored within from their dying spirits is a fraction of the millions of spirits contained by Alaitoc. Like all Exodite creations, it is a basic, rudimentary thing, which serves its purpose as a sanctuary for their departing spirits but nothing more.'

A figure, clothed in red and white, appeared at an archway ahead. Her hair reached to her knees, braided tightly and tied with plain thongs. A belt of reptilian hide held the eldar's robes in place. In her right hand she carried a staff of knotted, twisted wood, its top entwined about an irregularly-shaped green crystal.

'Well met, visitors,' said the stranger, opening her free hand in greeting.

'Well met, host,' replied Jair with a formal bow of his head. Aradryan copied his companion, keeping his eyes on the figure. 'Are you Saryengith?'

'I am Rijaliss Saryengith Naiad, the Pandita of Hirith-Hreslain. Please, come inside and join the others.'

SARYENGITH SPENT SOME time explaining what had happened to the seventeen rangers who had arrived ahead of the Alaitoc fleet. The orks had come to the maiden world thirty cycles before – Aradryan had a strange thought that the length of the cycles here were as fixed as the seasons – and while Alaitoc and the outcasts had readied their response, the settlement of Hirith-Hreslain had been overrun.

The Exodites of Eileniliesh were few in number, and not disposed to conflict. What armaments they possessed, and the warriors capable of wielding them, were sufficient to keep at bay carnosaurs and razordons that menaced their herds, but the orks had crashed down onto the planet with bikes and buggies, cannons and tanks: a horde of battle-hungry beasts bred for battle in an age long past.

Hirith-Hreslain had been invaded four cycles ago, and though Saryengith and her fellow elders had evacuated the town before the wrath of the orks had fallen upon it, there had been many of the warrior sects too stubborn to retreat. They had been slaughtered defending the town, rather than waiting the extra time for reinforcements to arrive from other settlements and nearby Alaitoc. From what little the scouts of the Exodites had seen, the orks were keeping themselves occupied and amused by looting and smashing up the ancient buildings; there were guarded whispers that some of the Exodite knights had been taken alive too. No party had been sent in the last cycle, though, so whether the orks had tired of their sport and started another rampage into the forest or not, was not known. What little that could be gleaned from the pain of the world spirit indicated the orks were still in Hirith-Hreslain in some numbers, but it was impossible to say if they had split their force.

Hirith-Hreslain was a paired-town located on a wide river, Hresh on one side of a connecting bridge, Selain on the other. After a quarter of a cycle with Saryengith and her scouts, discussing the best approach to the overrun town, it was down this water course that the rangers ventured, split into three bands. Dusk was some time away still, they had been assured, leaving them plenty of opportunity to reach Hirith-Hreslain and return.

Running effortlessly along the river path, Aradryan and the rest of his group covered the distance quickly. Though he enjoyed stretching his legs and the openness of the limitless sky above, the trek seemed a little pointless to him.

'Why do we not just take *Irdiris* and fly to Hirith-Hreslain?' he asked Naomilith, a female ranger who was running beside him to the right. 'Or one of the other ships, perhaps?'

'It is best that the enemy remain ignorant of our presence,' replied Naomilith. 'They must have arrived by starship, and so if we wish to destroy them we should give them no cause to return to their vessel.'

'How long have you been a ranger?' Aradryan asked. He glanced at Naomilith, admiring the way the shade and light of the tree branches overhead played across the delicate features of her face.

'Long enough to know when to keep quiet,' she replied with a cold smile.

Silenced by this retort, Aradryan ran on. Ahead, the smudge he had thought might be a storm cloud was revealed to be a column of smoke; several smaller columns in fact, merging into one cloud that lingered over the burning forest. They approached from upwind, and so the smell of the burning was absent, but the sight filled Aradryan with foreboding. It was obvious that Hirith-Hreslain had been set ablaze, and he was not sure how he would cope with the evidence of such destruction. What if he saw bodies? Would he be rendered almost incapable, as he had been all that time ago, before he had left aboard *Lacontiran*?

His apprehension increased as they neared the settlement. The roar of crude fossil fuel engines and raucous shouts and laughter announced from a distance that the orks had not left the town.

'That's that question answered,' Aradryan said to Naomilith. 'We can report now, yes?'

He was only half-joking, but the withering stare from Naomilith silenced further comment before it was made. A whistle from across the river attracted the attention of the rangers, and Aradryan looked over the waters to his left and saw another group beneath the eaves of the forest on the far side. He raised a hand in greeting, just as the communicator he wore as a piercing in his right ear tingled into life.

'Gahian is leading the third group around to the left, to come upon Hirith-Hreslain from the opposite direction,' reported Khannihain, the most experienced ranger in the group upon the far bank. 'I suggest that you move away from the river to explore the remnants of Selain, while we go into Hresh.'

All of the rangers had heard Khannihain's words and they looked at each other, seeking consensus.

'Seems a reasonable plan to me,' said Jair.

'I concur,' said Lithalian, from just behind Aradryan.

'Are there any objections?' asked Naomilith. She looked at the rangers in turn, each shaking his or her head, until Naomilith's gaze fell upon Aradryan.

'How would I know whether it is a good plan or not?' Aradryan said with a quiet, self-conscious laugh.

'Your voice is equal,' said Naomilith, 'despite your lack of experience.'

'What if I do not like this plan?' said Aradryan, bemused by the situation.

'If you have a counter-proposal, let us hear it,' said Jair, impatiently. 'If not, you are free to come with us or leave and follow your own course.'

'That does not sound sensible, I think I will stay with you.'

'So you are in agreement with Khannihain's suggestions? You will come with us into Selain?' said Naomilith.

'If that is what Jair or Khannihain say we should do.'

Naomilith let out a short hiss and shook her head in exasperation. She stalked away from Aradryan and whispered something to Jair as she passed. The older ranger approached Aradryan.

'I hope that you genuinely do not understand the proposition, and our situation,' said Jair, talking softly as he placed a hand on the younger eldar's shoulder and led Aradryan a short distance from the others. 'Naomilith wants to be sure that you are acting of your own will.'

'So I could really just leave now and do whatever I want?' said Aradryan.

'We hope you would not pursue a course of action that would endanger the rest of us,' said Jair. The other eldar frowned with thought as Aradryan stared blankly at him, still not quite comprehending why the others were so agitated about getting his approval. 'Let me see if I can make you understand. To be outcast is to make a choice, and to continue making choices without the guidance or the restraints of the Path. We are each free – free in a way that perhaps you still do not picture. We are free from everything. We are free from hierarchy, from any authority we do not choose for ourselves, free from orders and doctrine. Every spirit is equal as an outcast, there can be no coercion or subjugation.'

'Why is there such a delay? What are you discussing?' Khannihain asked over the communicator.

'I am sorry for the misunderstanding,' said Aradryan. He touched a finger to the ring at his ear, so that he could transmit. 'We are in accord with you, Khannihain. Explore Hresh while we see what there is to find in Selain.'

'Very well, it is advisable to reconvene here at dusk,' said Khannihain.

There came a chorus of affirmatives from the other rangers, and Aradryan added his own consent to the replies.

'Ready your weapon,' said Jair, turning away. 'We will be getting close to the orks.'

His fingers trembling just a little at this thought, Aradryan slung the rifle from his shoulder and carried it in both hands. The wind was turning and he tasted ash on the air, reminding him of the slaughter that the orks had already perpetrated. Licking his lips, which had become quite dry in the last few moments, he glanced around and then headed after the other rangers, whose coats were quickly disappearing into the scrub ahead.

THE RIVER CURVED sharply, and as Aradryan's group rounded the bend, the settlement of Hirith-Hreslain came into view. The town spread from both river banks, linked by a long bridge. On the far bank, the part known as Hresh rose up as a group of towers and elevated walkways from amongst the trees themselves. Selain was more open, and the buildings generally of fewer storeys.

Even from this distance the destruction wrought by the orks was plain to see. Some of the white buildings were marked with soot and burn marks, their shattered windows reflecting low flames still burning in the settlement. Smoke choked the air.

A splash drew Aradryan's attention to the river. Something long and grey, like a giant finned eel, slid through the water just below the surface. There were other things in the water too: corpses. The dead of Hirith-Hreslain floated amongst the reeds, bodies bobbing on the gentle waves.

Aradryan wanted to look away, but he could not. Morbidly, he watched as the river beast rose to the surface, jaws opening to reveal rows of small serrated teeth. It clamped around the arm of a floating corpse and turned, plunging into the water to drag its meal into the murky depths.

Hissing his breath through gritted teeth, Aradryan

looked along the river towards the bridge. He could not tell how many dead eldar were in the water, but there were a lot of them. Many were caught in the foam that broke against the piles of the span, turning over and around in the current.

Disgust welled up in the ranger, tainted with anger. It was the first time he had felt such deep revulsion, not of the dead but of their killers. The orks were still in the settlement, their raucous cries and guttural laughter easy to hear on the light breeze.

'Careful,' said Jair, laying a hand on Aradryan's wrist.

Aradryan realised that he had slipped his finger into the trigger guard, his grip on the longrifle tight. Noticing the alarm in Jair's eyes, Aradryan relaxed his fingers and nodded.

'Later,' said Jair. 'Later the orks will be punished for what they have done.'

The group moved on, slipping from the waterside into the forest surrounding Selain. They came upon an outbuilding, its windows and red-tiled roof still intact though the wooden doors had been broken in. Stealing inside, the rangers found the place had been ransacked. It was bare save for a few broken pieces of furniture and scattered shards of pottery.

Aradryan was intrigued by the construction of the building. He ran his hand over the walls, and could feel the slight joins between large blocks.

'What is it made of?' he asked.

'Stone,' said Jair, confused by the obvious question.

'Yes, but what type? Ghost stone? Firestone? W–'

'Stone, from the ground,' snapped Naomilith. 'Blocks quarried and shaped and assembled. The

Exodites fashion all of their settlements in the traditional ways.'

'Would it not be easier to grow their structures, as we do on the craftworlds?'

'I refer you to our earlier conversation,' said Jair. 'The Exodites eschew the easy path, especially those deeds we accomplish with our psychic abilities. They work with the physical, the labour of their works occupying their minds and keeping them from the temptations of flesh and spirit.'

'We waste time,' said Caloth, who was about the same age as Aradryan, though she had been a ranger for nearly two passes. A scar ran from the side of her nose to her right ear, a disturbing affectation that could have easily been remedied in any craftworld's Halls of Healing. 'We should enter Selain proper so that we can assess the strength of the enemy.'

That sounded like a dangerous prospect, but Aradryan kept his thoughts to himself, fearing more scorn from Naomilith, who had no qualms about displaying her dislike of him.

Reaching the outskirts of the town proved to be easy; the orks had set no patrols or sentries to guard against observation. In fact, the greenskins seemed wholly unconcerned by the possibility of attack. Aradryan thought that perhaps the aliens considered the eldar defeated, or perhaps too cowardly to return to their sacked town. If so, their error of judgement would be bloodily corrected that coming night.

'We should split into pairs,' suggested Jair. 'I will go with Aradryan, and head in the direction of the river.'

This received assent from the others, and the six rangers divided, heading in different directions to investigate the situation in Selain. Aradryan was happy to go with Jair, who had at least shown some patience with his questions and inexperience.

'I know that I said we have no leaders, and no hierarchy, but please do what I tell you,' said Jair as they cut through the trees towards a tower on the edge of the main clearing. 'I would rather we were not discovered.'

'Have no fear, I shall follow in your footsteps and do exactly as you bid,' replied Aradryan.

The sun was still some time from setting, but the shadows were lengthening. Jair and Aradryan flitted from the trees into the shade of an arched doorway. Aradryan tried the door but it was barred from the inside. A shattered window further along the wall provided ingress and the two rangers slipped over the sill. Inside was much like the first building. They ascended quickly to the top of the tower, coming to a bedchamber where blood had been daubed on the walls and spilled in sticky pools on the bare boards of the floor.

Ignoring the smell, Aradryan followed Jair as he stepped through the broken remnants of the windows onto a balcony. They crouched at the ledge and peered over, but could see little beyond the surrounding towers. Judging by the clamour of the orks – harsh shouts and the revving of combustion engines – the majority of the aliens were somewhere in the heart of the settlement.

They crept through the streets, heading in the direction of the river, occasionally searching the buildings they passed. They found no bodies, which worried Aradryan, and caused a thought to cross his mind.

'Do you think they have taken prisoners?' he asked. 'Should we try to rescue them if we find them?'

'I do not think they have prisoners,' Jair replied with a grim expression.

'How can you tell?'

'I do not hear any screams.'

With a shudder, Aradryan continued after Jair, who was moving more swiftly. The streets grew narrower and the buildings to either side were linked by skybridges and walkways in their upper levels. Once or twice Jair froze in place and Aradryan did likewise, pressing against the smooth walls as a brutish, hunched figure or two would pass along one of these aerial paths.

When they next paused, Aradryan could hear the gurgle of the river in the distance, even through the increasing noise of the ork occupiers. Jair signalled for Aradryan to join him where a high wall turned sharply around the edge of a garden. From here, the rangers could see into the open space at the centre of the town: a plaza that opened out from one end of the bridge.

'We need to go up,' said Jair, jabbing a thumb skywards.

The other ranger surprised Aradryan when he leapt onto the wall, pulling himself up to its top. With a glance back at Aradryan, Jair then sidled along the wall to the building adjoining it. Another jump and lift took him onto the small roof of a jutting turret. Aradryan realised he was meant to follow. Ensuring that his rifle was properly on his shoulder, he repeated Jair's actions, finding the climb easier than he had imagined.

From the turret roof, they leapt across an alley to a deserted balcony opposite. Checking inside, they found the room within empty. From there, they located a staircase winding up to a roof terrace at the summit of the tower. There was a pool at the centre of the garden, an arm floating amongst the lily pads, nibbled by the black-and-white fish. Putting this to the back of his mind, where all manner of unpleasant images were now hidden, Aradryan scurried across to the walled lip of the terrace. It was not very high, forcing the two rangers to sink to their bellies and slink along like serpents.

The plaza stretched below them, a massive pyre at its centre. On huge tripods and spits, chunks of a megasaur roasted noisily. The huge reptilian creatures were the staple herd of the Exodites, kept both to feed the local eldar and to trade with the craftworlds in exchange for goods and devices they could not manufacture themselves. Tatters of its scaled hide were being used as awnings on several of the ork vehicles, and covered a rough enclosure at one end of the plaza.

Around the fires the orks clustered, some of them exceptionally large, easily half again as tall as an eldar. Smaller orks lounged further from the centre. All were being attended to by a swarm of little creatures with pinched faces, large ears and shrieking voices. The servant aliens lugged crates and sacks, brought food and polished guns and boots. They were subjected to a constant barrage of growls, shouts and fists, and seemed equally eager to squabble amongst themselves as they were to see to their larger cousins' needs.

Disgust welled up inside Aradryan, masking the fear he had felt since entering the settlement. From birth he had been taught about the barbarous green-skins – worst amongst all of the lesser races – but to confront their nature personally was an affront to everything he was as an eldar. He listened to their crudes barks, grunts and howls, and knew that such a language could never conceive of the higher philosophies of life; it was a language for commands and subjugation and nothing more. That they destroyed what they did not desire, and desired little except war, was evidence of their base nature.

In an instant it was easy to understand the orks and their society. The larger creatures bullied the smaller, which bullied the even smaller. In just one glance at the plaza, Aradryan saw this social system played out a dozen times, will enforced by physical brutality and nothing else. There was cunning here, he knew from old tales, but no intellect. Though the orks walked on two legs and constructed vehicles and guns, that did not hide the fact that they were beasts in heart and mind.

Appalled at what the unthinking brutes had done to the settlement of the Exodites, Aradryan brought his rifle from his shoulder. He had never wanted to kill anything before – out of anger or sport – but deep down he knew there was no way to negotiate with the orks, or wait for them to pass on and rebuild. Unlike other natural cataclysms, the arrival of the orks could only be stopped with one means – to meet violence with a greater, more directed violence. Aradryan knew that he should not take pleasure in a cull, any more than one took pleasure in a firegull eating sandgrubs, but he could not stop feeling that an injustice needed to be addressed.

And there would be vengeance. It was not enough that the ork invaders were slain. Bitter experience had taught the eldar in times past that the greatest menace of an ork invasion was not the warriors. Orks alive or dead shed spores to breed and once these spores had a grip on a world, especially a young, burgeoning planet like Eileniliesh, they were almost impossible to root out. The only way to be rid of the green beasts was swift and utter annihilation. So it was that Alaitoc had mustered what strength it could and even the Avatar had roused itself from its dormancy to bring battle to Hirith-Hreslain. If just one ork was to escape into the forests, a few short orbits from now Eileniliesh might be overrun by a new green horde and be lost forever. The autarchs and farseers had not responded to make battle with the orks, for orks thrived on war as other creatures thrive on food and drink; the Alaitocii had come to exterminate them.

'Look over there,' said Jair. He had removed the sighting array from his rifle and was using it as a telescope. Aradryan followed suit and turned his gaze across the plaza in the direction his companion had indicated.

The buildings were in a far more ruinous state here, in the direction away from the river and away from the sunset. Many had collapsed, whether from bombardment or deliberate demolition he could not say. Rubble choked some of the streets and broken roof tiles, cracked balustrades and toppled walls littered the town. It was not this that Jair had noticed, though.

In the gardens of one of the towers were several crude-looking cannons, hidden in the shadow of a porch roof. They were crewed by the smaller green-skins under the watchful eye of an ork with a cruelly barbed whip, the former stacking shells against the garden wall; a lot of shells.

Aradryan remembered that he was not just here for his own edification. Using the gunsight, he scanned the surrounding streets and buildings, noting where barricades had been built and guns emplaced. There was some kind of vehicle pool at the far end of the plaza, and he set about counting up the buggies, open-backed trucks, large battlewagons and half-tracked bikes he could see.

Under the direction of Jair, he examined the defences on the bridge. This did not take long, as there were none that he could see. He also cast his gaze along the river banks, but this also revealed that the orks were taking no particular precaution to guard themselves against attack from along the waterway.

When they had seen all there was to be seen from their vantage point, Jair signalled for Aradryan to lead the way back down to the lower levels. This time they took one of the skybridges across the street to the next tower, moving from the shadow of one column to the next so as not to be seen from below.

They descended to street level, but had taken no more than a few strides from the door when Jair suddenly stepped back, moving against the wall. The sun was quite low by now, and the long shadows of a group of the smaller greenskins appeared at the end of the alley.

Though they were diminutive, no taller than

Aradryan's waist, the ranger felt a sudden panic gripping him at the thought of confrontation. They may be small, he thought, but they had vicious claws and fangs, and were used to fighting. He noticed that Jair had slipped his knife from his belt and unholstered his shuriken pistol; Aradryan had forgotten he carried such weapons.

The instinct to run tried to sweep away Aradryan's rational thoughts and his breaths became short and shallow as his body responded to the imminent threat. Jair must have detected something of his dread, for the other ranger turned around with a concerned expression and raised a finger to his lips.

Trying to remain calm, Aradryan pushed himself back against the wall as the shadows crept closer.

He could hear a smattering of high-pitched conversation growing louder. He couldn't move as the patter of bare feet on the paving stones came closer and closer, yet at the same time his brain was screaming at him that if he did not turn and run now it would be too late. Locked in stasis between the instinct to fight or flee, Aradryan gritted his teeth, his hands making fists at his sides.

Aradryan could smell them now, filthy and pungent. There was blood and smoke and rotting meat on the air, and he could imagine dirt-encrusted nails scratching at his flesh while jagged teeth sawed through his skin. His gut writhed at the thought, cramping painfully, but he kept his lips clamped shut despite the sudden ache in his stomach.

The greenskins came into view, four of them. They had beady red eyes. Their ragged ears and bulbous noses were pierced with studs and rings. Two wore nothing more than stained loincloths, the other two, ever so slightly larger, wore jerkins and boots of untreated animal hide, which added to their stink. One of them had a revolver-style pistol thrust into its rope belt, the others carried sharpened metal spikes to serve as daggers.

It was impossible to discern what they were saying, or to guess their mood from their nasal whining. They jostled each other and snarled, paying no attention to what was around them. Glancing to his left, Aradryan saw that Jair had his hood pulled across his face, his cloak drawn close about him. Moving gradually, Aradryan copied his companion, swathing himself with the cameleoline material.

Almost within arm's reach, the small goblin-like creatures walked past, oblivious to the presence of the two rangers. Aradryan dared not to breathe lest his gasps be heard, though the greenskins patrol, for such he guessed it to be, was making more than enough noise with its chattering to mask any such sound.

Then they turned out of sight, heading into a street that led back to the plaza. Aradryan almost collapsed with relief.

'Let's go,' hissed Jair, gesturing with his knife. 'We'll head back via the river.'

For a moment, Aradryan could not walk. He sank to his haunches, back against the wall, and took several deep breaths, eyes closed.

It was hard for him to believe that he was still alive. Aradryan chuckled, the sound coming unbidden from deep within him. The relief was so profound that he had to laugh to let it out.

Jair appeared over him, scowling. The other ranger grabbed Aradryan's coat and dragged him to his feet, clamping a hand over his mouth as more laughter threatened to erupt from his lungs.

'Control yourself,' Jair whispered. 'Remember where we are.'

Aradryan could not help it; his body was shaking, his mind overflowing with gratitude at still being alive.

'I will abandon you here, if you do not calm yourself,' warned Jair, stepping away.

The thought of being left alone in this ork-infested town sobered Aradryan immediately. He opened his mouth to say sorry, but Jair cut him off with a swipe of his hand.

'Apologise later,' said the ranger. He pointed to the sky, which was streaked red and purple by the dusk sun. 'We must regroup with the others.'

THE FOREST TOOK on a different air as night fell. Swooping winged beasts with long, toothed beaks screeched from the treetops. The roar of predatory carnosaurs broke the still night and the wind in the trees sounded like the whisper of dead gods as Aradryan waited in the darkness.

The sky glimpsed between the swaying canopy looked like brushed steel, the stars hidden by cloud and the smog of Hirith-Hreslain burning. The moons, of which two were currently creeping over the horizon, lit everything with a bluish gleam.

The other rangers had headed back into Hirith-Hreslain, to place webway beacons for the waiting fleet to fix on to. On the frigates and battleships waiting off-world, wayseers would detect these hidden markers and delve temporary passages into the heart of the town, allowing some of Alaitoc's warriors to attack from within the ork force.

Jair would signal to Aradryan when it was time for him to enter the town and assist in the attack with his longrifle. Alone in a small dell where the river was a half-seen silver sliver through the trees, the ranger considered his extreme reaction earlier in the day.

He was embarrassed by it now, but at the time he had been so certain of being discovered, and his subsequent butchery at the hands of the orks, that it had seemed miraculous to survive. Now it seemed so stupid, viewed with the benefit of hindsight. Had the greenskin sentries located them, there would have been ample opportunity to escape, even if Aradryan and Jair had been incapable of slaying them. The small creatures would have had no chance of keeping pace, and any resultant hue and cry would have been left far behind by the swift eldar.

It had been fear that had ensnared Aradryan: a true and deep terror that he had never felt before. The dread he had experienced on the quayside by the *Lacontiran* had been an intellectual, existential dread of being. The fear he had felt at the thought of dying, or worse being captured, had been a barbaric, instinctual response, as primordial as the world he was on.

Aradryan hoped that having gone through the experience once already, he would be better prepared for it next time – if there was a next time. If he was fortunate, he would never feel again that desperate moment and the frustration of inaction that had paralysed him. If the sensation did grip him again he was sure he would master himself and keep control. None of the other rangers had said it, but there was a name for his deepest fear: coward.

Jair's voice in his ear broke Aradryan's contemplation. He was on his feet and heading towards Hirith-Hreslain before Jair had finished speaking.

'I am with Assintahil, Loaekhi, Naomilith and Estrellian, in the building where we spied upon the orks. Can you remember the way?'

As he jogged, Aradryan filtered back through his memories, skimming past the trauma of their near-discovery, and found that the route was straightforward. One of the benefits of Dreaming was the honing of access to unconscious memories, so that dreams could be recalled. Those who persisted on the Path of Dreaming were able to relive past experiences, whether real or imagined, in minute detail, with a heightened reality when compared to the original experience. These memedreams were the greatest lure of the Path of Dreaming, allowing an eldar to constantly revisit past glories, loves and happiness without ever experiencing woe or setbacks.

In a way, Aradryan's experience on the *Lacontiran* had snapped him from a potentially dangerous journey into imaginary, wishful self-fulfilment.

'Yes, I know the way,' he replied, realising that he had been running through the trees for some time, on the brink of half-dream as he had examined his memories. 'I shall signal you when I am at the base of the building. Please do not shoot me by mistake.'

'Hurry up, if you wish to see something truly memorable,' urged Jair.

The sounds of the orks had been constant for some

time, but Aradryan realised there was other noise too, and that the bellows of the greenskins and the roar of their engines had changed in pitch. The boom of a gun made him realise that the Alaitocii had begun their attack already!

He sprinted through the forest, quickly reaching the buildings. Without pausing, he dashed through the streets, eyes and ears alert to the slightest sign of any alien foe in the shadows of the buildings. The firelight lit the sky above, ruddily dappling the clouds of oily smoke from the engines of the ork vehicles.

'I am almost with you,' Aradryan told the others as he leapt onto the wall from which he could access the secondary turret that granted access to the rangers' vantage point. He nimbly sprang from perch to perch, his muscles remembering the feat from earlier without conscious prompting.

Rather than cut through the tower, he continued up the wall, finding hand- and footholds on window sills and balcony balustrades. If he lost his grip, he would be dashed to a bloody pulp on the ground far below, but he moved without hesitation. This was a danger he could master, and he felt nothing but exhilaration as he climbed spider-like up the last section of wall and then swung himself over the parapet of the roof terrace, his coat and cloak fluttering.

'There!' Loaekhi was standing up, pointing directly across the plaza. His face was thin, cheeks hollow, eyes sunken, and his black hair waved in unruly wisps from beneath his hood. The rest of him was almost impossible to see, his cameleoline coat and hood blue and grey against the sky. From the ground he would have been impossible to see.

Aradryan looked across Selain and saw that the orks had been stirred; like daggerwasps roused from their nest they were gathering against the eldar attack. Already on the far side of the river there was fierce fighting, the sky torn apart by lasers and the trail of missiles. Below the rangers, the orks were assembling around the largest of the beasts: their warlord. The creature was clad in slabs of thick armour and in one hand carried an immense cleaver-like blade and in the other a gun that must have weighed as much as Aradryan. Clanking transports billowing choking exhaust smoke pulled up beside the hulking greenskins and they clambered aboard before the armoured battle trucks sped off towards the bridge in a cloud of oily smoke and dust.

It was not this that Loaekhi had seen.

In an alleyway on the far side of the main square, a glimmer of gold and blue lit the pale walls. Aradryan knew it immediately, for he had seen webway portals many times on his travels aboard *Lacontiran*. In a few moments more, a squad of ten Dire Avengers were heading into the ruins of a low building behind the orks, their exarch's azure-and-gold gonfalon flowing from the banner pole upon his back.

'I see something far more deadly,' whispered Naomilith. 'Look beneath the bridge. You will need your telesights.'

Intrigued, Aradryan raised the sight to his eye. It automatically enhanced his view, multiplying the dim light of the moons so that the image that Aradryan saw was as though it were midday. Directing his gaze towards the bridge, he saw nothing at first. As he increased the magnification and became accustomed to the bubble of water around the piles, he saw unmoving shapes, half-crouched in the shallow waters. Like statues they waited, their chainswords and pistols held above the water, no more visible than solidified shadows. They were Aspect Warriors lying in ambush: Striking Scorpions.

'I wonder if Korlandril is down there,' said Aradryan. He shrugged, it was impossible to see any markings that would identify any particular shrine, and Aradryan did not know to which his friend belonged.

Turning his attention back to the streets leading to the plaza beneath him, Aradryan saw that other Aspect Warriors were gathering – more Dire Avengers waiting in the darkness, while on the rooftops opposite he spied Dark Reapers moving into position.

'Take out the gun crews,' whispered Jair. 'The ones we saw earlier today.'

Aradryan nodded and found the garden in which they had spied the first battery of cannons. Through the shattered remnants of a gatehouse, the ork guns would be able to fire across the bridge, directly into the plaza on the opposite side.

He raised his rifle to his shoulder, easing the stock into place, trying to stay relaxed though his heart was beginning to race. He remembered what Jair and Athelennil had taught him as they had returned to Alaitoc, and put into practice the routine he had repeated hundreds of times when they had left the craftworld to come to Eileniliesh.

The movement felt natural, not forced, as he snapped the sight back into place on its magnetic lock and tilted his head to peer down its length.

Taking a breath, he moved the red-lit image until he could see the small alien creatures scurrying around their weapons. They were loading shells into the breeches of their cannons, somewhat poorly judging by the number of times their ork overseer cracked his whip. Shells were dropped and picked up, and fingers caught in the slamming breech lock.

Two of the silhouetted figures in his gunsight fell down. After a moment, he realised they had been shot by the others. There was more panicked movement, but he sighted on one of the smaller creatures kneeling near to the closest cannon, a trigger-rope clutched in its fist. The resolution of the night sight meant that he could see nothing of the creature's features, only its outline, and the faintest brighter patch of its open mouth as it exhaled into the cold night.

He had never killed anything before, he thought, as he touched his finger to the trigger of his longrifle. Earlier, when he had seen Jair pull his pistol and knife to the ready, he had been horrified by the proposition. This was a different matter entirely. All he had to do was apply a little more pressure through his index finger and the creature directly in the middle of his sight would be no more.

There was a slight hiss and the delicate whine of a powercell. An invisible laser bolt shot across the plaza, just a hair's-breadth in front a needle-thin crystalline projectile laden with toxins that would slay most creatures in moments.

Aradryan only realised he had fired when the figure in his sights suddenly reared up, one hand snatching at its shoulder. It spun once with flailing arms, somewhat melodramatically Aradryan thought, and then collapsed to the ground like a grotesque marionette that had snapped its strings.

He sighted again, smiling at how easy it was. He tried for a slightly harder shot, choosing a small alien that was crawling between two crates.

His shot took it in the head, felling the greenskin instantly.

Again and again he fired, hearing the telltale whine of his fellow rangers' rifles spitting death across the divide. The ork gangmaster was stomping to and fro, trying in vain to rouse its dying underlings. Aradryan missed a shot at the beast, the merest twitch in his arm causing his aim to go wide. Concentrating again, he fired once more, but the ork still did not go down.

'I'm sure I hit it,' Aradryan muttered.

'The ork?' said Naomilith. 'They're tough beasts. You might not have even penetrated the skin. Try again, and next time aim for the eyes.'

'The eyes?' replied Aradryan.

'Like this.'

Aradryan was not even sure where the creature's eyes were, until he saw the tiniest puff of droplets erupting from the line of its heavy brow, a heartbeat before the ork fell backwards, crashing into a stack of shells. The unstable ammunition spilled across the garden, and a moment before he pulled his eye away from the sight Aradryan saw a spark of ignition.

A series of explosions rocked the ork battery, blowing apart the garden wall and hurling stone blocks into the air. The front of the building, already weakened by previous impacts, toppled sideways, tearing away from supporting beams in a cloud of dust and rubble, burying the bodies and guns beneath a heap of broken debris.

Aradryan laughed, captivated by the destruction. The smoke and dust billowed across the square, and in the darkness he spied the Aspect Warriors moving forwards, readying to attack the orks from behind as they set off towards the river.

Turning his gaze that way, there was not much to see, save for the flicker of missiles, the muzzle flare of ork guns and the bright flash of lasers. He could not tell if the battle was going well or badly, but there was nothing he could do to affect the fighting on the far side of the bridge.

Returning his attention to enemies closer at hand, he lifted his rifle again and picked out an ork amongst a large group that were running towards the plaza, heading after the vehicles of the warlord. His first shot struck the ork in the shoulder. It stumbled, falling to one knee, and then rose up again, shaking its head as the nerve toxins coursed through its system. Aradryan's next shot missed as the ork bent to retrieve its dropped pistol. The third shot caught it in the leg, just above the knee, and this time the poison proved too much, the ork pitching face-first into the ground.

The plaza was filled with furious action as the Dark Reapers and Dire Avengers opened fire together, ripping into the ork mobs with a barrage of rockets and a storm of shuriken catapult volleys. A dozen orks were torn apart in moments, as many again losing limbs or suffering grievous wounds that would have felled lesser creatures.

A one-armed ork staggered from the throng, slumping against the burning remnants of a half-tracked vehicle. Aradryan could see its head through the twisted metal frame of the transport and took aim. His shot hit home just behind the ork's ear and the alien slid from view.

'Our task is done here,' said Jair.

Aradryan ignored him, taking aim once more to target another wounded ork limping past the body of the one he had just slain. Aradryan caressed the trigger of his rifle and the ork fell, its head bouncing off the chassis of the wreck as it spun to the ground.

'We have another mission,' Jair said, more insistent. The ranger laid his hand on Aradryan's arm, pulling his rifle to one side.

'There are plenty of targets still,' Aradryan said, snatching his arm away from Jair's grip.

'There are others that can deal with them,' said Jair, speaking calmly, though his eyes betrayed agitation in the flickering light of the battle. 'We have to move closer to the river, the Exodites will be arriving and we must ensure their path is clear.'

With some effort, Aradryan dragged his eyes away from the battle raging below. He nodded, some measure of clarity returning to his thoughts. Jair and the others headed to the stairwell and Aradryan followed reluctantly.

'Do you know why the Aspect Warriors must wear a war-mask?' Jair asked as the group descended the stairs, moving quickly to the lower floors.

'So that the grief and distress of battle does not consume them,' replied Aradryan. 'Do not worry about me, the death of these beasts is nothing. This is a cull, nothing more.'

'You are wrong,' said Jair. He stopped at the next

floor and stared intently at Aradryan. 'The war-mask allows the Aspect Warriors to shed blood in the name of Khaine, but when they remove their wargear they can forget the thrill of killing. The elation you are feeling, it is the touch of Khaine, and you must be wary of its grasp. To hold life and death in your hand is a powerful thing, and it can become addictive.'

Aradryan did not reply, but as he followed Jair down to the street, he realised that the other ranger spoke the truth. It was a sobering moment as he looked back at the joy that had filled him with the death of each ork. The sensation he felt as the group made their way through the moon- and fire-lit streets was different to the relief he had experienced following his first encounter with the aliens. There was a cold calculation about the death he brought, which in itself heightened his sense of superiority.

A shouted warning from Naomilith had all five rangers reaching for their weapons. Three orks came lurching around a corner ahead, no doubt fleeing from the slaughter unleashed by the Aspect Warriors. Unlike before, Aradryan did not freeze. His shuriken pistol was in his hand before he even thought about it.

The orks raised their crude guns as the rangers opened fire. The hiss of shurikens split the air, slicing into the alien trio, Aradryan's shots amongst the fusillade. His heart raced again as the monomolecular discs sliced into the nearest of the enemy, shredding the ork's jerkin and lacerating green flesh.

One of the alien beasts fell immediately, throat slit amongst scores of wounds, and another stumbled backwards, roaring in pain. The third ork unleashed a blaze of bullets, the noise of its gun thunderous in the narrow street, the flare of the muzzle almost blinding. Estrellian was flung back, his flailing arms masked by the camouflage effect of his cloak, blood spraying into the air. Bullet impacts cracked from the wall to Aradryan's right as he fired his pistol again, teeth gritted.

The ork that had killed Estrellian staggered and collapsed, leaking thick blood from across its face and body, gun falling from its spasmodic grip. The creature that had been wounded recovered its footing, but only for an instant; Jair and Naomilith's pistols spat another hail of shurikens, sending the ork thrashing to the ground. It convulsed for a few moments and then fell still.

Loaekhi stooped over Estrellian, shaking his head. The numbness of shock welled up from Aradryan's stomach, but he took a deep breath and stepped up to stand beside the dead ranger. He looked at Estrellian's blood-spattered face, realisation dawning that the battle was far closer than he had thought.

'That could have been any of us,' Aradryan whispered. He swallowed hard, mastering his fear.

'Stay alert,' Jair said.

'We cannot leave him here,' said Aradryan, his gaze drawn to the waystone half visible inside Estrellian's coat. It glowed with a warm blue light, pulsing softly. The four surviving eldar exchanged a look, and Aradryan was reassured by the composure of his companions. Loaekhi and Naomilith stowed their pistols and picked up Estrellian's corpse. The cameleoline masked the body still, so that it looked as though the pair of rangers were carrying nothing but distorted air, a disembodied face and hand floating between them.

'The two of us will have to meet the Exodites,' said Jair, as the other rangers disappeared into the darkness, bearing away the body of their fallen comrade. 'The orks are not yet defeated.'

APPEARING VERY DIFFERENT in her battlegear, Saryengith met Aradryan and Jair at the appointed place, in a clearing not far from the outskirts of Hirith-Hreslain. She was dressed in armour made of scaled hide, her head encased in a helm fashioned from the skull of one of Eileniliesh's giant reptiles. She had a laser lance couched in her right hand, a silver-faced shield in her left. The elder sat astride a dragon: a winged creature covered in red and purple scales that was more than five times the height of an eldar in length. Its tail ended in a diamond-shaped mace, its long, leathery wings folded back against its flanks for the moment, revealing the broad straps of the dark wooden riding throne in which the Exodite leader was seated.

Saryengith was not alone. There were more than a dozen other dragon riders, their mounts basking in the moonlight at the centre of the clearing. Several scores of Exodites were close by, riding on bipedal reptiles with harnesses studded by slivers of precious metal and flashing gems. Like Saryengith they carried shields and laser lances, though several had rifles too, similar to those carried by the rangers.

There were other creatures still, in the darkness of the forest: megasaurs. On their huge backs were howdahs similar in design to the towers of

Hirith-Hreslain. Crewed by dozens of Exodites, the behemoths had armoured plates on their chests and hanging down their flanks. Upon galleries surrounding the howdah were several large laser cannons, each directed by two eldar dressed in the distinctive scaled robes of Exodite armour.

Aradryan's previous experience of megasaurs had been sliced on a platter, and he had never encountered a dragon before. The air in the clearing was thick with the smell of dung and oiled harnesses, which whilst powerful was not totally unpleasant. The beasts made all manner of rumbles, growls, clicks, hoots and hollers, some of them muted, some of them ringing out across the forest in challenge. Some had long necks for reaching up to the trees, their legs as thick as trunks. Several had horny crests or bony frills to protect their heads and necks, and spiralling or curving horns jutting from nose and brow. All of them were larger than anything the orks had built.

Standing next to Saryengith, Aradryan was a little uneasy. Her reptilian mount leered at him with a black eye, ropes of saliva dripping from exposed fangs almost as long as his knife. The moonlight glistened on the creature's scales, green and yellow, and its claws were sheathed with silvery metal studded with sharp jags of red and black gems, so that they appeared like serrated, jewelled carving knives. Its bulk was enough to intimidate Aradryan, who had seen cloud-whales in the gaseous domes of Alaitoc, but only ever from a considerable distance. The creature almost within reach was a mass of scaled muscle and tendon, its ferocious temperament only held in check by the chains of its reins in Saryengith's gloved hands.

She wore a half-mask beneath her hood, shielding her eyes and the bridge of her nose. It was enamelled in red and black, the lenses made to look like flaming, daemonic eyes. A saddle pack was stowed across the back of her mount, just behind her throne-like seat. A longrifle was within reach, and a slender-barrelled fusion pistol hung amongst the baggage. Looking at the packs, Aradryan realised that everything that the pandita owned was in those bags; she would have lost home and possessions when the orks had overrun Hirith-Hreslain. For those on the craftworld, personal possessions were of little value except sentimental; lost or broken belongings were easy to replace, and fashions came and went quicker than seasons on Eileniliesh. For Saryengith, it would take considerable time and effort to fashion or purchase replacements for everything that had been destroyed or taken.

'What word from the battle?' asked Saryengith.

'Selain is almost empty of foes, their dead piled high in the streets,' Jair told her. Aradryan was content to allow his companion to speak. The journey back through the forest – after a hectic sweep of the streets close to the river to confirm that few, if any, orks had escaped – had been made in silence. Jair had seemed unwilling to talk about what had happened to Estrellian, and Aradryan thought that no good would come from forcing the issue.

The death of the ranger had brought about mixed emotions in Aradryan. He was sad to have witnessed another eldar die, especially at the hands of the brutish orks. Yet he did not feel as shocked or miserable as he thought he should; the fact that he was still alive outweighed his grief. As he had made his way between the trees, following Jair without conscious effort, Aradryan had relived the moment of Estrellian's death several times. Etched into Aradryan's memory was the cruel, angry glare of the ork and the brightness of the ranger's blood as it had erupted from the flapping folds of his cloak. The rattle of bullets beside Aradryan had been no more than an arm's-length away. If he had not stopped to speak with Jair on the stairwell, Aradryan might have been standing where Estrellian had died. Had the ork that shot Estrellian been the closest of the group, it would have been slain by the ranger's pistols and the creature in front of Aradryan might have opened fire.

In such situations, it was the narrowest of margins, the most fickle circumstances of chance, which made the difference between life and death. The thought should have terrified Aradryan, to realise that he had been so close to death. His actual state of mind was the opposite. The forest around him was alive with sounds and smells and sights, teeming with life that still flowed through his body. His first encounter with an enemy had frozen Aradryan; his latest had let him free.

Aradryan was drifting back into a memedream of the event when he realised Jair was speaking to him.

'The Exodites will ride out immediately, to push the advantage,' the other ranger was saying.

Looking around, Aradryan saw that the host of Hirith-Hreslain, less than a hundred who had survived the initial attack, was moving out of the clearing. The ground shuddered beneath the tread of the megasaurs, each footfall sending reverberations that fluttered the leaves of the trees.

'We can return to *Irdiris* if you wish,' said Jair, watching the Exodites depart.

'Not yet,' replied Aradryan. 'Let us see the battle to its end.'

'Are you sure?'

'Never more so.' Aradryan needed to return to Hirith-Hreslain, to see the orks destroyed. The town had been home to a vivid awakening for him, and he had to see how things would end. More than that, he needed to take part in that conclusion, to be an agent of the orks' defeat. If he left now, he might never find any meaning in the things he had witnessed and experienced. 'There are still orks to be killed.'

THEY FOLLOWED THE Exodites along the road as the dragon riders took to the night skies. The timing of their arrival was vital to the success of the plan laid out by the seers and autarchs. The Alaitocii and such rangers that had travelled on their battleships had slain the orks in Selain and were encircling the enemy left in Hresh. Through careful manoeuvring, the orks were being pushed back onto one of the main thoroughfares through the settlement, with only one seeming escape route. It was here that the Exodites would close the encirclement, dooming any orks that remained. If the warriors of Hirith-Hreslain arrived too early, the orks would realise their peril and try to break out into other parts of their town; come too late and the aliens would be able to escape into the forests.

Aradryan marvelled at his companions and their

scaled mounts. The Exodites looked like other eldar, perhaps a little shorter and broader than the Alaitocii, but still possessed of the same slender build, sloping eyes and pointed ears. It was in their dress and mannerisms that they were most different. Aradryan could see the delicate stitching on their robes, made by hand, and the polished scale armour and shields that protected them had similarly been fashioned by manual labour. They bore spears and swords in addition to their rifles and laser lances: weapons of honed metal, chased with inscribed runes but with no energy source for a power field or whirling chainblade teeth.

The Exodites wore knee-high boots, heavily strapped with buckles, and their hands and forearms were clad in gloves of the same heavy hide-like material, knuckles and fingertips reinforced with dark grey metal. Some wore surplices, bound with wide belts and pierced by metal rings. Their helms were tall and pointed, like those of a Guardian, with open faces. Many wore long, elaborately embroidered scarves around their necks and across their mouths.

As they approached Hirith-Hreslain, the sights and sounds of fighting stirred Aradryan from a half-reverie. He could see nothing of the battle from where he was, but the flare of guns and missile launchers punctuated the silhouetted landscape in front, and the wind carried the bark of guns and the whine of shurikens.

One of the Exodites at the front of the column rose up in his stirrups, standing high with his laser lance held aloft. He turned to look back at the following warriors.

'The enemy are cornered and their fate awaits them!' he cried out. 'The time to attack is upon us. Ready your weapons and steel your hearts. Slay those that must be slain, but take no pleasure in it. Guard against the lusts of Khaine, for they are no more than an iron voice giving word to the lies of She Who Thirsts. All desire is a trap, so kill without joy and strike down the vermin that have despoiled our homes. We will triumph and we will rebuild.'

'Hirith-Hreslain!' The Exodites raised their weapons in salute.

No sooner had the speech been made than ear-splitting screeches split the night air. Monstrous winged shapes dropped down from the clouds, silhouetted against the setting moons. Blasts of multicoloured lasers stabbed into the orks as the Exodite dragon riders plunged into the attack.

With a chorus of ground-shaking bellows and rasping cries, the Exodites' war-beasts entered the battle. Surging along the main road, the megasaurs and lithodons charged into the orks retreating from the attacks of the Alaitocii. There was nothing the orks could do against this new threat, though some turned their crude guns on the gigantic forces of nature bearing down upon them.

Jair and Aradryan followed as swiftly as they could, occasionally pausing to snap off shots at orks that were trying to lurk amongst the ruins, shouting warnings up to the crew of a nearby megasaur to direct their fire against alien mobs skulking in the shattered buildings. Lascannon and scatter laser and fusion lance fire erupted from the howdahs of the enormous beasts, screaming down like lightning from a storm of wrath.

Clearing the street and surrounding buildings with their first thrust, the Exodites pressed on, driving the orks back into the guns and blades of the pursuing Aspect Warriors. With laser lances and fusion pikes, the Exodites closed, determined to exact revenge for the destruction of the town and the deaths of their kin.

It was fitting that the autarchs and farseers had granted the warriors of Hirith-Hreslain the opportunity to deliver the killing blow to the occupiers of their town. They settled the bloody score with grim faces and dispassionate eyes.

Pulses of white fire and burning lasers strobed through the orks, cutting down a score in one salvo. The dragons soared above, their riders raining down more las-fire and showers of plasma grenades. Against the fury of the Exodites, the orks did not survive for long. They were cut down in short order, the wounded crushed beneath the feet of the advancing behemoths.

DAWN FOUND JAIR and Aradryan picking through the ruins, searching for wounded eldar and surviving orks with the rest of the rangers and squads of Aspect Warriors. They met up again with Athelennil, and Aradryan was pleased to see her, though he realised with some guilt that he had not thought about his lover throughout the battle. On reflection, his lack of thought concerning her wellbeing had been to his advantage, for he did not know if he would have been able to cope worrying about her life as well as his own.

Here and there they would find a casualty of one

side or the other; the eldar were taken to the healers, the orks despatched with pinpoint shots.

'You know that Thirianna fought here,' Athelennil told Aradryan as the two of them climbed down a broken wall from a ruined upper storey, having assured themselves that it was empty.

'And I trust that she is unharmed,' said Aradryan. 'That is all?'

Aradryan dropped down to the street, landing next to the sprawled body of an ork, one of its arms missing, bite and claw marks across its back.

'What else would I think? Thirianna and I are friends, if that.'

'So, you have no urge to return to Alaitoc with her?' Athelennil wrinkled her lip upon seeing the dead ork. 'Are you sure this is the life you wish to choose?'

Aradryan looked around. There were alien bodies everywhere, and smoke rising from dozens of fires. The stink of fumes and orks was all-pervading, and the glare of Eileniliesh's sun was harsh. Death hung like a shroud over Hirith-Hreslain, but it was not death that occupied his thoughts.

'It was fear of death that drove me to *Lacontiran*,' he said, grasping Athelennil's hand. 'I cannot let that fear rule my life. I have learnt here that death will come to us all, so it is in life that we must pursue our dreams and chart our own course. I cannot return to Alaitoc, for Thirianna or any other reason. There is no life there. Where there is no risk of death, life has no meaning.'

'Yet, death is so much closer out here,' said Athelennil. She reached out with her other hand and prodded a gloved finger against Aradryan's spirit stone. 'All that you are could be ended, far from home and friends.'

'If I am to die, it will be out here,' said Aradryan. 'Out amongst the stars where I belong.'

# BEGINNINGS

*The Black Library of Chaos – Deep in the weft and folds of the webway is a craftworld unlike any other. It was to here that the Laughing God, Cegorach, first travelled when he escaped the clutches of She Who Thirsts. The scholars who dwelt upon the craftworld were surprised to see the god appearing amongst them, but he stilled their excitement and related to them his tale, and that of what had happened to the other gods. The Laughing God finished his narrative and disappeared, instructing the scholars and their protectors not to forget what he had told them. Thus was the Black Library founded, and the first of the Harlequins created. From the Black Library the followers of Cegorach travel far and wide, searching for all knowledge of the power of Chaos and the manner of the dark gods of the Othersea. Artefacts of Chaos are brought here, for study and destruction, and within thousands of grimoires and tomes and volumes and tracts has been gathered an unprecedented literature concerning the warp and its denizens.*

'MADNESS!' SAID ARADRYAN, his gaze moving from one companion to the next, unable to believe what he had heard.

They were barely ten cycles out from Eileniliesh, where the hunt for orks in the wilderness still continued; Aradryan had left with some reluctance. Of all the places he would have chosen for their next destination, the Chasm of Desires would have been last. The thought was horrifying. At one moment he had been considering the boundless possibilities of his new life, the experiences he could seek out; at the next, his shipmates had announced that they intended to delve into the heart of the Great Enemy itself.

'It is not madness,' said Caolein. 'Other outcast ships have done it before.'

'Where do you think that came from,' said Jair, jabbing a finger at the waystone brooch on Aradryan's chest. 'The Tears of Isha fell only upon the crone worlds.'

'But why now?' said Aradryan. 'What about the winterfalls? The Mosaic of Kadion? Another Exodite world, perhaps? There are others who will throw away their lives for the Tears of Isha, we do not have to be numbered among them.'

'We do not even know if it can be done,' said Athelennil. 'It is an idea, nothing more.'

'It's a suicidal whim, that is what it is!' Aradryan

folded his arms defiantly. 'There is a reason it is called the Well of Sins, the Gulf of Utter Darkness, the Void of Eternal Damnation.'

'And despite those titles, it is also where the greatest rangers have gone before, to bring back the Tears of Isha so that future generations can avoid the hunger of She Who Thirsts. You wanted adventure, Aradryan. What greater adventure could we set upon?'

'I think I am prepared to aim a little lower, this early in my life as an outcast,' said Aradryan. He turned to Lechthennian, who had said nothing since Caolein had announced his intent to dare the Eye of Terror. 'What do you think of this insanity?'

Lechthennian had a lap-harp, which he strummed distractedly. He looked up at the mention of his name, shaking his head.

'I travel with the ship, nothing more,' he said. 'I do not choose its course.'

'You do not care where you go?' said Aradryan, frowning at the answer he had received. 'It has been suggested that we venture into the greatest warp storm in the galaxy, the physical embodiment of the bane of our entire people, and you don't have an opinion?'

His fingers picking out a jaunty four-note refrain, Lechthennian shook his head.

'We are not committed yet,' said Jair, reaching out a placating hand towards Aradryan. 'It may be impossible, or too difficult at least, as you say. We will not know until we reach Khai-dazaar. When we are there, you will be able to choose what you wish to do.'

'Khai-dazaar? I have never heard of it. What will I have to decide there?'

Athelennil sat down next to Aradryan, but he leaned away from her, disappointed that she would argue against him.

'Khai-dazaar is an interspace in the webway, where we can find those who would guide us to the crone worlds. If we are successful, you can always choose to remain there, or perhaps leave with another ship.'

'Leave? Would it come to that?'

'If we wish to go, we are not beholden to your view,' said Jair. 'There will be others willing to come with us, your presence is not required. Do not think like a Path-wrapped. Your destiny is no more attached to this ship than any other. *Irdiris* is but a vessel, its crews coming and going as they wish. It is not special, we are not special, and neither are you. You are outcast now, enjoy the freedom of choice that is laid before you.'

'From a maiden world to a crone world,' Aradryan murmured. 'Or abandoned to fend for myself. Madness.'

SITTING AT THE piloting console next to Caolein, Aradryan laid his hands upon the semicircular arrangement of jewel-like interfaces. It was not the first time he had steered the *Irdiris* since coming aboard, but he still felt a thrill as his fingers lightly touched the guide-gems. The contact brought a moment of communion with the energy of the ship's psychic network: formless sentience derived from the spirits of past eldar. Aradryan allowed himself a moment to settle, attuning his thoughts to the rhythm and flow of the vessel's pulse.

The display sphere in front of him showed the

webway tunnel curving gently down and to the right, realised in the glowing globe as an ethereal passageway of gold and silver. The *Irdiris* was quite capable of navigating the stretch on its own, so Aradryan sat back, feeling the control vanes of the starship adjusting to take in the sweep of the curve.

'Not far now,' said Caolein. 'Are you sure you're ready?'

'This might be the only chance I have to do this,' replied Aradryan. 'If you are intent on leaving me here.'

Ahead, the webway opened out into the interspace of Khai-dazaar. Dozens of webway passages intersected, forming a near-globular arrangement more than three times the size of Alaitoc's largest domes. The settlement that had grown up on the interspace looked like an inverted city, spires rising up from the artificial fieldwalls that kept the interspace together, pointing towards a glowing false sun at the centre. Bridges and concourses criss-crossed Khai-dazaar, forming a maze of quays and walkways, arcing over and looping around the turrets and towers that soared like gigantic stalactites. Lights of every hue shone from slender windows, and guiding lanterns blinked red and blue to form rainbow causeways between the labyrinth of structures.

A craftworld had landing protocols and the guiding hand of its infinity circuit to steer an arriving ship to its correct berth; Khai-dazaar was a free-for-all of ships coming and going, steering about each other on seemingly random courses. Small skyrunners cut past stately liners, while silver-hulled sky barges floated serenely from tower to tower.

Aradryan took in a deep breath, trying to figure out a way through the sprawling maze of arches and traffic.

'We should head to the Spire of Discontented Bliss,' suggested Caolein.

Aradryan felt the other pilot merging with him on the guidance matrix, their spirits coalescing briefly as Caolein highlighted a route towards their destination. On the display in front of them, a gleaming silver ribbon appeared, turning beneath a wide gantry before spiralling down towards one of the lower docks about a third of the way around the rim of the interspace.

Nudging *Irdiris* into line with the proposed trajectory, Aradryan enjoyed the sensation of movement afforded by the view of the city. In the webway, it was often the case that there was no sense of momentum, but as bright windows flashed past and roadways speared overhead he could feel the ship racing into Khai-dazaar. In fact, he felt they were going too fast and directed *Irdiris* to slow down, which required another course correction to keep them from heading into the higher levels of a spire.

Concentrating intensely, Aradryan was soon lost in the task of guiding the ship safely to its destination; always Caolein's presence was there with him to take over should he make a mistake. Determined not to embarrass himself, Aradryan pictured the elegant sapphiretails of the Dome of Enchanted Declarations, and in doing so *Irdiris* swooped gracefully down into the lower depths of the city, passing through the shadow of an immense battleship marked with tiger stripes of black and purple.

'Commorraghans?' he said in surprise, recognising the blade-like design of the energy arrays and steering fins.

'There are eldar of all kindreds here,' said Caolein. 'Rangers, corsairs, Commorraghans, traders from the craftworlds. And, of course, Harlequins, White Seers and others.'

Slowing the ship to a sedate glide, Aradryan made final adjustments towards the sweeping arc of the dock portal highlighted in the display. There were black stone runes embedded in the white stone of the gateway: 'Of all the Fates that Morai-heg wove, none was so damned as the life of Narai-tethor.' The reference was lost on Aradryan; a myth-tale he had not heard. He glanced at Caolein, who sensed his desire for explanation over the piloting interface.

'I have no idea,' laughed the pilot with a shrug. 'I think it might be from Saim-Hann, or maybe Thelthadris. The city has been built by people from every craftworld and beyond, each leaving their own mark and stories.'

A guidance beacon sprang into glittering life as they flew into the opening of the dock, connecting with the *Irdiris*. Aradryan latched on to this wave of psychic energy and allowed the ship to slowly slew sideways, adjustor vanes angled steeply to kill the rest of its momentum. With barely a shudder to indicate they had touched down, *Irdiris* extended her landing feet and settled on the concourse between two pearl-sailed pleasure yachts.

'Stylish,' said Caolein, leaning back from the controls with a smile.

Aradryan shut down the piloting controls and

directed his thoughts through the psychic matrix, informing the others that they had arrived. He felt a flutter of excitement emanating from the rest of the crew, and it was infectious. The viewing sphere enlarged, showing a real-light view of their surroundings. Aradryan could not see any other eldar on the broad apron, but the matrix of *Irdiris* buzzed with the life of the city.

'So this is Khai-dazaar,' he said, thoughts awash with the possibilities.

THE WEBWAY POCKET realm was initially bewildering. Every street was home to crafty-eyed hawkers selling wares ranging from cloaks and robes to ancient texts and supposed artefacts of the old eldar empire. Far from the polite traders on the Boulevard of Split Moons, these eldar haggled and competed, vying for the attention and patronage of visitors and each other. There seemed to be as many deals being struck between the merchants as with the other eldar who slowly wound their way between the stalls.

The goods put any craftworld trader to shame. Fine art pieces, some of them genuinely ancient, sat alongside processed ship stores. Exotic animals – mammalian, reptile, avian and indeterminate – lay in cages or blinkered or leashed, howling, yammering and hooting, while others watched the procession of potential owners with placid, intelligent eyes. Materials of every weave and colour and design were on show, together with jewellery of precious metals and ghost stone and cinderclay and shaped mineral; gems and semi-precious stones of every hue and shape, both natural and fashioned; statuettes and busts, ceramic tiles and beaten metal dishes. Aradryan saw treatises of philosophers next to popular poetry collections and political tracts; artists painting flattering portraits and not-so-flattering caricatures; plants and grasses, blossoms and bulbs, buds and petals from hundreds of worlds and craftworlds; animal hides and furs, treated skins and preserved horns, ground bones and polished skulls.

The open-fronted establishments behind the stalls were more reminiscent of the Bridge of Yearning Sorrows than anywhere else. Keeping close to Athelennil, who seemed to have a particular destination in mind, Aradryan passed narcotics dens and drinking houses, lyrical recitals and debating chambers, tattooists and bodypainters, dreamers and singers, ghost stone sculptors and flesh designers. The latter were a Commorraghan influence, offering their services for free in exchange for the opportunity to turn living eldar into works of art. Aradryan saw one old female wearing a sash marked by the runes of Biel-Tan sitting in a chair while a skeletal flesh designer fused bright blue feathers into her scalp, replacing her hair with an extravagant crest. Next to the eldar was an infant male, her son most likely, the skin of his exposed arms being redrafted with mottled snake scales.

'Not there,' said Athelennil, dragging Aradryan by the arm. 'If that is something you are interested in, I know a far more accomplished fleshworker over in the Crimson Galleries.'

'Not just now,' said Aradryan, pulling his eyes away from the bizarre vision, nose wrinkled in distaste.

'There is nothing wrong with expressing yourself

through a little body modification,' said Athelennil. She waggled the fingers of her free hand in Aradryan's face. 'I had talons for a few passes, if you can believe that.'

'Whatever for?' asked Aradryan, appalled rather than amused by the idea. 'And is that not very impractical?'

'I did not have them *for* anything,' said Athelennil. 'I had them because I could. Also, my consort at the time rather liked a little scratching in his lovemaking.'

'I really did not need to know that.' Looking around, Aradryan felt a twinge of concern. The contrast between Khai-dazaar and Eileniliesh was stark. He could see the Exodites' point of view; this was just the sort of behaviour that could lead to obsession and depravity.

'Do not be prudish,' warned Athelennil, mistaking his expression of apprehension for disgust. 'It is not for you to judge what others do with their lives.'

'It is just a shock, that is all,' said Aradryan, forcing a smile. He pulled Athelennil closer. 'I am still adjusting to life away from the Path. Does it not worry you? How do you maintain perspective and control?'

They continued along the street, passing underneath gaudy bunting strung between the balconies of the upper storeys. Aradryan swerved to avoid two scantily clad eldar in a heated discussion, whose melodramatic gesticulations were a hazard to those trying to pass too close. His last moment course correction forced Athelennil to duck beneath a low hanging garland of purple and white flowers.

'Control is definitely an area you need to work on,' she laughed, pushing Aradryan in retaliation for his bump. She stopped, her smile fading. 'The Path deludes us, teaching that we must curb our natural enthusiasm, blind our senses to the reality of our lives. To be outcast and wander from the Path is to accept yourself and to be free from the tyranny of self-perfection. The founders of the Path laid down an ideal, but it has become more than a goal to strive for – it has become a prison for our spirits.'

'The tales of the Fall, of the coming of the Great Enemy, are not simple propaganda,' replied Aradryan, with more vehemence than he expected. Though the prospect of a post-life existence in an infinity circuit depressed him, the thought of being consumed by She Who Thirsts was a genuine terror. His recent brush with indulgence during the fighting at Hirith-Hreslain had been a timely warning. 'We were possessed by our passions and it led to the destruction of our civilisation. Can we truly trust ourselves not to repeat the past?'

'Abstinence is a false philosophy, no better than the puritanical beliefs of the Exodites,' argued Athelennil. At Aradryan's nod the two of them continued on their way, side-by-side but not touching each other. 'With every generation, more become trapped. The society of the craftworlds survives because of those who fail on the Path. Seers, and exarchs, and Waywardens, all of them needed to pass on the lessons that they failed to learn. When does self-deprivation become an obsession in its own right? Must we wait until there are only teachers left and no pupils before we realise that the Path condemns us to stasis? It grants us no future.'

Aradryan was taken aback by the passion of

Athelennil's argument. He had never asked why she had decided to become outcast, and she had not volunteered the information. Now was not the time to inquire, he sensed, as Athelennil gestured for the pair to turn right into an alley lit by strings of blue and green parchment lanterns. Something bounded across in front of them: a small, white-furred primate of a species Aradryan had not encountered before. It leapt up onto one of the lantern ropes and swung away, moments before an eldar child came sprinting after it, shouting curses.

Stooping beneath the lamplines, Aradryan found himself coming out into a walled courtyard where glowing coal braziers and chairs of woven reed were arranged around a central fountain. Two eldar, garbed head to foot in heavy robes of scarlet, their faces and heads covered with scarves of the same, stood beside a doorway. The lounge area was otherwise empty. Ruddy light glowed through a slit window in the door between the two eldar, but the wall in which it was set was otherwise blank white.

'The Passage of Sunken Fears,' declared Athelennil. 'Let us not go in straight away.'

She reclined on one of the benches, close to the fountain. Aradryan lay down near to her, finding that the light sprinkling of water combined pleasantly with the ambient heat of the braziers. The coals smoked with sweet-smelling incense, while the water that fell on his lips had a tang of salt. He closed his eyes, trying to relax. He wore his ranger bodysuit, finding it more comfortable and practical than his old clothes, and the arms and legs shrank away from his skin to create a vest-like costume, responding to his desire to feel the heat and water on his limbs.

'The mistake of the Path is that it enables those upon it to dwell too long upon one aspect of themselves,' said Athelennil. Her quiet voice was hard to hear over the splashing of the fountain, and Aradryan realised he had quickly been slipping into a semi-slumber. He opened his eyes, experiencing a moment of vertigo as he stared up at Khai-dazaar's artificial sun, surrounded by a corona of jagged building peaks and curving skywalks.

'What is to stop the same happening to an outcast?' said Aradryan, pushing himself up on one elbow.

'The galaxy itself,' replied Athelennil. 'Away from the security and sanctity of the craftworlds is a dangerous, testing place. There can be little indulgence when you have to keep your eyes and ears open.'

'You are mistaken,' said Aradryan. 'I could slip into a memedream here and spend my life indulging in fantasy and phantasm. What is to stop me?'

'Thirst and hunger, for a start. You think that the people here will give you food and drink out of the goodness of their hearts? There is nobody on the Path of the Creator, none treading the Path of Service to bring it to your lap. And there are some very unsavoury types here. If you want to dream, you best not do it without someone to stand guard over you, unless you want to awake in the fleshpits or fighting arenas of Commorragh. Or somewhere worse.'

'I see what you mean...' said Aradryan, casting an eye towards the pair of eldar standing as sentries by the doorway.

'Them?' Athelennil laughed, cocking her head to

look at the silent guardians. 'They would never harm us.'

'Why are we here?' asked Aradryan. 'Who are they?'

'We are here to see Estrathain Unair, to see if a Harlequin troupe is currently in Khai-dazaar. They are the door wardens, who are here to greet visitors and inquire as to their purpose in coming.'

'Did you send word already?'

'That was not necessary,' said Athelennil. 'Estrathain knew my intent as soon as we arrived.'

'Indeed I did.'

Aradryan sat up abruptly as three figures stepped out of the doorway, garbed in the same all-enclosing clothes as the door wardens. They had spoken in unison, and as the trio advanced towards the fountain Aradryan noticed that they did so in step with each other.

'I am Estrathain Unair, mediator of Khai-dazaar.' The three figures stopped just short of Aradryan and raised their right hands, palms outwards and thumbs folded in greeting. The way that all three eldar spoke together was disconcerting, their voices exactly the same as each other. 'You must be very confused, Aradryan. Please come inside, have refreshments and allow me to explain.'

'Of course, I am your guest,' said Aradryan. He watched the red-swathed figures closely, noticing that there was something disturbing about their eyes. The ranger saw himself reflected in the black orbs and realised he was looking into gemstones, not organic visual organs.

'Please do not be disturbed by my kami, they cannot harm you,' said Estrathain, the three figures parting, hands directing Aradryan and Athelennil towards the now-open archway.

Beyond the plain wall was a short corridor, which led into another open space, almost exactly like the first, except that the incense on the braziers was more delicate and fruity, and the water that splashed from the fountain a pale shade of pink. There were seven identical arched doorways leading from the court-yard, and two more of the red-robed 'kami'. One of the doors opened and a third kami came into view, holding a tray on which was a pitcher of dark green liquid and two goblets, set beside a small platter holding a variety of confectionary treats.

'Welcome to Khai-dazaar, my home,' said Estrathain. Only one of the kami spoke, as it sat down and gestured for the rangers to do the same, voice slightly muffled by its scarf.

'Are you the real Estrathain?' asked Aradryan. He peered under the headscarf and saw the same glim-mering lenses as before.

'We are all the 'real' Estrathain,' said all of the constructs in unison. The single kami that had sat continued on its own. 'Only one of us will speak, to avoid further confusion. As I said earlier, I am the mediator of Khai-dazaar, and I know of your intent to dare the secrets of the crone worlds.'

'Do you rule Khai-dazaar?' asked Aradryan. He plucked a goblet from the tray held by the motionless kami. 'Do we have to seek your permission or make tribute?'

'You mistake me for a Commorraghan over-lord, Aradryan,' said Estrathain. 'I am no archon, be assured. As it appears that Athelennil has not furnished you with the nature of my existence, with her permission I shall digress from the immediate matter to enlighten you.'

All six kami looked at Athelennil, who laughed and nodded.

'Of course, please tell Aradryan your story,' she said. 'I forget how polite you always are.'

'Thank you,' said Estrathain, the attention of the kami returning to Aradryan. 'I do not rule Khai-dazaar. No individual or group has control of Khai-dazaar, and while I exist none ever shall. I founded this place, you see, and intended it to be a coming together of our disparate kindreds. Harlequins and folks of the craftworlds, Commorraghans and Exodites. Of course, the Exodites never came, but I invited them.'

The kami leaned back, its scarf slipping a little to reveal a plainly featured face fashioned from an off-white psycho-plastic. As Estrathain continued, Aradryan realised what had alerted him earlier to the unnatural nature of the kami: their mouths and eyes did not move when they spoke. In fact, their faces were simply masks, close approximations of an eldar visage but immobile.

'I was no bonesinger, and so my fledgling realm of equality and peace had no matrix, no equivalent to an infinity circuit. Instead, I possessed a considerable psychic talent of my own, furnished by a lengthy walk upon the Path of the Seer before I dispossessed myself from Ulthwé. I became the spine, the nervous system of Khai-dazaar, in a manner of speaking, putting myself at the service of those who wished to communicate, create and explore.'

'So you are somewhere else, controlling these

mannequins?' said Aradryan. 'A very good way to hide from those who might want to exert influence over you. It sounds as if you are powerful here, I would not condemn your paranoia.'

'That is amusing,' said Estrathain, raising a hand in demonstration. 'If the kami could laugh, I would. Alas, they are not capable. You must understand something about the nature of what we are. Those who have been seers understand the separation of mind, thought and form. Normally all are encompassed together, but not always so.'

The kami sat forwards and pointed a scarlet-gloved finger at Aradryan's chest, indicating his waystone.

'When your body is no more, your mind and thought persist,' Estrathain explained. 'Very shortly after, thought also dissipates, for it requires the physical form to operate. This leaves only the pure mind, the essence of each of us. It is our spirit, if you would accept such a term. It is mind alone that transfers to the infinity circuit of a craftworld. If given form again, the mind can give rise to thought once more, though often in limited fashion and of a temporary nature.'

'Of course,' said Aradryan. 'That form might be a starship or a skycutter, or a wraith-construct. Did you die, then? Is that why you have several forms?'

'I did not die, I was in the prime of my life when I became the kami.'

The puppet-thing swung its legs onto the couch and leaned back, hands behind its head. It seemed such a natural movement, but the unfeeling eyes and unmoving features twisted the familiarity into something much more disturbing. The other kami, except for the one that was standing at Aradryan's side holding the drinks tray, had departed; moving off on their other business, Aradryan assumed.

'Khai-dazaar started as a single ship, locked into the webway at this interspace,' Estrathain continued. 'I would send news to passing ships. Some of those ships remained, seeing the value of placing themselves at this intercourse between the stars. Traders came, and I brokered deals between the ships' crews, acting as an initiator and a confidant. Khai-dazaar grew, as ships became towers and gangways became docks. I could not be everywhere at once, and the demands on my time grew too great. So it was that I had the idea of the kami.'

'I understand,' said Aradryan, lifting up his goblet for it to be refilled. 'These are semi-autonomous creations, allowing you to be in more than one place.'

'You do not quite understand. They are fully sentient and autonomous.' The kami on the couch sat up and pulled back the front of its robe, revealing smooth artificial skin. In the centre of its chest glowed a spirit stone, blinking with tiny starlight, indicating that there was an eldar essence within. 'There were adventurers who were willing to trade Tears of Isha for information, contacts and berthing spaces. Over many passes, I assembled a score of waystones. With the flesh sculptors, my own psychic power and the aid of a self-exiled bonesinger, I became the kami. Each of them is me. We are all Estrathain.'

Aradryan laughed in shock, not quite sure he could comprehend what he had been told. He looked at the kami with the tray, scrutinising it closely. It tilted its head slightly and nodded. When Estrathain next spoke, it was through this body.

'Each of them is me, and I am all of them. One divided, and several as a whole. My disparate forms can act in concert or separately as we require. There are many of us now, all across Khai-dazaar.'

'And the answer to what you seek can be found in the Channelways of Saim Khat,' said the reclining kami.

'That is where we can find a Harlequin troupe?' said Athelennil, excited. She glanced at Aradryan. 'There are no others that can guide us to the crone world.'

'You are aware of my price,' said both kami.

'Three Tears of Isha, when we return,' said Athelennil, nodding in acknowledgement. 'We have an agreement.'

'You barter for waystones?' Aradryan was confused. 'Yet you said there was no infinity circuit here.'

'The kami are semi-organic and not immortal, and ever there are more demands upon me, so my numbers must continue to increase,' replied the kami with the tray.

'How many of you are there?' asked Aradryan. He stood up, placed his goblet on the tray and took up a piece of fruit-based confectionary.

'We do not know, we have not counted for some time,' said the kami on the couch. 'Several dozen, at least.'

'If the Harlequins agree to your request, I will be accompanying you,' said another kami, appearing in a doorway to Aradryan's left.

'You can leave Khai-dazaar?' It was Athelennil's turn to be surprised. 'I never knew that.'

'We are quite independent of each other,' said the

tray holder. 'There is not a particular bond to this place. We have never travelled to the crone worlds and we are intrigued.'

'You realise that it is dangerous,' Aradryan said to the kami. 'You might not return.'

'It is a loss we can bear,' replied Estrathain. 'That is the advantage of being multiply incarnated.'

'But as an individual, you must be afraid of your death,' Aradryan said, laying a hand on the thick sleeve of the kami who had just entered. 'If you are each autonomous, the Estrathain that I am touching risks the end of its existence.'

'That is true,' the kami replied, laying a hand on Aradryan's as if to comfort him. 'All things die, and I wish to see the Abyss of Shadows before this vessel is of no more use. It is an opportunity that few eldar will ever have.'

'I told you!' said Athelennil, looking at Aradryan. 'You are leaving behind a great chance if you do not come with us.'

'I sensed your hesitancy when you arrived, but in your mind you know that your fears do not outweigh your intrigue,' said the kami that was sitting down.

'It is true,' confessed Aradryan, looking at Athelennil. 'The more I have thought about it, the more the thought of the danger entices me. Perhaps it is just hubris, but there is a strong part of me that desires to truly claim to have seen the crone worlds and returned.'

'You wish to brag about it?' laughed Athelennil. 'That is why you will come with us?'

'If one is to brag, make it something worth bragging about,' replied Aradryan, indignant. 'We are getting ahead of ourselves. The Harlequins have not agreed to take us there.'

'And we will need to find others who will join us,' said Estrathain.

Both rangers looked at the kami who had spoken; the one with the drinks.

'Others?' said Athelennil. 'What others?'

'We are going to the crone worlds,' said Estrathain. 'A troupe of Harlequins, five outcasts and I are not sufficient for such an expedition. There will be considerable dangers and foes to overcome. Go to the Channelways and seek out Findelsith, Great Harlequin. If he consents, you will find a Commorraghan exile called Maensith Drakar Alkhask. She has a ship and warrior company that is sufficient for the venture.'

'You seem to know exactly what we need,' said Aradryan, growing suspicious of the mediator's motives.

'I facilitate the existence of Khai-dazaar,' replied Estrathain. 'At this moment, at least a handful of my other selves will be brokering similar deals for others, matching sellers to buyers, suppliers to markets, crews to ships, followers to leaders. It is our purpose to know these things and bring together interested parties in mutually-beneficial accommodations. Maensith desires a contract, one that will pay well, and a journey to the crone worlds will not intimidate her. You desire to go to the crone worlds, and so there is harmony. The unknown factor rests with the Harlequins. Findelsith and his kind are unpredictable and I know nothing of their intentions while they are here.'

'Then our next task is obvious,' said Athelennil. 'We must head to the Channelways. Please could you inform the other members of our ship's company that we will meet them there.'

'As you wish, I shall pass the word,' said all three kami. 'One of me will also join with your rendezvous, to help in the approach to Findelsith.'

'That is settled then,' said Aradryan, with a short, nervous laugh.

He had become accustomed to the idea of going to the crone worlds in no small part because he had thought the expedition unlikely to begin. Now it seemed there was an increasing chance that he might actually be setting out for the Eye of Terror and his uncertainty returned. He consoled himself with the notion that the whole venture relied upon the cooperation of some Harlequins, who were notoriously fickle in their loyalties and capricious in their schemes. This thought settled his nerves a little as he followed Athelennil out of Estrathain's chambers. The Harlequins would very likely turn down their petition.

After all, they probably had much better things to do than plunge into the nightmarish heart of She Who Thirsts.

THE AUDIENCE WAITED with hushed expectation, standing in small groups in front of the stage. The performance was to take place in one of Khai-dazaar's recital halls, where usually poets and singers and musicians would entertain the eldar of the city in exchange for gifts, passage or simple accommodation from appreciative onlookers. Black drapes hung over the windows, blocking out the light of Khai-dazaar's ever-present artificial star, and in the gloom of ruddy lamps, Aradryan and the rest of *Irdiris*'s crew stood to the right of the stage. As in the rest of the city, there were all manner of eldar in the crowd, including one of Estrathain's kami, who watched over the proceedings from a small dais at the back of the shadowed room.

The lights dimmed almost to darkness as a single figure walked out onto the stage. She moved with measured steps, the diamond patterning of her tight leggings and long hooded jacket difficult to see in the gloom. Under her raised hood, there was no sign of a face, only a bare silver mask that reflected the ruddy glow of the lamps, looking like distant nebulae. Streamers fluttered from her broad belt, twirling lazily in her wake as she came to a stop a little off centre stage. On her back she wore an elaborate device, sprouting two elegant funnels that rose above each shoulder, gems twinkling on its surface.

A whisper rippled through the audience, murmuring a single word: Shadowseer.

Poised, one foot crossed against the other, the Shadowseer bowed, and as she did so, a plume of glittering green and silver issued from her backpack, spreading quickly across the crowd. The sparkling fog drifted over Aradryan, tiny stars dancing in his eyes, the scent of fresh flowers carried on the breeze, filling him with a sense of peace.

Distracted by this, he had not seen a dozen figures appearing on stage. They wore brightly patterned bodysuits, decorated with diamonds and lozenges, stripes and whorls of rainbow colours. For the moment they were frozen in plateau, each holding a different instrument.

From the Shadowseer issued more light, a golden glow that illuminated the stage, bathing the Harlequins in its warm aura. Each wore a comic mask or half-mask with exaggerated features, gem-like tears and painted lips, and garish beading, while scarves, bejewelled bangles and headbands swayed and tinkled and twirled. Their heads were topped with vibrant multicoloured crests that fluttered gently as the dance began. As the gold fell upon each performer, he or she came to life, plucking at strings, tapping on small drums, slowly starting to twist and turn, moving about each other with effortless steps. From offstage came the sound of pipes and flutes, whimsical and mellow, causing Aradryan to relax further.

In his mind he pictured the World as Was, the eldar from before the Fall living in harmony and peace with themselves. For some time the music continued, breathing contentment, while the stars and mists swirled about the stage and audience, growing thicker and brighter.

Another handful of Harlequins entered with quick steps; they moved as a group through the musicians, passing effortlessly between them, showers of red sparks trailing from fingertips as they skipped and ran, surrounding the other performers with a maelstrom of colour. The music was quickening, Aradryan's pulse increasing with the tempo. The musicians separated, whirling away from each other, leaving one alone at the centre. She plucked the strings of her half-lyre with a gloved hand, while the Harlequins looked on appreciatively.

Then, with a discordant rasp, a windharp player stepped forwards, melodramatically thrusting the lyrist aside, the deposed musician falling gracefully to the stage with an arm outstretched in woe. The new musician took up the tune, fingers moving faster, while the drum beats grew louder. The dancers returned, spilling more red upon the players as the harpist was himself pushed away, tumbling head over heels to lie sprawling on the far end of the stage. The pair that had ousted him struck up a duet, their fingers becoming a blur as they faced each other, plucking and strumming faster and faster in an effort to outdo each other.

The other musicians brought up their instruments again as the Shadowseer's cloud turned to a darker mist, billowing heavily across stage and spectator alike, swathing the motes of silver and gold that remained. Aradryan looked at the Shadowseer and was shocked to see his own face beneath her hood, lips twisted in a cruel smile, eyes wide and fierce. It was a discomfiting sight; he glanced at the others around him, realising from their apprehension that each was seeing himself or herself mirrored in the Shadowseer's mask.

A sinking feeling took root in Aradryan's gut as the darkness descended. Foreboding filled him as he watched the musicians circling about each other, each now striking up his own tune. Where there had been harmony, now there was discord. Notes screeched against each other and the pipes had become a mournful dirge, weighing down Aradryan's mood even further. He felt as helpless as he had been on his first encounter at Hirith-Hreslain, rooted to the spot while the performers competed with each other; the music grew harsh and loud while the dancers flipped and rolled and spun, showing off their acrobatic prowess in extravagant style.

Two more performers had appeared unnoticed, cloaked and hooded with subtle pinks and pastel blues, their masked faces covered with silken purple scarves. Amidst the clashing notes and whirling dancers, they moved from Harlequin to Harlequin, stealthy and sinister, pausing to whisper in the ears of the other performers. Each Harlequin thus contacted paused for a moment, before renewing their efforts with even greater vigour. The cloaked mimes made great show of being amused and pleased by their interference; they laughed silently, pointing at the frenzied Harlequins as they skirled and danced and spun about each other, so fast it was hard for Aradryan to keep track, the display becoming a movement of light and darkness, colour and sound without figures or meaning.

Feeling dizzied and yet uplifted by the remarkable performance, Aradryan was rapt, unaware of anything else in the room. He realised he too was swaying with the music, his movements slightly jerky as he responded first to one tune and then another, his limbs twitching in rhythm to the different dancers.

A crash of drums and utter blackness set his heart racing. While the noise rolled away, echoing far longer than it should have done in the small hall, white light blazed from the Shadowseer, nearly blinding Aradryan. Narrowing his eyes against the glare, he saw a figure in black rising up at the centre of the stage as ominous notes flowed from the unseen pipes, low and beating like the pulse of some gigantic beast.

The figure was a Death Jester, her mask a bony visage, her suit studded with silver skulls. In her hands she held a miniature scythe, which she spun and twirled, its keen edge gleaming in the light cast by the Shadowseer. Aradryan wanted to cry out, knowing what was to come. Fear gripped him as that scythe-edge flashed around the other Harlequins, passing within a hair's-breadth of every performer as the Death Jester stalked and skulked, picking her first victim. The warning died in his throat and there was frightened, wordless breaths from those around him, barely heard by the ranger.

Finally Aradryan did cry out as the Death Jester's blade slashed across the throat of a moonharp player. There were other panicked calls from the audience as crimson specks marred the white light and the slain Harlequin collapsed, his instrument clattering to the stage. The Death Jester raised up her arms in triumph, and then spun on her heel, scythe flashing across the chest of a cartwheeling dancer. More red seeped into the whiteness, spraying up from the lethally wounded performer.

Again and again the Death Jester struck, until the stage was bathed with crimson, the musicians and dancers piled upon each other, entwined in their last throes, thrashing and wailing. Tears were streaming down Aradryan's face, his lips parted in horror. His whole body was trembling as he witnessed the carnage, while the cloaked mimes danced with glee, snatching up the bodies of the fallen, dragging them off the stage one-by-one as they died.

All fell to blackness and silence once more, making Aradryan's stomach lurch, his ears ringing from the cacophony that had been raised, the salt of his tears on his lips.

Gentle silver light prevailed again, revealing the Shadowseer alone on the stage once more. Aradryan had heard no patter or step of departing performers. The sound of weeping was all around Aradryan, and he realised that Athelennil was clutching his arm, her fingers painfully tight on his flesh.

With arms outstretched to either side, the Shadowseer bowed low, giving Aradryan one last glimpse of his own face as the hood fell, a wry smile on his image's lips as it gave him a wink.

He didn't know whether to applaud, shout, laugh or cry. He could feel his body shaking with expended energy, and was as fatigued as if he had been performing himself, every muscle clenched tight, his nerves jangling.

With silent steps, the Shadowseer left and the lights returned, revealing the numb crowd. Conversation, some heated, some subdued, erupted almost immediately, the sudden life and vitality of the audience making the display of the Harlequins seem even more ethereal and unreal, like a dream half-forgotten.

FINDELSITH JOINED THEM clothed in his full performance regalia. He had not taken part in the piece, as his role as the Laughing God was not required. His garb was an even more outlandish and extravagant motley than those worn by his troupe. His crest went through every colour of the spectrum, standing high from his scalpcap and cascading in streamers of increasing length to his waist. Precious metals glittered in the weave of his bodysuit, which was worn underneath a jacket with gem-glistening collar and cuffs. His mask was blank black on one side, save for a cross-shaped eye-lens behind which the Great Harlequin's deep red eyes glittered with mischievous intent. The right side was a blue face with a dagger-like pointed nose and upcurving chin, almost making a half-moon in shape. Red painted eyebrows and lips completed the face's features.

A kami stood close at hand. Estrathain had made the initial introductions, having fetched Findelsith from the backstage area, and now remained on hand to assist if needed. It was Jair who had been nominated to speak for the group, and he welcomed the Great Harlequin to the group with a bow.

'Thank you for the performance,' said Jair. 'For some of us, it is the first opportunity we have encountered to witness such a spectacle.'

'Your attendance is pleasing to the troupe,' said Findelsith, his deep voice resonant with a poetic cadence, 'and I am happy to listen to you. From Estrathain we learnt of your bold plans, I tell you now that we will not help you.'

'What?' blurted Athelennil, immediately disregarding the ban they had agreed on anyone but Jair speaking. 'How can you reply so quickly when we have not even told you our intentions?'

'Intentions are always the same, I find, and why should I not think the same of you? Waystones it is, every single time, always the same, and it is so boring. What performance is there for us to play that we have not yet played a hundred times?'

'We bore you?' Caolein took a step forwards, shoulders hunching. The Great Harlequin did not move, save to turn his head slowly and regard Caolein with that half-smirking mask.

'Do not play his games,' said Aradryan, laying a hand on Caolein's shoulder. 'He is the clown, he is meant to amuse us, so do not indulge him.'

Findelsith raised a gloved hand and pointed at Aradryan whilst still looking at Caolein.

'You I like, you have something special inside you, but even to you the answer is no.'

'I never thought I would see the cycle when a Harlequin dared not into the gut of the Great Enemy,' said Lechthennian, the other outcasts stepping out of his way as the elderly traveller approached. 'A poor excuse it is, to quote boredom and repetition, when one has the chance to be one with the Laughing God. Dare her lair, and laugh in his face. If it is not to tweak the nose of She Who Thirsts, what is it to be a Harlequin?'

Tilting his head in surprise, Findelsith stood up abruptly. He looked at each of the outcasts, lingering for just a heartbeat, before his gaze finished on Lechthennian, as inscrutable as ever.

'A chance challenge you lay upon my spirit, and a charge I cannot well deny,' said the Great Harlequin, turning away with an airy wave of his hand. 'You, friend, have the best of the argument, and you are welcome to it, I might say.'

'Tarry just for one more moment, and hear my debate, and you and I will be in accord, I grant you,' said Lechthennian, stepping quickly after the departing Findelsith.

The Great Harlequin paused a moment, allowing the outcast to catch him. Lechthennian's next words were softly spoken, and Aradryan could not hear them, nor see Lechthennian's lips nor read his expression. Aradryan looked at the others and their intrigued faces told him that they were as mystified as he.

There seemed to be a short debate, during which Lechthennian made imploring gestures several times, elbows tucked into his ribs, hands splayed out with a shallow bow. Aradryan was about to go over and ask the aging traveller to cease embarrassing himself, but before he took a stride he saw Findelsith take a step back and nod his head once in agreement. Lechthennian smiled briefly, bowed once more and returned to bring back the happy news.

'He seemed so adamant,' said Jair.

'How did you change his mind?' asked Caolein. 'He did change his mind, yes? We did see that?'

'All I had to do was employ a bit of flattery and dangle a proposition too exciting for him to decline,' replied Lechthennian. He motioned them to head towards the door. 'In part we can thank Estrathain for his agreement, as he was most intrigued by the idea of journeying with the kami.'

'And what else?' said Aradryan, thinking Lechthennian's account a little vague and unconvincing. 'You are not an agile liar, your concealment of something is plain to see.'

'I confess, I am reluctant to share,' said the musician. 'I dared Findelsith, you see, and now that we are committed, I fear I might have overstepped my bounds.'

'What dare?' said Athelennil, glaring daggers at Lechthennian.

'I challenged him to lead us somewhere he had never been before, to a world that caused even him a deep dread,' said Lechthennian. 'If he admits to fear, he cannot truly be an avatar of the Laughing God, for Cegorach laughs in the face of death and danger. To prove to himself that he is not truly afraid, he must take us to the place for which he holds the deepest fear, or give up his position as Great Harlequin.'

'We are going to journey to a world in the bosom of She Who Thirsts, at the heart of the Abyss of Despair, to a world so bad that a Great Harlequin of the Laughing God is afraid to go there?' said Aradryan, uttering the words slowly, unable to believe them himself. He sighed, and shrugged. 'Perfect. That is just perfect.'

# ADVENTURE

*The Crone Worlds – When the ancient empire stretched across the stars, the heart of civilisation was located at the Wheel of Destiny, our first world where Eldanesh was born at the hub. It was from the Wheel of Destiny that Morai-heg spun that fate of the eldar race, and about that wheel all things revolved, for good or ill. Populous were the worlds of the Wheel, and their art and fashions were considered the height of society. As with everything else, it was from the Wheel of Destiny that the strand of the Great Enemy was spun. The first of the sects and cults were created here, and from the Wheel of Destiny that poison spread through the empire. When the Fall came and the Great Enemy was born, it was Morai-heg that was consumed first, the Wheel of Destiny absorbed into the body of*

*She Who Thirsts. Ever they have belonged to her
and so now those worlds, once the heart of civilisation and now the heart of the Eye of Terror,
are known as the crone worlds.*

ARADRYAN LEFT THE business of organising the expedition to the more experienced members of *Irdiris*'s
crew, and spent the time exploring some of the
arcades and dens of Khai-dazaar. When the preparations were complete, he met with Athelennil, Jair
and the others at the quayside where the starship was
docked. From here, Caolein guided the *Irdiris* to the
large battleship they had passed on their arrival: the
*Fae Taeruth*.

The Harlequins had preceded them on board, their
gaily coloured webskimmer inside the *Fae Taeruth*'s
sizeable docking bay when the outcasts landed.
They were met by the captain, the female exiled
Commorraghan Maensith. She was not at all what
Aradryan had been expecting. The tales of the dark
kin of Commorragh had left an image in his mind
of cruel, sneering, whip-wielding torturers. While the
reputation was well-deserved, his first impression of
Maensith was of a cultured, polite starship captain.

She and her crew were dressed in black and purple and dark blues, it was true, but devoid of their
armour they seemed like any other ship's complement in Khai-dazaar. Maensith had white hair, swept
back from her face with a band of emerald-studded
metal, the gems matching the colour of her eyes.

Most remarkably, Maensith wore no waystone. This
realisation brought out a mix of dread and awe in
Aradryan, who instinctively touched his fingertips to

the brooch at his breast to reassure himself that his waystone was there. The thought of going through life exposed to the predation of She Who Thirsts horrified him, and he tried not to stare at his host.

Maensith might have noticed his gaze; she glanced at Aradryan for a moment, meeting his eye. There was a hardness to her that silently spoke of grim experiences, but the ship captain's smile was also quick and infectious as she introduced the notable officers from her two hundred-strong complement.

Aradryan had been warned by Estrathain not to inquire too deeply into her past, so he held his tongue despite the obvious questions that nagged him as Maensith explained the running of the ship and its layout. Of the *Fae Taeruth*, the only thing that marked it as significantly different from *Lacontiran* were the weapons bays and blisters. Running for most of the ship's length in the middle decks, the weapons batteries consisted of several dozen high-powered laser turrets, supplemented by shorter-ranged rocket batteries for anti-boarding defence. The crew that they passed on the tour, which took place as the *Fae Taeruth* slipped her moorings and headed into the webway, nodded deference to their commander and her guests, which was something that Aradryan had not encountered before, either on Alaitoc or further abroad.

'Do all of your crew hail from Commorragh?' he asked, slightly nervous of the company. They had returned to the landing bay to retrieve their belongings, and would be quartered with the officers of the mercenary company close to the ship's command bridge.

'Only a handful,' replied Maensith. 'Most are simply outcasts like yourselves, seeking some excitement and meaning in their lives. It is never wise to have too many kabalites in your crew if you are no longer in service to an archon.'

'Kabalites?' Aradryan had not heard the term before.

'If you wish, I could tell you more of the Commorraghan kabals, the wych cults and incubi of the Dark City, but that can wait for the moment,' said Maensith. 'My pilots and I need to speak to Findelsith regarding our journey.'

'This is your first foray into the Dark Abyss?' asked Jair.

'It is, though I have been close to its outer reaches in the past,' said Maensith. She lay a reassuring hand on the arm of Aradryan, noticing his apprehension at this revelation. 'I would say not to be afraid, but that would be a lie. Where we are going is dangerous, and I will not pretend otherwise. However, my crew and I have experienced battle and peril many times, and you are in good hands.'

With a nod of farewell, Maensith turned away. She stopped at the archway that led from the flight deck and turned.

'We are all going to profit well from this excursion, mark my words!'

When she had left, the outcasts boarded *Irdiris* to take up their possessions. Athelennil caught Aradryan by the arm when they were in the main passageway.

'Do not be tricked by pretty eyes and a welcoming smile,' she warned. Aradryan could not help but consider some of this to be due to jealousy on Athelennil's part, despite her prior declarations to hold no romantic claim to Aradryan or any other.

'I judge as I find,' Aradryan replied, laying his hand onto hers. 'It is good to know that you still watch out for my wellbeing.'

'Remember that, when we are in the heart of the Great Enemy,' said Athelennil. 'We all need to stand together if we are to return.'

Aradryan nodded, the warning reminding him of the course they were setting and the hellish destination at its end.

THE FAE TAERUTH made swift progress, keeping to the main arterial passages of the webway, heading towards the Eye of Terror. During the journey, the disparate groups that made up the expedition mingled little, so that Aradryan saw little of the Harlequins or mercenaries. On his forays from the cabin he shared with Athelennil, he was struck by something: all of the starship's crew went about their duties armed. Every mercenary he passed had a pistol and blade at his or her waist.

When he and the others were invited to be guests at a meal with Maensith, he raised this observation with the mercenary captain. Jair, Caolein and Athelennil were amongst the complement who joined Maensith and her handful of lieutenants in a dining area that more closely resembled a ballroom on Alaitoc than a mess hall on a battleship. Crystals glowed overhead, dappling the diners with red and gold and purple, and underfoot was a thick carpet, woven with a pattern of black roses on powder blue, their jade stems entwining to form mesmerising geometries.

The fare on offer was also better than he had

experienced on either *Irdiris* or *Lacontiran*. There were
meats cured in delicate spices, fresh fruit and cereals, lightly baked, sweet-tasting breads and bowls of
pungent broth. All was laid out on an oval table that
would have comfortably sat twice as many guests,
laden with silver and golden platters, amongst which
delicate ceramic dishes steamed while carafes of
wines and juices were freely passed amongst the
eldar.

'It is a necessary precaution in our lives,' Maensith
explained. 'It is better to be accustomed to the weight
of a sword at your hip, and to have your weapons to
hand if you need them. The webway is not safe, whatever your experiences in the past may be, and where
we are going it is far from a sanctuary.'

'Do you think we should be armed?' Aradryan
asked. He took a sip of a particularly azure wine
from a crystal goblet edged with delicate white gold.
The ranger had realised as soon as he had sat down
that much of his surroundings and what was on offer
were no doubt the proceeds of piracy, or at least
payment for less-than-moral deeds, but the notion
had not dampened his appetite or thirst, which had
been whetted by the festivities he had enjoyed in
Khai-dazaar.

'A ranger longrifle is of little use in a ship action,'
laughed Maensith. 'I am sure no one will take offence
if you choose to wear your pistols from here on.'

'I do not think I shall be of much assistance, if that
is the case,' said Aradryan, shaking his head. 'I am
comfortable with a longrifle, but encounters at closer
quarters have not gone so well for me.'

'Nonsense,' said Jair, who was on his second jug of

wine already. 'When we ran into the orks on the way to the Exodites, you showed no hesitation.'

'I fear that I did, perhaps for an instant,' said Aradryan. He shuddered as he remembered the red-eyed orks and the gush of blood from Estrellian's mortal wounds. 'I may have cost Estrellian his life in that brief moment.'

'Regret is as harmful as fear,' said Maensith. Her words were sharply spoken, the first time Aradryan had detected any harshness in her voice. 'To linger in the past invites doubt, and doubt eats away at the spirit.'

'And what of learning from the mistakes of the past?' asked Caolein. The question seemed innocent enough, but there was something about the pilot's words that hinted at accusation, and Aradryan, who was sat at Maensith's right hand, felt the captain stiffen slightly. He had almost forgotten that she hailed originally from the Dark City, so pleasant and convivial was the feast and its attendants. Why Caolein chose to ask such a barbed question of their congenial host was a mystery to Aradryan.

'The past cannot be changed,' said Maensith, keeping her tone even, though her eyes narrowed slightly. 'It is equally dangerous to cast one's gaze too far ahead, perhaps longing for something that will never come, missing the opportunities of the moment.'

'To experience the moment, and be nothing more?' Caolein asked, eyebrows raised.

'Just so,' said Maensith. Her fingers tapped a beat on the tabletop for a moment, before she reached out and grasped the stem of a golden goblet. She raised it a fraction and tipped the cup towards Caolein, before lifting it higher in toast to all present.

'Let us wish for a fruitful and uneventful expedition,' said the captain. 'The prize to those who dare!'

This last sentiment was echoed by her officers, and Aradryan murmured a late echo in response. There was an awkward silence, which was broken by the hiss of the door and the arrival of Estrathain's kami. The artificial being was clothed as always in its scarlet robes and scarves, and entered the feasting hall with quick steps.

'Apologies for the intrusion, my captain, but I come direct from the chambers of Findelsith,' announced the kami. 'This branch of the webway has almost taken us as far as it can, and we must make preparations for a transference to the material world. He must speak with you about the next stage of our journey.'

'Of course,' said Maensith. She set down her goblet as she stood and dipped her head to each of the diners in turn, finishing with a lingering look at Aradryan that he could not quite decipher. Her next words were almost a whisper, directed at the ranger. 'Come to see me, and I shall instruct you in the basics of swordcraft, Aradryan. You will feel the more confident for the lesson.'

With that she left, taking Estrathain with her. One by one, the mercenary lieutenants offered their apologies and excused themselves, claiming duties to attend, until only those of *Irdiris* remained. Aradryan noticed an absent member of their complement and wondered why he had not seen him earlier.

'What of Lechthennian?' he asked.

'I do not know where he is,' said Athelennil. There

was a quiet rebuke in her next words, which Aradryan knew were meant for him. 'I think he is more discerning of the company he keeps.'

DESPITE ATHELENNIL'S MISGIVINGS, Aradryan contacted Maensith during the following cycle. He arranged to meet the mercenary captain in one of the empty storage holds in the lower decks, and chose not to mention the rendezvous to Athelennil to head off any further chiding.

Maensith met him in her full battle gear. Over a black bodysuit she wore a shaped breastplate of silvered ceramic material, which fitted her body as snugly as the bodyglove. She had tassets and ailettes of the same design on her shoulders and thighs, edged with sharply tapered edges. About her waist was a skirt of purple laminar, split at the front to allow her to move with freedom. Her gloves went up to her elbows, and were lined with serrated blades on the outside of the hand and forearm, her fingers and thumbs protected with segmented armour. She also wore a helm that protected her skull and cheeks, with an aventail of scale. The armour shimmered like the carapace of a beetle or slick of oil, rainbows playing on the curved surfaces beneath the white strip lights of the cargo bay.

A pistol hung at Maensith's right hip, and on her left was a curved sword in a long scabbard. She held another blade of the same design in her hand, and proffered it to Aradryan without any word as he entered. He took the sheathed sword, feeling its weight approvingly. The scabbard was plainly decorated with a line of four red gems, the lower part bound with overlapping white cord.

'Wear it like this,' said Maensith. She stepped behind Aradryan and took the sword from him, releasing two lengths of binding. He was aware of her right next to him, the blades of her armour less than a hand's breadth from his flesh. She crouched, passing the thongs around his waist, looping them through ringlets on the scabbard before tying a firm but decorative knot. She tugged the sheath a little towards his thigh, settling its weight better on his hip. 'Now draw it.'

Aradryan reached across with his right hand as Maensith circled to stand in front of him, weight on one leg, finger held to her chin as she made her critique. The ranger grabbed the sword and tugged it free. His arm felt awkward, his elbow jutting at an odd angle, as he pulled the blade fully from its scabbard.

'Not like that,' said Maensith, stepping forwards with a purposeful look. She again stood behind him, reaching around so that her hand was on his wrist, fingers slightly splayed. 'Like this. Do not make a fist around the hilt, make the blade an extension of your arm.'

Aradryan did as he was told, keenly aware of her breath on the side of his neck. She had a peculiar presence, both disturbing and exciting at the same time. He could sense wildness kept in check by this veneer of civility. The sword certainly felt more natural after he had adjusted his grip.

'A little lower, towards the pommel, so that the weight balances easily,' Maensith continued. She stepped next to him, drawing her own sword, showing him the proper form. 'This is a slashing blade, used for cutting more than stabbing. Though if you find yourself in a tight fix, ramming the pointy part into your enemies might suffice.'

Her laughter was edged with just a hint of unkindness, which gave Aradryan pause. He turned to look at her.

'Why are you doing this?' he asked.

'Circumstance has thrown us together, my friend,' Maensith replied, swishing her blade back and forth a few times, stepping lightly from one foot to the other. 'It may come to pass that you and I must fight side-by-side. I would rather you did more damage to our enemies than to me.'

'Surely it would be better to leave me to fend for myself in that event,' said Aradryan, laughing at his own suggestion. Maensith did not laugh with him, but instead fixed him with a curious stare.

'Would you abandon me so swiftly?' she asked, her voice a soft purr. 'And I thought we had an understanding.'

'Oh no, you shall not trick me so easily,' Aradryan said, wagging a finger in mock disapproval. 'I know what you Commorraghans are like, and how fickle your loyalties can be.'

He regretted the words almost immediately, seeing the genuine hurt on Maensith's face. She sheathed her sword and turned away, shoulders tense.

'If that is all you see in me, a dirty Commorraghan, then perhaps I should just leave you to die,' she snapped, stalking towards the wide bay door. 'One less clueless Alaitocii to get in my way.'

'No regrets, you said!' Aradryan called after her, his

voice echoing quietly around the empty hold. 'Am I allowed to apologise?'

Maensith stopped but did not turn around or look back.

'You can admit to making a mistake, if you want,' she said, relaxing.

'I do not just see a filthy Commorraghan,' Aradryan said. 'Please, I need you to teach me how to at least defend myself. You never know, if I stay alive a little longer it might give you more time to get away.'

Turning with a half-smile on her lips, Maensith eyed him for some time, gauging him from head to toe. She evidently liked what she saw and rejoined him, sword in hand.

'There are four basic parries.' And so the lessons began.

For another sixty-eight cycles the *Fae Taeruth* forged across the galaxy, sometimes hopping across real-space from webway portal to webway portal, heading towards the Eye of Terror. In that time, Aradryan learnt swordplay with Maensith, spending whole cycles in the lower decks practising parry and cut, dodge and riposte. Maensith proved herself a capable teacher, though prone to toying with him during their sparring sessions. She had perfected her blade-craft over a long lifetime and he was but the barest novice; often he ended a session panting with exertion while she appeared unruffled.

Disapproving of his growing attachment to the ex-Commorraghan, Athelennil found quarters for herself, so that Aradryan slept alone. He and his fellow outcasts spent some time together, playing games of chance with the mercenary officers, and on two occasions they hosted a performance of storytelling, swapping exploits and anecdotes with some of those they had befriended amongst the *Fae Taeruth*'s company; none of them Commorraghans. Aradryan could see that they distrusted any kin of the Dark City on reputation alone, but knew better than to argue against this bias; the dark eldar were on the whole depraved and loathsome cousins to the Exodites and eldar of the craftworlds. It was perhaps his own yearning for a change in his life that guided Aradryan towards Maensith, who had been forced from her home and had adapted to life outside of Commorraghan society.

He saw Lechthennian little and the Harlequins even less. Occasionally he would hear the trill of a lip-flute or thrum of a mourning harp from the bowels of the ship, and once or twice he spied his fellow outcast outside his cabin, humming or whistling to himself, sitting in the corridor. He seemed utterly unconcerned by their current quest, though as time passed and they came closer and closer to the Maw of Eternity, the others in the company showed signs of increasing nervousness.

When Aradryan was not with Maensith, most of his time was spent with the kami of Estrathain. The half-living creation seemed to have inherited a disproportionate amount of his creator's curiosity, and asked endless questions on Alaitoc and *Lacontiran* that Aradryan was happy to answer. The kami's experience was all second-hand, but he regaled Aradryan and others with stories of those who had passed through Khai-dazaar during his life, and despite assurances of confidentiality to the contrary, shared a small amount of gossip and salacious tales of the more humorous and colourful disputes into which he had been brought for mediation.

On the sixty-eighth cycle, as the lights were dimmed for sleep, Aradryan was called from his chambers by Taelisieth, one of Maensith's lieutenants. Along with Maensith and her senior officers, the outcasts, Lechthennian included, were greeted in the navigational hall by Findelsith and his Shadowseer, Rhoinithiel. The whole chamber seemed to float in space, the walls, floor and ceiling covered with a psychogrammic projection of their location and the surrounding star systems. Opposite the door pulsed a seething wound of purple and crimson: the Eye of Terror.

'We come to the hem, the blurring of worlds,' said Findelsith, as the other eldar gathered in a circle around the two Harlequins. As he spoke, the view changed, coiling tubes of the webway overlapping the stars. Aradryan realised that the illusion was created by Rhoinithiel, the Shadowseer blending her abilities with the projections of the *Fae Taeruth*'s navigational network. 'Into the Womb of Destruction we pass, if on this course our hearts and minds are set. The webway corrodes, falling to nothing, and the raw bleeding of the warp remains. This is the Great Enemy before us, not just of legend but in form made real. Our goal lies within that maelstrom of woe, into the heart of the Prince of Pleasure. Speak now and be mindful of your desires, for even here She Who Thirsts can know you.'

It was odd the way Findelsith spoke this last sentence, indicating that he considered himself and his troupe apart from the other eldar in this regard. Aradryan wondered what made the Great Harlequin so sure that his own mind was free of the Doom of the eldar. He put such thoughts aside and considered the matter at hand. He had tried not to dwell on the prospect of entering the Eye of Terror, and in a way it had become secondary to the journey he had been making. It had not occurred to him that they might come this far and yet be baulked by the last effort, and so he had resigned himself to the quest with some misgiving. Having already spoken his mind at the outset and been overruled, he felt no desire to regurgitate old arguments. Instead, if one of the others was having doubts, let them be the first to raise it and he would support them.

The discussion was swift, though, and there were none amongst the outcasts nor the mercenaries who was of a mind to retreat from the task before them. In the fashion of outcasts, Aradryan was asked directly by Jair if he wanted to continue. If he desired, he offered Aradryan *Irdiris* to make the journey back to Khai-dazaar, or to wherever his wishes would take him.

It was a tempting offer, to have a ship and the freedom to go across the stars guided by only whim, and Aradryan was on the verge of accepting. He stopped himself, realising that a few swordcraft lessons and one battle with a longrifle was a woeful lack of preparation for life alone as an outcast. He might well make it back to Khai-dazaar, but if he was to leave now he would not only be abandoning his companions, he would be passing by an opportunity that might never come again.

Steeling himself to the decision, he declined the command of *Irdiris* and confirmed himself to the quest for the Tears of Isha. There was some amusement, misplaced to Aradryan's mind, in Findelsith's acknowledgement of this.

'So all are settled on the matter now, who will be undertaking this journey, to fetch the prize of Isha's Tears and in doing earn themselves high reward. Be silent and listen to my warning, for it shall be delivered only once. When we cross the veil we must take good care, so that not one of us is all alone. My troupe will watch over you for the time and so ensure that none are tainted. Many are the wiles of your greatest doom, heed not to any whispers of desire, for if not they shall be your undoing, and perhaps in your fall you doom us all.'

As FINDELSITH HAD promised, so it was. The Harlequins divided amongst the crew of the *Fae Taeruth* as the ship emerged from the webway and delved into the swirling vortex that was the incarnation of She Who Thirsts. In those first few moments, Aradryan felt something like panic gripping him, though it went deeper than just the fear of their environs. He became quickly convinced that he was not strong enough to resist the temptations and snares that the Great Enemy would surely set for him, and the warning of Findelsith rang loudly in his mind's ear, reverberating around his head.

Along with the others of *Irdiris*, he sat on a couch in one of the gathering areas above the starboard weapons batteries. With them was Taenemeth, one of the Harlequin masque's three Death Jesters, complete with bone-laden costume and skull-mask. The vision of death had said nothing since he had arrived, and his presence was more unsettling than it was reassuring. Thinking of death being amongst his companions sent Aradryan's train of thought careening into more self-doubt.

He was weak, selfish and cowardly, and had no place in such company. He would be the undoing of them all; the perpetrator of some chance act or remark that would open the way for She Who Thirsts to devour the entire complement of the *Fae Taeruth*.

All of these thoughts clustered into his brain at once, clamouring for his attention. He imagined the lurid whispers of the Great Enemy's daemonic servants, and wondered if he would be able to recognise them as such. Again and again his fingers fluttered to the waystone at his chest, seeking comfort in its presence, though its surface had turned icy cold to the touch. And then another fear took him: what if his dread was simply the whisperings of some daemonic voice, and not his own?

Circular fears whirled about, reinforcing his desire to be away from this place. He stood up, desperate to be on his own, where he could do no harm.

'I could kill you now if it would help out,' said a voice close to Aradryan's ear, mocking him. 'Such a cure might be considered drastic. But if that is what you truly desire, I will make your demise look fantastic.'

Spinning about, Aradryan came face to face with the death's head visage of Taenemeth. The Death Jester titled his head sideways, waiting for a response.

'Leave me alone,' muttered Aradryan, stepping to

one side to move past the Harlequin. Taenemeth moved to bar his path, shaking his head and wagging his finger.

'A shame it would be to leave you a ghost,' said the Death Jester, 'that is the tree of the seed you have sown. But you do not have to fear such a fate, if not by my hand then surely your own.'

What the Death Jester said was verging on nonsense, but Aradryan could not ignore the kernel of truth at its heart; it was in the company of the others that he was safest. There was no point running away from this, he had to endure whatever torments assailed his thoughts, for to be alone with such dark passions running through him would be to invite murder or suicide.

Taenemeth took a step aside, allowing Aradryan to sit down next to Lechthennian. Noticing his agitation, the musician winked and pulled a thumb whistle from his pocket. He passed it to Aradryan, who held it in his hands like it was a serpent.

'Just put the narrow end in your mouth and blow,' suggested Lechthennian. 'It will take your mind from other matters. If you want to get adventurous, there are three holes in the back you can cover with your thumb to make different notes.'

Aradryan laughed at the absurdity of it; Lechthennian's jibe on top of Taenemeth's morbid joking. He brought up the thumb whistle and blew a hesitant note. It warbled quickly and died away. The others were looking at him, but he could not feel ashamed, not now. He realised how ridiculous the whole situation was, and how close he had come to falling prey to his own fears. He tootled a few more notes and laughed again, looking up at the skull face of the Death Jester. He thought he understood, just a little bit, how the Harlequin felt, and what it must be like to be touched by the Laughing God. There was nothing he could do at the moment to preserve his fate, so if he died right now it might just as well be with a whistle on his lips as a frown on his brow.

INTO THE STORM that was the incarnation of She Who Thirsts plunged the *Fae Taeruth*. Aradryan did not suffer a repeat of the episode that had beset him on their first entry, but he was acutely aware of everything that passed. It was as if his life had been brought into a sharper focus, so that every word uttered by his comrades, every thought that entered his mind, was loaded with meaning, both obvious and hidden. His senses felt acute, so that the touch of his sheets at night was a lover's caress and the gentlest throbbing of the starship's engines felt like rumbling thunder. He was aware of the stares of the crew as they passed, and every eldar aboard seemed to be touched by a vague paranoia. The ranger felt his temper fraying, as were his nerves, but always when he thought he was about to burst with the tension there was a Harlequin nearby, distracting him with a quip, brief poetic recital or an improvised dance that burst the bubble of his agitation.

During the night cycle, his dreams were vivid and took him to scenes both remembered and imagined, and often both, so that he awoke with a start, unsure whether what he had felt was a real experience or just unconscious fantasy. He had expected nightmares, to be assailed by the visions of the Great Enemy, but the opposite was true. Aradryan's dreams were awash with romance and love, filled with happiness and belonging.

Sometimes he dreamed he was a bird, and would climb to the highest pinnacle of a tower that speared into a violet sky. There was no fear in him as he leapt from the parapet, and his wishes bore him aloft like wings, to soar amongst the purple clouds. Other times he was a fish, swimming with the shoal, one of many glittering bodies, enjoying the surge of current around him, drawn to the dappling light upon the surface of the raging river.

There were much more intimate dreams too, of Thirianna and Maensith and Athelennil and past amours, as well as associates of his own creation. Sometimes these were gentle encounters, other times wild and carefree.

Always after the dreams he was left with a slight melancholy, a sense of longing that was not wholly unpleasant. He spent much time in his cabin, seeking the dreams he had experienced, but despite his training he was unable to recapture them, their reincarnations never quite as satisfying as the originals. A sense of unreality crept into his waking life, coupled with the heightened sense of his surroundings, so that as he ate and talked and practised with pistol and sword he would feel dislocated from himself at times, only to be brought back to the dullness of realty with a jolt, bringing a short but profound sadness.

He saw nothing of Maensith in that time, and he assumed she was kept busy with the piloting and navigation of the ship. Thrice he had made inquiries after her, driven to distraction by the lingering moments of a remembered dream, seeking release from the gentle torment of dreamt promises, but she was incommunicado and he would return to his chambers with his ardour unchecked.

Once, and once only, he took himself to the viewing gallery on the highest deck, to look upon the Womb of Destruction for himself. The long, domed chamber was empty except for Findelsith, who sat on a stool by the arched windows staring into the abyss. He did not have his mask on, revealing a face that was younger than Aradryan had expected. The eyes were different too, with none of the playfulness that glittered behind the ornate mask. Findelsith's gaze was tired, and filled with woe. The red teardrop tattooed upon his cheek, the tiniest of rubies sparkling at its heart, summed up the Great Harlequin's demeanour.

Findelsith ignored Aradryan, so the ranger crossed to the other side of the narrow gallery and looked out. What he saw drew forth a choked gasp.

He had been expecting a field of stars, perhaps, but what he saw was a blend of both the real universe and the energy of the warp. Everything was shimmering, and stars burned with every colour, some of them seemingly so close that their coronal ejections of green and orange and blue must surely incinerate the vessel. As though he peered through the magnifying sight of his longrifle, wherever he looked came into stark focus, seemingly just out of reach.

He could see worlds circling around the flaming orbs, shadows passing across the light. Some appeared normal, simple globes or gaseous giants, some ringed, others with circling moon systems. Many were utterly strange: triangular pyramids or straight-sided cubes, or dual and triple worlds that spun crazily about each other while leering faces made storm clouds in their skies. Dozens of lancing flames erupted from one world to his right, streaming into the haze of the space between stars.

All seemed impossibly compressed, like a child's interpretation of the galaxy rendered in holographic form, so that it could be rotated and manipulated, allowing Aradryan to look behind stars and into the whirling nebulae that painted images of lurid congress or swept past as flocks of celestial birds that darted through the heavens.

Feeling dizzy and sick, Aradryan stepped back and looked away, fixing his gaze upon the toes of his boots to give himself a point of reference for reality and stability. It did not work, and he staggered to one side, losing his footing as the deck seemed to buckle and ripple beneath him.

'To stare into the void is no delight, and but a few have eyes for such a sight.' Aradryan looked up from all fours, seeing that Findelsith had replaced his mask and was coming towards him, a hand out-stretched to help Aradryan to his feet. 'It is too much for mortals to behold, to see nature's end where the warp unfolds. Such are the dark whims of a mad god's dreams, where once our towers rose and cities gleamed.'

Swallowing hard, Aradryan stood up with Findel-sith's aid, keeping his eyes away from the windows, focused on the mask of the Great Harlequin. He nodded his thanks and stumbled towards the door, unable to speak of what he had seen.

* * *

HAVING WITNESSED THE madness of the Chaos realm, Aradryan was consumed by trepidation when the announcement came via Estrathain that they were shortly to disembark. They had come upon their destination, the crone world of Miarisillion, somewhere in the depths of the Eye of Terror. The journey had not been without some tribulations – the Womb of Destruction was home not just to immaterial foes but also enemies of flesh such as the Space Marine Legions that had turned traitor against the will of the human Emperor. With speed sometimes, and with caution at others, the expedition had avoided these threats, moving into the depths of the Eye of Terror, always ready to turn and run lest they encounter some force or obstacle too great for them.

It was a harrowing time, made all the worse by the ever-present pressure of She Who Thirsts bearing down upon Aradryan's spirit. The *Fae Taeruth* was too large to enter the atmosphere of the planet, and so the expedition divided between *Irdiris* and the nameless vessel of the Harlequins. It was Aradryan's duty to take his place beside Caolein at the controls of the ship, and he entered the piloting chamber just as his companion was guiding the starship from the bay of the *Fae Taeruth*.

Miarisillion almost filled the navigational display, which was showing a true view of the vista ahead. Between grey scrapes of cloud Aradryan saw blue seas and white land. It looked like a frozen world, the landmasses encased in ice. Caolein shrugged at this suggestion, no wiser to the truth that Aradryan.

Entering the upper atmosphere, *Irdiris* swooped down on the tail of the red-and-green diamond-patterned Harlequin vessel. It was some time before they entered the cloud canopy, and Aradryan switched the spherical imager to a rendered version of their surroundings, the Harlequin ship appearing as a pulsing rune not far ahead.

Breaking out of the cloud at hypersonic speed, the two starships levelled, cruising above a wild ocean flecked with white crests of crashing waves. Daylight sparkled on the waters, though Aradryan could see no star to cast the light. Despite this, from the high altitude it was possible to see the terminator of night in the far distance, retreating towards the horizon.

It was some time before Aradryan sighted land, as Caolein guided the ship down in a decelerating glide. A high cliff of dark stone rose up at the edge of his vision, marked at this distance only by the massive fountains of surf that crashed upon its rocky foundations. As they swept closer, Aradryan could see the remains of a building along the summit of the cliff. Pillars and piles of masonry jutted from the waves, brought tumbling into the seas by an age of erosion.

The half-broken building continued along the cliff to the left and right, showing a remarkable cross-section of many-storeyed towers, stairwells and cellars. Aradryan could see the floors separating each level, linked by ramps and shafts, in places a maze of small chambers, in others becoming broad corridors and hallways.

Beyond the edge of the sea, the building continued; wherever it was that Aradryan looked he saw endless white stone, which from orbit he had mistaken for permafrost. Every scrap of land as far as he could see was covered with domes and bridges, towers and halls. Long and winding open staircases ascended solid pilasters that stretched into the sky, tipped with circular balconies, while curving roadways scythed between colonnaded forums and statue-filled plazas in elaborate loops and geometric swirls.

The whole edifice, save for that crumbled by the breaking cliffside, looked remarkably intact. Aradryan had been expecting a ruin, laid waste by the great tumult of the Fall, but the city looked no more damaged or decayed than if its occupants had simply departed peacefully a few cycles earlier. Pennants of grey and green snapped in the wind atop high banner poles.

'Look there,' said Caolein, pointing.

Aradryan had not been completely correct. The building did not enclose every last piece of earth, for off to the right a forest of blue-leaved trees broke the undulating white of tiled roofs and flagged terraces. It too seemed untouched by the ravages of time; an arrangement of circular lawns, spiralling towards a centre point, each a little smaller than the outer clearing, was clearly visible amongst the broad ring of trees.

There were other gardens, on the roofs and in gorge-like gaps between soaring halls. There were thousands of arched windows still glinting with panes, and doorways narrow and wide that led from hexagonally paved courtyards into the dark interior. Ponds and pools broke the monotony of the whiteness, some seemingly inaccessible except from the air. There were sculpture parks, their subjects too small to see even with the magnification of *Irdiris*'s viewer; streets were lined with much larger creations too, depicting naive interpretations of the eldar gods.

'This city must have been teeming with people in its prime,' said Aradryan.

'Not at all,' said Lechthennian. Aradryan had been so engrossed in the vista that he had not noticed the traveller coming into the piloting suite. Just behind him stood Estrathain. The kami's head slowly turned left and right, taking in the magnificent view with gem eyes. 'Only four thousand dwelt here. It is a palace, not a city.'

'That is fewer inhabitants than one of Alaitoc's habitation towers,' replied Aradryan, frowning. 'What of the other dwellings? How many lived outside the palace.'

'There is only the palace,' said Lechthennian, standing with his hands on the back of Aradryan's chair as he looked up into the display overhead. 'The whole world is the palace, every continent and island built to the design of one person.'

'To think that we had so many worlds that such vanity was possible,' said Estrathain. 'From such bounty and plenty come indolence and disaster.'

'It is unusual, even by the excesses of the empire in its greatest pomp,' said Lechthennian, eyes half closed as if in remembrance. 'There were those who built worlds in the webway, but for the creator of Miarisillion it was the dominance of the physical realm that stoked his pride.'

'How can you know this?' asked Caolein, twisting in his seat to look at the musician. 'Where did you learn such a tale?'

Lechthennian did not answer immediately, but looked at Caolein with a half-smile. The traveller shrugged, as if deciding that there was no secret to keep.

'How do the Harlequins know that it is here? In the Black Library, where all of our knowledge of the ancient empire and the Fall is kept, there are maps and atlases and charts aplenty, and journals both written and recorded survive from before the coming of She Who Thirsts.'

As Lechthennian mentioned the name of the eldar's doom, Aradryan felt a shiver run through him. He did not know whether it was a simple reaction to the use of the title, or whether the dark god that had destroyed the eldar could sense its name being spoken inside itself, even when only spoken in euphemism. The others had fallen quiet and Aradryan guessed he had not been alone in the sensation.

'You have been to the Black Library?' said Estrathain finally, turning his sculpted face towards Lechthennian. 'A most remarkable achievement, and one that can be claimed by even fewer than those who have come to the crone worlds.'

'It was a long time ago, and I am sure I do not remember the way,' said Lechthennian, still with the wry smile he had worn since raising the subject. 'If we survive this adventure, perhaps you could persuade Findelsith to take you there.'

'Looks like we will be landing nearby,' said Aradryan, as he noticed the Harlequin ship had begun a descending spiral towards the palace, bleeding off speed in preparation for touchdown.

Caolein returned his attention to the controls, guiding the ship along the vortex of a vapour trail left by the preceding craft. After a time-consuming descent, they eventually saw the Harlequins landing in a wide courtyard, lined with silver-barked trees with bright red leaves. Not far away was a massive dome, almost as large as one of Alaitoc's, though constructed of stone rather than an energy field, its contents concealed from view.

There was plenty of space to set *Irdiris* down beside the Harlequins, and as Aradryan let the engines decrease to idle, Caolein opened up the entry hatch and activated the boarding ramp. Aradryan took a last look at the view outside, noticing there were no birds or insects despite the mild clime and temperate conditions.

'I think we are the only creatures on this world,' said Aradryan, pushing himself from the reclining seat.

'Let us hope that things remain that way,' replied Caolein.

# PERIL

*The Womb of Destruction – When She Who
Thirsts came into being, roused from dormancy
by the depravity of the old civilisation, the
god's body took form where the ancient empire
had been at its strongest. So powerful was the
birth-scream of the Great Enemy, it tore open
reality, fusing the warp and the material universe together, creating a vast warp storm that
has raged to this day. This rift has many names,
for it is the most important feature in the galaxy.
The Womb of Destruction it was called at first,
for it was in the depths of this bleeding wound
that the eldar doom was born. Some refer to it as
the Abyss of Magic, as it is the Realm of Chaos
given physical property, a well of psychic power.
Another name there is; unusually it is a theft-
phrase taken in translation from the mon-keigh,*

*but it summarises the sense of despair one feels*
*when thinking of the warp rupture through*
*which the Dark Prince still jealously watches us:*
*the Eye of Terror.*

THE EXPEDITION MUSTERED under the branches of the
trees. Aradryan had brought his longrifle, pistol and
the sword gifted to him by Maensith, and was not
surprised to see the mercenaries more heavily armed
with rifles, shuriken cannons, brightlances and other
weapons that he could not identify. Slightly more
revealing were the Harlequins, who sported all manner of blades and pistols. Findelsith carried an axe
with a long, elegant blade across his back, and his
wrists were sheathed in bladed cuffs that glimmered
with energy fields.

The Death Jesters carried shrieker cannons, black-
painted versions of the shuriken weapons possessed
by Maensith's company, while several of the troupe
were armed with the tubular, glove-like harlequin's
kiss, which Aradryan had heard about from Jair.
The older ranger had claimed that when the harlequin's kiss was punched into a foe, it released a long,
molecule-thick wire into their innards, slicing them
apart from within. If true, it was a grisly weapon for
such gaily-appointed warriors.

The entrance into the palace interior was formed
by two trees at one end of the courtyard, the boughs
of which formed an arched, glassed gateway. Findelsith led the way with Rhoinithiel the Shadowseer
by his side and a cadre of harlequins not far behind.
Maensith followed with Aradryan and the others
close by, flanked by the mercenaries, while the rest of

the Harlequins brought up the rear. Passing into the glass-ceilinged entranceway, the padding of their feet echoed along the corridor, disturbing a silence that had persisted since the Fall.

Coming to a corridor that seemed to stretch into the distance to the left and right, the expedition split into two groups, each a mix of outcasts and harlequins. Aradryan and the others were in the group led by Findelsith, while Maensith took leadership of the other. Before they each went their separate way, Findelsith had a warning for them.

'Baubles and treasures aplenty there are, to turn a mind or hand to their taking. You must resist such plundering urges, for in this place there can be no desire. Take nothing but the Tears that you did not bring with you, and leave nothing that we bring to this place. Feel no yearning and lust for another, for through these things the Great Enemy strikes. He can feel us but he does not see us – give her no pause to turn her gaze this way.'

Another shudder gripped Aradryan at the reminder that despite the relative normality of their surroundings – as normal as a planet-spanning palace built by the arrogance of a single ruler could be – they were in fact on a crone world, steeped in warp energy, sustained by the psychic power of She Who Thirsts, who had fed upon the eldar since her birth during the Fall.

Aradryan paused, thinking that he heard whispering, but dismissed the noise as the breeze on the windows above. He felt as though they were being watched, but put the feeling down to the tapestries that hung on the walls, each a larger-than-life-size depiction of a noble-looking eldar with a narrow nose and high brow. In the closest, his white hair hung in braids across each shoulder, and around his neck was a tight choker studded with diamonds fashioned as tiny skulls. Aradryan sneered at the embroidered portrait, as if in accusation that it was spying upon him.

Turning, Aradryan realised that he recognised the face from a bust he had seen on a pedestal opposite where the entrance hall met the passageway. Examining the tapestries to the left and right, he saw that they all depicted the same person; though his hair and clothes and environs changed, the haughty features were unmistakable.

'A testament to aggrandisement and ego,' said Lechthennian. 'A whole world dedicated to the hubris of one, who doomed his family and friends to share in this self-inflicted confinement of pride.'

They continued to explore, finding several bedchambers and dining halls along the length of the corridor. As with the exterior, the inside of the palace was immaculate, with not a speck of dust, nor scratch or stain. The furnishings – portraits, sculptures, busts, tapestries and all showing the same overbearing face – were intact, with not a weave or stitch out of place in the carpets and chairs, the dark wood of the tables and mantels gleaming with polish.

It was impossible to explore the widening maze of rooms as one group, so one at a time, and in pairs, the band dispersed through the chambers. Aradryan did not know what he was looking for, if anything at all, and he found himself leaving Lechthennian in contemplation of an ornate fireplace, the mantel and surround of which was carved from green marble, forming intertwining figures and animals, with spears and bows in evidence. Yet whether they were hunting or doing something far less desirable was unclear to Aradryan, given the interconnectedness of the participants, and he looked away hurriedly, content to leave the musician to answer the question for himself.

Through various side passages, short stairwells and doorways Aradryan continued, always keeping a picture in his mind of where he was in relation to where he had come from, so that he could head back immediately if he needed to rejoin the others. This task was made more confusing by the abundance of mirrors he encountered. There seemed to be one every other room, and several in each passageway. Some were so large that at first he mistook them for branching corridors or additional chambers. The portraits at least had given way to this new form of vanity, but glimpsing himself every few steps, or seeing movement out of the corner of his eye, did nothing to help Aradryan relax.

He was sure that when he was not quite looking directly at them, his reflections pulled different expressions. Figures flitted where they should not, though in truth they were probably reflections of reflections. On the whole, it was a most unsettling experience, but there was nothing to do except to push on in the hopes of finding something significant to report.

The whispering seemed to have grown louder too, but Aradryan was almost used to it by now, it becoming a part of the background noise along with the pad of his feet on tile or hardwood floor, or the scrape of his scabbard as it caught on the corner of a table or shelf that he passed.

Aradryan found an answer to the riddle of the whispering in the next room. It was another arena-size bedchamber, the bed itself almost lost at the heart of a carpeted red sea and crimson hangings. Through a massive window he saw a seascape just a stone's throw from the palace, at the foot of a black-sanded beach. The waves seemed almost purple, and Aradryan realised with surprise that twilight was coming, the distant horizon darkening as he watched. The way the sea lapped, the sussurant hissing of the water, set his mind at ease. It was a comforting whisper, not a conspiratorial one.

Senses dulled by the mesmeric washing of the waves, Aradryan felt the need to sit down for just a moment. He had been searching for quite a time, and if he could just rest for a little while he would be rejuvenated to continue the search. He looked around but the vast chamber had no chairs or stools or chests, only the large bed at its centre.

Before he even realised what he was doing, Aradryan was beside the bed, stroking a hand across the silk-like covers. He did not need to sleep, he told himself as he turned and sat down on the edge of the bed. He would just sit here for a few moments, recharging his strength. He could see why such a place had been constructed; from the bed the sea seemed to come right up to the window, its wordless voice urging him to close his eyes and relax.

ARADRYAN MOST DEFINITELY did not sleep. He did not even close his eyes, and stayed sat on the edge of the bed staring out at the alien sea. Despite being very obviously awake, the ranger started to notice that

things were becoming decidedly dream-like. For a
start, his waystone was gleaming gold and hot to the
touch when he lifted his fingers to it. On top of that,
he was not alone on the bed. He did not dare turn
around, but he could feel the presence of someone
else behind him, their weight on the mattress.

Delicate music tinkled in the distance, soothing
and quiet, echoing along the empty corridors and
across abandoned rooms. Except the corridors and
rooms were not empty and abandoned. The figures of
eldar moved around the apartment, several of them
gathering by the window in front of Aradryan, holding hands with each other as they looked out across
the waves as darkness descended. They were a family,
two small girls with their mother and father. The person behind Aradryan called out a series of names and
the family turned with smiles, the children breaking
free to run to the bed. One of them leapt onto the
mattress, passing straight through Aradryan.

Bolting to his feet, Aradryan turned to look at the
ghosts. The eldar from the portraits, eyes lined with
greater age, lay beneath the covers, which were rucked
back to reveal his thin shoulders and shallow chest.

The music had stopped, and the small girl who had
leapt onto the bed was not smiling any more. Her
tiny hands were at the old noble's throat, and there
were shouts and rings of metal from across the palace
grounds. Old scores were being settled, the extended
families dividing into factions, sectarian violence
erupting between them to decide who should inherit
the luxurious planet-manse.

'Come with us.'

Aradryan turned to see a beautiful eldar female in

an elegant blue gown, the white of her thigh showing through a slit, her arms bare but covered in rings and torcs. Her black hair was heaped up upon her head, fixed by many jewelled pins. Her lips pouted at him and her eyelids fluttered ever so slightly as she sighed. He felt the light touch of her breath upon his cheek and smelt the fragrance of her perfume.

'It has been so long since we had visitors,' she said, her hand moving to Aradryan's arm. He could not feel her through his undersuit, but her fingers lay upon his forearm as if they were real. Behind the aristocratic-looking eldar, the girl on the bed had finished strangling the old noble and was pulling the heavy rings from his fingers, while her sister had joined her and was using a knife to cut his hair, pulling free gemstones from the bindings thus freed.

They were ghosts, Aradryan knew, but there was something alluring about the invitation that he could not shake. He knew in his heart that he could be content here. To live for eternity by the dying light across the sea was not such a bad fate. It was peaceful, nothing like the anarchy that had reigned elsewhere when the elderly ruler had drawn his last breath. It might have been coincidence, the birth scream of She Who Thirsts ripping apart the galaxy just moments after the self-proclaimed regent had perished, but the ghosts liked to think that their immortality was reward for the actions in bringing about the eruption of the Great Enemy.

'We will make you comfortable here,' she said, stroking Aradryan's arm. 'You will never hunger nor know thirst, and you shan't tire or be lonely. The children will play games forever, and you will never grow old either. Stay with us. Stay in our home by the sea.'

A screeching noise tore through Aradryan's thoughts. The ghosts snarled and fluttered away, becoming mist and then nothing. Aradryan was still sitting on the bed and he looked to where the noise had come from, seeing Lechthennian standing at the door with his finger upon the string of a half-lyre.

The screams of the dying eldar echoed in Aradryan's thoughts, carried by the after-echoes of that harsh note. It was not just those in the palace who had perished. Billions of eldar died, consumed by the god of the warp that had been created by their hedonism. Aradryan felt the tiniest fraction of their demise, his body quaking with reaction as the universe imploded around him, bringing into being She Who Thirsts, embodied by a storm thousands of light years wide that devoured the heart of the ancient eldar empire.

'Now is not the time to tarry with ghosts, Aradryan,' said Lechthennian, hanging his instrument from his belt. 'It is no pleasant fate to spend eternity trapped between worlds, lingering on the precipice between life and death.'

'What are they?' asked Aradryan. As he crossed the room back to the door, the shadowy figures were coalescing around him once more. Their whispering returned, almost beyond hearing, imploring and cajoling with soft words.

'They are the unfortunate ones who were trapped in damnation, their spirits remaining to be taunted by a life they can never have again, their torment a source of titillation to She Who Thirsts.' Lechthennian waved Aradryan through the doorway. 'Come, the time is nigh for the Witch Time and we will not have long.

The others are waiting for us in the garden dome.'

Aradryan did not have any idea what Lechthennian was talking about, but followed the itinerant musician as he hurried through halls and chambers. The ghostly after-images of the damned eldar flowed around them, young and old, male and female. Aradryan caught snatches of invitation and threat, but now there was no melancholy in the disembodied voices, only menacing hisses and snarled reproach.

The pair caught up with Maensith and the rest of the expedition by a grand gatehouse linking the residential wing with the massive dome Aradryan had seen earlier. The ghosts here were much in evidence, seeming more substantial though still semi-transparent, dozens of them drifting into the dome with agitated chattering.

'Where are the Tears of Isha?' asked Maensith. She had her blade in hand, and many of her warriors had their weapons ready also, perturbed by the apparitions that glided onto the carefully-trimmed blue lawns that covered the dome, a tree-lined road cutting from the entrance hall across the far side of the gardens.

Looking around, Aradryan saw more families, sitting beneath the boughs, while lovers stood hand in hand gazing at their reflections in ponds and pools. The small figures of children laughed shrilly as they chased about the trees and hid behind hedges and bushes, the noise bringing no joy to the ranger but putting his nerves on edge.

'It comes upon us, the Time of Witching,' said Findelsith, pointing towards the top of the dome. 'We must be quick, the Tears of Isha fall.'

Far above in the artificial cloud of the dome, a golden light shimmered. Like rain, the light descended and in its aura the ghosts of the doomed eldar grew bright, becoming auric silhouettes. They stopped and gazed upwards, reaching out with imploring hands as the light fell upon them.

The screams began at the far side of the dome, unearthly and distant but terrifying all the same. Aradryan gritted his teeth as the unnatural shrieking of the ghosts filled the air, the faces of the apparitions contorting with agony and despair as though the light burned them. Collapsing to their knees, the ghastly host's wails reached a deafening crescendo, their bodiless pleas for mercy echoing from the trees and dome wall, reverberating inside Aradryan's skull so that he felt as if it was his body that was disintegrating.

The first of the ghosts fell to the ground on a path not far to Aradryan's left, curling up in a foetal position, twitching and wailing. It shook the ranger to the core as others collapsed, like a cluster of dolls knocked over by a violent gale. Writhing and flailing, clasping immaterial hands to immaterial faces, the doomed eldar relived the moment of ecstatic torture that was the Fall.

The golden light was almost as bright as a sun now, and Aradryan could see little of what happened next. Each ghost wavered and shrank, losing shape and focus, becoming smaller and smaller until only a flickering star of gold was left. And then the light dimmed, leaving dozens of smooth, pearlescent stones lying about the dome.

'Be swift and sure and take your prizes now!'

Findelsith declared, sweeping an arm to encompass the gardens. Even as Aradryan started towards the closest Tear, where a robed young female had been standing a few moments before, he saw that the stones were shimmering, becoming as ethereal as the ghosts they had been.

The Tear of Isha was warm to the touch, its heat felt through the fabric of Aradryan's gloves. He lifted up the Tear and in the dancing patterns on its surface thought for a heartbeat that he saw the face of the dead eldar from whom it had been created. It felt wrong to take such a thing, but as his own waystone pulsed strongly at his chest he knew that it was a necessary task to protect the spirits of generations to come. The Tear would be gifted to an eldar infant, becoming their guardian from birth, attuning itself to their essence so that when later they passed from the mortal life, their spirit would be safeguarded from the hunger of the Great Enemy. Not until now had Aradryan known that the Tears of Isha were formed of the spirits of those who had been consumed by the Fall, and he could see why such knowledge was kept secret. It wrenched his heart to think of the unfortunates who had perished in this place, and to know that they relived that hateful moment again and again for the amusement of the Great Enemy brought a choking sob to his throat. It was a release he was giving the damned, to take them from this place.

In his hand the Tear was cooling, its surface solidifying into something more closely resembling the waystone it would become. He slipped it into a pouch at his belt and looked around for another.

Spying the glint of a Tear in a thicket of grass beside a pond, he stooped to retrieve it. It had almost disappeared but became solid at his touch. It followed the first into the pouch.

No more than twenty heartbeats had passed when the Tears of Isha faded from existence. There were cries of dismay from some of the others, for they had managed to gather less than a quarter of the stones that had materialised. The suggestion was made that they should remain for the Time of the Witch to return, so that more Tears could be claimed, but Findelsith shook his head and pointed back to the way they had entered.

'With daring we have entered the foe's lair, but she is not blind to us forever,' warned the Great Harlequin. 'The purity of the Tears protects yet we cannot remain here for too long. The eye of She Who Thirsts will turn this way, bringing retort from he who we steal from.'

This timely cautioning did not fall on deaf ears. Maensith quickly gathered her warriors and, forming up into two groups, they made one last search of the nearby dells and copses, but no more Tears were to be found. Findelsith and his troupe were already moving back towards the entranceway, and Aradryan followed close behind them.

'Remarkable,' said Estrathain, falling into step beside the ranger. 'This body cannot shed tears, but if it could I fear I would drown in them.'

Aradryan said nothing, unable to put into words the feelings stirred by the vista of misery that had surrounded him.

* * *

After the events inside the dome, the journey back to the courtyard where the expedition had landed was conducted in silence. The ring of the mercenaries' boots echoed hollowly along the passageways and Aradryan's thoughts seemed loud in his head. Gone was the disturbing background whisper, but the utter absence of noise in its stead was just as unsettling. This was truly a dead place, where the living had no right to trespass.

The harlequins led the way back to the ships, unerringly moving through the seemingly identical chambers and hallways. Aradryan found himself towards the back of the group, walking alongside Estrathain. The kami stared straight ahead, paying no heed to the artworks and furnishings, but Aradryan was again convinced that he saw flurries of movement in mirrors and window panes and silver decorations, movements that were not reflections of the eldar but possessed a life of their own.

He heard a scratching sound, for the briefest of moments and stopped, glancing back. There was a slight tremor in a curtained archway he had just passed. Aradryan would have dismissed it as a draught except that the air was still. Through the windows high in the walls of the corridor they were following the sky had turned to twilight, as he had first seen in the chamber by the sea. It should not have mattered whether it was night or day, but on a world with no sun the coming of dusk might portend something far more sinister.

Chiding himself for his paranoia, Aradryan took a few hasty steps to catch up with Estrathain. As he came level with the kami the ranger glanced to his left. He gasped, thinking he saw a pair of jet black eyes peering at him from the shadow of an alcove holding a silver statue with arms upraised. Looking more closely, Aradryan saw that there was nothing concealed behind the sculpture, but he could not shake the feeling of being observed.

They were not far from the entranceway that led to the courtyard where the ships had been left; Aradryan recognised some of the tapestries that covered the walls. It was with a sense of relief that he spied the glitter of the glass-ceilinged entrance hall some distance ahead, and he allowed himself a smile.

It was then that he heard the scratching again, and a distinctive click-clack, like a snapping twig. Some of the mercenaries ahead turned at the sound, so the ranger knew he had not imagined it. Maensith noticed the commotion and headed back.

'Why have you all stopped?' she demanded, glaring at her warriors. 'We must be gone swiftly.'

Before there was any reply, the skittering, scratching noise sounded again, like something running through the walls and ceiling. Aradryan caught a half-glimpse of something pale pink flittering across an archway ahead. He gave a shout and pointed, but the doorway was empty as the others turned.

'It is just the ghosts returning,' snapped Maensith, waving her pistol to move the group on.

Findelsith had now returned with some of the Harlequins to investigate the cause of the delay. The Great Harlequin was tense, his weapons in hand, his masked face turning left and right as he scanned the corridors and archways. Aradryan yelped as he thought he felt something brush against his back.

Spinning on his heel, he yanked out his sword and took a step backwards towards the others, the point of his blade making circles in front of him.

'Not all is as it once appeared to be,' said Findelsith, whipping around to stare at one of Maensith's officers, Thyarsion. The Great Harlequin extended his arm and tapped a finger to a sapphire-studded pendant hanging around the mercenary's neck. 'Your throat was not adorned with this trinket. Did you not heed the warning that I gave?'

'Where did you get this?' snarled Maensith, ripping the jewellery from Thyarsion, the silver chain parting with a scatter of glinting links.

'It was wasted, lying unwanted in a drawer,' said Thyarsion. He made to take back the necklace but Maensith snatched away her hand.

'Who else has broken the ban of thievery?' she demanded, holding the pilfered jewel aloft. There were muttered confessions from several of the mercenaries, and a variety of gems and artworks were revealed, stuffed into pouches, bags and pockets.

'Nobody will miss them, there is nobody here,' said one offender.

'Tis fools who steal the treasures of this place!' said Findelsith, striding through the gathered warriors to confront the individual who had spoken. 'Your greed is like a beacon blazing bright, did you not heed my words of dire warning? They will be coming to reclaim their gilt. This trove is not for mortals to ransack, it is the vault of the Prince of Pleasure.'

There were angry retorts and exclamations as the Harlequins moved through the throng, demanding the treasures from those who had taken them.

Aradryan looked horrified as some of the mercenaries raised their blades and pistols to defend their ill-gotten prizes. Through the clamour of raised voices, Aradryan heard Lechthennian beside him speaking, but the words were lost.

A piercing screech from the musician's half-lyre silenced the arguments.

'Run,' he said, pointing to the windows ahead of the group, his voice cold and calm. 'We are discovered.'

Aradryan looked down the corridor and his blood froze and his skin prickled with a chill of utter dread. At the arched windows stood dozens – hundreds – of pale-skinned figures. They had androgynous faces and single-breasted bodies, with eyes like polished coal that stared at the eldar with rapt hunger. Forked tongues slithered in anticipation over needle-thin teeth. They were bereft of clothes save for bangles and loops of beads, and each sported a crest of hair of purple or red or dark blue, splaying dramatically from their scalps. Instead of hands they had elongated claws, like some monstrous lobster, and these they tapped against the window panes while narrow faces snarled and grinned and leered.

Aradryan's waystone was like a nail being driven into his heart, piercing hot as it burned through his chest. A chorus of voices sang in his head, beautiful and terrible, alluring and yet filling him with disgust. Though he had never laid eyes on the creatures before, he had heard tales from his earliest memories and knew in his gut, in the deepest pit of his spirit, the nature of the apparitions that confronted him: servants of the Great Enemy, daemonettes of dread Slaanesh.

* * *

With a splintering crash, the horde of daemons burst into the palace, laughing and screeching, taloned feet rattling on the tiled floor, claws snapping. A warning shout caused Aradryan to turn, just in time to see more daemonettes scuttling from the archways behind, scalp-fronds waving madly as they ran down the corridor.

Remembering Lechthennian's words, Aradryan thought to run, but the way towards the ships was barred by the enemy. Maensith and her warriors opened fire with las-bolts and shuriken, filling the passageway with glittering discs and actinic blasts. The hiss of shuriken cannons and crack of fusion pistols added to the noise.

'Move on,' said Estrathain, gently pushing Aradryan aside as the kami stepped forwards, one arm raised towards the daemonettes rushing from the back. 'It has been some time, but I have a little of my power left.'

A blaze of white light burst from the kami's upraised palm spreading to become a burning coruscation that shrieked through the approaching daemonettes. Where the flames touched, the daemons turned to crystal and shattered, spraying shards that sliced down more of their kind. Estrathain was thrown back by the strength of the blast, staggering into Lechthennian. The kami held up his hand in surprise, blackened scraps of red cloth falling from the charred remnants of his glove. Smoke wisps rose from his ceramic fingers, the artificial flesh discoloured by burned whorls.

'We are at the heart of the Gulf of Magic,' said Lechthennian, supporting Estrathain as he straightened.

'It would not be wise to open up your mind again.'

'I miscalculated, but it is not a calamity,' said the kami. He threw off his scarf and discarded his robe and gloves, revealing a white form, which looked like liquid stone, flowing and rippling as he stepped forwards again. Hundreds of tiny silver runes glowed in his artificial skin, crackling with psychic power. 'I have not served Khai-dazaar for so long as its spirit conduit without taking some precautions.'

Though the daemonettes had been thrown back by the kami's first assault, they had gathered again, even more numerous than before, and came hurtling down the passageway. Gone were the expressions of cruel delight and covetousness, replaced with glares of deepest hatred.

Lightning forked along the corridor from Estrathain's fingers, leaping from one daemon to the next, turning every foe touched into a shower of ebon sparks. The psychic storm was not enough to keep every enemy at bay, and the daemonettes raced swiftly closer, claws opening and closing with excitement.

Glancing over his shoulder to see if passage to the ship had been cleared, Aradryan saw that the rest of the company fared little better. Maensith and her warriors had managed to band together into three groups, their rifles and pistols enough to keep most of the daemonettes at bay. Amongst them, Jair, Caolein and Athelennil fought on, though Aradryan felt a moment of concern as he saw blood dripping from a cut across the cheek of his former lover.

Those daemonettes that survived the fire of the mercenaries and outcasts had to contend with the dazzling skills of the Harlequins. Just as he had been at the performance in Khai-dazaar, Aradryan was momentarily transfixed by their display. Somersaulting, cartwheeling and pirouetting, the warrior-troupers danced around the daemonettes, dodging and ducking snapping claws, their chainblades and power swords licking out to cut away limbs and sever necks. That such carnage was wrought by the brightly-dressed performers, their faces covered with grinning and snarling masks, added to the surrealism of the scene. The skull-faced Death Jesters swept and twirled their shrieker cannons like batons, powered blades on the stocks and muzzles flashing, slicing apart the foe, giving themselves room to unleash hails of shurikens.

At the centre of the Harlequins stood Findelsith and his Shadowseer, shouting commands in his their sing-song tones like joint conductors of a lethal orchestra. Now and then Findelsith would level his pistol to shoot into the face of a pouncing daemonette.

The display was fascinating, but Aradryan forced himself to turn away, concluding that there would be no retreat just yet. He returned his attention to the daemonettes closing down the corridor. Shurikens and laser fire sprayed past him from some of Maensith's warriors, but the daemons were almost upon the ranger and kami. Aradryan was aware of Lechthennian just behind him, and could not recall seeing any weapons on the musician. He was defenceless, unless a quick skirl of his half-lyre could banish the daemonettes.

Estrathain leapt forwards, fists blazing with energy, to meet the daemonettes head on. Protective wards flared into life as their claws sparked from his artificial body. Aradryan had no attention to spare for his companion as lightning flared from his hands, for the daemonettes would be upon the ranger in moments.

Aradryan tried to remain as calm as if he were in the bay of the *Fae Taeruth*, sparring with Maensith. He took a shallow breath and raised his blade in readiness for the first attack. Looking at the daemonettes, he was shocked, his blade trembling in his hand as he saw in their pale faces glimpses of likenesses of his loved ones. The glaring black eyes were the same, but there was something in the tilt of the head and cheeks of a daemon to his right that put him in mind of Thirianna, while a creature pulling back its claw to swipe at him reminded Aradryan of Maensith; here and there he saw lovers of his past, including Athelennil.

And then he saw the face of his mother.

With a scream of rage, Aradryan lashed out at the daemon that dared to wear the face of his mother, slashing his sword across its throat. As its incorporeal body shimmered into a cloud of pastel blue mist, Aradryan stepped up to catch the claw of another on the edge of his blade, deflecting the blow aside. He whipped the tip back-handed across the daemonette's chest, opening up a wound that bled silver across its single breast. Spitting, the creature fell back, giving Aradryan space to lunge forwards beneath the claws of another daemon, pulling his sword up to slice through the leg of his attacker.

He felt a hand grabbing his arm and he staggered back a step, glancing to see Lechthennian pulling him away from the fight. Beyond the musician, the passageway was clear for the moment and, without waiting for their rearguard, the mercenaries were heading back to the courtyard.

'What about Estrathain?' said Aradryan, but his worries were unfounded. A white sheet of fire exploded from the kami, hurling back the daemonettes that had been surrounding the psyker.

'Run!' said Lechthennian, pushing Aradryan towards the others.

The ranger needed no second invitation and sprinted down the corridor with long strides, Estrathain at his heels. The enemy were not totally destroyed ahead; a glance through the broken windows showed more and more of them spilling from other palace wings, converging on the ships in the courtyard. There were other creatures coming too: six-limbed fiends with lashing tongues stalked towards the pair, coming between them and the remains of the entryway.

'Shortcut,' said Aradryan, leaping over the sill of a shattered window to land in a shrub-filled border. Estrathain followed him out into the courtyard and the two of them cut across a lawn, heading directly for *Irdiris*.

THEY WERE HALFWAY towards the ships, the mercenaries not far ahead plunging over flagstones and grass, when something burst from the palace to Aradryan's left. Masonry and glass erupted as a gigantic daemon exploded into the courtyard.

Aradryan staggered, his waystone flaring with white light, his mind and body awhirl with dislocation. The ranger was not the only one affected; mercenaries tripped and fell, some of them crying out in pain at the daemon's appearance. Those that stayed on their feet clutched hands to heads and waystones, moaning and snarling. Only the Harlequins were unaffected, forming a ring around the stricken warriors and outcasts.

The creature towered above the eldar, two of its arms ending in larger versions of the claws of the daemonettes, while another two ended in slender-fingered hands that grasped scimitars as long as Aradryan was tall. Its unnatural flesh was pierced with rings, and chains of gold and silver hung with runes and pendants that glittered hypnotically. Into its incorporeal hide were sunk gems of every colour, which Aradryan realised with horror were the spirit stones of dead eldar, scores of them. The stolen spirit stones gleamed with dark light, eldar essences trapped within. Its face was elongated, with razor teeth, looking oddly bovine except for its eyes; these were many-faceted orbs of black that reflected back Aradryan's face a dozen different ways. Spiralled horns, two above each eye, arched back from its brow, and two more curved around its pointed ears from the back of its head.

The creature was surrounded by an aura like the golden rain that had fallen during the Time of the Witch, only denser, more cloying. The air around the greater daemon shimmered with its power, and the ground under its tread cracked and sparked with Chaotic magic. Aradryan could hear his name being called, over and over, sometimes in a mocking voice, sometimes enticing.

'A Bride of Perversion,' hissed Estrathain, though Aradryan did not need to be told the title of the monstrosity that was charging towards the starships, swords flashing. The greater daemon was a monstrous embodiment of the Prince of Pleasure's power, known by many names in the craftworld myths: a Warden of Spirits, King of Hearts and Decadent Lord amongst others. 'Run for your ship!'

Before Aradryan could grab Estrathain, guessing his intent and knowing the folly of confrontation with the greater daemon, the kami broke into a run, heading directly for the Decadent Lord. The kami's body blazed with psychic fire as he sprinted across the courtyard with sparks trailing from his fingertips. The greater daemon turned at the kami's defiant shout, raising up its twin scimitars as it rounded on Estrathain.

A shining shield of silver sprang up around the kami as he held an arm up towards the Decadent Lord. The greater daemon laughed, a high-pitched, chilling sound that froze Aradryan to the spot despite the kami's instruction to run. The two daemonic swords swept down, turning Estrathain's shield into falling shards like a broken mirror. The blades continued on their course, slicing into the shoulders of the kami, spraying silver blood-like fluid as they quartered him from neck to waist, the body parts sent spinning through the air.

Claws snapping, blades weaving a complex pattern through the air, the Decadent Lord advanced on the other eldar, its pale skin spattered with the silver of Estrathain's vital fluid. The greater daemon stopped for a moment to extend a long, thin tongue, which flicked along its swords, tasting the essence of the dead kami. Hissing in distaste, the Decadent Lord reached out a clawed hand towards the Harlequins, who were massing behind Findelsith, their weapons ready. The creature beckoned to them with its claw, laughing again.

'Do as he said, my companion bold.' Aradryan heard Lechthennian right behind him. The voice was unmistakeably that of the musician, though the meter of his words was more poetic than normal. 'Run swift now and let the old tale unfold.'

'I thought you had been caught,' replied the ranger, turning. His next words remained unsaid, as he saw the manner of the person who had spoken.

Lechthennian was dressed in the garb of the Harlequins, in a manner. A hood and cowl covered his head and shoulders, chequered with red and black. He had discarded his robes, revealing a bodysuit of purple and white and yellow, patterned with stripes and dots and banding. His face was hidden by a plain mask, totally blank and black except for a single rune in red upon one cheek: the symbol of Cegorach the Laughing God.

'I was caught, a long time ago, my friend,' said Lechthennian. There was jest in his tone. 'Yet I wriggled free and here I am still. The friendless and lonely traveller; fell guardian of the Black Library; webway wanderer without a sprit, my life hostage to the Great Enemy. I am Solitaire.'

A bellow of anger, terrible and long, reverberated around the courtyard. The Decadent Lord sensed the presence of the Solitaire and turned, clashing its swords together in challenge.

'Cometh unto me, thee pretty prancer,' called out the greater daemon, in a voice deep and luxurious.

The words were ancient eldar, the language spoken before the Fall. 'Cometh unto me and dance the dance of eternity. Your spirit is ours already.'

Lechthennian stepped past Aradryan, two golden daggers seeming to appear in his hands as he broke into a run towards the Decadent Lord.

'We shall whirl and twirl and see who is best,' Lechthennian replied, performing a flip over a line of bushes. 'There is nought of true heart in your foul breast.'

The greater daemon pounded over paving and through hedgerows in a headlong charge, its roar of ancient hatred still echoing from the broken walls of the palace. Seeing that it was intent upon Lechthennian, Aradryan was able to run too, circling around the gardens towards the rest of the expedition, who were being shepherded towards *Irdiris* and the Harlequins' vessel.

As he ran, Aradryan cast glances back towards the Decadent Lord and Lechthennian, thinking that despite the tales he had heard concerning the Harlequin Solitaire, a single eldar would last only moments against the greater daemon of She Who Thirsts; the shockingly swift demise of Estrathain was proof of that.

The Decadent Lord skidded to a stop, its clawed feet throwing up splinters of stone from the ground. Lechthennian dived beneath its right-hand blade, the sorcerous weapon missing the Solitaire by the tiniest of margins. Leaping to one side, Lechthennian dodged the claw that swept out towards his gut, hand-springing away as the Decadent Lord turned and lashed out with its other blade.

Reaching the Harlequins, Aradryan came to a stop beside Maensith and Findelsith. It was impossible to see what the Great Harlequin thought of the unfolding confrontation, and Maensith looked on with wide-eyed fascination.

'We have to help Lechthennian,' said Aradryan, pointing his sword back at the greater daemon. As he did so, Lechthennian somersaulted over a clawed foot aimed at his head. His daggers flashed, drawing a slender line across the greater daemon's clawed right arm.

'It is not our purpose to interfere, it was for this that he wanted to come,' replied Findelsith, holstering his pistol. 'This dance has been danced for a long, long time. The Solitaire always dances alone, for he has been taken by She Who Thirsts. The Laughing God will watch over our friend, watch and you will see that I am not wrong.'

Aradryan and the other eldar were not the only audience to the dramatic fight unfolding in the courtyard. The lesser daemons and beasts were gathering at the periphery, watching the duel between the Solitaire and Decadent Lord. There were hundreds of daemonettes and fiends and beasts, and like the Harlequins they did not intervene. Aradryan assumed that the moment the greater daemon or Lechthennian was slain the immaterial host would descend upon the surviving eldar, and he edged towards *Irdiris* as he watched the unfolding scene.

The Decadent Lord and Lechthennian moved with fluid grace, weaving about each other, sometimes so fast their weapons were a blur. It was like the performance of the Death Jesters on the stage, weapons whirling close but never quite touching, like an elaborately choreographed dance. The greater daemon was at least four times Lechthennian's height, its reach far longer, but the more agile Solitaire nimbly spun and ducked and dodged its attacks, nipping close to the greater daemon with his daggers ready, only to be sent somersaulting or cartwheeling away before he could land a telling blow. The four arms of the Decadent Lord were in constant motion, claws and swords slashing and swinging, while its tongue lashed out, cracking like a whip.

Aradryan watched transfixed, the interplay of the two fighters creating a mesmeric scene. The golden cloud that surrounded the greater daemon trailed in its wake as the two moved from lawn to patio to pathway, the ground churning beneath the tread of the greater daemon, the Solitaire's acrobatics leaving spiralling trails in the creature's misty aura.

As the two moved back and forth, Aradryan realised that Lechthennian did have a plan. Slowly, subtly, the Solitaire was luring the Decadent Lord towards a copse of trees. Beneath the boughs of silver branches, the greater daemon would be disadvantaged.

As Aradryan had guessed, so the fight unfolded, with Lechthennian retreating towards the cover of the silver-barked trees. Turning, he ran the rest of the short distance, running straight up the closest trunk into the lower branches, leaping through the blue leaves from limb to limb. The Decadent Lord followed, sending up a shower of leaves and splintered wood as it slashed both swords after the Solitaire.

Though the woods gave Lechthennian some cover, his ascent into the branches brought him up to a level where the greater daemon's horns could be used. The Decadent Lord flung its head at the Solitaire as he jumped past its shoulder, catching the Harlequin in the leg. Aradryan gave a cry of dismay as Lechthennian lost his footing and tumbled, spinning at the last moment to land awkwardly on his feet.

With a triumphant shout, the Decadent Lord thrust out its right sword, seeking to skewer Lechthennian. The bellow was answered by a laugh, as the Solitaire's ploy played out. Flipping out of the blade's path, the Solitaire avoided death by a hair's-breadth. The point of the sword passed into the trunk of the tree that had been behind Lechthennian and stuck fast for a moment.

It was all the hesitation Lechthennian needed. Using the Decadent Lord's outstretched arm as a step, the Solitaire skipped from the ground to the greater daemon's shoulder, ducking beneath its swiping claw. Twisting in mid-air, the Harlequin jumped up and hooked a leg around one of the daemon's horns, swinging across its face.

The Solitaire's daggers blazed as he plunged them into the eyes of the Decadent Lord. The daemon howled in pain, letting go of its sword to flail at the Solitaire, who leapt free into the treetop again, escaping retribution.

Aradryan ran again, turning his back as the demented screeches of the greater daemon and its servants swept across the courtyard. He dared not look back, and joined a throng of mercenaries speeding up the ramp of *Irdiris*. It was not designed for so many to embark swiftly, and Aradryan was forced to wait at the foot of the ramp. Caolein had already boarded and the ship's engines whined in preparation for take-off as Aradryan darted one last look back at the host of Slaanesh.

Lechthennian sprinted back towards the ships, the still-twitching form of the greater daemon lying beneath the trees behind him. The daemon horde raced after the fleeing Solitaire, his laughter goading them into enraged screams and wails.

'Come on!' Maensith grabbed the sleeve of Aradryan's coat as she sped past, dragging him up into *Irdiris*. Lechthennian was heading for the Harlequin ship and so Aradryan was the last to board. He sent a message to *Irdiris* to close the entryway, and looked out to see the ground already dropping away as a tide of pink and red and purple spilled over the lawns and pavement below. A daemonette leapt up, claw seeking to grab a purchase on the lifting ship, but the ramp was withdrawing too quickly and the daemon fell back into the mass below. A sea of faces – the devilish likeness of Aradryan's family and friends amongst them – stared back at the ranger.

And then the door iris closed, cutting off the view, and *Irdiris* sped away from Miarisillion, the crone world, Planet of the Pleasure Palace.

# CRAVINGS

*Commorragh – When the Fall consumed the eldar and the Vortex of Misery engulfed the ancient empire, those who had not departed with the Exodites or craftworlds were forced to flee into the webway. For long generations the webway had been expanded and great palaces, beautiful estates and entire cities had been birthed in the links between dimensions. The most wicked and depraved of the Fall's survivors took over these interspaces and pocket worlds, and in time the twisted kin of the dark eldar built a city to rival their pride and evil: Commorragh. Here the worst excesses and most depraved practices of the ancient days continue, and the sects that once tore apart eldar civilisation grew into the mighty kabals that now rule the Dark City with intimidation and incessant violence.*

THE JOURNEY DEPARTING the Eye of Terror was strangely more peaceful than the expedition's entry, though Aradryan would have expected the Great Enemy to have plagued the eldar with nightmares and pursuit now that they had revealed themselves. Instead, a quiet air of contemplation settled upon the starship. Perhaps it was in this self-reflection that the Great Enemy sought to do the most damage, leaving her victims free to consider their own dooms and desires, the seed having been sown in aeons past.

For the first few cycles back aboard the *Fae Taeruth*, Aradryan spent time alone in his cabin, relieved and drained in equal measure. Nothing he had been expecting or had previously experienced could have prepared him for the episode on the crone world, and the heart-chilling encounter with the daemonettes and Decadent Lord would linger in his dreams for as long as he could sleep.

Yet for all the fear and desperation that had clutched at his spirit in those moments, Aradryan had been invigorated by the venture. As with the battle with the orks, his sense of freedom, his appreciation of life, was enhanced by the trauma of Miarisillion. In comparison to the deadly foes of the crone worlds, the brutish greenskins that had invaded Hirith-Hreslain seemed laughable. It was as if Aradryan had passed through fire and not been burned, and the latest blaze had been hottest of all and yet had left him physically unscathed.

In purely material terms, the expedition had also been a qualified success. They had recovered nearly two hundred waystones, though Maensith had lost sixteen of her warriors to the daemonic attack. Efforts had been made to bring their spirit stones back, but four had been left behind in the final rush for the ships, no doubt to suffer torment in the grasp of the Great Enemy. One of those who had fallen had been a Commorraghan, who had possessed no waystone, his spirit most likely enduring untold tortures at the hands of the daemonettes.

Two Harlequins had perished also, one the Death Jester Taenemeth, and for some reason the loss of these warrior-dancers struck Aradryan as particularly sad, for they had brought joy and awe to him in their performance and would never dance again. Findelsith was sanguine about the losses, and assured Aradryan that the spirits of the fallen Harlequins were safe, sneaked away from the Great Enemy by the Laughing God they had served and emulated in life.

And there was the loss of Estrathain too, torn asunder by the greater daemon. In a sense, the kami was but a single facet of Estrathain, who would continue to live, but the experience the divided eldar spirit had sought had been lost on the crone world, and all the memory therein, and so while the other kami would endure, they would be lessened by the loss.

To think about those who had not survived was perversely encouraging to Aradryan. It reinforced his belief that the manner of one's death was unimportant, it was the life that one led beforehand that was defining; not to others but to he who was living the life. All things passed, even the greatest and longest legacies would eventually fail and be forgotten. Aradryan thought of what Maensith had said about regrets, and realised that despite the horror and death and his misgivings before setting out, he did not regret the adventure. He had survived and the experience had enriched his life; if he had died it would no longer matter as he would be in no position to be aware of the loss.

After breaking back into the webway, the Harlequins took their leave of the *Fae Taeruth*. Lechthennian had chosen to go with them, and so the outcasts of the *Irdiris* gathered on the launch deck to say goodbye to their companion. Lechthennian was dressed in his normal travelling clothes, his Harlequin suit and mask concealed once more amongst his belongings. The musician seemed happy, and when he had been questioned on the fight with the Decadent Lord he had simply shrugged and laughed away the encounter.

'You could stay with us,' said Athelennil, holding a hand to Lechthennian's chest in a sign of deep friendship. '*Irdiris* is your home.'

'It is not the nature of the Solitaire to have a home,' Lechthennian replied, patting the ranger on her shoulder. 'I shall spend some time with Findelsith's troupe, and we shall perhaps go to Ulthwé to perform the Dance without End, for it is the first and perhaps only time Findelsith will have a Solitaire in his masque.'

Aradryan felt his skin crawl at the thought of watching the Dance without End. He had only heard and read about it, for not in his lifetime had a Solitaire travelled to Alaitoc to perform the dance – at least not to Aradryan's knowledge, for now that he had seen the way that Lechthennian had kept his true identity hidden, the ranger wondered if any of the other eldar he had met or known were Solitaires in disguise. The performance in Khai-dazaar, as shocking and disturbing as it had been, was only an overture, a preamble to the true Dance without End, in which the Great Harlequin took the role of the Laughing God and the Solitaire played the part of She Who Thirsts.

'We could meet you again in Khai-dazaar,' suggested Caolein. '*Irdiris* is not the same without Lechthennian.'

'Lechthennian will be no more, when I set foot from this ship,' said the Solitaire. 'I am the Laughing God and I am the Great Enemy, and I travel where fate wills me. My true persona cannot be known, for I would become a lodestone of temptation, luring those around me to share my dark fate. *Irdiris* will find new stories to tell.'

Aradryan had not known the musician as long as the others and so did not feel quite the sense of loss that they did, though he was aware that Lechthennian's departure did represent something of the end of an era for the ship.

'Thank you, for your wisdom and protection,' said Aradryan, raising a hand in appreciation. Lechthennian nodded in acknowledgement but did not smile. He leaned close and whispered so that only Aradryan could hear.

'Each of us dances to the tune he hears, played out in our hopes, ambitions and fears. Some of us are bold, some of us meek, where one sees strength, another seems weak. Whether you fight or whether you run, She Who Thirsts calls out the beat of the drum.'

With that perplexing riddle delivered, Lechthennian stepped away, bowed with a sweeping arm and trotted up the winding boarding gantry to the door of the Harlequin's starship. He turned at the last moment and something silver flashed in the air, spinning down from the Solitaire. By instinct, Aradryan caught it: the silver thumb whistle. By the time he looked back to say thank you, Lechthennian was gone from sight and the door of the ship was closing fast.

MAENSITH CAME TO Aradryan after a few days of the *Fae Taeruth* being back in the webway proper. She was her relaxed, playful self again, in stark contrast to the state in which she had been during the descent into the crone worlds. Though her words were as teasing as ever, her actions were more forthright than before the expedition, and Aradryan found himself a guest in her chambers often over the coming cycles. After one such liaison he came across Athelennil, who gave him a look of disdain but made no outright accusation. It was easy to attribute her behaviour to jealousy, and Athelennil's mood was probably all the more depressed following the departure of Lechthennian, so Aradryan ignored the slight and left his former lover in the companionway aft of the officer's quarters.

Ten cycles from Khai-dazaar, Maensith had the *Fae Taeruth* break into realspace, exiting from the webway via an oval portal of shimmering white. They had entered a star system called Assain-alei-Nemech, which was on the rim of a swirling nebula that Maensith referred to as the Lake of Sorrows. Aradryan was with the mercenary commander in the viewing deck when Jair and Athelennil entered, seeking the ship's captain.

'Why have we come here?' asked Jair, who darted a disapproving look towards Aradryan. 'We should be returning to Khai-dazaar with the waystones.'

'What is there for us in this place?' said Athelennil. She looked out of the row of broad windows, seeing a few gas giants orbiting a pale blue star. 'It looks like a dead system.'

'If my dallying here delays you, feel free to depart whenever you wish,' replied Maensith. 'I am here to add a little extra to the spoils for the markets in Khai-dazaar. You may enjoy the company of outcasts who are willing to share in the burden and cost of ship life, but I have a complement that demand a fair reward for the risk of their lives and labours. The waystones we took, our share of it, are not sufficient compensation for the resources we have expended so far.'

'Piracy?' Aradryan had harboured suspicions since he had first come aboard the *Fae Taeruth* but had not broached the subject with Maensith. She laughed at the shock in his voice.

'Where do you think all of this pretty finery comes from?' she asked, her waved hand encapsulating the ornate chairs and couches, low tables and cabinets that furnished the observation deck.

'I am not so naive as you think,' said Aradryan, scowling at the flippancy of the answer. 'I am just surprised that you would bring us here so soon after risking your life in the crone worlds. Would it not be better to recuperate before embarking on more conflict?'

'We do not have that luxury, my dear Aradryan,' said Maensith. 'If we wish to berth at Khai-dazaar, and compensate Estrathain for the loss of his kami, our profits are severely cut. Besides, compared to the company we have been keeping recently, a few haugri-alim will hardly be any threat at all.'

'The haugri-alim?' It was Jair who asked the question before Aradryan had the chance. 'An alien species? Is that what you wish to find here?'

'More than wish, we will find them here. In fact, we will not have to wait at all,' said Maensith. Touching her hand to a plate beneath one of the windows, she magnified the view. The sliding display brought into focus a starship unlike anything Aradryan had seen before – and he realised that seeing sights for the first time was becoming something of a theme since he had become outcast.

The name of the haugri-alim Aradryan guessed to be a play on haugrilim, a race from the oldest myths who had dwelt at the bottom of the seas and were tricked by Eldanesh into revealing the secrets of how to breathe water. Their craft was a simple cylindrical shape, with an outer ring supported by long spars on which its engines were located. Though it was still quite small in the magnified image, Aradryan could see blocky structures arranged in rings around the central superstructure, which he assumed to be weapons of some kind.

'Their ships pass through this system on nearly every journey,' explained Maensith. 'They are gas-dwellers, and have a holy site in the clouds of the world below. It is sort of a pilgrimage, or an homage or something. I do not quite understand it myself, but it makes them terribly predictable and vulnerable.'

'We will take you up on the offer to depart,' said

Jair. Athelennil nodded her agreement and the two rangers looked at Aradryan expectantly. 'To be an outcast does not force one to become a corsair.'

'No, but it makes life a lot more comfortable if you do,' said Maensith. The ship captain also turned her gaze on Aradryan, an eyebrow lifted in query.

'This is not a life you will want,' said Jair, shaking his head sadly.

'This Commorraghan fascinates you, but there will be sights and experiences of unimaginable beauty and power if you come with us,' said Athelennil. 'Do not become a pirate, Aradryan, it is a pointless, repetitive existence.'

Aradryan thought about it for a few moments. There would likely be more safety aboard the *Irdiris* and, despite recent divisions, he liked Jair and Caolein, and still had fond thoughts for Athelennil. He did not wholly trust Maensith; he did not trust her in the slightest if he was being honest with himself. His new company would be corsairs and Commorraghans, who were not known for their loyalty. It was a life of danger, of strife and fighting, and it was likely to be shorter as a pirate than a ranger. As the latter he could visit Exodite worlds and distant craftworlds, explore alien planets and seek out new experiences.

But would it be worthwhile? Would he have the satisfaction he had felt on their successful escape from the crone worlds. Life on board the *Fae Taeruth* would be more exciting, the contrast between life and death brought into sharp relief. Aradryan did not feel particularly bloodthirsty, but on the other hand it was battle that had given him his greatest thrill, and nothing else he had ever experienced, no dream or journey, came close to filling him with the same heady mixture of excitement and fear.

'I do not think I will be as welcome as you say,' Aradryan told the rangers, an apologetic expression on his face. 'And I feel that you will be more content without me in your company. That is, if Maensith wishes me to stay.'

'You are more than welcome to join the crew of the *Fae Taeruth*,' said the captain. 'I will offer you the same deal as everybody else aboard. Stay for a cycle, stay for a thousand, as your heart desires, no onus is placed upon you and no oath binds you to this ship. Fight for me and earn equal share. Protect your companions and they will protect you. I will ask nothing of you that I would not do myself, and if you have any complaint you can bring it to me openly. I spent half of my life in a kabal, watching for the dagger of an ally aimed between my shoulder blades, kicking those beneath me to keep them down whilst reaching up with one hand to grasp the ankles of those who climbed above me. That is not the life I want on the *Fae Taeruth*.'

'I shall stay aboard, for a cycle or a thousand,' said Aradryan. He turned back to Athelennil and Jair. There was sadness on their faces, genuine and deep. Aradryan smiled to lighten the mood of their departure. 'You look as if you mourn for me, but I am not dead yet. I promise I will see you again, and I owe you a debt that cannot be easily repaid. Athelennil, you took me from Alaitoc and showed me what was possible. Jair, you watched over me when I took those first steps, guiding me away from the structure of the Path into a universe of possibilities. I cannot thank you enough for what you have done, but I hope that it does not seem disloyal of me to seek a future that will allow me to spread my wings ever further.'

'Take care,' said Athelennil. Then, taking Aradryan by surprise, she took a few steps and embraced him, pulling him tight to her body. He wrapped an arm around her shoulders and squeezed back. When she stepped back, Athelennil glared at Maensith. 'If you wrong him, I will find you and make you pay, Commorraghan.'

Maensith's laugh was short and harsh but she said nothing as she strode from the room, leaving Aradryan with his former companions.

'Good fortune and prosperity,' Aradryan said to the other rangers, and left them to follow Maensith.

GHOSTING CLOSE UNDER the mask of its holofields, the *Fae Taeruth* manoeuvred behind the haugri-alim ship as the alien vessel turned into the gravity well of its destination planet. Maensith had tackled several such targets when she had been a kabalite officer operating out of Commorragh, and she ran her ship with smooth efficiency.

Some rogue scanner flicker or stray sensor return spooked the haugri-alim, and their engines flared into full fury as they tried to run for the safety of the gas giant's upper atmosphere. Swinging after the fleeing vessel, the stellar sail of the *Fae Taeruth* catching the full force of the system's stellar winds to speed them after their quarry, the eldar closed quickly, outpacing their lumbering prey by a considerable margin.

The control deck of the warship was different to

that of *Lacontiran*. On the merchant cruiser there was only a small weapons station, and her scanning array was far less sophisticated. Aradryan and the other pilots had been situated in an isolated compartment high in the ship and communication took place over the psychic network. On the *Fae Taeruth*, the crew were all located in one large space, subdivided into a rosette of decks surrounding a central command pod; engines, piloting, navigation, weapons, sensors and damage control were all within sight of each other so that Maensith and her officers could monitor the situation with sight and hearing as well as feedback over the internal matrix.

Like the ship she pursued, the majority of the *Fae Taeruth*'s weapons systems were to port and starboard, with a single high-powered, long-ranged laser turret directed from the bow. Aradryan watched with fascination as Maensith summoned a floating display in front of her, created by glittering projectors located in the floor beneath the command pod. Her left hand rested on a glowing network interface, while the fingers of her right danced across the runes of a projected holo-pad. The main holographic display was centred on the target ship, dark against the swirl of orange and red of the gas giant's atmosphere. Runes danced across the image, highlighting various systems on the fleeing ship detected by the scanning team. Maensith guided aiming reticules into position; glowing red diamonds flashed as target trajectories and ranges were laid in by the eldar manning the weapons consoles. The ship's captain provided a narration for the benefit of Aradryan.

'A ship of this size will be carrying more than a

thousand haugri-alim,' she explained. 'Coupled with their dense and gravity-heavy artificial environment, that makes it virtually impossible for us to successfully board. This is a fight we must win from a distance.'

'Why do they not turn and attack?' asked Aradryan.

'Instinct, I suppose.' Maensith shrugged and manipulated the image in front of her, magnifying the view of the vessel's engine housings. More target runes sprang into life. 'Some of us are predators and some of us are prey. haugri-alim are the latter.'

Maensith fell silent for a moment, communing across the network with other officers. A few moments later a startling burst of white beams sprang from the bow turret, flashing across the gulf between the ships in an instant. Red energy flared where they struck – defensive shields. Maensith hissed in annoyance.

'Most of these traders forego shield generators for more hold space,' she said.

'Is that a problem?'

'Not of the kind you are thinking,' replied Maensith. She made some adjustments to the target matrix, focusing on a jutting piece of superstructure above and forward of the engines. The laser lance fired again. This time the red spark of the shields was less intense and several of the beams broke through, burning into the targeted area of the enemy ship. Clouds of molten metal glittered and the next salvo met no resistance, tearing through the shield mast and the hull around it. Maensith turned with a wry smile. 'It just means less cargo for us to take.'

With its shields compromised, the haugri-alim ship finally began to turn, trying to bring its weapon batteries to bear on its pursuer. The *Fae Taeruth* was too swift to be caught so easy, sliding to port as the enemy turned to starboard, staying in the wake of its quarry's engines. Another flash of laser beams cut through the engines of the desperately turning ship, causing plasma explosions to ripple through the circular section. Crippled, the cylindrical vessel started to spin while fitful plumes of escaping gas caused the ship to yaw back and forth, creating a sporadic spiral of trailing debris.

With her prey crippled, Maensith and the crew guided the *Fae Taeruth* closer, matching their target's erratic course as best they could whilst bringing the broadside weapon batteries to bear. Laser and plasma sprayed from the gun decks, converging at three points along the top of the haugri-alim ship, burrowing through armour plate and reinforced bulkheads.

'The haugri-alim are as good at engineering as they are at fighting,' said Maensith as Aradryan watched more glowing slag jettisoned from breaks in the damaged ship's metal carcass. 'Another couple of salvoes and we will...'

As she spoke, the enemy ship started to crack open, sending spinning fragments into space, chasm-like tears opening up along one side of its hull. There seemed to be dust or mist venting into the vacuum, until Maensith increased the magnification of the view and Aradryan saw many-limbed, squid-like shapes drifting out within the escaping artificial atmosphere; distance and scale had made them appear no larger than floating motes of debris. The haugri-alim were clad in silvery, banded suits that allowed their dozens of flailing tentacles free movement. Their torsos were protected within heavily reinforced domes of transparent material, allowing them a view in every direction.

'Each is three times as tall as you or me,' said Maensith, shaking her head. 'They favour microwave-based weapons. Very nasty at close range. Anyway, they will not be posing any further threat. We will take our time before we board, to ensure that they have all been blown out or asphyxiated. The last thing we need is to run into a few survivors. When that is done, we can go down and take what we like.'

'And what do they have that we want?' asked Aradryan. 'They seem so crude, I cannot believe anybody would want anything made by these creatures.'

'They have access to many valuable ores and elements that are difficult to acquire by other means,' said Maensith. She stepped out of the command pod, signalling to one of her lieutenants to take charge now that the enemy had been dealt a fatal blow. 'Also, you will be surprised at the items that generate interest in markets like Khai-dazaar. haugri-alim skin is very tough, and there are some in Commorragh who swear that there is no material as thick yet flexible, ideal for working with to make undersuits and armour joints. Some of their digestive organs are also rich in certain rare minerals. It is a shame that we have to waste so many.'

Aradryan said nothing as he watched the corpses of the haugri-alim dispersing through the void, their tattered suits and cracked protective domes glinting in the light of the distant star. He was not sure how he felt about their deaths. From so far away it was easy to dismiss such casual slaughter. It had been almost laughably easy to defeat them, and Aradryan wondered if he had made the wrong choice. He had stayed with Maensith for the promise of excitement and life-defining battle, but all he had witnessed so far was a cold, calculated massacre.

Perhaps it would not all be like this, he told himself. It was probably better to think of the haugri-alim bodies drifting away from their ship in the same way as the others on board the *Fae Taeruth*: lost profit.

# Part Three

---

## Pirate

# ALLIANCES

*The Winter Gulf – There was a time when the lands of Eldanesh and Ulthanesh were sundered from each other. A torrent as wide as an ocean divided the Houses of the great founders, and so it was that they would never come to meet. However, seeing that her children would forever be divided, the Goddess Isha gave thanks to Mighty Asuryan the All-seeing and asked that he part the rapids and allow the folk of Eldanesh and the folk of Ulthanesh to meet. This the Great Pillar of the Heavens did not do, for he was of the opinion that by their own efforts should Ulthanesh and Eldanesh come upon each other. Yet he tempered his judgement with a cooling breath, with which he stilled the waters of the Winter Gulf for a time. The torrent froze and the people of the two Houses were able to*

*cross over. At times the waters thawed and they
were divided of people and purpose, but at times
they were united and the Winter Gulf served as
a union between Eldanesh and Ulthanesh, as
well as a barrier.*

THE ATTACK ON the haugri-alim was only the first of
several raids by the *Fae Taeruth*. After exchanging
their spoils for more supplies at Khai-dazaar, Maensith took the ship out to a stretch of star systems
along the arm of a nebula known as the Winter Gulf.
Some of these engagements were won from afar,
as had been the case with the haugri-alim, but on
two occasions Aradryan was amongst the boarding
crew. With each encounter his confidence grew; the
humans who provided such easy pickings were slow
and clumsy, with weapons as crude as their wield-
ers. After the sheer terror of his daemonic encounter,
Aradryan viewed these combats as little more than a
chance to practise his marksmanship and swordcraft.

Even though the challenge posed by these untrained
adversaries was slim, the hack-and-slash of mortal
combat was still exhilarating. Aradryan grew accustomed to the excitement of coming conflict as the *Fae
Taeruth* would close in on her crippled prey, boarding boats sent screaming across the void to swiftly
finish any survivors from the precision strikes of the
weapon batteries. After each raid, he would return
to the ship and the welcoming embrace of Maensith, temporarily sated but soon expectant of further
excitement.

His favoured position with Maensith did not earn
him many friends amongst the ship's officers, all of

whom had served on the *Fae Taeruth* for a considerable time. Although bound together in battle, the company of the corsair vessel were not averse to veiled insults and threats; a very different atmosphere than aboard *Lacontiran* and *Irdiris*. Knowing that he could not rely upon the capricious whim of Maensith to protect him against all harm, Aradryan gathered about him a complement of self-interested eldar, freely lavishing his own share of the spoils upon them to guarantee their loyalty. Amongst the regular mercenaries such generosity was welcomed, and when others amongst the officers saw his popularity they wisely chose to align themselves with the up-and-coming corsair. Aradryan had never been one to bear grudges or ill wish and found it easy to accept such allegiances, his magnanimous attitude earning yet further influence. Such precautions meant that he had yet to be forced to bare a blade against a rival, and long he hoped that situation would prevail; he could face a party of humans without qualm but there were some amongst the *Fae Taeruth*'s crew who far surpassed Aradryan in swordsense and fighting experience.

The successes enjoyed by the corsairs quickly healed any divisions, and Maensith was keen to have a lieutenant like Aradryan. A Commorraghan by birth, she was feared and respected by her crew but rarely liked, despite her easy-going disposition towards them. Aided by Aradryan's quick wit, she was able to keep her fractious underlings from falling out too often and it was agreed across the company that they could expect fine and profitable times ahead.

Such was the optimism aboard the *Fae Taeruth* as

they headed for another foray into human space. The webway gave the eldar the advantage over their foes; humans were forced to traverse the astronomical distances between stars using the perilous, untamed warp. Only able to travel a relatively few light years at a time, hopping from system to system, the human merchants who plied their trade along the rim of the Winter Gulf were easily found and run down.

Moving through the webway in preparation for a convoy raid into a system known as Naimh-neilith, the *Fae Taeruth* came upon an extraordinary gathering of ships. Summoned to the observation gallery, Arad-ryan met Maensith. Several holo-displays showed a vast interspace at the confluence of two arterial webway tunnels, and in that juncture a fleet was assembling.

Aradryan counted eight other ships, three as large as the *Fae Taeruth*, the others being smaller frigate- and destroyer-sized vessels. Two of the other cruisers, menacingly black and midnight blue, clearly bore the markings of Commorragh, which Maensith quickly identified as coming from the same kabal – the Ascendant Spear. The rest were displaying a variety of bold and colourful patterns, tiger-striped and mottled with blues and whites and oranges. The matrix of the webway was thrumming with communication, and the *Fae Taeruth* was hailed as soon as she appeared.

One of the holo-images changed at Maensith's command, switching from a view of the largest cor-sair ship to show a tall eldar dressed in a long coat of shimmering gold over a bodysuit of purple and white. His hair was raven-black, styled in a high crest that cascaded past his shoulders. There was a scar on his upper lip that twisted his mouth into what resembled a permanent sneer, an expression that was matched by the look in his eyes.

'It seems we have an uninvited guest,' said the eldar. 'Perhaps you catch the scent of the scraps we will leave you.'

'I am Maensith of the *Fae Taeruth*.' The captain kept her calm despite the insult. 'Please do me the courtesy of naming yourself.'

'Saidar Yrithain, Prince-Commander of the Azure Flame,' said the other with a mocking bow. 'My ship is the *Sathaisun*. I am sure you have heard of me.'

'I have now,' said Maensith. 'I have raided the Winter Gulf for a dozen passes, but I do not recall the fleet of the Azure Flame.'

Before Yrithain could retort, another holo-figure shimmered into existence. The armour-clad figure immediately put Aradryan in mind of Maensith in her full battledress; he wore black, bladed plates over golden mesh, segmented gauntlets sheathing long-fingered hands. The newcomer's face was gaunt and pale, his eyes dark and piercing, and his head was bald except for a white scalplock threaded with silver skull-shaped beads.

'Maensith of the Crimson Talon is known to me,' said the Commorraghan.

'And Khiadysis, Hierarch of the Ascendant Spear needs no introduction to me,' replied Maensith, touching the fingertips of her right hand to her left shoulder with a quick nod of the head. Though the captain kept a passive face and calmly clasped her hands behind her back, Aradryan sensed a sudden nervousness in the mannerisms of his lover. 'It has been a long time since I laid claim to any membership of the Crimson Talon.'

'Your self-exile is a matter of little remark any more,' said Khiadysis. 'You were one of the most promising dracons, but memories can be cruelly short in Commorragh.'

'Success in the kabals breeds its own kind of peril, hierarch. I did not expect to meet with such a lord of Commorragh so far from the Dark City. I hope that it is good fortune, as it would be a great inconvenience to locate new raiding territories.'

Khiadysis laughed, short and sharp, and waved a benevolent hand in Maensith's direction.

'I understand your worry. It would not serve any purpose to disclose our meeting to your former kabalites, so harbour no concerns on that account. Your present location shall remain unspoken to those in the Crimson Talon who might desire to know it.'

'You have my thanks.' Maensith nodded again, though she did not relax.

'Perhaps the two of you could reminisce at your pleasure when we have concluded our purpose here,' cut in Yrithain. His holo-image turned towards Maensith. 'Your timing is unfortunate, and if you sought to conduct some action at Naimh-neilith you must re-evaluate your plans.'

'Nonsense, Yrithain,' said Khiadysis. 'Another ship of the *Fae Taeruth*'s size, which I am sure is more than ably commanded by Maensith, would be a notable addition to our firepower.'

Yrithain glowered at the kabalite but did not argue. Aradryan watched the exchange in silence, unsure of the comparative authority and agendas of the two commanders. At a guess, he thought that Khiadysis held the upper hand in the conversation, though his ships were outnumbered by the corsairs. The arrival of the *Fae Taeruth* may have altered the power balance in the ad-hoc fleet, and they would do well to keep both Yrithain and Khiadysis happy.

'If that is to be the case, we must adapt our strategy,' said the prince-commander. 'Maensith, please ready your ship for communion with the *Sathaisun* and we shall be able to locate a role for you and your vessel.'

'Of course, Yrithain. And what is the purpose of this gathering? Is there a convoy en route?'

'Nothing so dull,' said Khiadysis. 'I have not come all of this way for a few ships. We will be raiding Naimh-neilith itself.'

'Attacking the planet?' said Aradryan, his surprise getting the better of him. His outburst was not seen by the others – his form was not part of the holo-projection from the *Fae Taeruth* – but he earned himself a scowl from Maensith. The captain turned back to the others with a sly smile.

'It is good fortune indeed that brings us here at this time,' she said. 'I shall begin the communion shortly.'

With nods of parting, the images of the other two commanders flickered into nothing. Maensith looked at Aradryan, her displeasure dissipating.

'You, my lover, are about to experience the greatest thrill this life can offer,' she said.

LASER FIRE STROBED across the ether, ripping livid wounds of flame and debris across the armour of the human's orbital station. Missiles flared from the battlestation's defence turrets, sweeping past the voidcutter piloted by Aradryan, targeted at the larger eldar ships behind the flotilla of boarding craft. Aradryan did his best to focus on the controls of the small single-sailed vessel, but it was impossible to totally ignore the mayhem that was going on around the boarding parties.

The wreckage of system defence ships drifted across his view, billowing gas and fire as they were drawn into the gravity well of the planet below. The shimmering shape of an eldar frigate enclosed by holofields stole around the periphery of the battle, its laser batteries intercepting a swarm of bombers launching from a dock set high in the battlestation's superstructure. The tracery of laser fire and blossoms of explosion lit the huge orbiting platform, highlighting the cave-like opening that was the pirates' point of attack.

The station looked like an inverted, four-storeyed ziggurat in general shape, with a single command tower extending far beneath its shadowed bulk, navigation lights and sensor arrays jutting from the shaft of the control spire. Stubby defence emplacements dotted its surface and the space around it shimmered red with powerfields overloading as the fire of the eldar fleet converged on the platform.

Shockwaves of energy rippled past the voidcutter, but Aradryan dealt with each successive buffering with practised control, riding through the expanding clouds of radiation and glittering particles.

Maensith had been right: this was one of the most beautiful and terrifying acts Aradryan had performed. The interplay of the fleet, the web of laser fire lancing from turrets and gun decks, created mesmerising patterns against the dark circle of the world, with the station a glittering ruby at their centre. As when he had been at Hirith-Hreslain and the raid on the haugri-alim, Aradryan felt detachment, and had the time and space to admire and be awed by the spectacle of war. Yet there was also the danger of the encounter with the orks and the flight from the daemonettes, for there was genuine peril as laser beams seared across the cockpit display and missiles as large as the void-cutter powered past. And at the end was the promise of the close-fighting that Aradryan found so thrilling.

The *Fae Taeruth* had been added to the part of the fleet tasked with silencing the battlestation, so that the Commorraghans and Yrithain's cruiser could close to low orbit and launch their raid on the planet itself. The orbital platform was more than a tactical objective; it housed weapons magazines and extensive storage holds full of potential plunder. Yrithain had assured Maensith that he already had a party interested in the acquisition of these items, and delivery of the guns, ammunition and food packs would ensure the *Fae Taeruth*'s crew would share in their allotment of the spoils.

Along with a dozen other voidcutters and star-runners, Aradryan's craft arrowed through the emerging streams of laser fire. As the range to the battlestation closed, shell-firing cannons opened up, their high-explosive rounds filling the vacuum with spinning shrapnel. Their holofields as effective against the crude human sensors as they were the naked eye, the assault boats sped through the furious defensive fire, trusting to speed to keep them ahead of the enemy's targeting matrices.

The opening that Aradryan was aiming for grew larger and larger on the display. With enough power in the voidcutter's engines to continue the mission, Aradryan furled the stellar sail and outriggers as the flotilla passed beyond the minimum range of the defence turrets. White light blazed from the open bay, from which a squadron of fighters had launched at the first sign of attack. Those craft had been dealt with by the initial eldar wave of Nightwing fighters, and the way was clear for the boarding parties to land.

Guiding the voidcutter on a curving path beneath the upper levels of the platform, Aradryan steered towards the bay opening. As the craft plunged into the bright docking lights within, the landing area could be clearly seen. Several dozen humans were in the bay, dressed in white trousers and long blue coats. They wore no helmets, their shaven heads glinting in the glare of the lights, but they had rebreather masks on, connected by ribbed piping to air tanks on their backs. Aradryan's second-in-command on the mission, Taelisieth, activated the twin bright-lances mounted in the nose of the voidcutter. From the other attack boats spewed more laser fire, joined by the flare of blue plasma stars. The combined fire scythed through the waiting humans as the station's defenders opened fire with their lasguns and crude automatic rifles. Miniature warp vortexes, no wider than Aradryan's outstretched arms, appeared in the midst of the humans; the distort cannons on two of the raiders had been activated. The defenders caught in the grip of these pocket warp gates were pulled apart by the crashing forces, some sucked directly into the warp. Aradryan had no time to contemplate the hideous fate of those unfortunate enough to survive the transition into warp space; their torment would not last long.

Braking heavily, brightlances still spitting beams of blue energy across the dock, Aradryan brought the voidcutter to a sharp stop, dropping to the bay floor. Even as the craft settled down, the main door was opening and he was rising from his seat. He snatched his sword from the console and clipped the scabbard to his belt as he hurried down the voidcutter's central passageway.

Emerging into the landing bay, nose and mouth covered with a lightweight breathing mask, Aradryan found that there were no survivors of the assault boats' barrage of fire. To his right, several corsairs were guiding an anti-grav dais down the ramp of their star-runner, another distort cannon mounted on the floating platform. Other groups were heading to secure the entry routes into the bay – two of them – ensuring that the humans could not counter-attack.

Under Aradryan's direction, the distort cannon was steered across the bay and aimed towards the wall to the left. The weapon opened fire at the wall, its metal and rock-like substance engulfed by a whirling sphere of flickering energy. The small portal collapsed after a few moments, leaving a perfect circle burrowed through the thick bulkhead, leading into an access corridor not directly connected to the launch bay.

Aradryan drew his sword and pistol and waved for his team of forty warriors to move through the newly created opening, the d-cannon gliding under the control of its gunners. With a last glance to assure himself that the rearguard were set to defend the voidcutters and star-runners, Aradryan stepped through the bulkhead, calling for his raiders to head to the right.

On the last leg through the webway Aradryan had memorised the internal layout of the station – he had not asked how Yrithain had come by such information – and knew the allotted roles of the corsairs aboard his vessel and the others to the finest detail. Surprise and timing were key if they were to be successful; the larger ships would be making their run to orbit at a precise time and the battlestation's main weapons had to be rendered ineffective by then or the whole raid would have to be abandoned. Knowing that Yrithain's patience had already been tested by the *Fae Taeruth*'s arrival, and that the favour of Khiadysis would be fickle, Aradryan had no doubts regarding the price of failure.

PLOTTING A ROUTE through the station's interior, Aradryan was struck by the inelegance and artificiality that formed the basis of the humans' sense of space and architecture. There was nothing of nature in the design, no flow or grace to the simple grid layout; it was purely functional. The doorways and arches passed by the corsairs were broad and low, often marked with red and yellow stripes to denote hazards, indecipherable stencilled lettering on the walls beside them.

Using the d-cannon, Aradryan and his party were able to bypass the worst chokepoints and defensive bottlenecks, moving from one line of attack to another in a few heartbeats, so that the humans were easily outflanked and cut down. The masked soldiers would form a line ahead of the advancing eldar, ready to defend a junction or crossing. Aradryan would have a handful of his warriors engage the humans from the front for long enough for him to devise another route of advance. Sometimes the eldar would simply disengage from the defenders, having slipped into a secondary access tunnel, or dropped or climbed up a level. Most of the times, though, Aradryan led his corsairs on the attack, striking the defenders from the side or rear while their attention was drawn by those left behind.

The humans' communications systems and command structure seemed woefully inadequate in the face of such a threat. Aradryan was surprised by the continued success of this tactic, as he slashed his sword across the throat of a human officer defending a stairwell that led to the innermost decks of the battlestation. Ducking beneath a pistol swung as a club, Aradryan kicked out at his attacker's knee, sending the man sprawling to the floor. The gleaming edge of Aradryan's blade bit into the side of the human's head, stilling his resistance.

Firing a flurry of shurikens from his pistol into the throat of another foe, Aradryan stepped over the corpses of the fallen and glanced down the stairwell. There appeared to be no defenders on the level below, but he was not about to take any chances.

As the last of the humans died, a gurgling rasp emerging from his shuriken-ripped throat, Aradryan parted his company with gestures from his sword. The d-cannon crew understood his intent, and pointed their machine at the landing at the top of the stairs.

Aradryan's skin crawled and his hair rose up with

static energy as the distort cannon opened fire, punching a hole between reality and the warp. Part of the landing collapsed, sending a slide of broken masonry and twisted metal reinforcing rods plummeting down into the floor below. There were a few cries of shock and pain amongst the rumble of the tumbling landing.

Leaping down into the hole with his followers close behind, Aradryan landed on top of another human, who had been crawling across a tipped slab of flooring. Losing his footing, Aradryan rolled to one side, his pistol spitting discs that shredded the fallen man's jerkin, droplets of blood spraying through the cloud of dust that surrounded Aradryan. In the gloom, Aradryan saw shapes moving – too slow and cumbersome to be his companions. He slashed at the disorientated soldiers with his sword, cutting down three enemies in quick succession.

As the dust cloud dispersed, the corsairs came leaping through the hole and Aradryan regained his bearings. The d-cannon floated down last, its gunners standing on the anti-grav platform. Aradryan double-checked their current position against his mental map, fixing the junction ahead in relation to the image in his mind. A left turn would bring them to where they needed to be.

Suited men came running around the corner ahead, no doubt responding to the noise of the collapsing stairwell. They were taken unawares as Aradryan and the rest of the corsairs opened fire, sending out a hail of shurikens and las-bolts. Sword held ready, Aradryan sprinted to the junction with Taelisieth at his shoulder. The passages to the left and right were clear for the moment, so Aradryan sent his lieutenant to the end of the corridor on the left, to secure the distant archway with a handful of corsairs. Turning his attention to the right, Aradryan sent another party to the far end of the passageway, where an armoured door had descended across the hall; he did not know whether the door could be raised again and it was best to assume the worst.

The walls and floor gently vibrated, set to a faint tremor by hidden power cabling. The passage and its surrounds were atop the power plant of the station: a crude plasma chamber that held an artificial star in check with magnetic fields and ceramic walls. The thrum that resonated around Aradryan was a lifeless, mechanical vibration, with none of the potency of an infinity circuit or world spirit. It was purely electrical energy, converted from the plasma reactor and sent along metal wires to distant gun posts and laser arrays. As basic as the system was, the electromagnetic flux created by the plasma chamber was enough to distort the scanners of the eldar warships, making its exact location impossible to fix.

This was where Aradryan and his team came into the plan. Bringing forth a trio of beacons similar to those the rangers used at Hirith-Hreslain, the corsairs looked to Aradryan for guidance on their placement. He paced out the required distance along the corridor and, as he had expected, there was a door to his left, hung on hinges that creaked a little as he pushed open the rudimentary portal.

'One in there,' Aradryan told one of the beacon-holders, nodding towards the doorway. 'Another at the sealed archway ahead. Bring the third.'

A little further from the junction was a small access panel. It came off to Aradryan's prising fingers easily enough, revealing a circular cableway just about wide enough for an eldar to crawl into. Aradryan crouched and looked into the hole. There was a metal band holding a cluster of cables in place at roughly the right place, and he pointed out this feature to the corsair with the beacon. There was no need to be absolutely precise; Yrithain's instructions had left some margin for error.

Ushering his companions back to the junction, Aradryan heard a commotion from the direction of Taelisieth and he saw fighting had broken out at the far end of the corridor. He sent reinforcements to his second-in-command as red las-blasts seared the walls around the eldar, two of the corsairs falling back from the passage junction with cries of pain. It seemed the humans were aware of the corsairs' location and were about to launch a concerted assault. The enemy could not have any idea what the eldar planned – Aradryan had been astounded and amused by the suggestion – but the timing of the counter-attack was inconvenient.

Activating the beacons remotely, all Aradryan could do next was wait and hope that Maensith had been able to manoeuvre the *Fae Taeruth* into position. Like the group that had delved into the heart of the battle-station, the corsair's leader had been put into the risky but pivotal lead position of the second wave. She would have to rely on skill and speed to outpace the fully operational cannons of the orbital platform.

Once in position, and this was the ingenuity of Yrithain's plan, Maensith would activate the cruiser's webway portal, burrowing a tubular breach through realspace to create a temporary extension of the webway. Normally such a thing would have no impact on the material universe and would pass unnoticed through solid matter. With a small modification in the webway's flux, and the target of the beacons, the web passage could be used to isolate the station's plasma generator. If Aradryan had tried a conventional attack against the plasma reactor – assuming he and his companions had been able to fight their way through the massed layers of security blockades and hundreds of soldiers, and been able to penetrate the thick walls surrounding it with something like a distort cannon – any breach of the chamber would have resulted in a catastrophic feedback and meltdown event.

As if coming to a cue on a script, a shimmering wall bisected the tunnel behind Aradryan; streaming, half-seen energy cascaded at a slight diagonal to the angle of the walls. He knew from vast experience that he was looking at a webway manifestation, though the speed of its pulsing and partially temporal nature were new to him. Almost immediately, the webway tunnel appeared and raucous klaxons sounded along the passage, deafeningly loud.

Everything plunged into blackness, and all went still and silent.

Somewhere in the plane between realspace and the warp, a star blossomed into life and died in a heartbeat as the breached plasma chamber ran riot for an instant before being snuffed out by the impossible physics of the webway.

Aradryan stood absolutely still, knowing that in the

moment that the plasma generator had been spirited into the alternate dimension, all of the major systems of the platform would have crashed. Along with the all-important weapons systems, environmental controls would be compromised too. Soon the air would be growing staler and the temperature was already slowly dropping, gradually being leeched out through the structure of the battlestation. Artificial gravity had ceased, hence Aradryan's immobility for the moment, and all lights had been extinguished.

The battlestation, to all intents and purposes, was dead.

The sudden loss of power had interrupted the fighting between Taelisieth and the humans, neither side sure of what to do next. Aradryan blinked three times in rapid succession, activating the artificial lenses over his eyes. They were not as powerful as a proper visor, but there was enough reflected heat from the eldar and the cables within the walls to create a fuzzy image of Aradryan's surrounds, while his fellow corsairs stood out like yellow silhouettes.

Kicking lightly off the floor, Aradryan did a slow cartwheel until his feet touched the ceiling. Rebounding towards the floor, he twisted again, splaying his arms to slow his descent. Touching down lightly, he stepped again, and in this way he made safe progress along the passageway towards Taelisieth.

The silence had not lasted more than few heartbeats before the shouted panic and the curt snarl of commands echoed along the corridor. Taelisieth reacted swiftly, leading his warriors against the humans in the darkness, making the most of their fear and confusion. Like ghosts, the bright images of the eldar pirates floated out of sight around the corner.

'Onwards, the enemy will be converging,' Aradryan told his warriors, pointing after Taelisieth. Turning to plant a foot on a wall, Aradryan pushed himself around the junction.

Ahead, the flash of laspistols and the whirr of shurikens punctuated the fight between eldar and human. Propelling himself down the corridor as fast as he could, Aradryan reached Taelisieth and the others as a sprawling melee broke out. Using his momentum, blade held out in front of him like a lance, Aradryan threw himself into the humans. The tip of his sword scored across the neck of a man struggling to gain his footing, the strap of his rifle tangling his arms. Blood jetted slowly from the wound, painting Aradryan's arm red as his mass carried him past the dying soldier.

Twisting to avoid a swinging rifle aimed at his head, Aradryan found himself spinning out of control towards the floor. He punched down and turned, correcting his fall. Pulling up his knees, he was able to get his feet under himself and push up, leaping over the human who was pulling back his rifle for another swing. Aradryan lashed out with his sword, severing the man's wrist. As the human fell back, pain wracking his features, Aradryan stretched out a leg, catching the wall with enough force to spin him towards the ceiling feet-first. Landing cat-like on the tiles above the two sides, Aradryan looked down on the unfolding fight.

The humans were utterly unable to deal with the change in conditions; they could not react quickly enough to prevent themselves colliding with walls, floor or ceiling, nor were they supple or dextrous enough to use their weapons whilst in mid-air. The eldar were like a flock of predatory birds, moving though their enemies with pistols and blades, shooting and cutting at leisure while their victims flailed helplessly in response. The cries of the wounded and dying humans formed a bass foundation to the light and lilting laughter of their superiors.

Aradryan spied a human trying to get away, using the lip of a ventilation cover for purchase as he pulled himself along the wall. With a turn and a kick, Aradryan somersaulted down to the floor just ahead of the fleeing soldier. The eldar drove his sword point between the shoulder blades of the human, the force of the blow sending Aradryan back to the ceiling once more. Using light fittings as hand- and footholds, Aradryan sped along the ceiling to the next junction. Checking to the left and right, he assured himself there were no further reinforcements coming for the moment.

Glancing back, he saw Taelisieth and his party binding a number of humans with gossamer-like fibres, made more difficult because their prisoner's struggles caused human and eldar alike to spin through the air.

'What are you doing?' Aradryan demanded, somersaulting back down the corridor to confront the lieutenant.

'Maensith's command,' replied Taelisieth. There was a hint of humour in his voice. 'Did you not hear?'

'I did not,' said Aradryan. 'They will only slow us down. We have to get to the weapons lockers as quickly as possible.'

'No need to worry about carrying all of that bulky stuff, when you can plunder something that moves under its own power,' said Taelisieth. He placed a foot against the wall to brace himself as he hauled a bound human to his feet and pushed the man down the corridor. The human wiggled helplessly as he floated along the passageway. Taelisieth took a step after, but was stopped by Aradryan's hand on his arm, causing the two of them to begin to slowly turn head over heels.

'And what use are prisoners going to be when it comes to getting our share of the spoils? You heard Yrithain the same as I did. He has already arranged payment for the stores of the battlestation. What is Maensith's game?'

'You should ask her,' said Taelisieth, his shrug causing him to turn away from Aradryan. 'I thought you were the one she confided in. You are her favourite, after all.'

Aradryan said nothing, pushing himself away from his second. If Maensith had a plan, it was better to keep to it than cause further delay and disruption. The battlestation had no secondary systems of any import – why would it when normally the loss of its reactor would also be the cause of its destruction – but the corsairs were still outnumbered by several thousand humans. It was clear the way back to the ships would not be easy, even though the loss of light and gravity no doubt favoured the raiders.

'So be it, we shall see what we can do,' said Aradryan. He lifted a finger to the communicator stud in the lobe of his ear. 'For those who have not yet been informed, we will be taking prisoners if possible. Do not risk your lives for them, but if you can take any enemies alive, then do so. There will be no attack on the upper storage levels; we head back as a group to the landing craft.'

As the party set off once more, half a dozen captured humans in tow, Aradryan considered Maensith's instruction, and wondered why she had not chosen to share her orders, or her rationale, with him. There was only one reason Aradryan could think of for Maensith to refuse Yrithain's wishes, only one group of people that were interested in live prisoners: the Commorraghans.

THE CORSAIRS HAD a running battle back to their landing craft, and though they lost nearly a quarter of their number, Aradryan and his company managed to capture several scores of humans for whatever bargain Maensith had struck with the Commorraghans. In the zero gravity and darkness, such encounters were harsh, brief affairs of flashing laser and shuriken volleys, sweeping swords against bayonets, power mauls and knives. The eldar brought their dead with them, taking their spirit stones into safekeeping before forcing the captives to pull the lifeless remains.

Corridor by corridor, hallway by hallway, Aradryan guided his warriors back to the ships. The d-cannon had been destroyed, its anti-grav platform rendered inoperative after the loss of the station's artificial gravity field; Aradryan would not leave such technology to be studied by the humans and so the workings of the cannon had been melted with a fusion charge.

Without the means to create their own shortcuts and doorways, the corsairs were harder pressed to outmanoeuvre the human soldiers, who had managed to recover some of the organisation and structure they had lost following the destruction of the power network. Even so, they were poorly equipped to deal with the conditions, and though the losses of the corsairs were growing in number, they did not encounter irresistible odds.

Approaching the docking area where the void-cutters and star-runners were located, Aradryan signalled the parties he had left defending the ships. As he expected, they had faced fierce counter-attacks and had been forced to withdraw to the craft, using the ship's weapons to destroy the occasional forays from the human forces. They reported that no attack had been made since the plasma chamber's destruction, but the ships' sensors detected large bodies of troops guarding the approaches to the landing bay, waiting for the pirates to return to their vessels.

It was a tricky situation, but one that Maensith and Aradryan had considered. After receiving as much information as was available concerning the positions of the humans, Aradryan devised a plan of attack. It was not necessary to destroy all of the defenders; the corsairs merely had to punch a hole through the cordon and withdraw under the cover of their vessel's guns. As with their initial response to attack, the humans displayed a short-sightedness in their deployment, and gave no consideration to the possibility that their attackers might choose not to follow the routes already dictated by the architecture of the station.

Sending a group of a dozen corsairs to scout the path ahead, Aradryan contacted the warriors on the ships. Since the removal of the plasma core, the pirates had been circling back to the dock from the opposite direction to their departure. This put them in an ideal position to make a last run for sanctuary, with only one guard outpost in their path. Aradryan called on the ships' crews to target their weapons at two particular points in the wall to their right, on the other side of the bay from the hole created by the d-cannon. The first was the rear wall of a defensive emplacement guarding an access conduit; the second was a junction with that conduit.

When the scouting party returned to report that there were no enemy between the pirates and the junction, Aradryan gave the order to his warriors. Setting off at speed, pushing and dragging lines of bound humans tied together with hair-thin polymer strands, Aradryan and the corsairs made their final dash.

On coming within sight of the junction, Aradryan told the ships' crews to open fire. A combination of brightlances, scatter lasers and d-cannon blasts smashed into the dividing bulkhead, ripping a new opening through the wall. The way was not yet clear, however, and as the pirates reached the smoke-filled juncture of corridors, heavy las-fire erupted from the manned posts to their right. Chunks of debris glided along the corridor away from the previous fusillade, but not enough to provide significant cover against the lascannons and lasguns of the defenders.

As Aradryan had hoped, the humans were too cautious and had drawn their men into an embrasure overlooking the passageway. Gun slits and murder holes pierced the walls, and anyone trying to make it across to the breach in the bulkhead would be cut down in moments.

'Fire again, second position,' said Aradryan, peeking a look around the corner of the junction. His infrareceptor lenses picked out the body heat of several dozen humans clustered in the bunker-like rooms either side of the corridor. A moment later he saw the clashing, ravening sphere of a d-cannon detonation tearing out a portion of the bulkhead, sucking half a dozen defenders into the maw of its warp vortex. Through the newly-created gap erupted a storm of fire from the other ships' guns, and in that first moment of anarchy, as humans were cut down by the searing lances of laser and hails of shuriken cannon fire, Aradryan signalled for his warriors to make the run across to the blasted hole in the bulkhead.

A few humans were competent enough to snap off las-shots from their fortification, but their aim was poor and Aradryan made it across to the opening without so much as risking a near-miss. He ducked into the landing bay through the gouge in the wall, to see that some of the other pirates had emerged from the ships, lasrifles and shuriken catapults ready to cut down any defenders entering the dock; thread-like tethers held them to the ships in the zero gravity.

Not waiting to see how the others fared, Aradryan backed up against the wall and then kicked himself forwards, sailing through the air towards his void-cutter. The air coming through his rebreather mask was already beginning to taste stale and he knew that the atmospheric quality was dropping rapidly. For a moment he considered the possibility that the human prisoners were the lucky few; their comrades would suffocate to death in the following hours, with perhaps only a few fortunate commanders and upper echelon officers having access to emergency air supplies. Aradryan soon dismissed the notion, knowing that even a lingering, dreadful death by asphyxiation was probably better than whatever fate the prisoners faced at the hands of the Commorraghans.

Aradryan had misjudged his course slightly and was forced to reach out to grasp the hand of a pirate standing at the top of the voidcutter's boarding ramp. Grabbing the other eldar's wrist, Aradryan pulled himself down into the opening. As soon as he was within the grip of the vessel's smaller artificial field, weight returned, catching him by surprise. He managed to land on his feet, but his awkward fall jarred his sword from his grip, which clattered to the deck, accompanied by a laugh from the pirate on the gangway. Ignoring his embarrassment and retrieving his weapon, Aradryan picked his way to the piloting chamber and made ready to take off as the other crews soared across the landing bay, trailing lines of prisoners like squirming serpent tails.

When Aradryan received word that all were aboard the voidcutter, he sealed the doorway and guided the craft into the air. Just as with their arrival, humans were heading into the dock, bringing with them heavy weapons that spat missiles and laser pulses after the departing pirates. Under Aradryan's deft fingers, the voidcutter jinked to the left and right, making itself an impossible target as the stellar sail unfurled and the holofield shimmered.

Passing out of the docking bay, Aradryan turned the viewsphere to the rear, so that he could see the

*Fae Taeruth* and other ships converging on the planet below. They had already attained low orbit, pulses of laser fire spewing from their lance turrets towards the surface. A cloud of tiny stars was pouring from the Commorraghan warships: fleets of attack craft plunging into the atmosphere of the world intent on loot and prisoners.

Aradryan turned the voidcutter out-system, trimming the sail to catch what he could of the stellar winds, recharging the engines of the ship. Behind him the dark shape of the battlestation was silhouetted against the star's light creeping around the edge of the world, hanging lifeless in the void.

As with his previous encounters and fights, Aradryan felt enormous relief and satisfaction. The audacity of the attack, the cunning and ruthlessness employed in its execution, was stronger than any drug or dream he could remember. Even the revelation of Maensith's double-cross of Yrithain partway through and the rapid change of plans only added to the drama after the event. Laughing, Aradryan leaned back in his chair and closed his eyes, reliving the moments of near-death, the clash of sword on rifle and the flicker of las-fire across his vision. There would be a time when Morai-heg would cut his thread and seal his fate, but that time had not yet come and while he lived, Aradryan was determined to enjoy everything his life offered him.

A RUDDY LIGHT suffused the landing bay, bathing the voidcutter with scarlet. Stepping down the craft's ramp, Aradryan felt like he was striding into permanent twilight. He and Maensith were aboard

Khiadysis's flagship to attend a captains' council convened at the insistence of the Commorraghan hierarch; Khiadysis had refused to conduct the meeting by holo-communication but had not mentioned the nature of the discussion he desired.

Since the raid on the battlestation, the *Fae Taeruth* had joined forces with the corsairs of the Azure Flame and the Commorraghans of Hierarch Khiadysis for three more attacks. Each had gone well enough, but it became increasingly obvious with each raid that the target of the attacks were not the ships but their crews, and after each attack the Commorraghans took their share in aliens and left the corsairs to squabble over the meagre remains of the spoils. Maensith's support of Khiadysis had firmly swung the balance of power within the fleet towards the Commorraghans, and though he did not express his nervousness to his captain, Aradryan believed this to be a mistake. As untrustworthy and arrogant as Yrithain was, he was still born of the craftworlds. The Commorraghans were not just outcasts, they were barbaric and savage, and allying himself to their cause, even through the proxy of Maensith, made Aradryan shudder more than once.

For all that, Maensith had been able to manage her relationships with both Khiadysis and Yrithain to the advantage of the *Fae Taeruth* and Aradryan knew that now was not the time to withdraw from the pirate fleet to set out alone again – Khiadysis had made it clear he expected Maensith's support for some time to come. Less clear, but suspected by Aradryan, was an underlying threat; any attempt by Maensith to turn on Khiadysis or otherwise leave would result in her former kabal swiftly learning her whereabouts. Though the pirate captain never spoke to Aradryan of those times, it was painfully clear that she had fled Commorragh in less-than-ideal circumstances and had hidden away for good reason,

Aradryan hoped that the coming meeting would reveal the hierarch's greater intent – for it was obvious that he had one, and the raids they had been conducting were building up to another large expedition. With that completed, Aradryan hoped to persuade Maensith to leave the fleet and forge a lone fate; he was tired of answering to the whims of a soulless predator even if the cost was the risk of retribution from the past, and the thought of becoming one of Yrithain's followers threatened to be just as bad.

'Why does it have to be so dark?' asked Aradryan. Six armed Commorraghans fell in behind the pair as they left the voidcutter, saying nothing. Ahead, a door hissed open and a robed, bald-headed eldar appeared. He bowed and beckoned for Maensith and Aradryan to approach.

'This is captured light from the tame star at the heart of Commorragh,' said Maensith. She walked with long, nonchalant strides, but like Aradryan she was armed with pistol and sword at her waist and her eyes were constantly moving, alert to all around her. In the glow, her skin was tinged with red, her eyes glittering with the same. 'It is not called the Dark City simply because of its inhabitants' lifestyles.'

'Dracon Maensith,' said the dark eldar at the door, bowing again, his expression slightly leering as he regarded the shapely captain. 'I must ask that you submit your weapons to me.'

'Never,' snapped Maensith. 'Step away from me, casket-born. Convey me to Khiadysis Hierarch immediately. And I am no longer dracon, you can dispense with the flattery.'

Cowed, the attendant nodded and headed out of the door. Following, their escort a few steps behind, Aradryan and Maensith were led to an elevating chamber. During the short walk, Aradryan noticed that there was something other than the lighting that lent a mood of oppressiveness to the atmosphere. On Alaitoc or a ship, he was used to the ever-present warmth and energy of the infinity circuit. Even at Hirith-Hreslain there had been the unconscious touch of the world spirit. On the Commorraghan ship there was nothing. A glance at their guide and the warriors behind reaffirmed Aradryan's initial observation that none of them were wearing waystones.

Apart from the coldness emanating from the lack of a psychic network, there was another sensation that dragged at Aradryan's spirit as the group boarded the ascending chamber, which rose soundlessly up through the levels of the ship. The Commorraghans deliberately cultivated an air of malice about them. There was an undercurrent of misery, which lingered on the edge of perception like a half-heard scream of torment. The whole ship was steeped in torture and agony, and its stench dripped like oily sweat from the dark eldar around Aradryan. He felt unclean just standing this close to them. Their presence tainted the air and he wanted to choke, suddenly able to taste pain and depravity in his mouth, cloying in his throat and filling his lungs.

He felt a movement close to him and relaxed,

feeling Maensith's hand brush against his for the briefest moment.

There was none of the depraved filth about her, though once she had been hailed as a leader amongst the Commorraghans. Aradryan harboured no illusions about his lover's past; she had undoubtedly committed acts of evil and taken part in perverse rites that would turn the stomach of any sane eldar. Yet now, as Aradryan considered her amongst her former kin, he realised that she was no longer one of them. She had spoken the truth when she had claimed to have left behind the double-dealing and predatory behaviour of her birthplace. Even though she would ever be a pirate and a mercenary, she had somehow managed to cleanse the taint of her history.

Without a sound, the conveyance slid to a halt and the doors opened, revealing an opulently decorated and furnished hall. The Commorraghan functionary bowed and waved for Maensith to exit. Aradryan followed after her, and glanced back to see the doors closing, in a moment becoming invisible behind velvet curtains.

The escort of kabalite warriors had been left behind but Aradryan felt no more secure. On a gilded throne at the far end of the hall sat Khiadysis, and the Commorraghan lord was flanked by a dozen white-helmed warriors with lyrate horns twisting from their crests. Each bodyguard wielded a dual-handed blade almost as tall as an eldar and was garbed with heavy plates of dark armour painted with small Commorraghan runes. Though he had never seen them before, Aradryan guessed that these were the deadly incubi, believed by some to be the followers of the Fallen

Phoenix, Arhra, who had founded the Striking Scorpion Shrine of Aspect Warriors. To see so many of the sinister mercenaries aboard Khiadysis's ship was testament to the wealth and power of the hierarch.

The incubi were not alone in attending the kabalite commander. Sitting on a stool at his feet was a female eldar, dressed in a black robe banded with silver rings, her hands and forearms sheathed in silken gloves. Aradryan noticed the glint of partially concealed blades on fingers and within the folds of the courtesan's dress.

'Lhamaean,' said Maensith, her voice barely a breath. 'Poisoners without equal. Do not get too close. And look, in the shadows to your right. Urghuls from the depths of Commorragh.'

Aradryan glanced as directed and saw indistinct, grey-skinned shapes in the ruddy darkness between the huge rib-like columns that lined the hall's wall and ceiling. The things crouched in the shadows, turning eyeless heads in his direction as he passed.

On a long couch on a lower step in front of the Commorraghan hierarch sat Yrithain. With him were two of his captains. The self-proclaimed Prince-Commander of the Azure Flame looked less than comfortable, and he fidgeted with the collar of his blue robe with a hand heavy with rings, his wrist clasped by a silver torc. The pirate prince glanced often towards the incubi standing silent sentry around their employer.

'Come in, my guests, come in,' said Khiadysis, lifting a hand in greeting. His words emerged from hidden speakers around the hall, so that he did not have to raise his voice yet it was heard across the large chamber.

A raised path ran the length of the hall towards the throne dais, and it was along this thickly-carpeted runway that Maensith led Aradryan. To either side were deeper enclosures, some of them fitted with cushions and sheets where naked eldar were locked together in passionate contortions; others were barred and dank, and Aradryan heard whimpering and mewls from the prisoners kept within.

Stopping for a moment, he looked down into one of the cages. A round, human face stared up at him, blood matting her hair, her forehead and cheeks scarred with dozens of tiny scratches. She opened her mouth, pleading, revealing the ragged stub of a tongue shorn away. Nail-less, broken-fingered hands reached out in supplication. Despite her obvious pain, the human had dry eyes, and Aradryan remarked upon this to Maensith as they continued towards the dais.

'The haemonculi will have removed the tear ducts first,' replied Maensith, keeping her gaze on Khiadysis, her tone deliberately devoid of emotion. 'Lack of lubrication will eventually blind her, and she cannot cry.'

Ignoring the displays to either side, Maensith strode up the aisle towards the platform on which Khiadysis's throne was situated, Aradryan following close behind her, keeping his gaze ahead. As much as he did not have to look, he could not block out the sounds of pleasure and pain that surrounded him. More than just the noise, the hall seethed with passion and punishment, making Aradryan's skin crawl with its slick touch, even as Khiadysis luxuriated in it. The hierarch's eyes were half closed, his lips trembling gently with pleasure as his gaze followed the pair from the *Fae Taeruth*.

Sitting opposite Yrithain, Maensith directed a satisfied glance at the prince-commander. The look Aradryan shared with the lesser officers of the Azure Flame was not so assured. Still, Aradryan was confident that Maensith knew what she was doing, and obviously she had judged it to be in their better interests to lend support to Khiadysis rather than Yrithain.

As he seated himself, Aradryan caught a glimpse of a serpentine face staring at him from a curtained alcove behind the throne. The bright red-scaled visage disappeared almost immediately, but it had been unmistakeable. Some of the sounds issuing from the cages under the hall were definitely not eldar or human in origin, and it was with some effort that Aradryan forced himself to listen to Khiadysis.

'I am pleased with the outcome of my latest adventure,' said the hierarch. He lifted up a hand and a small, smoking dish was placed in his palm. Inhaling the fumes deeply, Khiadysis's eyes opened wide, the pupils shrinking into tiny black dots in twin pools of green. Veins darkened beneath his pale skin, sketching a pale blue web across throat and face.

'We are not so pleased,' said Yrithain, folding his arms and darting an angry glance at Maensith. 'I have made promises that will go unfulfilled.'

'Ah yes, your deal with Commander De'vaque,' said Khiadysis. The title and name was unfamiliar to Aradryan, but to his surprise they sounded human. 'I would not worry about him any more. In fact, that is why I have brought you here, to discuss an attack on Daethronin.'

'Out of the question,' said Yrithain, standing up. His officers followed suit, more uncertain than their leader. 'The deal I have brokered with Commander De'vaque is both profitable and stable. I see no need to risk antagonising the Imperial commander with a raid on his home system.'

'You have become his lackey, Yrithain,' said Khiadysis. The words were spoken in a matter-of-fact tone, devoid of malice or accusation. 'He takes half of your spoils, in return for what?'

'Without the information we were given by De'vaque, we would not have enjoyed our recent success. The safe harbour he provides at Daethronin shields us from the attention of Imperial Navy patrols, and the targets he has guided us to have been weakly protected.'

'Yes, it is all very safe, isn't it?' Khiadysis looked at Maensith. 'Safe and sound, nice and friendly. These are not concepts that are common amongst my people. We take what we want, without the permission of others. You were a hound, Yrithain, hunting the game of the humans. De'vaque feared you and has managed to leash you with these agreements and pacts. Now you hunt the prey he chooses, and you have forgotten what it was like to run free.'

Yrithain did not argue, but his face was a war of emotions as he sought to counter what the hierarch had said, but knew that there was truth to the accusation. Instead, the prince-commander turned his anger on Maensith.

'I brought you into my plans, offered you a part to play and a share of the spoils, and this is how you repay me?'

'It was Khiadysis Hierarch that brought me into the raid,' Maensith replied calmly, meeting Yrithain's accusing glare. 'I do not owe you any loyalty.'

'And so you support this half-witted scheme to attack Daethronin? You think to turn the tables on my ally?'

'I know nothing of your allies, or of Daethronin,' said Maensith. 'Khiadysis Hierarch simply asked for a tribute from me as a sign of my gratitude.'

'Tribute?' Yrithain almost spat the word, and Aradryan empathised with him. Handing over the prisoners they had taken to the hierarch was tantamount to paying their own ransom. Aradryan kept his lips tightly sealed, however, wishing to show no discord with his captain.

The argument continued, to little end, and Aradryan started to entertain different thoughts to those he had enjoyed before, namely whether he had been right to join with Maensith. For certain he had benefitted from the relationship, and the unconstrained life of a corsair suited him better than the half-duty of the rangers. Conversely, that freedom was always at the behest of another, whether that had been Maensith or Khiadysis. Ambition – insomuch as it related to the imposition of his will over others – had never been part of Aradryan's goals, and life growing up on a craftworld eradicated most desires along such lines, emphasising the qualities of cooperation over competition.

With that in mind, the freedom to do as he wished was strong in Aradryan, and that freedom could be ensured with a ship and crew to follow his will. He had been fortunate so far in finding sponsors such as Athelennil and Maensith, but if he was ultimately to take control of his own fate, Aradryan needed to literally take control too. He glanced at Yrithain and wondered if the corsair prince would be vulnerable to a newcomer taking his place. After all, it was Yrithain who had brokered the first deal with the Commorraghans, which had now gone so badly wrong for the Azure Flame.

Aradryan did not want to betray Maensith, it was not in his character to be treacherous, but perhaps some kind of joint-leadership could be arranged. He was virtually co-commander of the *Fae Taeruth* already, so it would not be so much of a leap as might be imagined.

Turning his attention back to the ongoing debate, Aradryan reminded himself to be patient and to develop his plans one step at a time. There was no point in expending too much effort or thought on Yrithain just yet – Khiadysis was the immediate concern. As he listened to the conversation, Aradryan heard that the hierarch had been able to bring Yrithain on board with a plan to attack Daethronin, wherever that was; the three pirate commanders were arguing over the exact detail of the assault.

'I think it may be useful for a neutral party to be the first to make contact,' said Aradryan, sensing an opportunity. If he could somehow get *Fae Taeruth* separated from the rest of the fleet without violence, he and Maensith could consider their options. Khiadysis turned a questioning look on Aradryan, and he suppressed a shiver at being the subject of the cold-hearted stare.

'Prince Yrithain has already had dealings with this

De'vaque person,' Aradryan continued, smiling apologetically at the commander of the Azure Flame. 'Far be it from me, being just a humble officer of the *Fae Taeruth*, to cast doubt on the character of my superiors, but it would seem unwise to me, hierarch, to allow Yrithain to approach De'vaque without monitor.'

'You think I would concoct some kind of double-deal?' Yrithain's lip trembled with anger at the proposition.

'I would no sooner let you out of my sight than turn my back on my dracons,' said Khiadysis, darting a murderous look at the prince-commander before returning his steady gaze to Aradryan. 'Why can we not travel to Daethronin together?'

'That is a perfectly sound strategy for attack,' said Aradryan, looking at the others. 'However, the longer and greater the surprise of our coming, the better it will be for all of us. The *Fae Taeruth* can act as scout and messenger, travelling to Daethronin just a few cycles before the rest of the fleet. We can bring back word of the enemy strength, if anything has changed since the Azure Flame last travelled there, and if encountered by the humans we can rightfully claim to be emissaries of Prince Yrithain. In fact, I would seek out such contact, to lure the humans into a misplaced sense of familiarity.'

'That might work,' said Khiadysis, rubbing the side of his nose with a bony finger. Yrithain caught something of Aradryan's brief look, and his eyes narrowed with suspicion for a moment. Aradryan thought that perhaps the pirate prince would say something to the hierarch, but instead Yrithain's lips twisted in a lopsided smile.

'That is a far better plan, Khiadysis Hierarch,' said Yrithain. 'The *Fae Taeruth* can arrive first and make contact with Commander De'vaque on my behalf. The humans will prepare their port facilities for the incoming cargo, making them vulnerable. I will then travel to Daethronin under the guise of bringing the commander his share of our latest spoils. The Azure Flame and the *Fae Taeruth* will be in position to attack the enemy immediately when your ships break from the webway as the third phase.'

Maensith watched the exchange impassively, eyes flicking between the prince and the hierarch before glancing at Aradryan. She licked her lips quickly, and was about to speak when Khiadysis cut her off.

'I did not rise to the position of hierarch, nor have I maintained it for so long, by allowing myself to be lured into potential ambushes.' Aradryan's chest tightened around his heart and he fought the urge to glance at the incubi spread across the stage. If Khiadysis deemed it more to his advantage to kill his allies now, all the hierarch had to do was give the word to his hired slayers. There was little he or Maensith or Yrithain could do to prevent their deaths in a few heartbeats; it was why they had been allowed into the throne chamber even though they were still armed.

'There is no need to suspect such a thing,' said Maensith. 'To ensure that nothing is amiss, the *Fae Taeruth* will leave Daethronin as soon as the Azure Flame arrive. The greater strength of the fleet will still be with you, hierarch.'

Khiadysis considered this as Aradryan tried to keep his breaths regular and calm. He wondered if the hierarch would speak, or whether a simple gesture would be sufficient to bring down the wrath of the incubi. Perhaps even that would not be needed; the mercenaries may have some other means of discerning their master's wishes.

'I concur,' said the hierarch, nodding briskly. 'The burden of risk will lie with Prince Yrithain.'

Yrithain murmured a few protests at this conclusion, though whether out of genuine concern or simply so as not to appear too happy with the outcome of the meeting, Aradryan could not tell. The pirate prince took his leave soon after. Maensith rose to accompany him but was stayed by a gesture from Khiadysis.

'Remain with me for a little while longer, child,' he said. 'Forgive my paranoia, but I would prefer it if you and the good prince do not engage in any discussions without me present. I will be monitoring the holonetwork to assuage my anxiety and do not expect you nor any of your representatives to meet with any of the Azure Flame. Is that agreeable?'

'I am glad that we have an opportunity to discuss the future without Yrithain present,' said Maensith, sitting down again, leaning ever so slightly closer to the hierarch than she had been previously. She looked with narrowed eyes at the back of Yrithain as he stepped from the hall. 'It seems to me that we have an opportunity to not only take what we wish from Daethronin, but also rid ourselves of some dead weight.'

# ASCENSION

*The True Stars – There is a band of star systems, a great swathe of the galaxy, that lies between the Eye of Terror and the ring of the Exodite worlds. Many of these star systems were once home to eldar planets before the Fall. The inhabitants of these worlds perished when She Who Thirsts was born screaming into the galaxy, but their cities and technologies still survive. These places are known as the True Stars: the last remaining evidence of the Empire That Was. Great are the treasures hidden on these worlds, and powerful are some of the weapons that still defend them. Some True Stars have fallen to alien invasion, inhabited by humans, orks and others. Some are wildernesses, never to be found again. Many harbour treasure troves and vaults from the time before the Fall, and rangers from the craftworlds, Commorraghan expeditions and alien explorers often seek out these ancient and majestic worlds.*

As ARADRYAN PREPARED to shift the *Fae Taeruth* from the webway into realspace, he ran over the plan in his head, endeavouring to find any flaw or missed opportunity. In theory, the scheme he had concocted with Maensith was simple enough: forewarn the humans of the attack and aid in the destruction of the Commorraghans. With Khiadysis and his ilk disposed of, the *Fae Taeruth* would be free to stay with the Azure Flame or leave as the corsairs saw fit. The complications came when one considered the humans. They were a fickle race at best, and downright stubborn and contrary at worst. There was every chance that Commander De'vaque would try to imprison or kill Maensith and her crew.

It was to forestall any negative reaction that the *Fae Taeruth* was exiting the webway far out-system from Daethronin's star. The ship would coast in at cruising speed without holofields, hailing the humans from the outset. Maensith's hope was that there would be no surprises on either side. Once the peaceful intent of the eldar was established, a meaningful discourse could be held with the Imperial governor.

In discussions with Yrithain, at which Khiadysis had been present, Aradryan had learnt that Commander De'vaque ruled Daethronin in the name of the Emperor; the humans called the system Carasto. From a previous, fortuitous encounter, Yrithain had run afoul of the Imperial commander's starships, but had been able to broker a deal with the human. In return for safe berths and information about nearby Imperial convoys and transports, Yrithain gave a proportion of his spoils to the Imperial commander and left alone fleets and vessels leaving and destined for Daethronin. In this way, Commander De'vaque grew in power over his Imperial neighbours while the Azure Flame corsairs were given free rein to attack other star systems and merchant flotillas.

Aradryan wondered if there was some deeper reason behind Khiadysis's desire to attack Daethronin. As one of the True Stars, it had once been part of the great eldar empire before the Fall. There were many Commorraghans that still harked back to those glory days, seeing themselves as the true inheritors of the old empire. It would not be a stretch of the imagination to believe that Khiadysis wished to strike back at the humans, who had built their Imperium on the ruins of the eldar civilisation.

With this in mind, Aradryan slipped the *Fae Taeruth* across the veil that separated the physical galaxy from the webway. Half distracted by thoughts of True Stars and whether there was a way in which Yrithain could be deposed from his position in charge of the Azure Flame, Aradryan was shocked when his sensor bank came alive with readings. He had been sure the *Fae Taeruth* would emerge a good distance from the orbit of Daethronin's primary world, but as soon as the ship had broken into realspace the scanning arrays detected five human ships all within half a cycle's travel of the cruiser.

There was no need to relay this information to Maensith. Via the psychic conduits running the length and breadth of the ship she was aware of the situation as soon as Aradryan. Contrary to instinct, Maensith ordered the crew to remain steady and did not order the holofields to be raised or the weapon batteries armed; she stayed true to the guise of an Azure Flame raider returning to its home. To this end, the *Fae Taeruth* had recoloured its hull to blue and black tiger stripes, and at Maensith's insistence began broadcasting several crude human ciphers and hails passed on by Yrithain.

The simple radio wave messages took some time to be detected and for responses to be broadcast; time during which the *Fae Taeruth* came to a stop and allowed the human ships to form a cordon around her. There did not seem to be much urgency about the humans' manoeuvres and Aradryan shared Maensith's confidence that the *Fae Taeruth* was being treated as an unexpected but not unwelcome visitor.

Eventually the responses to the eldar's transmissions were picked up. It took moments to run the garble of noises through the translator banks, which revealed a demand for the *Fae Taeruth* to meet the flagship of the human flotilla at a designated co-ordinate. There was no hint of suspicion in the message received, which was undersigned by a human calling himself Darson De'vaque. The repetition of the surname, Maensith explained, indicated that it was likely that the human fleet was under the command of a genetic relation of Commander De'vaque, though Yrithain had not furnished her with any information regarding siblings, parents or children.

Routing a brief acknowledgement through the translators and transmission systems, Maensith ordered the *Fae Taeruth* onto her new course, to rendezvous with the humans in one-quarter of a cycle. Aradryan was intrigued and excited. This would be the first time he had met a human without trying to kill or capture it; the prospect of a fresh experience raised him from the gentle lethargy that had plagued him during the last few raids.

THE HUMAN SHIP stank.

Aradryan had always been aware of the stench during raids and boarding actions, but he had never really considered it having been occupied with more pressing matters of life and death. Though not tinged by the ozone of laser fire or the iron of spilled blood, the small frigate onto which he had been brought – along with Maensith and Iriakhin, one of Khiadysis's warriors – was filled with a disgusting array of aromas. There was the filthy perspiration of the humans themselves, mingling with the smell of fossil-based lubricants. Metal and corrosion assaulted Aradryan's sensitive nostrils alongside human effluent, unsubtly and ineffectively masked by olfactory-scourging anti-bacterial chemicals and artificially-scented detergent surfactants.

As if the stench was not enough to make Aradryan dizzy, the ship was in a state of constant vibration, both gentle and strong. Every corridor they passed along was abuzz with electrical charges from cabling within the walls, while crude light fittings fizzed with power. A more deep-seated resonation shook the ship from its plasma engines, creating an ever-present rumbling that unsettled Aradryan's stomach. The thump of their escort's heavy boots on bare metal decking pounded in the eldar's ears, as did the rasping breaths of the 'armsmen' that had met the corsairs' shuttle.

To complete the sensory assault, the artificial light flickered at a painfully slow frequency, so that to Aradryan and his companions' eyes they seemed to strobe rather than provide the constant glow afforded by the more advanced, organic lighting used on craft-worlds and the eldar's ships. The contrast of glaring light and sharp shadow made strange, harsh angles out of the undecorated bulkheads they passed.

Without the distraction of deadly combat, Aradryan noticed all of these unpleasant sensations and more. They were conveyed to a primitive mechanical elevation chamber that clanked and clattered on chains as they ascended through the ship, the clunk of each passing level ringing through Aradryan's ears. He focused on the humans, who wore ill-fitting pressure suits and bore short-barrelled, chemically-powered laser carbines; he could smell the laughably inefficient acidic compounds used in the weapons' power packs. The men did not have helms or hats, but all were shaven-headed, bearing tattoos on their scalps akin to clan or House markings; their meaning was lost on the corsair.

At least a head shorter than the eldar, the soldiers of Darson De'vaque had flat faces and noses, their mouths wide, their eyes small and porcine. They glared with barely repressed anger at the eldar, their faces screwed up in clownish grimaces and sneers, but in their eyes Aradryan could see the touch of fear as well. The humans hated their eldar charges because they feared them, and they feared them because they did not understand them. Aradryan smiled at one of the humans in an attempt to alleviate his discontent, but the change of expression was misinterpreted and the soldier raised his gun a little higher, the comically deep frown creasing his forehead becoming even more contorted.

Amongst the stink and the clatter, it was not surprising that humans could barely think, Aradryan realised. It was almost impossible for him to concentrate for more than a few moments with such distractions. As if being short-lived was not curse enough for the people of the Emperor... It was no surprise that they had reverted to such barbarous ways, in the absence of genuine philosophy and culture.

Eventually they reached their destination, somewhere in the heart of the Imperial frigate. Other than a perfunctory welcome issued by Darson De'vaque upon the *Fae Taeruth*'s arrival at the rendezvous, they had heard no message of importance from their host. It seemed unlikely that hostilities would ensue, considering the dispositions of the other human ships in the vicinity, and Aradryan was hopeful of a cordial if not enriching experience.

They were brought to a low-ceilinged room lit by burning wax lamps. The effect of the lighting was not entirely unpleasant, in a prehistoric sort of way, and the lack of illumination was of no concern to the eldar, who could see far more clearly in the dim light than their human companions. At a long table that ran lengthways along the room sat Darson De'vaque, or so Aradryan presumed. He was a slender person, in comparison to the stocky guards that had formed their escort, and a little taller than the average human Aradryan had encountered. There was a softness to his face that indicated he was better fed than his subordinates, and his carefully trimmed facial hair also indicated a slightly higher standard of personal hygiene. Some flowery fragrance, overpowering in its own way, had been used in an attempt to obliterate the man's inherent smell, and Aradryan detected the sheen of perfumed oil in De'vaque's slicked, shoulder-length hair.

The man was dressed in a formal-looking blue frock coat with high collars around his neck, hemmed and braided with golden thread. There was a piercing in the side of his nose, of a small human rune made from silver, which connected by a slender chain of the same metal to a ring in his lower lip. His hands were bare – a pair of black gloves were laid on the table in front of De'vaque – and his hands showed signs of care and attention, with neatly cut and buffed nails that glistened with a dark red polish. On seeing this, Aradryan examined the man's face again and detected a powdery cosmetic that had been applied to smooth away some of the blemishes and discolorations that marked his skin; it had not been immediately apparent in the dim lighting.

De'vaque had bright blue eyes, surprisingly engaging and alert for one of his species. Blubbery lips turned upwards in an exaggerated parody of a smile as those eyes moved from Aradryan to Iriakhin to Maensith. The human stood up and raised a hand to his chest, presumably in a gesture of greeting, and then spoke. Aradryan knew enough of the human language to understand De'vaque's words – though the human tongue was incredibly disparate and diverse across the galaxy, its underlying principles and sounds were easily learnt in comparison to the complexities of the Eldar language – but like his companions Aradryan had a translator device fitted to his shoulder. It was better that the humans believed that their 'guests' could not understand them without the devices.

'Welcome aboard the *Invigorating Glory*, my allies,' said De'vaque. Aradryan wondered whether the translator had worked properly, having indicated the name was that of the starship. It seemed a pompous title for such a small vessel. 'I am Darson De'vaque, Viceroy of Carasto, Rogue Trader of the Chartist Captains and heir to the Imperial Command of this star system.'

Quickly deciphering the meanings of the titles, Aradryan realised that Darson was the eldest son of Imperial Commander De'vaque. Though no expert in human physiology, he guessed Darson to be of middle age, if not a little older, and surmised that his father would be entering his final span of life shortly, if he had bred at the usual age for humans. While that much was clear, the concept of 'rogue trader', if the translation had been correct, was lost on Aradryan.

'We accept your welcome,' said the eldar pirate. It had been decided that he would act as spokesperson for the *Fae Taeruth*, which the humans would mistake for seniority, thus affording Maensith a degree of protection should matters turn sour. The translator spat out a few guttural syllables before Aradryan continued. 'I am Aradryan, of the *Fae Taeruth*, lately of the Azure Flame corsairs with whom I believe you are already acquainted. It is a pleasant surprise to encounter you in these circumstances.'

De'vaque listened to the translation with his fixed idiotic smile and then nodded.

'Please, be seated while I send for refreshments and food,' said De'vaque, waving a hand towards the seats opposite him.

The odour rising from the plates and cups that were subsequently brought forth was nauseating in the extreme. Even the clear liquid that on casual inspection might be mistaken for water had a chemical taint to it, and despite such anti-microbial efforts was somewhat cloudy in the crudely-cut crystal bottle. Aradryan offered thanks for the repast, but did not eat or drink anything that was offered.

What followed was a drawn out and increasingly tedious conversation, made all the more painful by the subterfuge of waiting for the translator; Aradryan was forced to listen to each meaningless platitude twice before replying while Darson had to genuinely wait for the device to render Aradryan's lyric replies into his crude language. Try as he might to subtly indicate through word and posture that all was not well with De'vaque's allies, the garbled nonsense spewed from the speaker of Aradryan's device conveyed nothing of his implicit warnings.

With Iriakhin listening to everything that was being said, it was impossible for Aradryan to be more overt in his cautioning. Khiadysis's minion would have to be waylaid or otherwise removed for a short period in order to be blunt with Darson De'vaque, in such a way that Iriakhin would not suspect that anything was amiss.

As Darson's inquiries regarding the business of the *Fae Taeruth* became more insistent, Aradryan was at a loss to parry the human's questions with meaningless pleasantries. There were few enough goods on board to offer as trade – due to the change of plans on the orbital station – and without Commander De'vaque's cut of the spoils there was no reason to come to Daethronin.

Struck by the genius of desperation, Aradryan picked up one of the curious cubes of food that had been left in a platter on the table close at hand. Not pausing to think what he might be consuming, Aradryan popped the morsel into his mouth. As he had feared, it was horribly overspiced and barely cooked, so that when he feigned a choking fit he was not far from genuinely retching.

Doubling up, one hand slapping the tabletop, Aradryan imitated a paroxysm of suffocation, holding his breath until he felt quite dizzy. The humans clustered around him, Maensith and Iriakhin stood protectively over him. Out of instinct, Aradryan took a proffered cup, the near-stagnant water he almost gulped down throwing him into a new and entirely unplanned bout of choking. Eyes streaming, Aradryan forced himself to his feet for a few moments. In doing so, he managed to turn his back to Iriakhin and meet Maensith's gaze. The moment their eyes met there was a flash of understanding between the two eldar.

'What is the nature of this food?' the pirate captain demanded through her translator. 'Are you trying to poison us?'

Catching the theme and thinking that some human plot was unfolding, Iriakhin snarled accusations at Darson, who was quite taken aback by the turn of events, though he remained seated throughout. In his remonstrations, Iriakhin became highly animated, forcing the human guards to intervene, their weapons pointed at the eldar.

'Calm yourself, we cannot cause an incident,' Maensith told Iriakhin in their own tongue, while Aradryan continued to hack in fraudulent asphyxiation. 'Let us quickly reappraise the situation before we lose control.'

Lulled by her calming words, Iriakhin allowed himself to be backed towards the door by Maensith. As a wall of men surrounded the two retreating eldar, Aradryan leaned across the table. With a thought, he muted his translator before hissing his words directly at Darson, low enough to be inaudible to Iriakhin.

'Say nothing, we are spied upon. When Yrithain comes, he will be followed by others who are not friends. Have your ships ready to strike. We will assist.'

The man's eyes widened with shock, though whether at hearing his own language rolling from the tongue of the eldar or the message given was unclear. He nodded quickly in understanding as Aradryan flopped back into his chair, still coughing. The eldar reactivated his translator and said a few words between gasping breaths, directing them towards Iriakhin.

'It is no heinous conspiracy, companions,' he said, holding up a hand. 'The human food was not to the liking of my palate, and nothing more sinister. I am recovered now, I assure you.'

'Clear away this mess,' said De'vaque, waving at the attendants who had gathered around Aradryan.

Within a few moments the plates and goblets were gone, leaving the wooden table bare save for a single cup in front of Darson. 'My most humble apologies. Please, return to your starship immediately, to seek assurance that your health has not been affected. Thank you for bringing word of Prince Yrithain's arrival, I will ensure that my father greets your coming ships in a suitable manner.'

Listening to these words, Aradryan did not know whether his warning had been understood or not. He had to believe that the warning had been delivered.

Nodding, Aradryan turned to the other two eldar. Maensith came forwards, offering her shoulder for Aradryan to support himself. Iriakhin darted Aradryan an annoyed glance, but irritation was preferable to suspicion. Aradryan allowed himself a moment of satisfaction; that he had managed to warn Darson of the Commorraghan attack and fooled Iriakhin into thinking no such thing had happened.

WHEN THE FAE *Taeruth* rejoined the rest of the pirate fleet, there was time only for a brief conference with Yrithain and Khiadysis, to confirm that the humans were expecting the eldar's arrival. There was no means to convey to Yrithain that a warning had been sent, and as the ships of the Azure Flame disappeared along the webway, Aradryan was left with a feeling of unease.

Iriakhin left to report to Khiadysis on the events aboard the *Fae Taeruth*, leaving Aradryan free to voice his doubts to Maensith. The two of them spoke in one of the sub-chambers adjoining the command hall, furnished with a circle of armchairs around a low table, the walls lined with crystal-fronted cabinets holding a variety of drinks decanters and trophy pieces taken from raided vessels. Maensith sat, while Aradryan took a short-bladed, bone-hilted knife from one of the cupboards, idly twisting the dagger between his fingers.

'We have overlooked a possibility,' said Aradryan. 'In all our concern for what Khiadysis might do, and our efforts to allay any suspicions he may harbour, we have neglected to fully consider the options open to Yrithain.'

'Yrithain is under the same constraints as we are,' said Maensith. 'If he turns on us as well as Khiadysis he will be outgunned.'

'Not now, with the humans as his allies,' Aradryan said quietly.

Maensith's lips parted and then closed again, her argument dismissed. She shook her head slightly, brow creasing gently.

'Do you think Yrithain will have the humans turn on us as well?'

'If we were in the same position as Yrithain, would we not sense an opportunity to rid ourselves of *all* our rivals? It would be prudent to expect Yrithain will convince the humans to attack all of the vessels in the second wave, including ours.'

'We cannot warn Khiadysis about the humans' forewarning without implicating ourselves in the treachery. What are we to do, Aradryan? It was your idea to caution the humans against our plans, and now we are caught again between Khiadysis and Yrithain.'

'I do not know what to do!' snapped Aradryan, slamming the tip of the knife into the deep red wood of a cabinet top. He took a deep breath. 'We have half a cycle before the rest of the fleet moves to Daethronin. That is not much time for the humans to prepare; their ships are very slow. We must think of something in that time.'

'Or we can hope that Yrithain remains true to our common goal of dispensing with Khiadysis's alliance, without any action against ourselves.'

'I would prefer we took hold of our own threads of fate than leave them to dangle in the grip of Yrithain. I cannot believe we are utterly trapped with no third option.'

'You are right.' Maensith stood up and crossed the chamber to lay a hand on Aradryan's cheek. Her skin was cool to the touch, but the softness of her fingers sent a flare of pleasure through Aradryan. Since the chance meeting with the Azure Flame and the Commorraghans, Maensith had been much preoccupied, and the two of them had enjoyed little intimacy. 'Between us we will find a solution, I am sure of it. Maybe, if we take our minds from our immediate problems, an answer will present itself.'

Aradryan smiled, a moment before Maensith's lips met his.

EVERYTHING AT DAETHRONIN was as agreed between the pirate commanders. Yrithain and the Azure Flame were in position behind the escort of small human ships that came out-system to greet the *Fae Taeruth* and the Commorraghans. The handful of destroyers were little match for the weaponry of the three eldar cruisers and the journey towards Daethronin's primary world was uneventful.

For all that Aradryan could see, the humans were ripe for the ambush and had taken no precautions at all against attack, despite the warning given. The timing of the Commorraghans' arrival had been determined to ensure the humans would be caught between the two waves of eldar ships. When the flotilla arrived above the human world, the *Fae Taeruth* and Khiadysis's ships would attack, driving the human escorts against the fleet of the Azure Flame.

It would take at least five cycles to reach the prime world, probably more when accounting for the ponderous nature of the human vessels. Aradryan was not looking forward to such a tense time, wondering when they would receive the order from Khiadysis; at the moment it looked like there was nothing the humans could do to defend themselves, which would effectively leave the battle to Yrithain and Maensith against the Commorraghans. The odds were too close in that event, which was why the aid of the humans had been required in the first place. Not only that, the *Fae Taeruth* was in the most dangerous position, situated between the two dark eldar cruisers. In the event of the Azure Flame turning their guns on the Commorraghans, the most prudent course of action would be to side with Khiadysis.

As soon as the second wave slipped into realspace, Aradryan left his position in the piloting chamber and joined Maensith in the main control hall. At a nod from her, he relieved Taelisieth at the main gunnery controls; to ensure security, neither of them had shared their plans and doubts with the rest of the crew and immediate action would be required whatever circumstances arose.

After a series of customary hails had been exchanged, the combined human and eldar fleet started towards the heart of Daethronin. As the *Fae Taeruth* unfurled her stellar sails and turned gracefully in-system, Aradryan noticed that none of the scanner returns of the human ships corresponded to Darson De'vaque's vessel. In fact, comparing the sensor sweep with those retained in the ship's matrix indicated half a dozen ships were now unaccounted for.

Aradryan sent this information across the matrix to Maensith, but the reason for the discrepancy became immediately obvious. Warning tones chimed across the control chamber, indicating multiple warp breaches. Maensith brought up the visual display, the globe of stars circling slowly above her command pod. Kaleidoscopic whorls broke the fabric of space-time as raw warp energy poured into the material universe. Aradryan counted six rifts opening, and from each emerged one of the missing human ships, directly behind the *Fae Taeruth* and Khiadysis's cruisers.

As the warp breaches closed, the holo-images of Khiadysis and Yrithain burst into view on the main chamber floor. It was the hierarch who spoke first.

'We are surrounded,' snarled the Commorraghan leader. 'It is of little advantage to the humans. Their reinforcements are out of range at the moment. We will obliterate those close at hand first, and then turn our guns on the new arrivals. They cannot match us for speed and firepower.'

'Those reinforcements are merely the lid on the trap,' said Yrithain. In the revolving system display, the Azure Flame vessels were tacking hard, turning across the stellar winds towards the Commorraghans. Plasma flared as the human ships also reduced speed for tight manoeuvres, though far more laboriously than the eldar vessels.

'Traitor!' rasped the hierarch. 'We will see you destroyed first!'

Maensith said nothing, but looked across the chamber at Aradryan. He nodded in reply and activated both weapon batteries, locking on to the Commorraghan cruisers to either side even as Maensith sent the commands that would pull up the *Fae Taeruth*.

Aradryan's fingers danced across the gems of the console, unleashing a barrage of laser and missile fire into the neighbouring cruisers. The aftsail of Khiadysis's cruiser turned into golden shreds flittering across the firmament, while the gun decks of the other erupted with fire and debris. Aradryan's heart raced as he expected a destructive reply, but none came, such was the surprise with which the opening blow had been struck. The *Fae Taeruth* dipped sharply at the prow and rolled to starboard, giving Aradryan one last salvo at Khiadysis's flagship before the weapon batteries could no longer bear upon their targets.

Turning from the weapons controls, Aradryan fixed his gaze on the display, anxious to see what their new enemies would do. The view in the sensor sphere spun rapidly to keep the two cruisers in view as the *Fae Taeruth* turned sharply away from both the Commorraghans and the humans. Yrithain was far from the fight, and his loyalty questionable when he was able to intervene, and if Khiadysis was set on retaliation, the *Fae Taeruth* had little chance against two adversaries. It had been a desperate plan Aradryan and Maensith had concocted during their second voyage to Daethronin and whether it had been successful or not was far from established.

The Commorraghans had been trimming their sails to counter the approach of the Azure Flame, and the attack from the *Fae Taeruth* left them caught between two courses of action. Khiadysis's ship, with its damaged stellar sail, stayed on its course change towards Yrithain's ships; the other stuttered mid-manoeuvre as its captain sought to turn onto the tail of the fleeing *Fae Taeruth*.

The holo-image of Khiadysis disappeared with a howl of rage. Yrithain's apparition remained, arms crossed, his expression a little agitated.

'Well done,' said the prince of the Azure Flame, his smile mocking rather than good humoured. 'I had told Darson De'vaque that you might not be trustworthy, but making the first strike has ensured he will not turn his guns against you. I commend your ingenuity and courage.'

'And do not forget that it was we that first issued warning of the attack, not you,' said Maensith. 'I am sure the Imperial commander and his son will take that into account when the negotiations begin.'

Aradryan briefly returned his attention to the scanner globe. Despite his threat of retribution, Khiadysis was breaking away from the combat as quickly as possible, abandoning his second cruiser, which was now continuing a sweeping turn away from the *Fae Taeruth*; her commander had no doubt realised that his damaged ship was outgunned by the other cruiser without the aid of the hierarch.

The human ships did their best to take up

intercepting courses, but there was little doubt the Commorraghans would escape the trap unless the Azure Flame gave chase. Yrithain must have noticed the same, judging by his next question to Maensith.

'Are you going to let them escape? I would not like to list Khiadysis amongst my enemies.'

'He will not return,' said Maensith. 'He is far from Commorragh already, and there is no guarantee we will be here still when he has affected his repairs. Regardless of any hurt he might feel, he also cannot return to the kabal and admit he was the victim of such a simple trick. No, he will return with a tale of overwhelming odds barely escaped, and keep to a life within the towering spires conniving against his archon and stepping on the lives of his underlings, as most hierarchs are content to do.'

'What did you mean by negotiations, which you mentioned a moment ago?' said Yrithain.

'Is it not obvious?' said Maensith. 'Your arrangement with Commander De'vaque is compromised. You brought an enemy to his star system, and you cannot be trusted. We will have to make a new offer, a much more generous offer, on behalf of the Azure Flame to ensure we are welcome at Daethronin.'

'There is no reason to assume the commander will conclude I was complicit in any attack,' said Yrithain.

'Believe me,' Maensith said with a smile, 'that is exactly what I will endeavour to make him conclude.'

She broke the holo-link, isolating the ship's network to prevent Yrithain establishing any further contact without permission.

'Yrithain was right, in part,' said Aradryan, gesturing for Taelisieth to take command of the gunnery console again. When the officer was at his station once more, Aradryan crossed the floor of the command chamber and took the hand of Maensith.

'How was Yrithain right?' she asked.

'The threat that Khiadysis held over you still exists. He will tell your old kabal where to find you, and I fear that will not go well.'

'It is true that I parted from the Crimson Talon as a thief and a fugitive, but there is no reason to be concerned for my future,' replied the captain. She lifted her hand, still gripped in Aradryan's fingers, and kissed the inside of his wrist. 'Let us set course to intercept Darson De'vaque's ship before Yrithain has a chance to get a step ahead of us again.'

WITH A SWAGGER in his step, Aradryan strode down the carpeted aisle of the Imperial commander's reception chamber. It was located aboard a pleasure yacht of some kind – a stubby, plasma-powered tugboat in comparison to any eldar ship worthy of that name – located in high orbit over the principle world of Daethronin, which the humans insisted on calling Carasto.

Aradryan was feeling supremely confident, despite the rows of soldiers that stood to attention to his left and right, and the small company of marksmen he had spied stationed amongst the metal beams that held aloft the high-arched ceiling. He felt their magnified sights upon him like evil eyes, as once he had looked from afar through his ranger longrifle.

As well as the men-under-arms, Imperial Commander De'vaque had a mass of advisers, scribes and heralds loitering in the audience chamber. Their whispering was as clear to Aradryan as if he was in conversation with them, but their exclamations and utterances were entirely dull and revolved mainly around Aradryan's appearance – both his being aboard the yacht and his mode of dress.

This latter was indeed remarkable, for Aradryan had taken some time over his clothes for such an important meeting. Yrithain had seen fit to depart rather than risk the displeasure of the humans, and the remaining ships of the Azure Flame had been keen to broadcast their thanks and loyalty to the warriors of the *Fae Taeruth*. It had become clear soon after that Yrithain had not been a popular leader, and the increasing demands made by Commander De'vaque had stretched the patience and fealty of his underlings almost to breaking point. The arrival of the Commorraghans had provided a common adversary to rally against, but with that particular problem solved, the other corsairs were happy to join Maensith and Aradryan, once more promised fair division of spoils and a voice in any debate.

Aradryan had suggested to Maensith that they maintain the fallacy of his command, protecting her from any double-dealing De'vaque might contemplate, and so he came to the court of the Imperial commander in his finest regalia, as befitted a prince of the corsairs. He wore a skin-tight undersuit of purple and gold, beneath a knee-length black coat that flared wide at the hips, the shoulders studded with tiny stars of wintersilver. The wide lapels were edged with more silver and hung with fine chains of the same material, stretching across Aradryan's chest in refined mockery of the gold braiding and frogging that was heaped upon De'vaque's uniform. Boots drawn up to his thighs, of supple dawn-leopard skin in black, red and yellow, completed the ensemble, along with numerous rings, bracelets and an elongated skull-shaped piercing in the side of his brow. Aradryan had drawn his hair up into a high crest, further emphasising his height over the stunted humans, and his face was subtly painted to accentuate the shape of his eyes, which were wide and bright compared to the sunken orbs of his host.

The Imperial commander stood next to a high-backed chair, the man as solid as the wood and velvet throne on which he leaned. His cheeks and upper lip were hidden by a bush of thick, greying hair, his chin clear of the growth to display three slender scars. De'vaque wore a peaked cap, of dark blue, the same as his dress coat, its visor coming down over straggling eyebrows. A flat nose and mauled ears betrayed a history of physical conflict – probably recreational, Aradryan guessed, judging the scars on the man's chin to be from some kind of slender duelling sword – and the man's hands were balled into fists with rough knuckles, thumbs tucked into a broad belt that was hung with a pistol on one hip and a tapering, curved sword on the other.

Aradryan was armed also, pistol and sword like the commander, but only for display; if he was required to use his weapons his plan would have failed and he'd be swiftly slain by the several dozen men with guns trained upon him. Well aware of the dashing figure he must pose to the gangling, awkward humans, Aradryan gracefully progressed along the black and gold carpet towards the Imperial commander, timing his strides so that he covered the ground at a sedate but purposeful pace.

The chamber itself was furnished with a heavily-grained wood lacquered with deep red. Various eagles and other Imperial insignia adorned the banners that hung from the ceiling every twenty or so paces. The floor was tiled with intricate mosaic, though from his position Aradryan could not tell whether it was simply a patterned design or some more illustrative image; there was a balcony above the throne stage from which the view would undoubtedly be more suited.

Stopping some ten paces from the throne, Aradryan cast his gaze above the crowd of gaudily-dressed human males and females clustered to his right; courtiers, family and other hangers-on, the eldar pirate surmised.

'Forgive my lack of introduction,' said Aradryan, once more speaking through the face-like translator brooch upon his breast; his spirit stone was mounted in a gold sunburst on the other side. 'Your herald, as willing as he was to accommodate me, was quite unable to pronounce my name. The mangled sounds he made reminded me of a bovine animal in distress. Thus, I must present myself. I am Prince-Commander Aradryan Iadhsuan Adiarrin Naio of the Azure Flame, Admiral of the Winter Gulf.'

'It is customary for petitioners to bow in recognition of the Imperial commander's rank.'

This rebuke came from a younger human standing just behind De'vaque. He was a little taller than the commander, and much slighter of build. Aradryan could see no family resemblance between the two and categorised the man who had spoken as some kind of functionary. He turned his eyes – purposefully coloured a startling violet for the encounter – back on the Imperial commander.

'Your pet appears to be squawking out of turn,' said Aradryan. 'Please silence it.'

'I am Antoine Nallim, Chief Steward of Carasto, and you will not treat me with disrespect, pirate scum.'

Aradryan turned slightly and allowed his gaze to roam across the other people in the hall. In the civilian men he saw the odd cut on brow and cheek, and amongst the officers of the soldiers he saw the same, reinforcing his opinion that duelling was an acceptable sport on this world. Turning his attention back to De'vaque, who had remained grumpily silent so far, Aradryan smiled thinly.

'Am I correct in the belief that duelling with blades is regarded as a suitable means for settling dispute?'

'We duel, yes,' said De'vaque, folding his arms across his chest. 'What makes you think I will allow you the honour of duelling with my chief steward?'

'If your culture believes it is appropriate to establish superiority through violence, surely you must allow me the opportunity to seek redress against the insult I have suffered from the words of your underling?'

'I'll give this arrogant thief a scar to remind him of his manners,' said Nallim, unbuttoning his coat. The man beneath was athletically built, by human standards. Rolling up the sleeves of his undershirt, Nallim drew a sword from its sheath at his hip, exactly the same in design as the one worn by the Imperial commander.

'Would it be allowed for me to use my own weapon, or must I use one of those flimsy skewers you call swords?' asked Aradryan.

'You may use whichever blade you feel best suits you,' said De'vaque. His jaw was clenched tight, and he clearly did not feel that his chief steward's challenge had been wise. Nonetheless, he held his tongue; it was probably bad manners for him to intervene on either side's behalf.

'Feel free to remove your coat, pirate,' said Nallim, bounding across to the carpeted aisle, his booted feet slapping on the tiles. 'You should not encumber yourself unnecessarily.'

'Style before purpose, I am afraid,' Aradryan said as he slowly drew his sword. He looked at De'vaque and tried to find the human words for what he wanted to say. 'Is there some official start to the violence, or do we just start swinging?'

'Raise your blade to your brow in salute, and then you may begin,' replied the Imperial commander. Aradryan noticed that De'vaque's eyes had not left him throughout the exchange. For a human, he was very focused and attentive.

Aradryan did as he was bid, bringing the flat of his sword to touch his forehead just above the bridge of his nose. Nallim did likewise, and the two stood as still as statues for a heartbeat, staring at each other.

Aradryan noticed the tiny dilation in Nallim's eyes as he thought about the strike he would make. The skin of his knuckles paled a fraction more and there was a twitch of a tendon in his wrist. It was a signal as clear as day to Aradryan that his opponent was about to attack.

Bringing his sword down to a straight lunge, Aradryan took a long stride forwards. So swift was the strike that Nallim's sabre was barely a finger's width from his face when the point of Aradryan's sword lanced through the human's throat, twisting slightly to avoid the blade being chipped on the man's vertebrae before the point erupted form the back of his neck.

What seemed like an age later, there were shouts and screams from the gathered men and women. De'vaque was bellowing madly for his men to hold their fire, while several of the courtesans fainted to the ground, eyes rolling in their sockets as blood sprayed over the carpet and tiles.

'A duel is only to first blood!' roared De'vaque, turning towards Aradryan with balled fists, his face reddening.

Aradryan let go of his sword, so that Nallim's body crumpled to the ground, the blood spurting from the wound creating rivulets in the gaps between the mosaic pieces.

'He is certainly bleeding,' said Aradryan, clasping one hand in the other at his waist.

'I should have you killed here and now, and your ships blown out of the stars,' continued the Imperial commander, but Aradryan knew the threat was empty; why would De'vaque stop his men from shooting if he wished the pirate commander dead?

'It would be unwise to try such a thing, Commander De'vaque,' said Aradryan. He stepped over Nallim's twitching corpse and took three more strides, his height advantage over De'vaque becoming even more pronounced in such close proximity.

'What do you want?' De'vaque backed away and slumped into his chair while a squad of soldiers picked up Nallim and carried him from the hall, trailing a spattered line of crimson. 'The same agreement as Irrithan?'

Aradryan suppressed a wince at the mangling of the name, and shook his head.

'There will be no further arrangements with the Azure Flame,' said the eldar, earning a scowl, but he continued. 'The Azure Flame will no longer take sanctuary in Daethronin, nor will the ships that pass through this system be vouched any safe passage. Any relationship between you and Yrithain is over. You will allow me and my fleet to depart this star system unmolested. We will no longer be your tamed hounds, Imperial commander.'

'You think to double-cross me again?' De'vaque's jowls shook and he spat the next words. 'I'll see you gutted and skinned before I let you out of here.'

'I would reconsider, commander, if I were you,' said Aradryan. He reached out his right hand, activating the holo-projector set into the ruby ring on his index finger. A ruddy vignette sprang into life between him and De'vaque, of Maensith and Darson sitting at a table together. The two of them were tasting long strands of confectionary and sipping gently effervescing wine from crystal goblets. 'You see, I was kind enough to invite your son on board my ship before I departed. As you can see, he is being looked after. For the moment. He will continue to enjoy our hospitality until we are ready to leave this place.'

'Darson, you idiot!' bellowed De'vaque, shaking a fist at the image. 'What do you think you are doing?'

'It is only an image, commander, there is no audio relay,' explained Aradryan.

'Trickery. Any fool can conjure up a moving hololith.'

'Please make whatever inquiries you require to confirm my statement, Imperial Commander De'vaque. The officers of your son's ship will inform you that he is aboard my vessel, as are several of his bodyguard. Trust me, the guards will not prove very useful if you choose to act against us.'

'Why? Why did you not just leave? What was the point of coming here, to see me, if all you wanted to do was leave safely?'

'It is not in my nature to slip away like vermin in the night, commander, especially in the face of a lesser species,' Aradryan said. 'I want you to know that it is only by my will that you are still alive today. Had it not been for my actions, my twisted kin would have attacked your world and exacted a far more agonising retribution for your occupation of it. They take unkindly to upstart barbarian-apes squatting on one of our planets, you see. I am less troubled by the past, and you are welcome to stay at Daethronin as long as you wish. I thought you might appreciate my permission on the matter.'

'Your... permission?' A vein was throbbing dangerously in De'vaque's forehead as he squeezed the two words between gritted teeth. The man inhaled deeply and flexed his fingers, forcing himself to visibly relax. 'I will make sure you pay for this poisonous act, pirate. You will not get away with this.'

'Oh, but I will, Imperial Commander De'vaque,' said Aradryan, smiling broadly. 'In fact, I already have.'

Saying the words made the feeling a reality. It had been as much to gratify himself as to arrange a ceasefire that Aradryan had answered the Imperial commander's summons. Here he was, standing in the middle of De'vaque's domain, surrounded by men who would kill him as soon as blink, and there was nothing they could do about the situation. He had known from the outset that Darson would be the man's weakness; despite their prolific breeding, humans of status set great value on their heirs and to have one taken in such cavalier manner would be a massive loss of prestige and honour. The moment was to be savoured, and Aradryan enjoyed the looks of dismay and fury on the humans as he stepped lightly back towards the hall's doors.

Stepping through the open portal, Aradryan laughed, leaving a lilting echo in the hall behind him.

WHEN THE *Fae Taeruth* and the other ships of the Azure Flame were safely away from Daethronin and the breaches into the webway were prepared, Darson De'vaque and his guards were escorted back to their shuttle. Aradryan stood at the gunnery controls and watched the small craft jet away from the cruiser.

'I am sure that Imperial Commander De'vaque will not take kindly to this treatment,' said Maensith, her voice coming from the command pod at the heart of the chamber.

'He should know his place in the galaxy better,' said Aradryan. 'He may rule a world in the name of the human Emperor, but he is but a speck of grit – no, a tiniest fragment of a miniscule particle – in the grand design of the galaxy. Commander De'vaque should be taught that ultimately he is powerless and worthless, and that he should not underestimate us.'

Aradryan looked over his shoulder and saw that Maensith was smiling, her lips twisted in a cruel expression. It was not quite as intimidating as the half-insane grimaces of Khiadysis, but it was a reminder that Maensith had been brought up with a very different view of the universe.

'You have something in mind, my dear?' asked the ship's captain.

In reply, Aradryan returned his attention to the console and activated one of the laser cannon batteries. He locked on the targeting network to the signature of the departing shuttle.

'De'vaque would have hunted us down like wild animals,' said Aradryan, remembering the look on the Imperial commander's face as he had watched Aradryan cut down his chief steward. He had wanted to control the pirates, at one and the same time desiring their loyalty yet thinking of them as expendable tools. Aradryan's finger hovered over the firing gem as he looked again at his captain.' He knew that we were of no more use to him and would have thrown us to his allies in order to benefit himself. Such treachery should not go unrewarded.'

Maensith nodded once and Aradryan fired the laser cannons. In the spherical display at the centre of the chamber, the human shuttle exploded into a ball of fire and gas, utterly obliterated.

'Make shift to the webway, as swift as you can,' Maensith declared, transmitting her message to the rest of the fleet. 'The leash is off, and wolves must hunt!'

# THEFT

*The Forge of Vaul – At the heart of the galaxy lies the Forge of Vaul, where the stars and planets and nebulae were brought into being upon the anvil of the Smith God. Here, the hottest furnaces of the oldest stars burn to fuel the fires of the Forge. Starmetal and sunbronze are the materials with which Vaul worked, and mighty were the artefacts he created. It was here that Vaul was chained by Khaine to labour in atonement for freeing Isha and Kurnus, and it was in the Forge of Vaul that the Godslayer, the Sword of Khaine, deadliest weapon in all the worlds, was created. When Khaine was torn apart in the duel between She Who Thirsts and the Lord of War, it is said that the Widowmaker flew from his hand and returned to the place of its birth. It waits there now, biding the long aeons until a hand worthy of wielding it pulls it from the anvil in which it rests.*

FOLLOWING THEIR DEPARTURE from Daethronin, the Azure Flame, now under the joint command of Maensith and Aradryan, found great sport and spoils across the star systems of the Winter Gulf. Having been held back by their agreements with De'vaque, some of the captains of the Azure Flame delighted in targeting ships coming to and from the Imperial commander's star system. It was not only around Daethronin that the pirates made their presence felt. From Eldaseth to Taerinnin, a stretch of nearly three thousand light years, the Azure Flame swooped upon lone merchant ships and isolated outposts, dared the guns of convoy escorts and the cannons of orbital platforms.

Aradryan earned himself a reputation amongst the corsairs as a brazen, daring adventurer. He could barely believe the transformation in himself, from the weak-willed, terrified ranger who had cowered at the approach of a diminutive orkoid, to the carefree and courageous pirate prince he had become. Despite Aradryan's popularity amongst most of the Azure Flame fleet, there were some aboard the *Fae Taeruth* who were not so indulgent. Chief amongst his critics was Taelisieth, who missed no opportunity to raise objections and doubts about Aradryan's leadership, decisions and motives with Maensith. Such an argument came to a head aboard the *Fae Taeruth* as the three eldar discussed an upcoming raid on a convoy mustering point.

The three of them were in the observation gallery,

surrounded by the glowing fabric of the webway shimmering beyond the window interfaces. Aradryan saw a curving wall of purple and blue held aloft by white columns that burned with ember-like runes. The *Fae Taeruth* had travelled this part of the Winter Gulf frequently, and Aradryan had dubbed this particular weave of tunnels the Golden Gate due to its proximity to a number of warp routes used frequently by the human Imperium. There were rich pickings indeed to be had, if one did not mind risking the Imperial Navy patrols.

'It is too reckless, for little reward,' protested Taelisieth. 'We have already drawn too much attention to ourselves in this area, we need to move on.'

'But the convoy staging area is nearby, in Laesithanan,' replied Aradryan. 'It is ripe for us. Darson De'vaque spoke of it before his departure.'

'The more dangerous, the better for you,' snarled Taelisieth. 'I know what drives you, Aradryan. This system, it will be well-guarded, and you want to spite the humans by taking their ships from under their noses. It is not worth the risk; not for your further aggrandisement.'

'My aggrandisement?' laughed Aradryan. He turned to Maensith, laying a hand on her arm. 'Who was it that led the attack at Niemesh? It was me! Who saw the opportunity to outwit that battlecruiser commander at Caelosis? Me! If it was not for my wit, this fleet would have seen half as much action.'

'And the *Laethrin* and *Naeghli Atun* would both still be with us,' countered Taelisieth. 'Yrithain never lost a single ship, and you have lost two in less than a hundred cycles. The captains follow you still because they are excited, but their patience will wear thin soon enough. This convoy, it carries nothing of importance – weapons for some human warzone far away. Without De'vaque to take them, what use are they? Will you find another corrupt Imperial governor willing to trade for them? And for what?'

'We will be taking prisoners,' said Aradryan, earning himself sharp looks from both Maensith and Taelisieth. He enjoyed their surprise, but suppressed his smile. 'It is just an idea of mine, but hear me out. It is only a matter of time before the Crimson Talon seek revenge on Maensith, now that Khiadysis is bound to have told them of her whereabouts.'

'You think to pay them off with prisoners?' said Maensith.

'I am sure we could find an intermediary at Khaidazaar who will be able to negotiate on our behalf,' said Aradryan. 'I know that it might not be easy, but it is worth considering.'

Maensith's face showed that she was considering the idea, and at some length. Her expression changed subtly from doubt to interest to thoughtfulness, and back again several times as she weighed up the possibilities. Her gaze fell upon Aradryan and they locked eyes, sharing a moment of common purpose and understanding. The hint of a smile twitched the corners of Maensith's mouth.

'And the rest of the fleet, what do they gain from this attack?' said Taelisieth, holding out his hands.

'By which you mean the rest of the crew,' said Aradryan, breaking his stare from Maensith's bewitching gaze to turn it upon Taelisieth. The lieutenant did not blink to show any sign of shame at the accusation.

'All get equal share that is the rule. I have no use for clumsy humans, do you? If you wish to offer a love gift to our captain, feel free to do so with your own share, but do not empty our pockets for your gesture.'

'I would have thought you owed our captain a little more respect and loyalty, considering all that she has given you, and how far she has carried you,' said Aradryan.

Taelisieth snapped to his feet, eyes wide with anger.

'Carried me?' he shouted. 'You have been nothing but a chain around our necks since your arrival, Aradryan of Alaitoc. If you are so magnificent, perhaps you would deign to repeat your performance of De'vaque's court?'

One hand on the hilt of his sword, Taelisieth stepped back and gestured for Aradryan to rise. Aradryan was about to comply, filled with indignation, but Taelisieth continued his tirade and gave Aradryan pause to reconsider drawing his weapon.

'It is one thing to puncture a sluggish lump of a human, it is quite another challenge to match your sword against one of our kind. Do you dare that?'

'My skill at arms is not the subject of debate,' Aradryan said slowly, keeping his gaze fixed on Taelisieth's sword hand. The moment the pirate looked to draw his weapon Aradryan was ready to leap aside. His words were spoken calmly, trying to defuse the irate lieutenant's mood. 'If it is my leadership you doubt, then give us an alternative.'

'Have you a more profitable suggestion, perhaps?' said Maensith. 'One that is better than this convoy?'

'The Gallows Stars, near Khebuin, where anasoloi traders make a dash from the Indiras Gap to reach the safety of the Naeirth cluster.' Taelisieth said the words quickly, as if he had been rehearsing them repeatedly. 'We can be there in three cycles, and back with a prize within ten.'

'Lone anasoloi traders?' Aradryan's laugh was sharp and short. 'What challenge is that?'

'Easy pickings, captain,' insisted Taelisieth. He took his hand from his sword and knelt on one knee beside Maensith, eyes fixed earnestly on her face. 'Think of what they might be carrying – Cthellan spheres, cudbear hides or perhaps even Anasaloi devil-wyrds. All can be bargained at great profit at Khai-dazaar. We are corsairs, not Commorraghan arena fighters. We do not need a challenge to prosper or prove ourselves.'

Maensith stroked her chin and looked between Aradryan and Maensith. Aradryan gave her hand an encouraging squeeze, but she drew it away and stood up.

'We shall see who is the better leader, not by deciding here but by a test in truth,' said the captain. She smoothed her long black robe with pale fingers and smiled thinly. 'My cherished Aradryan, I shall leave you in command of the *Fae Taeruth*. Taelisieth and I will transfer to the *Haenamor*, under his command. Whichever of the other ships' captains you can persuade to your cause will accompany each endeavour. In ten cycles' time we will return to the Cradle of Moons to see who is worthy of commanding the Azure Flame with me.'

'And what happens to the loser?' asked Taelisieth.

'What do you suggest?' Maensith asked.

'Winning will be reward enough,' said Aradryan.

'Taelisieth's shame will be sufficient punishment for the wrongs he has spoken against me.'

'And I will see you humbled, for my part,' said Taelisieth. 'Should I bring back the larger prize, you will never set foot again on the command deck of a ship.'

'So be it,' said Maensith as she strode from the room, leaving Aradryan alone with Taelisieth. The lieutenant smiled coldly.

'You have gone too far this time, Aradryan.' Standing up, Taelisieth patted Aradryan on the shoulder in condescending fashion. 'This is exactly what I wanted. Without Maensith and me to protect you from your rash impulses, I do not expect you to return. It is a shame that we might lose the *Fae Taeruth*, but at least you will have a grand tomb for your corpse.'

'If I lose the *Fae Taeruth*, I will gladly step aside for you,' said Aradryan. He ran a finger down Taelisieth's cheek and winked. 'Have fun popping anasolois for cudbear hides. When I have finished humiliating you in front of the whole fleet, you can wrap yourself up in them for comfort.'

THREE SHIPS OF the Azure Flame slid from the webway not far behind the cluster of human ships gathering in high orbit over the fifth world of the system. Alongside Aradryan on the *Fae Taeruth* were *Naestro*, under the leadership of Kharias Elthirin, and Namianis aboard the *Kaeden Durith*. With the three most powerful ships of the Azure Flame under his command, Aradryan was confident that the gaggle of merchantmen would be little threat.

Though he longed to prove himself against a foe

more challenging, the initial sensor sweeps indicated only a single warship to protect the flotilla; by its size it would be outgunned by the eldar cruisers.

'I came looking for sport, but it appears we shall have little of that,' Aradryan said, turning to smile at his second-in-command, Laellin. She nodded but said nothing, her focus set on the gunnery panel. Aradryan allowed a sliver of his consciousness to slip into the *Fae Taeruth*'s matrix. It was an empowering feeling, to be at the heart of so many systems. Beforehand he had only interfaced with the piloting networks, but now he had access to every component of the cruiser. His thoughts touched briefly upon those manning the various stations around the command hall, acknowledging them one by one.

Establishing a contact with Aerissan at the sensor controls, Aradryan felt for a moment as though he looked through the *Fae Taeruth*'s eyes. It was a bewildering experience, momentary but intoxicating. Aerissan guided Aradryan's attention to the scanner readings. The warship they had detected was attached to one of the cargo ships, although its plasma reactor, weapons and shields showed a spike in energy output as they were brought up to full strength.

With a thought of thanks to Aerissan, Aradryan slipped from the sensory banks into the communications suite. Immediately his holo-image appeared in the control chambers of the other two ships, while the slightly translucent ghosts of Kharias and Namianis materialised on the deck of the *Fae Taeruth*.

'Morai-heg has seen fit to spin us a rich thread, my friends,' declared Aradryan. 'Eight ships to be plundered and only a single worthy adversary to protect them. We shall split, so that the escort cannot protect the fleet from one direction. Avoid engaging the enemy, for as small as it is, I expect this guard dog's bite to be fierce. There is no need to be hasty, we can pick off the prizes in turn, after all.'

As the Azure Flame closed in, the freighter commanders tried to make a run for freedom. There was no coherent plan as cargo haulers, gas carriers, bulk transporters and superlifters split from each other in a flurry of blazing plasma trails, falling back on the ancient survival instinct of the herd: the predators cannot catch us all. The human warship broke its docking and turned towards the incoming eldar ships, forcing the *Naestro* to break away her attack, but leaving the *Fae Taeruth* and *Kaeden Durith* a clear run into the heart of the spreading flotilla.

As the *Fae Taeruth* overhauled the closest ship, Laellin targeted its aft sections with the starboard lasers, scoring a flurry of hits across its engine housings.

'Careful,' warned Aradryan, focusing the scanner sphere on the stricken ship. 'These human ships have fragile plasma drives. We do not wish to detonate our prize, do we?'

The *Kaeden Durith* swept ahead, gravity nets extending towards the crippled freighter. Aradryan did not mind the audacity of Namianis in taking the first prize; his goal was the much larger vessel at the heart of the convoy. The enemy warship was staying close to the biggest freighter, and three other ships of the convoy had decided that the guns of the light cruiser were a better defence than open space. They were wrong, Aradryan told himself in triumph. There was no way a single ship could protect every vessel in the convoy, especially against much swifter foes.

It was not long before the commander of the human escort came to the same conclusion and brought his ship onto a bearing that cut between the eldar and the ships trying to escape out-system. It was a wise move, forcing both the *Fae Taeruth* and *Naestro* to abort runs toward the fleeing vessels. However, it did mean that the cluster of four ships it had been protecting were now vulnerable.

Despite the urge to plunge in for the kill, Aradryan held himself and the *Naestro* in check for the time being. There was something about the way the warship had suddenly abandoned its charges that made Aradryan suspicious. There was also the unanswered question of why it had been docked with the large cargo ship when the eldar had arrived.

The four ships that had been left to their own protection were clustered together. They would be armed, no doubt, and although their weapons were little match for the holofields of the *Fae Taeruth*, in order to board their prize, the eldar would have to slow down, increasing the chances of being successfully targeted. There was safety in numbers for the moment, and though Aradryan desperately wanted the largest ship for himself, he remembered the mockery of Taelisieth. Only a fool would take on four vessels with a lone ship, no matter how poorly armed the more numerous vessels were. If he had wanted to destroy the cargo haulers, it would be easy enough, but he had to take them intact. Even more than that, Aradryan needed to capture as many of them as possible if he was to offer the kabal of the Crimson Talon sufficient pay-off to forget Maensith's past indiscretions. Aradryan held his tempestuous mood in check and resolved that he would not be caught out by making rash decisions.

Turning his attention back to the ships that had scattered, Aradryan used the infinity network to plot the intercept routes required to catch them. With the position taken up by the escort, there was a good chance that the portion of the convoy that had held together would be able to flee in-system before the *Fae Taeruth* could disable the scattering ships and return.

With a grimace of frustration, Aradryan looked back and forth across the display globe, trying to decide between the two options. Then, as if Morai-heg had not granted him enough fortune, he saw the largest ship suddenly expelling a cloud of plasma from emergency exhausts along its starboard flank. Yawing violently away from its companions, the ship started to fall behind, its engines flaring and dying fitfully, leaving scattered blooms of expanding plasma in its wake.

'That is our first prize!' Aradryan declared in triumph.

Chasing the running cargo haulers for a while longer, Aradryan drew the escort further and further out of position. When he was confident that he could outrun the warship back to the stuttering freighter, he ordered the *Fae Taeruth* to come about. Though the route back to the largest vessel was more circuitous, the higher speed of the eldar ship would give Aradryan plenty of time to affect an attack. To ensure that he and his crew were not disturbed, he ordered the *Naestro* to close towards weapons range of the human light cruiser, to dissuade the enemy captain from turning after the *Fae Taeruth*.

It was soon clear that the strategy had worked. Sails glittering gold in the stellar winds, the *Fae Taeruth* sped towards her prey.

PULLING ALONG THE starboard flank of the erratically powered freighter, the *Fae Taeruth* extended her gravity nets, binding herself to the larger ship. Half a dozen boarding tunnels latched on to the hull of the target vessel, high-powered lascutters in their tips melting through the outer shell to allow the boarding parties to dash aboard.

Normally Aradryan would have been at the forefront of the attack, leading the corsairs into deadly combat. This time he would not take part in the hack and thrust of the fighting; he was a leader not a warrior now. The initial parties reported minimal resistance – a couple of dozen humans swept away by the impetus of the attack. Securing a foothold across several decks, the pirates brought on reinforcements, Aradryan moving across to the human ship with them.

There were two main objectives – the control bridge and the storage holds. Dividing his force into three, Aradryan sent the greater part forwards to look for the captain and officers. Another descended the stairwells to the lower decks, seeking the cargo containers. Aradryan remained where he was, with twenty more pirates to guard the route back to the *Fae Taeruth*.

Through the communications stud in his ear, Aradryan monitored the progress of the boarding parties. They were under instruction to take prisoners wherever possible and soon there was a steady flow of unconscious or wounded humans being brought back to the staging area. The attack was progressing smoothly, although no sign could be found of the ship's captain; Aradryan knew things would go more smoothly if he could arrange an orderly surrender.

It was then that things started to go wrong. Naphiliar, who had been leading the search for the command crew, reported that his party had encountered heavily armoured warriors. They were being cut down by devastating firepower and had to fall back towards the boarding area.

'Armoured warriors?' replied Aradryan. 'What sort of armour? What weapons do they have? Tell me more!'

In response Aradryan heard his lieutenant panting heavily, punctuated by groans. Evidently he had been wounded. Over the open feed of the communicator, Aradryan heard sharp cracks and thunderous detonations. Something heavy thudded on the decking close to Naphiliar.

'This one is still alive.' The voice was deep, tainted by artificial modulation. Aradryan could hear a dull hissing, which was suddenly blotted out by the horrendous roar of a crude engine. Naphiliar screamed, his voice drowned out by the rasp of a chainsword and the snap of shattering bones.

'Praise the Emperor and abhor the alien.'

The tone of the voice was unmistakeable, as was the heavy tread that receded into the distance. Aradryan had heard many horror stories of the Emperor's Space Marines, but had thankfully never encountered the physically-enhanced warriors of the Imperium.

On board *Lacontiran* he had talked to warriors who had seen the genetically-altered soldiers and been fortunate enough to survive. Their presence was a shock, and a hard blow against Aradryan's desires to prove himself superior to Taelisieth. A ship-borne combat suited the Space Marines perfectly, and Aradryan suddenly realised that the escort ship had to be a Space Marine vessel. With that being the case, there was no telling how many more of them there might be; his corsairs were poorly matched for the coming battle.

Their presence changed everything, and Aradryan filtered through the tales of the Space Marines from memory, trying to find something that would give him an advantage. Everything he recalled merely emphasised what a terrible proposition they were to face in combat. The Space Marines would fight to the death rather than allow the ship to be taken, that was certain. In his ear-piece he could hear more reports of the deadly warriors' counter-attack, and he knew he had to react quickly to avert a disaster.

Aradryan quickly told the rest of his corsairs about the nature of their foes, and ordered them to avoid direct confrontation if possible. Evasion and ambush would be the best tactic against the hulking Space Marines – Aradryan's warriors possessed a few fusion pistols and powered blades capable of penetrating their armour, but they would have to bring across some heavier weaponry from the *Fae Taeruth* if they were to wipe out the Emperor's elite.

There were more encounters with the Space Marines by the parties moving aftwards, working through the hold space. Forewarned, these groups were able to swiftly retreat from their heavily armoured adversaries before any fighting broke out. To make matters worse for the raiders, the crew were still roving randomly across the ship, running into bands of corsairs as they tried to lay in wait for the Space Marines or retreat from their counter-attacks.

The situation was rapidly becoming confused, and Aradryan had only the scantest information regarding his enemies and the layout of the ship. With the *Fae Taeruth* grappled alongside, the cruiser was too close to perform anything but the most basic sensor sweeps of the vessel. What these told Aradryan was not encouraging – the Space Marines seemed to be gathering in strength in the lower decks towards the prow, most likely to push up to the corsair's landing area. There was nothing Aradryan could do against a determined attack except to fall back to the *Fae Taeruth* and disengage. He paced back and forth along the metal corridor beside the boarding tunnel entrances, trying to think of some way to outwit his foes. The sound of fighting – the distinctive noise of the Space Marine's boltguns and the detonation of grenades – echoed up the stairwells and along the passages. It was difficult to tell exactly where the noises were coming from, but they seemed to be getting closer. Aradryan tried to gather reports from his warriors over the communicator but their replies were fragmentary and hurried.

'Look at this!' Aradryan turned to see Laellin hurrying along the corridor, dragging something behind her. It was one of the crew, a large and bloodied hole in his chest. Before Aradryan could ask her what was so important about a dead human, Aerissan contacted him from the *Fae Taeruth*.

'We have detected significant warp breaches at the system limits. Human ships breaking from warp space, I would say. Nearly a dozen of them.'

'The escort for the convoy or more freighters?' Aradryan asked, gesturing for Laellin to wait before speaking. His second dropped the corpse on the deck and folded her arms impatiently.

'Too distant to say for certain, but warships would be my assumption,' replied Aerissan.

'What is it?' Aradryan demanded, distracted by Laellin's agitated fidgeting next to him.

'Look,' said his second-in-command, pointing at the dead crewman's chest. Aradryan looked into the ragged hole, seeing ribs splayed outwards, the internal organs turned to a mush.

'It is a dead – very dead – human,' said Aradryan. 'There will be more of them around if you want to start a collection. Now, I have something important to attend to.'

'Do you think a lasgun or shuriken did this?' snapped Laellin, grabbing Aradryan's arm, forcing him to look at the opened carcass again. 'This wound was blown open from the inside by a small explosion.'

'So what could cause such an injury, if it was not one of our weapons?'

'A Space Marine's boltgun, of course,' said Laellin, clenching her fists in exasperation.

'Why...' The question faltered on Aradryan's lips as he reached an answer for himself. 'Take me to see these Space Marines. Quickly now!'

Aradryan followed Laellin as she turned and

sprinted back up the corridor. They passed a handful of corsairs guarding the open bulkhead at the end of the passage and stepped out into a narrow landing. Turning right, Laellin headed up the open stairwell, her light tread barely making a sound on the metal mesh of the steps. She turned through a small doorway that led into a thin conduit barely wide enough for the eldar to run along. The air was humid and hot here, pipes running along the floor sprinkled with droplets of condensation.

'I think this is one of their artificial atmosphere exchanges,' explained Laellin as she ducked beneath another pipe running across the corridor at chest height. She stopped above a grate and glanced down. Her lip twisted in consternation. 'They were here before. They must have moved down a level.'

She pulled out her laspistol and fired at the bolts securing the grating. It fell with a loud clang on the deck below. Aradryan jumped through first, hand moving to the hilt of his sword as he landed. He could hear the thump of the Space Marines' boots close at hand. Landing lightly next to him, Laellin pointed towards a stairwell to their left.

Moving swiftly and silently, Aradryan ran to the top of the stairs. He glanced over the rail and then stepped back immediately, seeing a mass of blackened armour at the bottom of the steps. As quick as it had been, the brief look had confirmed what he had suspected. He moved back to where Laellin was keeping watch in the corridor.

'Pull everybody back, half to protect the boarding tunnels, the rest to somewhere spacious,' he told his lieutenant.

'There is some kind of communal mess three decks up. Will that suit?'

'Perfect,' said Aradryan, 'I shall come with you.'

'What are you thinking?' Laellin asked when she had disseminated the necessary information via her communicator.

'The Space Marine I saw had black armour, hastily and badly painted,' explained Aradryan as they moved silently up the stairwell, leaving the Space Marines behind. 'There was a crude motto written on his shoulder guard, and no icons. I think we are dealing with renegades.'

'Ah, renegades,' said Laellin, with a smile. 'So, they are protecting the convoy for themselves? They would not like to be caught here by the real escort any more than we would.'

'Exactly,' said Aradryan.

It took them a little while to reach the mess hall Laellin had mentioned. More than fifty corsairs were already there and a few more were entering from the doorway at the opposite end of the long room. The mess hall was a wide open space, divided by long tables and benches riveted to the floor. Hatchways and doors to the kitchen lined one wall, and lighting was provided by four strips that ran the length of the room, flickering and fizzing in an annoying fashion.

'Please give me your communicator,' said Aradryan, reaching out to Laellin.

Laellin complied, pulling the stud from her ear to pass it over. Aradryan used a fingernail to pry open the tiny cover, splitting the device like a pea. A minuscule reflective panel glistened inside and he pressed the device between thumb and forefinger. A quiet but high-pitched tone sounded from the device as it began to scan the different frequencies, seeking a signal. It was only a few moments before static hissed and then Aradryan could hear gruff voices.

'Heynke, use the auspex.'

The following words were accompanied by short bursts of static, which Aradryan guessed to be interference from some kind of scanning device.

'Most have reached the upper decks,' said a different voice. 'Too much interference from the superstructure for an accura... Hold on, something strange.'

'What is it?'

Aradryan reassembled the communicator and held it up to the translator face he had affixed to his coat. He smiled at his warriors, and held a finger to his lips to hush their chatter.

'I think this conversation is too dull,' said Aradryan. 'Let us give these fools something worth talking about.'

'Look for yourself.'

'What do you think they are up to?'

'Commander of the Space Marines,' Aradryan said, the communicator picking up the harsh words from the translator. 'I am monitoring your transmissions. Listen carefully to me. This loss of life is senseless and is not of benefit to myself or to you. It occurs to me that we do not need to fight. I detect your simple scanner and know that you can find me. I know something that would be valuable to you. Meet me where we can hold conference and we will discuss this matter like civilised creatures.'

'Was that...?' said a third human voice. 'Did that bastard override our comm-frequency?'

There was laughter from the corsairs as the translation echoed from Aradryan's device.

'How?'

'Forget how, did you hear what he said?' another voice cut in. 'He wants a truce!'

HEARING THE CLUMP of boots outside the far doors, Aradryan leaned back against the end of a table and waited for the Space Marines to enter. Around him several dozen eldar waited, some of them with weapons ready, most of them lounging across the tables and seats. Aradryan caught a glimpse of himself in the scuffed metal of a cabinet. He was dressed in a long coat of green and red diamond patches, which reached to his booted ankles. A ruff of white and blue feathers jutted from the high collar, acting as a wispy halo for his narrow, sharp-cheeked face. His skin was almost white, his hair black and pulled back in a single braid plaited with shining thread. Aradryan smiled at what he saw, but grew serious as the doors hissed open in front of him.

The two creatures that entered were as tall as Aradryan, and more than twice as broad in chest and shoulder. Both were clad shoulder to foot in thick plates of powered armour, daubed black in the same manner as the Space Marine Aradryan had spied earlier. One held a heavy-looking, double-barrelled weapon in one hand, its outer casing inlaid with golden decoration against a blue enamel. The other had no helm and his face was flat, his chin wide and his brow heavy. His head showed a thin layer of blond stubble. He carried a crystalline sword in his huge gauntleted hand, and a pistol in the other. There was something about the bare-headed Space Marine that unnerved Aradryan, but he could not identify what it was as the two hulking warriors stomped up the mess hall.

They stopped a dozen paces from Aradryan, weapons held easily. The pirate captain moved his eyes to meet the red-lensed gaze of the first Space Marine. He stood a fraction taller than the other, holding himself more upright, and was several paces closer than his companion. Aradryan assumed he was in charge.

'What is the name of he who has the honour of addressing Aradryan, Admiral of the Winter Gulf?' Aradryan barely made a sound as he spoke; the hard-edged tone of his speaking-brooch sent the words across the mess hall.

'Gessart,' said the helmeted Space Marine. 'Is that a translator?'

'I understand your crude language, but will not sully my lips with its barbaric grunts,' replied Aradryan.

The helmetless Space Marine moved up next to Gessart and Aradryan saw clearly what it was that had disturbed him before. The Space Marine's eyes were flecked with churning gold. He had psychic power, of that much Aradryan was certain. There was something about that golden light in his eyes that reminded Aradryan of the Master of Magic, the most manipulative of the Chaos Gods. It was ever-changing, like the Grand Mutator, flickering with azure and violet shadows. There was something unnatural; even more unnatural than psychic power. The resonance it left in Aradryan's mind reminded him of the Gulf of Despair, where he had faced the daemonettes. That was it, Aradryan realised. The second Space Marine was touched by the presence of a daemon!

Aradryan looked at Gessart with a furrowed brow, disturbed that he seemed to be parleying with devotees of the Dark Gods. Strangely, Aradryan did not catch the same scent of corruption from Gessart, but that did not settle his fear.

'That you consort with this sort of creature is ample evidence that you are no longer in service to the Emperor of Mankind,' Aradryan said, wishing to swiftly conclude his business here. Alaitoc had a long history, and the memory of the eldar stretched back to the dawn of the human's Imperium when half of the Emperor's warriors had been tainted by Chaos. 'We have encountered other renegades like yourselves in the past. My assumptions are proven correct.'

'Zacherys is one of us,' said Gessart with a glance towards the psyker. 'What do you mean?'

'Can you not see that which dwells within him?' Aradryan could not believe that Gessart was oblivious to the creature possessing his companion. There was far more to this situation than appeared, but Aradryan did not want to get drawn into whatever was going on with the Space Marines.

'What do you want?' demanded Gessart.

'To save needless loss for both of us,' Aradryan replied, opening his hands in a placating gesture. 'You will soon be aware that those whose duty it is to protect these vessels are close at hand. If we engage in this pointless fighting they will come upon us both. This does not serve my purpose or yours. I propose that we settle our differences in a peaceful way. I am certain that we can come to an agreement that accommodates the desires of both parties.'

'A truce? We divide the spoils of the convoy?' It was hard to tell Gessart's mood through the mechanical modulation of his helmet's speakers. Aradryan thought he detected hope rather than incredulity.

'It brings happiness to my spirit to find that you understand my intent. I feared greatly that you would respond to my entreaty with the blind ignorance that blights so many of your species.'

'I have become a recent acquaintance of compromise,' said Gessart. 'I find it makes better company than the alternatives. What agreement do you propose?'

'There is time enough for us both to take what we wish before these new arrivals can intervene in our affairs. We have no interest in the clumsy weapons and goods these vessels carry. You may take as much as you wish.'

'If you don't want the cargo, what is your half of the deal?' Gessart looked at the assembled pirates, finger twitching on the trigger of his weapon.

'Everything else,' said Aradryan with a sly smile.

'He means the crews,' whispered Zacherys.

'That is correct, tainted one,' said Aradryan. The eldar pirate fixed his eyes on Gessart, pleased that he detected a note of agreement although the Space Marine was hesitant, perhaps not trusting Aradryan's intent. The pirate leader sought to encourage Gessart to the right conclusion. 'Do you accede to these demands, or do you wish that we expend more energy killing one another in a pointless display of pride? You must know that I am aware of how few warriors you have should you choose to fight.'

'How long before the escort arrives?' Gessart asked Zacherys.

'Two days at most.'

'You have enough time to unload whatever you wish and will not be hampered by my ships or my warriors. You have my assurance that you will be unmolested if you offer me the same.'

Gessart stared at Aradryan for some time, but it was impossible to discern the alien's thoughts behind his helmet. Aradryan kept his own expression impassive, giving nothing away though inside he was rejoicing at the chance to sweep up the crews of the ships without undue aggravation.

'The terms are agreed,' said Gessart. 'I will order my warriors to suspend fighting. I have no control over the crews of the convoy.'

'We are capable of dealing with such problems in our own way,' said Aradryan. Indeed, Maensith had taught her warriors many techniques for subduing recalcitrant foes, having learnt from the best slave-masters of Commorragh. 'Be thankful that this day you have found me in a generous mood.'

Gessart hefted his weapon and fixed the eldar pirate with the cold, red stare. As Gessart spoke, Aradryan saw himself reflected in the helm lenses, one hand raised expressively, lips almost forming a sneer.

'Don't give me an excuse to change my mind.'

THE FAE TAERUTH built up speed, turning towards the last of the freighters to be boarded. Gessart's ship was powering away from the vessel, the renegade Space Marines having completed their own pillaging. Aradryan watched the strike cruiser through the holo-orb, thoughts touching lightly upon the psychic matrix to monitor the *Fae Taeruth*'s manoeuvre.

A sudden panic gripped Aradryan, flowing into him from the cruiser. The *Fae Taeruth* roared in alarm, sending a psychic shockwave rippling across her decks. Aradryan felt the semi-sentience of the ship spearing into his thoughts, his mind awash with scanner readings. The passing Space Marine vessel had targeted the *Fae Taeruth* with a variety of high-density sensors emanating from its weapon batteries: its guns were locked on!

The distress of the cruiser was matched by Aradryan's own dread as he saw gun ports sliding open along the starboard side of the strike cruiser. There was no time to activate the holofield, no space in which to manoeuvre away from the worst of the coming bombardment.

Laser, shell and plasma flared from the gun batteries of Gessart's ship, pounding the flank and mast of the *Fae Taeruth*. Still enmeshed with the infinity matrix, Aradryan felt every blow as a faint wound on himself, an ache spreading up his spine as the pounding continued, smashing the mast of the primary stellar sail. Secondary flares of pain registered in Aradryan's mind as gun decks exploded and holds filled with human prisoners were breached, belching atmosphere and corpses into the void.

Reeling, Aradryan staggered from the command pod, gasping heavily. The lights in the chamber had dimmed as the *Fae Taeruth* struggled to redirect her available power to maintaining the integrity of her compromised hull. Warning chimes and voices sounded a barrage of alerts.

Everything went dark and the ship plunged into silence. Somewhere, on a deck below, Aradryan could hear prisoners distantly shrieking in terror. He staggered back to the interface and laid his hand upon the dull gems. Nothing happened.

'She is dead,' muttered Aradryan, numbed by the realisation. '*Fae Taeruth* is dead.'

# ESCAPE

*The World of Blood and Tears – When the End of the Universe comes, there shall be a great battle to decide the fate of the spirits of the eldar. The Rhana Dandra will see the might of the eldar pitted against the Great Enemy, the Final Battle against Chaos, and all shall perish. The Herald of the Death, Fuegan the Burning Lance, agent of the Rhana Dandra, will call together the Phoenix Lords who forged the Path on which all eldar tread, and they shall be brought as one to Haranshemash, the World of Blood and Tears. Here they will fight their last battle, and the universe shall know peace once more.*

GESSART'S PARTING GESTURE, a bitter repeat of Aradryan's slaying of Darson De'vaque, had not quite slain the ship as Aradryan had feared. Minimal life support and the barest vestiges of the psychic matrix were still operational. Communication was compromised – only Kharias's voice could be heard as the captain of the *Naestro* offered assistance.

'Sensors report that the Imperial escort ships are less than a cycle away,' reported Kharias. 'Do you wish us to take your survivors on board?'

'No, we can manage,' Aradryan snarled in reply. He refused to accept that the *Fae Taeruth* was finished. 'There is still time to affect repairs. If we can bring the webway slipstream back to life, the human ships will not be able to follow us.'

'Such repairs would require many cycles and full dock facilities.' Kharias spoke patiently, but Aradryan knew that his fellow captain would not remain too long to offer assistance. The risk of being caught by the vengeful human ships increased the longer they remained. 'See sense, Aradryan.'

Still feeling soreness in his body from the psychosomatic connection he had shared with the ship when it had been damaged, Aradryan was in no mood to back down. He could remember clearly the words of Taelisieth; to return without the *Fae Taeruth* would be the deepest humiliation.

'Come alongside to take possession of the prisoners,' he snapped. Aradryan addressed the other eldar in the dim light of the command hall. 'We are not abandoning ship. There is time enough to repair the webway slipstream, I am sure of it.'

He saw several of the other officers shaking their heads despondently.

'Kharias is right,' said Laellin, stepping away from

her console. 'There is nothing to be salvaged here. Our prisoners outnumber us by four to one. If any of the holds have been breached internally, they will attack us. We cannot stay.'

'Nonsense!' Aradryan looked for support from some of the others, but in the twilight he saw only sad faces and shaking heads. 'I can't...'

With a heavy sigh, Aradryan slumped to the floor of the command pod, his back against the main console. He could feel the tiniest tendrils of the *Fae Taeruth*'s energy circuits stroking gently at his thoughts. Tears filled Aradryan's eyes; not for himself but for the ship that he had lost. For generations she had survived and it had been his hubris that had destroyed her.

Aradryan tried to speak, but the words stuck against the lump in his throat. He swallowed hard as tears ran down his cheeks. His voice was barely a whisper.

'Take the survivors aboard, Kharias. Ready weapons batteries to destroy the *Fae Taeruth*. We will not abandon her to the scavenging grasp of the humans.'

As Aradryan watched the hull of the *Fae Taeruth* breaking apart under the laser cannonade, part of him wished that he had stayed aboard. He had been tempted, but at the last moment he had crossed the boarding bridge to the *Naestro*, driven by an instinct to survive that was deeper and stronger than his desire to avoid the humiliation that awaited him when they returned to the rest of the Azure Flame.

Not only had he failed to bring back the *Fae Taeruth*, nearly a thousand prisoners had been lost with the ship; there was neither the room nor the supplies to keep them on board the remaining two vessels.

Aradryan had not been so callous as to leave the humans on board the cruiser during its destruction. Drugged so as not to risk any trouble, they had been ferried back to their ships and left to the attention of their arriving allies. With so many to be abandoned from the *Fae Taeruth*, it had been pointless taking the others on the *Naestro* and they too had been deposited unconscious on their vessels.

Leaving the viewing gallery, he headed back to his cabin. There were stares of disgust and pity from the eldar that he passed; disgust from former crewmates and pity from those who served aboard the *Naestro* and *Kaeden Durith*. Regardless of whatever retribution Taelisieth decided to impose upon Aradryan, the loss of reputation was absolute, and without it Aradryan knew he was worthless to himself and Maensith.

Aradryan took to his cabin, sealing the door with a mumbled word before he lowered himself onto his bed. On the floor beside him was a small shoulder bag, containing the few possessions he had decided to salvage from the *Fae Taeruth*. Reaching inside, he brought out a folded packet of dried purple leaves: dreamleaf. He had not dreamed since he had joined *Irdiris* and for a moment the scent of the narcotic was unfamiliar and frightening. The fear passed as old memories surfaced, of dreams and remembrances filled with joy and wonder.

Licking his fingertip, Aradryan dabbed at the dreamleaf and brought it up to his mouth. He smelt it again, this time the fragrance reminding him of soaring amongst dream-woven clouds and looking upon galaxies of blinding stars. It was dreaming that had set him on the road to where he was now, he thought. A road that had ended in ruin and despair. He took the dried leaf from his finger with the tip of his tongue and laid back, head against the hard surface of the mattress.

The dreamleaf did its job, flowing through his body, relaxing his muscles and dulling his mind. Closing his eyes, Aradryan blocked out external sensation, quietly speaking the mantras he had learnt to disassociate his senses from the rest of his body. It was as if darkness and silence cocooned him, but not in a frightening, cold way. The numbness was a warm embrace, allowing him to slip into the deep meta-sleep of the memedream.

LAUGHING AT NOONSPARROWS courting in the bushes, sat with Korlandril on the flower-decked hillsides of Etherian Tor in the Dome of Magnificent Tribulations.

THE LOOK OF resignation on Thirianna's face as she said goodbye, and the warmth of Athelennil beside him.

THE TOUCH OF Maensith on the first night he had been welcomed aboard the *Fae Taeruth*. Her joy did not last long; blood started to weep from Maensith's eyes, forcing Aradryan to retreat, seeking sanctuary in pure fantasy.

A VOLCANIC ERUPTION spewed glittering green fire into the heavens, bearing Aradryan up as ash on the superheated winds. Nothing more than a mote of dust in the raging storm, the winds howling around him, he was borne higher and higher, until the fiery plains spread out beneath him. He fluttered for a long time, flicked from one wind to the next, never falling, always carried upwards until the ground itself disappeared and the stars surrounded him.

Now the stellar winds took hold of his immaterial form, swishing him from star to star, sliding his incorporeal body along the clouds of nebulae and through the rings of supernovae. He became starlight itself, as fast and light as thought, and then became nothing; a part of the fabric of the ether that bound together the universe.

And here was peace and freedom.

SOMETIMES ARADRYAN ATE, and sometimes he drank, though such intermittent breaks in his dreaming barely registered. When wakefulness threatened to hinder his return to the meta-sleep – true waking prompted by physical needs – he returned to the dreamleaf again, forcing back the conscious world so that he could continue to explore the depths and heights of his unconscious. Here he could evade the pain of failure. In the world of the dreams, there was no laughter from Taelisieth. Beyond the veil of consciousness, Aradryan could turn away from the horror and the hurt in Maensith's eyes when she asked what had become of her ship.

He fled, cycle after cycle, into the dull embrace of the memedreams. Some kind spirit – perhaps ordered by Maensith or perhaps not – left food and drink by his cabin door. Aradryan never turned on the lights, but ate in darkness and silence, his last dreams and his next imagining drifting together, turning every meal into a potential banquet, every glass of water and juice into lavish wine.

It was better this way, he told himself in the few lucid moments between doses of dreamleaf. He was of no use to anybody, least of all himself; too afraid to die and too pointless to live.

Her laughed at his own moroseness and enjoyed the sadness that gripped his heart. His dreams became vistas of Alaitoc's infinity circuit, trapping him between life and death. He was nothing but a spark of energy in the great craftworld, and it nothing but a glimmer of lights in the galaxy.

Commander De'vaque's face returned to haunt him, rage incarnate, throwing back Aradryan's taunts that he was nothing to the universe. Now Aradryan could see that all of life was for nothing. There was no purpose other than to exist, to continue on until the end came, touching briefly upon other lives but leaving no lasting impression on the great turning of the universe.

Aradryan's dreams became more evocative and less rooted in reality. He knew that he should not indulge any longer, that the dreaming and the dreamleaf would break apart his thoughts. Faces from the past swam together. He saw Rhydathrin as he had been during that last meeting on the Bridge of Yearning Sorrows. Yet Rhydathrin shared Aradryan's face, and he realised that it was not Rhydathrin at all, but the mirrored mask of the Shadowseer Rhoinithiel. The laughter came then, so hard and loud that Aradryan thought he would rip apart his stomach and chest.

And so he did, pulling apart ribcage to expose his beating heart. Except his heart was no longer there. In his dream, he followed the trail of bloody droplets, and found that his heart was being fought over by tiny figures: Thirianna and Korlandril, Athelennil and Maensith. They bit and clawed at each other, pulling and ripping at Aradryan's heart with minute hands, their fingers digging into the red flesh.

With a wet popping noise, the heart split asunder, showering Aradryan with sweet nectar.

On the ground where his heart had been lay his waystone, pulsing slowly. He tried to pick it up, to force the stone back into his chest to fill the void left by his missing heart, but his fingers passed through the waystone.

Childish giggling sounded from the shadows of the room, and half-seen, androgynous figures crept in the darkness, their black eyes fixed on Aradryan.

The chamber was huge, as Aradryan found himself asleep on the bed by the sea, in the ancient haunted palace. There were pictures everywhere, images from his life, his friends and family and strangers and enemies; every face he had ever seen. He bounded across the immense room with sudden energy, to lift a silver-framed image from the floor.

'I am several and one,' said the picture of Estrathain. The kami's blank face filled every image around Aradryan, thousands of eyeless, noseless visages staring down at him from the walls and ceiling, glaring up at him with accusation from the tiled floor.

In the distance Aradryan could hear the tootle of Lechthennian's flute and the strum of his half-lyre, but the Solitaire was becoming quieter, moving away. He was not coming to help.

* * *

THE DREAMS CAME and went, and Aradryan did not care for the real world.

THE DREAMS CHANGED more over time. Aradryan went back again and again to his liaisons with Athelennil. Only he did not spend those moments of passion with Athelennil but with Thirianna. All else was the same, the places and the mood, the laughter and the heat, but Thirianna played the part of his lover in a way that she had never done so in fact.

'THEY ARE COMING to kill us,' Thirianna whispered as she lay next to Aradryan. The heat of her body warmed his arms as she lay cradled against his chest. 'We will all burn.'

'I do not understand,' replied Aradryan, sitting up.

HE COULD HEAR screams; distant shouts of pain and terror echoed around the room. Aradryan was sure he was awake. The effect of his last dose of dreamleaf had worn off. The dream persisted, though, leaving the stench of burning in his nostrils.

He looked down at the dreamleaf pouch, now only half-full. It did not matter, he told himself. Most dreams meant nothing. He reached for another pinch of dreamleaf, and was soon swept away on a silver cloud of pleasure, Thirianna laughing by his side.

'THEY ARE COMING to kill us,' Thirianna whispered as she lay next to Aradryan. The heat of her body warmed his side as she lay cradled against his chest. 'We will all burn.'

Sitting up, Aradryan found himself on Alaitoc. It

was the Dome of Crystal Seers. Around Aradryan were the glittering statues of seers past, their bodies turned from flesh to glassy immobility. Every face was the same, and the lips of all the seers moved. Every single one had become Thirianna and they all issued the same warning.

'They are coming to kill us. We will all burn.'

ARADRYAN REACHED FOR the dreamleaf with a shaking hand. No matter how much he took, or how many exercises and mantras he put himself through, he could not rid himself of the nightmares. Whatever venue he took himself to in his dreams, Thirianna was there, with the same message every time.

Fingers touching the pouch, Aradryan stopped himself and rolled back onto the mattress. He stared up at the slowly shifting purple and red that dappled the ceiling. Once he would have been able to turn the shapes into the foundation of any landscape he desired, channelling the gently changing patterns into mountains and seas, cities and forests. Now they just reminded him of burning.

He pushed himself to his feet, trying hard to focus. He had been dreaming for a long time – how long he was not sure, but many cycles. Reality was hard to grasp and he stumbled, his legs weak from inactivity. Bracing himself against the wall with one hand, he arched his back, taking in three deep breaths.

Slowly, painfully, a degree of clarity returned. The light hurt his eyes and the touch of the air on his skin was rasping and cold. He embraced the sensation, drawing it into himself to drive out the vestiges of the dreaming.

Still he heard Thirianna's warning, a whisper in the air around him.

'They are coming to kill us. We will all burn.'

Making his way out into the passage, Aradryan took slow steps, acclimatising himself to his waking state. His head throbbed and his gut ached. The taste of dreamleaf was acrid in his mouth and his skin felt stiff and dry. With aching eyes, he peered down the corridor.

'Wait,' he croaked, reaching out a hand as a shape flittered from one archway to another ahead of him. The figure stopped and turned in surprise.

'Aradryan? I thought you lost forever to the dreams.'

The voice was familiar, but Aradryan could not place it. He took a few steps closer, the other eldar's facing resolving into the gaunt features of Nasimieth. The gunnery captain was frowning, more from confusion than anger.

'Where is Maensith,' Aradryan said, forcing the words to form with dead lips and thick tongue. 'I must speak with her.'

'I do not think she wishes to see you,' said Nasimieth. Aradryan straightened as best he could, forcing himself to concentrate on Nasimieth's face.

'I can find her through the matrix,' said Aradryan, stepping past the other eldar.

'Not in that state.' Nasimieth held out an arm to stop Aradryan. He laid a hand on his shoulder. 'She is in her chambers.'

It seemed as if Nasimieth whispered something else – 'They are coming to kill us. We will all burn.'

Shaking his head, Aradryan stumbled on.

\* \* \*

MAENSITH'S CHAMBERS WERE a suite of rooms situated above the command deck, adjoining the observation gallery. Aradryan recovered some of his composure and sense as he walked the length of the *Naestro*, which had become the new flagship of the Azure Flame. The ship was quiet, the stillness filtering through his dilapidated mind.

It was the stillness of pre-battle tension.

The door to Maensith's chamber opened to his approach, revealing a circular common area. The captain, Taelisieth and several other lieutenants were sat in the collection of chairs and couches set upon a thick rug that dominated the room. All eyes turned to Aradryan as he entered, apathy in some, outright hostility in others.

'You should not be here,' said Taelisieth, getting to his feet. 'Crawl back to your dreams, cursed one.'

Ignoring the jibe, Aradryan focused on Maensith. She looked on impassively as Aradryan stiffly walked across the carpet and stood before her.

'We need to speak,' said Aradryan. 'In private.'

'Now is not the time, Aradryan.' Maensith's tone was stern rather than cruel. She shook her head softly. 'You are in no state for any conversation, and we are about to embark on an attack.'

'You look like a corpse,' remarked another of the officers, Sayian.

Picking up a silver plate from one of the tables, Aradryan looked at himself. His eyes were shrunken in dark sockets, all life leached from them to leave them bloodshot and red-rimmed. His skin was like creased and cracked parchment, flaking away as he lifted a finger tip to prod at his stiff flesh. His fingernail was half-chewed and bloody, and his knuckles prominent and rubbed raw. His hair sat in a tangled mess upon his head, the natural black colour coming through, the white ends still showing artificial pigment.

He felt as bad as he looked. Aradryan's spine ached as though the bones had fused together from so much time spent lying down. His breath wheezed in and out of his dry mouth and down a raw throat into shrivelled lungs. His spirit stone was a grey oval on his chest, with the barest flicker of light. Every joint flared with pain as he stooped to place the plate back where he had lifted it from, the dish falling onto the tabletop with a clatter from his numb fingers.

'An attack? Where?' He asked, turning his bleary look on to Maensith. The words were little more than a wisp of breath from shrivelled lips.

'It is none of your concern,' said Taelisieth, shoving Aradryan. The former steersman had no strength to resist and tottered awkwardly backwards for half a dozen steps. 'You do not belong here.'

'I have to go back to Alaitoc,' said Aradryan, clumsily dodging Taelisieth's next thrust, pain flaring through the muscles of his legs and back. 'Please, a moment of your time is all I ask.'

'When the raid is finished,' said Maensith. 'Whatever you have to say can wait until then.'

Dizziness struck Aradryan and he staggered to his left, almost colliding with Taelisieth. The officer struck Aradryan in the chest with an elbow, sending him sprawling onto a couch. Aradryan lay there, only half aware of what was going on. Thirianna's warning whispered in his ears.

'They are coming to kill us. We will all burn.'

'Leave him for the moment,' he heard Maensith say. The looming shadow of Taelisieth withdrew. Aradryan lay still, breathing quickly. He dimly heard the conversation continuing, but could not make any sense of it.

A name struck him, heard amongst talk of strategy and manoeuvres: Nathai-athil. It was a star system not far from where he had lost the *Fae Taeruth*. Through the fugue of his exhaustion, he recalled that it was a dead system, of no interest at all.

'Why Nathai-athil?' he asked, pushing himself upright. 'There is nothing there.'

'It is a new convoy mustering point,' said Maensith, waving for Taelisieth to silence his protest.

Aradryan absorbed this without comment, slumping to one side, head pounding. The conversation continued around him. Something nagged at him, trying to pierce his thoughts through the constant whispering that threatened doom and fire. There was something about Nathai-athil that unsettled him.

'There is nothing there,' he said, straightening once more.

'You are babbling, cretinous wretch,' said Taelisieth. 'Please, Maensith, let me eject this wreck.'

'Wait a moment,' said Aradryan, fending away Taelisieth's grasping arm, focus returning. 'How did you learn of this place?'

'We captured a fast freighter moving out of Daethronin three cycles ago,' said Maensith, again waving for Taelisieth to halt. 'Its systems showed a rendezvous at Nathai-athil. Seven ships, poorly escorted.'

'Nathai-athil is a terrible mustering point,' said

Aradryan. 'It is nothing but dust clouds, gas and asteroid fields. There are no navigation markers or landmarks. The humans will find it difficult to gather there.'

'But it is an ideal place to hide if you do not want to be caught,' said Maensith. 'You do not know this, but we have continued to reap great success in your absence. The humans will try anything to avoid or catch us.'

'Anything?' said Aradryan. 'Would they sacrifice a ship for that?'

'An ideal place to hide...' muttered Taelisieth. He looked with narrowed eyes at Aradryan, but some of the aggression had gone, replaced with curiosity. 'You think we are being lured into an ambush?'

Aradryan shrugged. The effort of staying coherent amidst the after-images and echoes of the long dreaming was becoming more and more taxing.

'We cannot simply turn away,' said Maensith, her gaze moving across her officers. 'If it is not a trap, we waste a great opportunity.'

There were no replies from the others. Maensith shook her head in irritation, darting an angry glance at Aradryan.

'A dream- and drug-addled fool, you are, and paranoid too,' she said. 'A doom-monger no less.'

'Yet we should act with caution,' said Taelisieth. 'Send the *Kaeden Durith* to investigate first.'

'And risk warning the flotilla and escorts of attack?' Maensith was scornful. 'They would scatter into the clouds and be lost.'

'We do not have to separate the fleet,' said Taelisieth. 'Just send a ship first before committing full strength from the safety of the webway.'

Aradryan could barely hear what was said next. The dreaming was beckoning to him, dragging him back from reality. He remembered why he had come here, and fought against the lure of the dreaming. His body was almost dead, the exhaustion dragging him down into dark, cold depths. Aradryan managed to summon the energy to pass on the warning.

'I need to go back to Alaitoc,' he said. 'They are coming to kill us. We will all burn.'

ARADRYAN WOKE UP feeling more refreshed than before, though his throat and lips were still dry and there was an ache in the back of his head that pulsed dully down his spine. He found himself lying on one of the couches in Maensith's chamber – the same seat on which he had passed out, he recalled with some difficulty. His mind was blurred, as was his vision, and it was hard to remember what had happened. He was left with a recurring thought, as of a half-dream.

'They are coming to kill us. We will all burn.'

Sitting up, Aradryan was relieved that there was no fit of dizziness. He found a carafe of water on the floor next to him, and a small crystal tumbler. As he reached out for the drink, he noticed the yellowish stains on his fingertips and wondered at the amount of dreamleaf he had consumed over the cycles following his humiliation by Taelisieth. It was no wonder he had lost sense of himself. Despite his slightly improved physical condition, he was still ashamed to his core at his recent failures; his indulgences with the Dreaming would have done nothing to repair his shattered reputation.

Swinging himself around to sit properly on the couch, Aradryan leaned forwards, hands on knees. There was a tingle in his mouth, an itch of craving for dreamleaf that was easy to ignore. Less accommodating was the nagging whisper in his ears. If he paid attention, Aradryan would swear it sounded like Thirianna's voice.

Recalling the mix of dream and nightmare, the presence of Thirianna and the dread warnings she brought with her, Aradryan's head swam again. He squeezed his knees tight and stamped his foot on the floor, trying to assure himself that he was not dreaming again. It was impossible to tell, of course. With so much dreamleaf and his long expertise, any dream he underwent could well be indistinguishable from reality. For all that he knew, this was a memedream that he was experiencing, and not a new awakening at all. He tried hard to remember if he had woken before and subsequently returned to the dreaming, but he could not tell.

Such thoughts threatened to send him down into a spiral of insanity. He drank a tumblerful of water, savouring the liquid as it slipped over his swollen tongue and down his parched throat. If this was not reality, his imagination was doing him proud, he thought.

'More coherent this time, I hope.' Aradryan looked towards the door and saw that Maensith had returned. She wore her battle armour, her weapons hanging from her belt. Seeing her sent flashes of recollection through Aradryan's skull.

'Did I...' He did not know how to ask the question.

'Have I dreamt long?'

'Thirty cycles and more, with barely a mouthful to eat and drink every cycle,' said Maensith, her face showing pity rather than sympathy. Her look sent barbs into Aradryan's pride and he straightened up and looked her in the eye.

'And what else did I do?'

'Nothing much,' said Maensith. 'You asked me to return to Alaitoc. You did not say why, but it seemed very important to you. Who is Thirianna?'

'They are coming to kill us. We will all burn.' Aradryan spoke the words without thought, letting them free from where they had been fluttering around inside his head.

'That is what you kept saying as you dreamt,' said Maensith, her face now showing genuine concern. She sat beside him. 'What have you seen?'

'Alaitoc aflame,' replied Aradryan. He shuddered as images from the dreaming floated through his thoughts: images of death and burning and misery. He could not shake the feeling that it was somehow his fault. He looked at Maensith, a deep dread gripping his heart. 'It is a warning, I am sure.'

'We shall see soon enough,' said Maensith, standing up. 'In seven more cycles we shall be there.'

'What do you mean?' Aradryan stood also. 'We are returning to Alaitoc?'

'Yes, we are, which is why you need to bring yourself back to a state that at least vaguely resembles sanity and hygiene. There are still some of your clothes in my bedchambers, if you wish to change.'

Maensith took three steps towards the door before Aradryan spoke her name and stopped her.

'Why are we going to Alaitoc? This is not because of me, is it?'

'Yes, in more ways than one,' Maensith replied. 'Even in your dream-woven state you saw something was wrong with our attack at Nathai-athil. Taelisieth went first with the *Kaeden Durith* and found more than a dozen Imperial ships waiting for us. It seems we have agitated the humans enough for the moment, so I decided we should leave the Winter Gulf. Between your babbling about fires and Thirianna, and my desire to seek out somewhere a bit safer than open space to collect myself, Alaitoc seemed the natural choice.'

'I do not want to go back, not now.'

'It is not your choice, Aradryan. Morai-heg cast a loose thread for you, and now it is unravelling. You have already lost me one flagship, the ship I stole from my kabal to earn my freedom, and you are not welcome on this one. The crew speak out against you, and I must listen. Even the passion I once shared with you does not turn me to your cause any more. I will be returning you to Alaitoc, or setting you on a small moon somewhere; it is your choice as long as you do not stay aboard.'

Aradryan flopped back onto the couch, limbs limp. Maensith twitched her head in irritation and left him to his dark thoughts.

WHEN HE SLEPT, Aradryan did not dream. It was better to fall into the utter blankness of unconsciousness than to risk the return of the nightmarish Thirianna and her whispered warnings. Aradryan slept and woke, and regained something of his strength and dignity, if not his pride.

When he awoke again he felt a strange tension in the air. The chambers were empty still, but a note thrummed through the ship, keening across its fabric and along the crystal lines of its psychic network. It was this that had roused him from his deep slumber and it took a moment for Aradryan to realise what the sensation was. The *Naestro* was at full stretch, every part of her engines running at the highest power. Aradryan's nerves resonated with the force flowing through the matrix, sending the ship speeding through the webway.

Leaving Maensith's chambers, Aradryan headed for the control hall. The doors opened for him – he had wondered if there had been a psychic bar put in place – and he stepped inside. Maensith was in the command pod, her face screwed up in intense concentration. Taelisieth glanced up from the weapons console. A frown creased his brow when he recognised who had entered, but he said nothing, nodding his head towards the display sphere at the heart of the hall.

The holo-image showed the webway behind the *Naestro*. It looked like they were rushing up a gleaming silver tunnel towards the surface, a black lattice of rune-carved wraithbone keeping the walls of the webway in place. Two dark shapes stood out against the streaming silver fabric, their hulls mottled midnight blue and black, their prows studded with curving sensor blades, hulls jutting with barb-like cannons: Commorraghans. The livid white marks along the lengths of their hulls spoke of recent repairs and Aradryan's gut shrivelled into a tight knot.

'Khiadysis,' he muttered.

'It was not just the humans waiting for us at Nathai-athil,' said Taelisieth. 'Khiadysis must have heard something of the trap being laid. They were waiting for us to bolt back to the webway, but we spotted them two cycles ago. They have been following us ever since.'

'Where is the rest of the fleet?' asked Aradryan. 'We have two cruisers outgunned.'

'The cowards scattered as soon as the Commorraghans appeared,' Maensith snarled from the centre of the chamber. Aradryan looked at her, but her eyes were focused on the console gems. 'Our only hope is the sanctuary of Alaitoc. Even Khiadysis will hesitate to attack us there.'

'And how long before we reach Alaitoc?' asked Aradryan. He started towards the stairway leading up to the piloting suite, but Taelisieth broke from his console to stop him.

'You are not a pilot or officer,' said the corsair, eyes narrowed. 'It is no small fault of yours that we are pursued.'

'We will be at Alaitoc shortly,' replied Maensith.

Aradryan felt impotent as he watched the dark shapes of the Commorraghan cruisers closing slowly with the *Naestro*. Forward gun turrets extended from the prow of the ship, revealed by lines of sliding shutters that opened up like the gills of some monstrous shark.

'Baring their teeth for nothing. They are still out of weapons range,' announced Taelisieth.

'Keep them out,' snapped Maensith.

In the holo-display two small stars appeared, each deep red in colour, jettisoned into the wake of the

*Naestro*. Aradryan realised they were some kind of munitions, but was not sure of what type. The pursuing pair of cruisers had time and space to avoid a direct contact with the two stars, though they lost some momentum doing so. When the lead cruiser – it looked like Khiadysis's own ship to Aradryan – was level with the closest star, Taelisieth gave a satisfied growl and manipulated a control on his console.

The star expanded into a ball of red lightning, flaring from one side of the webway to the other. The detonation caught the second star in its arcs of energy, causing a secondary explosion. The tubular passage of the webway was filled with a storm of power that sped along the walls and rippled along the hull of the Commorraghan cruiser. The energy wave expanded, catching up with the *Naestro* in a few moments.

Aradryan felt the shock of the webway's shuddering through the psychic network, a moment before the ship physically shuddered, causing him to sway on his feet. Looking back at the display, he saw that both Commorraghan cruisers had ploughed on through the psychic storm, the flares of energy dripping from their hulls like water off the oiled skin of a marine beast. Taelisieth cursed loudly and looked over to Jain Anirith at the sensor controls.

'Some kind of psychic shielding,' Jain reported. 'No lasting damage detected.'

The chase continued endlessly. Aradryan was rooted to the spot, unable to tear his gaze away from the holo-display. He was not sure if it was reality or his imagination, but he thought he could see the Commorraghans eating up the gap between the ships. He did not know how they could move faster than the *Naestro*, which was one of the most efficient ships he had ever been on, but somehow they did. Aradryan sensed the Commorraghans getting closer and closer, creeping up on him like a slow death. Eventually their forecannons would come into range and the chase would rapidly end.

'Sending warning to Alaitoc of our approach,' announced Maensith. 'We will be coming out of the portal at full speed.'

'Let us hope that there is no ship trying to come back in,' said Aradryan. Maensith scowled at him for pointing out the obvious danger.

Aradryan could not bear the tension – both in his body and the fraught psychic power being channelled through the ship. As much as it pained him to stay and not be able to do anything, he could not leave and simply wait for the outcome. He lived every moment, etching the sight of those two black predators into his memory like nothing else.

This is vengeance, he thought, as he looked at the Commorraghan vessels. This is the payment I make for the decisions I have made. It would all catch up with him in the end, he knew that. Ever since Hirith-Hreslain he had stayed one step ahead of his doom, trying his best to outwit fate. Now it was not up to him. He would perish or live by the actions of Maensith and the others.

Looking back he realised he had craved freedom but had enjoyed none. Always had he been in the thrall of someone or something else. First it had been his fear of death, and then his lust for Athelennil. His desire for danger had mingled with Maensith's passion to create an intoxicating and addictive combination that had steered his life for a while. And then his shame had been his prison, locking him into his fears as much as the dreamleaf.

'Freedom is a myth,' he said, to nobody in particular.

He was startled when he realised that the ships in the holo-display were getting smaller. Suddenly they were replaced by the snarling face of Khiadysis.

'Run, you pathetic worms, run!' growled the hierarch. His right eye twitched with a tic that Aradryan had not noticed before. 'You cannot stay at Alaitoc forever, you conniving bitch. I will find you, or the Crimson Talon will.'

That image disappeared to be replaced by a golden wheel of energy, the brightness of the webway gate causing Aradryan to put his hand in front of his eyes, blinking hard. When he could see again, the soaring towers of Alaitoc were racing past, silhouetted against the slowly turning disc of the craftworld's webway portal. The *Naestro* swept over domes and bridges, almost brushing the forcefields and gravity nets that covered Alaitoc. It was a view of the craftworld that Aradryan had never experienced before, seeing her racing past in all of her glory; he had previously been too occupied with piloting to notice the size and grandeur.

'I am back,' he whispered and he realised he was crying.

# RESOLUTION

*Alaitoc – One of the major craftworlds that survived the Fall, Alaitoc is known for the strength of its inhabitants' adherence to the Path. This strict regime can be too much for some, and so many depart Alaitoc seeking the life of the Outcast, and thus it has a large diaspora of rangers, corsairs and other adventurers across the galaxy and other craftworlds. The name of the craftworld derives from the legend of Khaine and means 'Sword of the Heavens'.*

THE COUNCIL OF Alaitoc sat on the stepped seats of the amphitheatre-like Hall of Communing. It was a column-lined dome set close to the rim of Alaitoc, and Aradryan felt very small as he stood at its centre, surrounded by nothing but a transparent force dome and the stars of the galaxy. The council consisted of the seers and autarchs of Alaitoc, joined by a few other select individuals of exceptional wisdom or age.

Farseer Anatharan Alaitin had been nominated as spokesman, though in truth the eldest councillor's role had been more of interrogator than mouthpiece. There were shining motes of crystal in the ancient farseer's skin and eyes, and his hair was as white as snow. Aradryan had been questioned for several cycles, pausing only for refreshment, concerning his exploits since he had left the craftworld. He was still not sure why everybody was so concerned with his business, and as the fourth cycle of questioning began his exasperation became vocal.

'What do you want from me?' he demanded, turning a circle to look at the assembled councillors. 'I feel as if I am on trial for some charge that has not yet been levelled.'

'In a way, you are.' This came from one of the eldar sat on the lowest step of the hall. Aradryan recalled the lengthy introductions that had preceded the inquisition and brought up a name: Kelamith. 'Purposefully or unwittingly, your actions have brought about great destruction to Alaitoc. We are here to divine the nature of that threat and whether you are complicit in its arrival or simply a victim.'

'Destruction?' Aradryan looked around, hands spread wide in innocent appeal. 'I see no destruction. What have I done?'

'The humans are coming,' said Alaitin. 'Soon, we fear. They bring war with them.'

'And what has that to do with me?'

'This Imperial commander, De'vaque, tell us more about him,' said Kelamith. 'We see your thread and his tightly bound together. On the skein we have seen that the bloodshed stems from your line, but there are too many fates to count at the moment. We need your help, Aradryan, to avert disaster for our craftworld.'

Taken aback by the farseer's humble tone, Aradryan nodded. He felt ashamed of what had happened with De'vaque, realising that his pride and self-opinion had fuelled his confrontation with the governor more than sense or desire for freedom. He carefully explained the circumstances that brought him into De'vaque's circle, firmly placing the emphasis on the existing relationship created by Yrithain. Alaitin delved deeper, demanding to know what happened at Daethronin. With some chagrin, Aradryan related the encounter on the Imperial commander's yacht. There were whispers and mutters amongst the councillors, who felt that they were now hearing something that would explain how such a doom was being brought down upon Alaitoc.

'And so you held his son hostage until you were free, yes?' said Alaitin. 'That was the last you saw of the Imperial commander?'

Aradryan swallowed hard, painfully recalling his actions that had followed. He looked at Alaitin, who regarded him sternly with slate-grey eyes.

'That is not what happened,' said Aradryan. At that moment, he desperately wanted to wake up. This dream had gone on long enough, it was beyond tiresome and had now becoming frightening.

'What happened, Aradryan?' Alaitin's question was like a blade slicing into Aradryan's heart, through flesh and bone into the core of his being. Aradryan remembered a cloud of exploding plasma and gas. In his heart he felt the galaxy trembling with the affront he had done to De'vaque. He could not believe his own callousness, and his head swam at the recollection.

'What did you do, Aradryan?' Alaitin was relentless, his eyes boring into Aradryan.

'We killed them,' he replied softly, meeting the gaze of some in the assembled audience. As he spoke, Aradryan saw dismay and disgust written on their faces. '*I* killed them: De'vaque's son and bodyguards. I blasted their shuttle apart and scattered their ashes into the ether. It was unnecessary and cruel, and the greatest hurt I could have inflicted on Commander De'vaque.'

Silence more condemning than any shouted accusations swallowed Aradryan. He felt the scorn of the councillors washing over him, stripping away the last tattered vestiges of his dignity. Their silent charge echoed over and over in his mind: cold-blooded murderer.

'So now we perhaps come to understand the why,' said Kelamith. He laid a hand on Aradryan's shoulder, eyes soft with pity. 'Thank you.'

'There is as yet no explanation as to the how.' This came from a tall, well-built figure who had been sitting opposite Kelamith. His robes were dark and light blue, threaded with white, and his face was narrow with flared nostrils and bright blue eyes. Aradryan knew who he was – everybody on Alaitoc knew Arhathain, chief amongst the autarchs. He stood up now and approached Aradryan, fixing him with that pale stare.

'Commander De'vaque knows nothing of your connection to Alaitoc, nor where the craftworld might be found?'

'That is correct, autarch,' said Aradryan. He wanted to flee from that piercing glare, but was pinned to the spot by its intensity. 'My place of birth never arose in conversation with him or his son, and Alaitoc is far from the eyes of the humans. I cannot see how he...'

Aradryan's voice died away as he thought about the question. His heart sank even further, though he had thought it impossible. Even his confession about Darson De'vaque paled in comparison to the revelation that was coursing through his thoughts. Panic gripped him as he looked into the uncaring eyes that regarded him from every direction, dozens of them judging him silently.

'The Commorraghans.' Aradryan squarely met Arhathain's. 'They had been waiting in the webway for the Azure Flame to flee from the ambush at Nathai-athil. We thought it was simply opportunism, but...'

He let them draw their own conclusion, unable to voice it himself. It was Kelamith who spoke next. When Aradryan turned in the direction of the farseer, the pysker's eyes were ablaze with energy.

'Bitter and spiteful, filled with hatred for the betrayal against him, Khiadysis Hierarch will lead Commander De'vaque after the one he despises.' The farseer's unnatural gaze fell upon Aradryan. 'The Imperial commander brings allies with him, for he has persuaded others that Alaitoc is a nest of pirates that has been plaguing their star systems of late. A fleet he brings, and soldiers of the Emperor's army.

And with them comes another, a titan of a man who leaders a Chapter of the Emperor's Space Marines. He is called Achol Nadeus and it will be by his hand and his word that Alaitoc will be doomed.'

Aradryan shuddered at the prophecy, remembering the dreams of fire and Thirianna's warning. He felt a tremble, not from within but from Alaitoc itself. It was as if a great drum had pounded in the depths of the craftworld and reverberated to its outer edge in moments. The sensation brought with it a quickening of Aradryan's heart. His pulse raced and an image flickered in his vision; a memory from Hirith-Hreslain, of a giant of fire and wrath that wrought carnage wherever it trod.

The Avatar of Khaine was awakening and war was coming to Alaitoc.

THE DOME OF Crystal Seers was bathed in twilight from the dying star that Alaitoc was orbiting. The orange light glinted from the faces of past farseers, their flesh absorbed by the infinity circuit of the craftworld, so that now they stood as crystalline statues, dozens of them across the dome, set into sweeping, beautiful parklands of silver and blue.

Aradryan flexed his fingers, trying to work off some of the tension that gripped his body. Every joint felt stiff, every nerve taut. His mind buzzed with what might come to pass. And all he could do for the moment was wait.

'You may like to know that Thirianna is doing well,' said Alaitin, who waited with him. The two sat on a curving white marble bench, their backs to a glittering pool of black. Alaitin was garbed in battle dress, his robes covered with rune armour, his head encased in a jewelled helm that hid his face. He was unarmed, as was Aradryan. The farseer had explained several times that this was essential, but Aradryan felt naked without his sword and pistol. He wished he still had his longrifle. For one who had not known battle for so long, he realised he had swiftly become accustomed to its accoutrements.

'It will not be long now,' said the farseer. He turned his head away for a moment.

Earlier Aradryan had watched the fire and strife of the space battle unfolding through the dome. Las-fire and plasma had flickered across the firmament and ships like cathedrals and swans had duelled against the stars. The humans had not been stopped – could not be stopped – and they had boarded at the docks two cycles ago. Since then, they had been pushing steadily towards the core of the craftworld, the spearpoint of their attack formed by the Sons of Orar Space Marines led by Achol Nadeus.

'What of Maensith and the *Naestro*?' asked Aradryan. 'She told me they would stay to help in the fight against their starships.'

'The *Naestro*... survives for the moment,' replied Alaitin. 'She was badly damaged in a duel with an enemy frigate, but the ship and her captain are still with us.'

Aradryan nodded, relieved by the news. Whatever happened to him – to Alaitoc – the ships would be able to escape. There was a little comfort in knowing that.

The silence that followed was not quite complete. Aradryan could hear the distant sound of shells and explosions. Now and then a tremor would ripple through the infinity circuit. Here, in the Dome of the Crystal Seers, that ripple was magnified, and it seemed that the ancient farseers would whisper amongst themselves for a moment as the wind stirred around them. The rustling was no more than a breeze in the trees, Aradryan told himself, but it was no less disturbing to hear.

He found himself listening for the next sussurant exchange, but instead he heard something entirely unexpected. It was jolly, chirping notes, though no bird made its home here. His hand strayed to his pocket, and there he found a thin, silver tube – the thumb whistle Lechthennian had given him. It had been amongst the possessions he had taken from the *Fae Taeruth*, and throughout his adventures Aradryan had never once thought about it before now.

He lifted the thumb whistle to his lips and blew a few stuttering notes. A flurry of a reply sounded to his right and he stood up, playing a little more. Sat on the edge of a fountain not far away Aradryan saw a figure garbed in outlandish colours and patterns, his face hidden behind a blank mask beneath a diamond-studded hood. Something silver glinted in his gloved hand.

'Lechthennian!' Aradryan cried out the name and ran over to the Solitaire. Mischievous eyes glinted in the dark beneath his hood, looking at Aradryan through the lenses of the mask.

'Not just I, my wayward companion,' said the Solitaire, pointing with his thumb whistle. 'The stone you cast has rippled far and wide.'

Aradryan recognised Findelsith's motley costume

immediately, and with him were his troupe, leaping acrobatically from two skyrunners. The Harlequins bounded lithely across the grey turf and formed a group behind their leader. Findelsith pointed dramatically at Aradryan and shook his head. His finger then moved to Lechthennian, and the Great Harlequin gave an exaggerated, resigned shrug.

'For you I would not cross the voids of space,' Findelsith said in his sing-song way. 'Yet the Solitaire has brought me to you, and to you I must now pledge my service. In his company his debt is now mine, and the Laughing God will not be denied.'

'What debt?' asked Aradryan, looking at Lechthennian. 'You do not owe me anything.'

'Not knowing me, you defended my back, when we fought the daemons of She Who Thirsts,' explained the Solitaire. 'You were a brighter spirit at that time, it is a woe to see the darkness now.'

'I have travelled many dark paths since we parted, and I have none but myself to blame for taking them.'

'For Alaitoc we will fight our battle,' declared Findelsith. 'The humans will be our clumsy partners in the Dance of the Bloody and the Bold.'

Sensing someone behind him, Aradryan looked over his shoulder to see that Alaitin had joined him.

'Did you know they were coming?' Aradryan asked the farseer, who shook his head. The Harlequins returned to their skyrunners, Lechthennian waving a farewell as he bounded aboard the open-topped skimmer. The two vehicles rose into the air and hissed past, heading towards the rimward side of the dome.

'The Laughing God prances lightly up the skein,

and it is a rare seer that can follow his trajectory. I count us amongst the blessed that Cegorach's servants have come, but they step lightly and will not alter our fate for the better or for the worse. There are, however, some others who have come who are known to you. The *Irdiris* arrived ten cycles ago and her rangers even now lure the humans into our trap in the Dome of Midnight Forests.'

'Athelennil is on Alaitoc? Can I see her?'

'There is not time,' replied Alaitin. He raised his head, as if looking at the stars above. 'Thirianna has done well indeed. The attack in the Dome of Midnight Forests is halted, and so the next and final blow will come here, to the Dome of Crystal Seers. All is in motion as we predicted.'

'And my part?' asked Aradryan, mouth becoming dry as he contemplated the fate the seers had decreed for him.

'It will be as we explained.' Alaitin took Aradryan by the elbow and led him back to the bench, but the outcast could not sit down. He was too agitated to stay in one place and started to pace back and forth across the paved area surrounding the dark pool.

'You cannot be certain we will succeed,' said Aradryan.

'Nothing is ever certain, but this course grants us the greatest chance of success. It is too late now to avert what must be done. Since your arrival events have been set into motion that must be guided to a satisfactory conclusion. You cannot escape your fate any more than we can guarantee it.'

'So all I can do is wait?' said Aradryan.

'Yes,' said Alaitin. 'But you will not have to wait long.'

Aradryan forced himself to sit down, pulling his coat tight around him though the air was warm enough. He looked at generations of seers around him, their cold crystal bodies gleaming in the light of a dying star, and felt utterly alone. It had been pleasant to see Lechthennian, who still held some measure of regard for Aradryan, but there was nobody else in his life who would spare him a moment's thought. The only reason he was still on Alaitoc, and not formally banished, was because the craftworld needed him. He was the centre of this catastrophe and it would only be through him that final oblivion could be averted.

'There is a moment of imbalance,' announced Alaitin, his tone worried. Aradryan shot a look at the farseer next to him.

'What sort of imbalance?'

'A human psyker, one of the Space Marines, has been protecting the enemy against our interference, masking his part on the skein.'

'You mean that something has been hidden from us all along?' Aradryan swallowed hard. 'There is not time to change the plan now!'

'Do not be afraid,' said Alaitin. 'Thirianna sees the threat and moves to thwart it. The attack across the Dome of Midnight Forests can still be halted, forcing the enemy here.'

'Thirianna? She has no experience, how can she possibly prevail where others have failed?'

'Through her love of her friends and her duty to Alaitoc,' the farseer replied, regaining his air of equilibrium.

Time seemed to pass slowly, and Aradryan's skin

crawled as he thought of all the plans of the autarchs and seers going awry, sent off course by the actions of one Space Marine. It was too late to change now, though; the fate of the craftworld had been set in motion the moment Aradryan had been told what he must do by the council.

'Thirianna prevails,' said Alaitin. Although the farseer had waited as calmly as the immobile statues around the pair, there was a hint of relief in his voice.

Aradryan gazed morosely at the blue moss creeping through the cracks between the paving slabs under his feet, still not convinced that all would proceed as the farseers had predicted. There was much still that could go wrong and doom him to a painful death, and see Alaitoc destroyed.

He felt a tremor of energy course through the infinity circuit. The whispering of the farseers started again, but this time it did not quieten within a few moments. He thought he caught words amongst the gentle murmuring.

'The wanderer returns.'

'The wanderer returns.'

'The wanderer returns.'

Over and over the phrase echoed through Aradryan's thoughts.

'Thirianna has cast the rune and sent the signal,' said Alaitin, sitting next to Aradryan, hands in the lap of his seer's robe. Rune-incised rings glinted on his fingers. Aradryan twitched as an explosion rolled across the dome, from somewhere to his right. He looked and saw a pall of black smoke rising towards the stars. Alaitin did not react at all. 'The humans have been halted and their new offensive brings them here, seeking the core of Alaitoc. Sensing victory, Achol Nadeus will lead the attack. Our doom approaches.'

LAS-FIRE SCORCHED ACROSS the plaza, blasting fragments from the surrounds of the ponds and fountains. Aradryan sat rooted to his spot on the bench, hands white from clenching the edge of the seat as a hail of shuriken fire whistled in front of him, ripping apart the arm and shoulder of a human soldier, his grey uniform torn to thin tatters.

Aradryan repeated to himself the assurance that Alaitin had given him moments before the first humans had crested the hill behind them – they cannot see us.

Lechthennian somersaulted over the head of another human, his harlequin's kiss punching into the back of a second. The pierced soldier spasmed, near-invisible tendrils of wire erupting from his mouth, ears and eyes, scattering bloody mist for a moment before they were drawn back into the Solitaire's weapon.

'They cannot see us,' Aradryan whispered to himself, flinching as a Death Jester's shrieker cannon fired behind him. A human fell to one knee, a gaping wound in his thigh. His pained expression turned to one of horror as his skin reddened, the accelerating toxins in the shrieker round spreading through his system. Veins and eyes bulging, the man somehow staggered to his feet, his lasrifle dropping from his bloating fingers.

The human exploded, the detonation fuelled by his own biochemistry, shards of bone slicing into the other humans around him. Aghast at their companions' deaths, the squad of warriors started to fall back from the plaza, only to be caught by a hail of shuriken fire from a squadron of jetbikes arriving behind them.

The battle had spread across the dome, which was lit by fires and las-light, plasma and human flare shells. Aradryan had been in many raids and boarding actions, but nothing compared to the terrifying thunder and roar of the human assault. Big guns pounded in the distance and the wind brought the stench of tank engines; Aradryan was reminded of his first encounter with the orks at Hirith-Hreslain.

Alaitin had said nothing since the humans had broken into the dome. He might be concentrating on concealing their location, Aradryan guessed, or he might just as likely be asleep. It was impossible to tell either way.

Their engines humming, a trio of Vyper jetbikes sped past, their gunners directing the fire of their scatter lasers against a company of soldiers advancing from Aradryan's right. As shells started to create a line of fiery blossoms along a hillside not far away, the thought occurred to Aradryan that artillery could fall anywhere: it did not have to see him to kill him.

'They come,' said Alaitin.

Aradryan did not know what the farseer was talking about at first, and then he heard a different timbre of engines approaching. Miniature rockets screamed across the plaza and he saw boxy troop transports rearing over the surrounding hills, painted in quartered swathes of red and white. Spewing smoke from quad-exhausts, their tracks clacking and clanking and grinding in an awful cacophony, three of the slab-sided, unwieldy troop carriers hove over a nearby crest like armoured whales beaching themselves. Each had an open cupola in the roof manned by a Space Marine clad in armour of the same colours: the Sons of Orar.

Further away, there were other variations of the crudely angled tanks ploughing across lawns, crushing crystal statues under their garish bulk: some with slope-armoured turrets and side sponsons, others with multiple-missile ranks on their roofs and two with single, large-bore cannons mounted in their frontal armour. If the Falcon grav-tank was so named for its swooping grace, effortless speed and streamlined hull, the Space Marines' vehicles were wheeled and tracked blocks that bulled their way across the ground, smashing through any obstacle with brute force.

Aradryan glanced at his companion, to see if he reacted at all to the incoming attack, but Alaitin was as placid as if the two of them were merely enjoying the landscape of the dome. The eldar fell back from the Space Marines' assault; the Harlequins leapt upon their skyrunners and were away swiftly, followed by a stream of jetbikes darting away into the maze of bridges and silver streams. Wave Serpents carrying guardians and aspect warriors pulled back enclosed within the glimmer of their protective shields.

Slabs cracking beneath their weight, the Space Marine vehicles rumbled between the pools, their gunners tacking left and right, searching for targets. After them came an even larger tank, which seemed more like a mobile bunker than a vehicle. Sponsons on its sides mounted a plethora of heavy weapons, while the lenses of artificial eyes gleamed from sensor arrays mounted atop its back.

With a wheeze of hydraulics and a puff of air that washed over Aradryan and caused his hair to flutter, the front of the vehicle opened up, spilling red light from its interior. A single warrior walked down the ramp that was dropping to the ground, as the other part of the hull lifted up to create an opening taller than an eldar.

The warrior's armour was even heavier than that of the other Space Marines, his heraldry augmented by rubies and scrolls carved from white marble. He wore no helm, revealing close-cropped black hair that topped a heavily tanned face criss-crossed and puckered with pale scar tissue. Slate-grey eyes swept the plaza and then turned to stare across the dome, towards the hub of Alaitoc. His shoulder pads were adorned with gold script, and from the powerpack on his back rose a pole from which a long rectangular pennant flew, embroidered with more human writing in red on black, the edges bound with gold thread.

Chapter Master Achol Nadeus of the Sons of Orar; the man who held the doom of Alaitoc in his grip.

A squad of Space Marines from one of the other transports assembled on their leader. Aradryan detected a faint buzz of communicators activating but he could not hear what was being said. The Space Marines divided into two groups of five, one of them returning to their vehicle, the other remaining with the Chapter Master.

As one, Nadeus and his warriors turned towards

Aradryan. The Space Marines had their weapons raised, and there was a look of shock on the face of the Chapter Master. Cupolas and sponsons on the vehicles whirred in Aradryan's direction, the glimmer of sighting arrays appearing as a collection of multi-coloured dots on his chest.

'They can see me now?' said Aradryan.

'Yes,' replied Alaitin. 'They can see you now.'

'PEACE, PEACE!' ARADRYAN called out in the human tongue, flinging his arms out and slipping to his knees. 'I have no weapons.'

Within a few moments filled with the crunch of heavy boots and whine of armour, he was surrounded by the Space Marines, their boltguns and other weapons pointed directly at him. That they had not opened fire on instinct was surprising enough.

'Do you understand me?' said Aradryan, a note of pleading in his voice. He had known this was the part he hated, but the seers had assured him there was no other option. They had traced the thread of his life and this route, contrary to appearances, offered Aradryan and the craftworld the best chance of survival. Outright resistance would not prevail against the might of the human forces, and so Aradryan was left with only this humiliating salvation. 'Please, I have no weapons.'

There was another buzz of communication. Nadeus towered over Aradryan, like a colossal statue silhouetted against a ruddy sky filled with the light of the dying star.

'Speak, xenos, and quickly,' said the Chapter Master. Aradryan was not sure what 'xenos' meant, but from the tone employed by Nadeus he assumed it was not an honorific.

'I have important news and an offer of peace,' said Aradryan. He resisted the urge to glance at where he could see Alaitin sitting out of the corner of his eye but still invisible to the Space Marines. The farseer stared at him through unblinking crystal lenses. Aradryan took a breath, long and deep.

'You are being tricked, Chapter Master. Your enemies have placed you exactly where they want you. I must speak with Imperial commander De'vaque in person, or we are all dead.'

Nadeus reached down and grabbed the front of Aradryan's robe, easily lifting the eldar to his feet with one arm.

'What do you know of De'vaque?' asked the Chapter Master.

'Tell him it is Aradryan! Aradryan! I know him, and I am repaying the debt I owe him.'

Holding his breath, Aradryan studied the Space Marine's face. There was disbelief written there, and anger. The Chapter Master's grip tightened, almost crushing Aradryan inside his robe. Aradryan was convinced Nadeus was going to kill him that moment, and closed his eyes.

'Please, Chapter Master, you have to tell De'vaque it is Aradryan.' It was the most demeaning thing Aradryan had ever done, grovelling to this murderous barbarian, but he wanted to live so badly he would do anything. 'He knows me. Do not kill me, please. Do not kill me.'

'Keep this filth secure,' said Nadeus, hauling Aradryan from his feet to pass him to one of his warriors.

Fingers stronger than a vice gripped Aradryan's arms as he was lifted away, but he breathed a sigh of relief as he saw the Chapter Master striding back to his command vehicle.

THE BATTLE FOR the Dome of Crystal Seers continued to rage and Aradryan feared that he had been too slow or that the farseers had made a mistake. Airburst detonations left clouds of smoke in the upper air, showering shrapnel on the eldar Guardians below. Grasslands older than the Imperium of Mankind were churned to filth beneath the treads of tank columns, and the remains of seers who had guided Alaitoc to safety for generations before any of the humans had been born were shattered by shell strikes and lascannons. Aradryan wanted to weep, but he kept his emotions in check. Despite his protestations and begging, his mind was alert and clear; if he was to come out of this encounter alive he needed all of his wits about him.

Chapter Master Nadeus had returned after making his inquiries, and stood silently in front of Aradryan, boring holes through the eldar's skull with his stare. There was little doubt that he would kill Aradryan without hesitation. For his part, Aradryan hung his head and avoided the commander's gaze as much as possible.

De'vaque's arrival was heralded by a squadron of four tri-rotor aircraft soaring across the dome. Bubble-like gun mounts dotted their underbellies, twin-barrelled cannons swivelling to survey the scene below. Behind them came a smaller craft with a single rotor, flitting left and right as it evaded possible anti-aircraft fire. A blue blazon was painted on the nose of the craft and Aradryan saw that it was a leaping fish leaving a trail of sparkling diamonds. Seeing this, Aradryan realised that the design was the same as the mosaic that had been on the floor of De'vaque's yacht: a personal symbol or family heraldry.

De'vaque's craft landed amidst much wind and whirling dust, as the other four aircraft kept watch for attack above. When the Imperial commander was safely deposited, the patrolling aircraft spread out, lifting higher into the air. De'vaque stomped across the plaza, gaze immediately drawn to Aradryan, who was being held between two Sons of Orar.

It was hard to follow the emotions that swept across the commander's face. First there was surprise and then anger. His scowl intensified as he came closer, but then was replaced by a twitching of the lips and the hint of a triumphant smile.

Unprompted, Aradryan fell to his knees again, hands lifted towards the Imperial commander in supplication.

'Lord De'vaque, thank the stars!' cried Aradryan.

'Kill it!' snarled the governor, his hand resting on the pommel of the sword at his waist.

'I have a warning,' said Aradryan, desperation making his voice almost a screech. 'You are being tricked, Imperial commander. I know I have wronged you harshly, but I swear for atonement and my life that you must listen to me!'

'It is a cowardly, treacherous wretch,' said De'vaque, directing his words to Nadeus. 'Nothing it says can be of value.'

Aradryan felt an armoured gauntlet on his shoulder, about to pull him to his feet. He wriggled from its grip before the fingers closed, prostrating himself on the cracked slabs in front of De'vaque.

'I am so sorry for the death of your son,' squealed Aradryan, eyes fixed on De'vaque's face. The words were truthful, though used now in guile. 'Darson was killed by my hand, and it should not have been.'

De'vaque's eyes opened wider into a murderous glare and he bared his teeth, spittle erupting from his mouth. Drawing his sword form its scabbard. the Imperial commander stepped forwards.

'Halt your men, Nadeus, I shall kill this filth myself.'

'That would be a mistake, Master Nadeus,' said Aradryan, turning his imploring gaze to the Space Marine leader. 'I have vital information.'

'Wait,' said Nadeus, putting a hand to De'vaque's chest to stop him. 'I still do not understand how this creature knows you, Imperial commander.'

'He is a captain of the pirates we are here to destroy, Nadeus,' replied De'vaque. 'I almost had him before, but he escaped.'

De'vaque stepped around the Chapter Master's outstretched arm, sword raised for the killing blow.

'There are more ships coming!' yelped Aradryan, flinching away from the sword.

Nadeus's fingers enveloped the wrist of the Imperial commander as the blade descended, stopping the sword before it hit Aradryan. The former pirate breathed out in relief, but the moment was short-lived as the Chapter Master turned his stare back to Aradryan.

'What ships? Where?'

'We are almost victorious,' said De'vaque, trying unsuccessfully to shake free from the Space Marine's grasp. 'We need to slay this creature and press on. The infinity core is not far from here.'

'What ships?' Nadeus demanded again. He plucked De'vaque's sword from his trembling grasp, the thin duelling blade looking like a piece of cutlery in the Chapter Master's huge fist. 'Tell me or I will kill you here and now.'

Aradryan did not have to reply. Nadeus tilted his head to one side as the communicator bead in his ear rattled into life. The Chapter Master looked up, through the dome above their heads.

'How many?' he growled.

'Just kill him!' snarled De'vaque. 'He betrayed me! He killed my son!'

The Imperial commander lunged for his sword and was knocked to his backside by a swipe from Nadeus's free hand. The point of the blade was only the length of a finger from Aradryan's face, unwaveringly directed towards his right eye. He swallowed to moisten his throat.

'One moment, please, Chapter Master.'

Aradryan felt the surge of power beneath him, coursing along the matrix of the infinity circuit. Alaitoc trembled with energy and it sent a surge of strength through Aradryan's fatigued body.

The Dome of Crystal Seers burst into brilliant white light. Every statuesque seer was glowing with psychic power and the floor itself gleamed with them. Traceries of the infinity circuit could be seen like veins throughout the dome, connecting and interconnecting the seers with their craftworld.

As his eyes swiftly adjusted to the light, Aradryan noticed something else: the silence.

There was not a crack of gunshot, shout of anger or blast of shell. The entire dome was quiet. Looking up, Aradryan saw the streak of laser and the flare of missile frozen in the air. Like a lightshow, beams and tracer rounds criss-crossed the dome, an immobile rainbow of violence.

Aradryan stood up as Nadeus looked around in disbelief. The entire battle had frozen. Jetbikes hung in the air above some trees to their left, while a squad of Space Marines were in mid-charge down a slope to the right, the flare of their bolters held in stasis. The white light of Alaitoc's power penetrated everything.

'Look up,' said a voice behind Aradryan.

Out of instinct, Nadeus did so, as did Aradryan. Against the backdrop of the stars he could see the plasma flares of spaceships stuck against the firmament. Bombers and fighters were locked together in a twirling dance, looking like the frozen plateau of a painting.

'The stasis will not remain for long,' said Alaitin, stepping up beside Aradryan. 'We must conclude this business swiftly or all be killed.'

'Slay them, Nadeus,' barked De'vaque, pushing himself to his feet. 'They are an affront to the Emperor. Do your duty, Chapter Master.'

'Ships from a dozen craftworlds have exited our webway portal, Chapter Master,' said Alaitin. 'At the moment they are held in stasis with your fleet. When I draw this veil back and time resumes, they will destroy your fleet utterly.'

'Do not think that Alaitoc stands alone,' Aradryan snarled at De'vaque. 'You cannot bring war to one craftworld without threatening it against all others. Your miserable army will not leave this star system unless we decree it.'

'Mutual annihilation,' said Alaitin.

'I am comfortable with that,' replied Nadeus. 'To rid the universe of this abomination would be reward enough.'

'A tainted reward, and ultimately driven by the vanity of one man,' said Alaitin. The farseer pointed at De'vaque, who stepped back, aghast, expecting some psychic bolt to strike him down. 'There is no justice or honour to be found here, Chapter Master.'

'Everybody knows that the eldar are liars and thieves,' said the Imperial commander. 'They are trying to fool you. Attack now and we shall have victory and glory!'

'When our ships have finished destroying your fleet, Alaitoc will kill herself,' Alaitin continued. 'She will implode her webway portal and consume us all in one conflagration that will briefly outshine the star we currently orbit.'

'But not before our surviving ships have departed,' added Aradryan, still staring at De'vaque. 'They know where there are weapons that can scorch entire worlds in moments and extinguish stars. Destroy Alaitoc and the whole eldar race will respond, and a hundred human worlds will die.'

'More lies,' growled De'vaque. 'Empty threats.'

'If you are so much of a threat, why should I not destroy you now while I have the chance?' asked Nadeus.

'You would perish in vain and for vanity,' said Aradryan. 'Ask the Imperial commander who Yrith-ain is. Or perhaps he will tell you of his dealings with Khiadysis? Go ahead, ask him.'

Nadeus looked at the Imperial commander, who suddenly had lost much of his bravado.

'Meaningless gibberish,' said De'vaque.

'Names of his conspirators,' said Aradryan. 'If you wish further proof, I can tell you the places and times when attacks took place, not only sanctioned by this traitor, but only made possible by his collusion. He seeks me for killing his son, I cannot deny that. Are you to be the instrument of his personal vendetta, Chapter Master? Will your Sons of Orar perish for the pride of this weak-willed hypocrite?'

'Pirate filth!' roared De'vaque. He tried to snatch a boltgun from the grip of one of the stasis-bound Space Marines, but it would not move.

'Stand back, Imperial commander,' said Nadeus. The Chapter Master's bolt pistol was in his hand and pointed at De'vaque's chest. 'Tell me that these are more lies. Let me see your face when you do it. And tell me how you came to find this place, or how this pirate came to know your name?'

'They cannot turn you against the Emperor's will,' said De'vaque, holding his hands out in front of him as a barrier to the pistol.

'How many thousands have died already?' whispered Alaitin. 'How many of your warriors have fallen to clean the blood from this man's hands, Chapter Master?'

The boom of the pistol caused Aradryan to jump. De'vaque's head disappeared in a cloud of blood and bone and his headless corpse collapsed to the pavement.

'Too many,' snarled the Chapter Master. 'Call off your ships and I will cease the attack.'

# EPILOGUE

THERE WERE THOUSANDS of dead, too many for the Dome of Everlasting Stillness. Those Aspect Warriors who had fallen were laid to rest in the catacombs of their shrines until the Guardians and civilians had been conducted through the ceremony of internment. Only seven of Alaitoc's spiritseers had survived the battle, and so they were aided by the others of the Path of the Seer. They moved silently along the long rows of the dead, followed by floating caskets into which they placed the glowing spirit stones of the fallen. There was not time to give thanks and bear witness to the passing of every individual – to do so would take hundreds of cycles.

Aradryan drew up the hood of his white robe and stepped across the threshold of the dome. Just as there were too few spiritseers to conduct the dead to the infinity circuit, there were not enough Mourners for there to be one for every fallen eldar.

When the humans had eventually left, four cycles after the showdown in the Dome of Crystal Seers, Aradryan had been faced with the awful truth of what had happened. There was no way to extinguish the guilt; it was so great it would crush the greatest of minds and the most patient of philosophers. He had known, as he had watched the first of the bodies being lifted from the blood-slicked field, that he would tread the Path of Grieving. There was no other way to deal with the loss and the hurt that was created by the knowledge that so many had been slain because of his actions.

It was easy to cry. Tears rolled down his cheeks in a constant stream, every droplet shed in memory of a lost life. The magnitude of what he had perpetrated threatened to overwhelm him, and his tears became choking sobs. To Mourn came easily; he trod the Path of Grieving to learn how he might eventually stop.

Nearly a third of Alaitoc lay in ruins, from rim to core, the swathe cut by the Imperial troops a scar that would take generations to heal. Some domes would never recover. They would be let free from the base of the craftworld and sent into the fiery heart of dying Mirianathir, to be reborn one day as particles that would fuel the craftworld again.

He thought of so many spirits to be absorbed by the infinity circuit. The thought had horrified him before, and sent him into the stars to seek escape from his own mortality. The irony was not lost on him; of how everything had come full cycle and here he was again surrounded by corpses. This time he was not afraid. He had come to terms with death,

and thoug... ...
atoning for wha...
release when it eve...

'We must all bear a hea...

Aradryan stopped and turne... ...life without
following him along the path betwe...
the dead. Her seer robes were overlaid w... the
and sash of white, and after her came one o...
spirit-caskets.

'There are not enough tears in the universe to wash
away the guilt of what I have done,' said Aradryan,
choking back his sobs. 'Not just those here, but the
blood that I spilled by my own hand, and the lives
that were taken by my words. The fallen will never
have justice.'

'There is no justice, just fate,' said Thirianna, 'and
I have found that even fate is not so immutable as
we might think. I must share the blame for this cata-
clysm, for I have been guilty of one of the grossest
crimes of the seer.'

'I do not understand,' said Aradryan. He motioned
Thirianna to a bench and the pair of them sat down,
heads bowed. They did not look at each other.

'It may have been your actions that set in motion
events that would bring down the hatred of Commander De'vaque, but it was my actions that ensured
those events culminated in the disaster that befell our
home. Without my intervention, Alaitoc would have
been safe.'

'I am still unclear what you mean,' said Aradryan.
He produced a square of linen from a pocket inside
his sleeve, its corners embroidered with runes of
comfort, and dabbed at his eyes. He pushed a wisp of

his hood. 'If you think ... ...de me stay on Alaitoc, then ...ness. You cannot feel guilty for that – ...no responsibility for my subsequent actions.'

'It was not that of which I am guilty, though thank you for reminding me,' Thirianna replied with a soft laugh. 'When you became involved with Yrithain, confrontation with De'vaque became a distinct possibility. I glimpsed the narrowest of futures, possible only by the most complex chain of events, and hence far more unlikely to happen than likely. Yet for my own selfishness, I manipulated people and fate to satisfy my curiosity and sate my fear, and in doing so I brought about the very catastrophe I sought to avoid.'

'There must be some kind of seer's logic in your words, because I do not know what it is you have done.'

'I manipulated Korlandril, and through him Arhathain, to make the council of seers investigate my glimpse of Alaitoc's doom. From that moment, a sequence of thread came together which turned a remote possibility into a self-fulfilling prophecy. The more we looked, the more we were likely to bring it about, because as soon as we found the danger and saw your part in the doom that would come, I sent warning to you, across the gulf of space through the eternal matrix that underpins the webway.'

'My dreams... They are coming for us. We will all burn. Such nightmares I have never known.'

Thirianna stared at him, hand lifted to her mouth in shock.

'I meant to warn you, not to torment you.'

'Yet it is still not such a grave transgression as I have

committed,' said Aradryan. 'If it were not for that warn-ing, I would not have been on Alaitoc, and present to intervene against De'vaque. Without me, our people might never have stopped the humans. And that brings to mind a question I have not yet been given clear answer to. Why is it that I could not tell the tale of De'vaque's treachery to Nadeus earlier? If he had known from the outset what a venal creature he was allied with, the attack might never have taken place.'

'You heard it from the lips of De'vaque: our words cannot be trusted. De'vaque had to betray himself, to show his guilt to Nadeus, in order that the Chapter Master would be convinced. We tried many threads to bring about that fate, but the only one that had any measure of success was to draw the human forces on, to allow them to sear into the heart of Alaitoc. Only at the moment of apparent victory would De'vaque himself come to the craftworld, and only by placing him alongside the thread of Nadeus and yours could we bring about the conclusion we so desired.'

'And so it was well that you sent me warning,' said Aradryan, standing up. He offered a hand to Thiri-anna and helped her to her feet. 'Many have died, but annihilation has been averted.'

'Had I not implanted that psychic message in your dreams, you would not have woken from the Dream-ing that gripped you,' Thirianna whispered, laying her head against his shoulder. 'I did not realise this at the time, but that act brought grave consequences, and I should have known not to interfere in such a delicate matter. Had you been Dreaming when the *Naestro* came to Nathai-athil the fleet would have been caught in the ambush laid by De'vaque and Khiadysis.'

'Wait,' said Aradryan, stepping away from Thiri-anna. 'You mean we would have been killed there? If that is the case, I owe you my life!'

'When you survived Nathai-athil you were set on a course, driven by my dream-borne warnings, to return to Alaitoc. With your return to Alaitoc you brought Khiadysis to the craftworld.' Aradryan fol-lowed the logic and a sickness began to well up in his stomach as he realised the import of Thirianna's words. 'Once Khiadysis knew you were at Alaitoc, he passed this to De'vaque and the human warriors who had been mobilised to hunt you down came here also.

'I became a seer to know what would happen to my friends, and I doomed us all. Korlandril was taken by his anger and consumed by the Phoenix Lord Karan-dras. You might never overcome the grief and guilt of what you are responsible for. And me... I saved your life, yes, but almost at the cost of Alaitoc...'

There was no comfort for Aradryan to offer his friend. Each in his way, he and Thirianna and Korlan-dril had been victims of their own nature. The Path and all its protections could only offer a means by which they might survive themselves. Whatever call-ing, whether of Commorragh or the maiden worlds, on the Path or Outcast, no eldar could fully escape himself or herself. They had been the seed of their own doom, and thus would it be until the Rhana Dandra and the end of all things.

Aradryan stood up and could not look at his friend. He looked at the lines of the dead that had been the victims of their mistakes, and walked away.

The greatest truth about the Path is the simplest to say and yet the hardest to comprehend. In this profound moment comes a realisation of the genius of the Asuryas, and the flaw in their genius.

There is only one Path, and it binds all of us together.

We seers may pick apart the strands, until we reach the infinitesimally small details, but their presence is a distraction to the overall flow of the skein. Be you Poet or Dreamer or Mourner, Warrior or Seer or Outcast, as the events in your life are but threads in the cord of your fate, so your whole life is but a thread in the cord of the fate of the eldar. We all walk the Path as a single species, and as a collective we must learn to control our passions and our fears together, or face destruction from one and the same.

>     —   Kysaduras the Anchorite, afterword to
>         *Introspections upon Perfection*

# ABOUT THE AUTHOR

**Gav Thorpe** has been rampaging across the worlds of Warhammer and Warhammer 40,000 for many years as both an author and games developer. He hails from the den of scurvy outlaws called Nottingham and makes regular sorties to unleash bloodshed and mayhem. He shares his hideout with Dennis, a mechanical hamster sworn to enslave mankind. Dennis was recently apprehended trying to mesmerise the populace from his Twitter account *@DennisHamster*.

Gav's previous novels include fan-favourite *Angels of Darkness*, the Time of Legends trilogy, *The Sundering*, and the Eldar Path series amongst many others.

You can find his website at:
*www.gavthorpe.co.uk*

*An extract from* Path of the Renegade,
*the first instalment in the Dark Eldar Trilogy*
*by Andy Chambers*

'LET THE GAMES begin!'

The horns and sirens sounded out in a shriek that rose into ultrasonics before crashing out in a explosion of bass. White light flared on the thirteen rotating outer platforms before dying away to reveal thirteen slaves. Some wailed and gibbered, others dashed around helplessly, some prayed and others stood defiantly screaming. Young, old, fat, thin, male female, they all swung smoothly around the central stage in their individual bubbles of captivity.

The platforms began to float higher or sink lower in response to the audience's interest in them. Those the audience found most intriguing would be matched against combatants by the beastmasters. The least interesting would be fed to warp beasts if their platforms sank low enough, something that often increased their number of viewers markedly.

After a few seconds the occupant of the highest platform – a hook-armed, red-furred specimen – vanished and reappeared on the central stage to be met by a single wych a moment later. The nearly naked wych looked slender when measured against the brutish human but she moved with a fluid grace that made the human look positively comical. The wych picked up on the possibilities and led the lumpy human around like a shambling ogre chasing a nymph. She improvised a series of slick engagements that sliced the man up so slowly that he wound down like a clockwork toy, quick trysts that left him only kissed by the edge of the blade each time.

Before she could finish him a white flash erupted and another slave appeared. This one was a shaven-headed, tattooed fanatic that rushed straight at her with a hooked knife held low. The wych pirouetted lazily out of reach before lunging just the tip of her blade into the fanatic's eye socket. He screamed and staggered, dropping the knife. Flash. A third slave appeared and was hamstrung a heartbeat later. Flash. The wych seemed to barely avoid the sweep of a cleaver; her counter left her opponent dragging his entrails in the sand. Flash. A second wych joined the first, the two of them leaping and cavorting together like lost lovers reunited as they ripped through the injured slaves. Flash. More slaves. Flash. More blood.

The voice of the crowd rose and fell like surf against a shore, enraptured as they drank in wave after wave of pain and suffering. The first batch of slaves had vanished from the outer platforms, one way or another, and were rapidly replaced. Five wyches were working the central stage by now and they left an ever-speeding influx of slaves leaking their lifeblood out on the sand. Xelian felt satisfied that the opening warm-up was well under way and turned her attention to her two allies.

Kraillach looked somewhat recovered, his lined face showing patrician features instead of the death mask of a mummy. Yllithian was hunched forwards, careless of the entertainment but obviously eager to talk. The dimension-warping technologies artfully concealed within the arena structure permitted a spectator to cast their presence into the midst of the action, feeling the blood drops on their face and hearing the death-screams ringing in their ears. They also permitted Xelian, Kraillach and Yllithian to converse together inside a co-sensual reality safe from outside observation.

'I have found the key to ridding ourselves of Vect,' Yllithian began without preamble. 'The answer lies in Shaa-dom as I suspected.'

'How can you know this? Are you telling me you went there yourself?' Kraillach sniffed derisively.

'I did go there, as you well know from your own spies.'

'Well, I don't believe it. You're still alive after all.'

'Enough,' grated Xelian. She promised herself that one day there would be a reckoning for moments like these. 'Speak. Tell us what you found out on your... expedition, Nyos.'

'With the right preparations it may be possible to recall El'Uriaq from beyond the veil.'

'El'Uriaq!' Kraillach spat, his face blanching at the name. 'What madness is this? The old emperor of Shaa-dom has been dead for three millennia!'

'It can be done,' Yllithian insisted with surprising vehemence, 'and it is our path to victory. With one of Vect's most deadly enemies at our side the kabals would abandon the tyrant in droves. The value of someone who has defied the tyrant previously cannot be over-estimated.' The sudden tirade seemed to wear Kraillach out and he fell back in his throne waving one hand feebly as if to brush Yllithian away.

Yllithian lapsed into silence. On the central stage the wyches' dance of death was almost over. Now they skirmished with each other over the crimson dunes of sliced meat they had made, skipping grotesquely over the still screaming, quivering piles of maimed slaves.